MATT BROLLY

Following his law degree, where [illegible] criminal law, Matt Brolly comple[illegible] Writing at Glasgow University. H[illegible] author of the DCI Lambert crime novels *Dead Eyed* and *Dead Lucky*. Matt lives in London with his wife and their two young children. You can find out more about Matt at his website www.mattbrolly.co.uk or by following him on twitter: @MattBrollyUK

Also by
Matt Brolly

Dead Eyed

Dead Lucky

Matt Brolly

ONE PLACE. MANY STORIES

This novel is entirely a work of fiction. The names, characters and incidents portrayed in it are the work of the author's imagination. Any resemblance to actual persons, living or dead, events or localities is entirely coincidental.

HQ
An imprint of HarperCollins*Publishers* Ltd
1 London Bridge Street
London SE1 9GF

This paperback edition 2019

1
First published in Great Britain by
HQ, an imprint of HarperCollins*Publishers* Ltd 2019

Matt Brolly asserts the moral right to be
author of this work.
A catalogue record for this book is
available from the British Library.

ISBN: 978-1-84845-800-0

This book is produced from independently certified FSC™ paper to ensure responsible forest management.

For more information visit: www.harpercollins.co.uk/green

Printed and bound in Great Britain by
CPI Group (UK) Ltd, Melksham, SN12 6TR

For my nan,
Eileen Burnell

Chapter 1

He tried to stretch. His back was pushed tight against the wall, his covered head snagged between two coat hooks. Every other breath brought with it the stench of foot odour and moth bombs.

He'd been in the flat for three hours, the last two of which had been in the wardrobe. Preparation was important. The woman was predictable, she would return after work, the husband less so. His behaviour was erratic of late. He'd been spending more time at the bar than at work.

He stretched once more, savouring being alone, going over the plan again and again until it was so embedded in his mind that it was almost a memory.

The woman arrived on time. His pulse didn't alter as he listened to her move around the room, the strange noises she made, thinking she was alone.

Eventually she left the room. Realising he'd been holding his breath, he let it out in a rush, his lungs filling with the trapped, musty air of his hiding cell.

It was another two hours before the husband arrived. He heard the front door click open, the heavy steps as the husband walked into the living room, the muted voices as the couple exchanged pleasantries.

He was about to leave his confines when he heard the woman

enter the en-suite bathroom. He edged the wardrobe open. The bathroom door was ajar and he tiptoed across the bedroom floor in time to see the woman pulling up her garments.

As she left the room, he placed his right hand on her shoulder. She jumped, and rounded on him thinking he was her husband. She stared at him for a second, her mouth agape. A look of confusion crept across her face and for a heartbeat it was as if she'd been expecting his arrival. Then, realising what was happening was all too real, she went to scream.

With a practised move, he reached out and covered her mouth before she could give sound to her situation.

Chapter 2

Lambert sensed the decay as he entered the building.

He'd been here before.

Inside, the cloying stench of antiseptic and bleach did little to mask the subtle odours of illness and death which permeated from the walls of the hollow reception area.

He knew where he was going, he'd visited the same ward on numerous occasions many years ago. His body guided him along the route without him having to think, a homing instinct he'd thought long extinguished. He tried to ignore the people he passed. An elderly man, wisps of dry grey hair atop a wrinkled skull, wheeling a bag full of yellowing liquid which seeped into his veins. An obese teenage girl, pushed along in a wheelchair by two similar sized youths, her plastered leg protruding in the air like a weapon. And finally a man he'd hoped to avoid, leaving the lift as Lambert was about to enter.

The man, immaculate in a pinstriped suit and coiffured hair, froze. Lambert had to suppress a smile as the colour literally drained from the man's face. His healthy St Tropez tan faded into a ghost-like white.

'Michael,' said the man, holding out his hand.

Lambert ignored the outstretched limb, not yet ready to be fully grown up about the situation. He entered the lift and turned to watch Jeremy Taylor, partner of Price Barker Solicitors, shake himself as if from a daze and walk away.

'Michael Lambert,' he said, into the box outside the ward. 'I'm here to see Sophie Lambert.' He remembered a time twelve years ago when he'd said the very same thing into what looked like the very same box. Only then he'd been visiting on happier terms.

The screams started as soon as he was buzzed into the ward, the sound of tortured women, flesh being torn. The nurses' desk was empty. Lambert considered walking the corridors in search of Sophie but didn't want to risk intruding on the other patients. Eventually, a smiling nurse gave him directions to Sophie's room. The woman beamed at him as if this should be the greatest day of his life.

He ambled down the corridor, debating whether or not to turn and flee the scene, until he reached the entrance to Sophie's room.

Taking a deep breath, he stepped over the threshold. For a time he just stood there dumbstruck, forgetting to breathe. Sophie sat upright in bed, cheeks pinched red, a tiny figure clamped to her breast. Smiling, she beckoned him over.

It was too late to leave. He took a seat next to her bed. 'How did it go?' he asked, not knowing what else to say.

Lambert had been virtually estranged from his wife, Sophie, for the last three years following the death of their daughter, Chloe, though they had continued sharing a house together. During that time Sophie had had a brief affair with Jeremy Taylor, the solicitor Lambert had just encountered, who was the father of the child his wife was holding.

The child released itself from Sophie with a smacking sound

and looked in Lambert's direction. 'Do you want to hold her?' asked Sophie, as unsure about the situation as he was.

'No. Thank you. I'm okay.'

Tears welled in Sophie's eyes. 'This little thing is Chloe's sister,' she whispered, stroking the baby's head.

Lambert choked back his own tears. The baby was the closest thing there would ever be to Chloe but there was no avoiding the fact that she wasn't his. He poured a beaker of water, taking some time to think. 'Do you have a name for her?' he asked, his voice coming out as a squawk – like an adolescent boy's.

'I wanted to call her Jane.' Sophie hesitated, looked down at the baby for support. 'If you will give me permission, Jane Chloe.'

Lambert looked away, forcing back tears, picturing his little girl before the accident. Her curious smile and unending joy for the world, and how he had destroyed it all by losing control of his car. He didn't know if it was a good idea giving this new child Chloe's name. He didn't want her to be haunted by her dead sister, or for her to grow up feeling she was a replacement, but he knew Sophie would never ever let her feel that way. 'If you think that is best,' he said.

'What do you think, Michael?'

'I think it would be wonderful,' he said, darting his hand across his eyes, turning to face them. The child looked back at him as Chloe had done all those years before.

He left ten minutes later, refusing to be overwhelmed by his growing sense of loneliness. He'd left the family home three months earlier, informing Sophie that it wouldn't be appropriate for him to stay. He'd even discussed divorce proceedings with her but she'd wanted to get through the pregnancy before making any decisions. Although he was happy for her, he knew he should have been the father of that little girl back in the ward. As he took the lift, he envisaged a future without Sophie. He imagined her raising Jane without him.

His vision blurred as he entered the main lobby of the hospital. Fiery lights danced in front of his eyes. The dizzying colours – flickers of burning ember, a multitude of shades and sizes – signified the start of a hallucinatory episode. From research on the internet he'd self-diagnosed his condition as a form of hallucinatory narcolepsy. It was the same type of episode he'd suffered when driving Chloe.

The episodes had occurred more often in the last few months, ever since Sophie's pregnancy and the Souljacker case. The trigger was usually a lack of sleep, or stress. At the moment, he was suffering from both.

He sat down on a bench, the material cold and hard against his flesh, and closed his eyes. He told himself he was in a good place. The episodes normally occurred at home in bed, a smooth precursor to sleep. Knowing it was unwise to fight, he lay his head against the rough textured wall and fell asleep.

'Sir, sir.' The hand pulled at his shoulder, the accent foreign. 'I'm sorry, sir, I need to clean here.'

Lambert darted awake and took in his surroundings. He was still in the hospital. He checked his watch. He'd been asleep for three hours.

'Sorry, sir,' repeated the cleaner, switching on a floor polisher which whirred into life with a deafening drone.

Lambert stood and stretched. The place had thinned out with normal visiting hours over. Lonely patients walked the floors like ghosts, occasionally passed by a hurrying doctor or nurse. The three hours had refreshed him and had evaporated, for a time, his worries over Sophie and the new child. It was eleven p.m. He considered calling Sarah, but decided it was too late. She would either be sleeping, or out working on the case. Either way, he wouldn't know what to tell her. He didn't fully understand how he felt about the situation at the moment, and was in no mood to analyse his feelings. Knowing he wouldn't get back to sleep that evening, there was little option but to return to work.

Lambert had resumed his position within the National Crime Agency two months previously, following his unofficial pursuit and capture of the notorious serial killer, dubbed the Souljacker. Since returning, he'd been working on an international drugs case. The case had proved challenging, and there was still months of work ahead.

Lambert was part of a small specialised team, his NCA team working with the Met's joint Organised Crime Partnership. So far they had arrested a number of small time dealers, and inroads were slowly being made into the main distributors.

Lambert caught the tube to Westminster and made the short walk to the NCA's headquarters, the June night air still thick with heat from the day.

His office was deserted. Lambert often survived on three to four hours' sleep a night so was often alone in the neon-lit open-plan office. He opened up The System, an unofficial amalgamated database of police computer systems, traffic systems, CCTV images, and social media back ends. The System had been created for the now defunct organisation called The Group and was only available for select officers within the

NCA. He was about to log in when the office doors exploded open.

'Just the person,' said the rotund bulldog-like man who had barged through the doors as if they were an unnecessary obstacle.

Chief Superintendent Glenn Tillman stood in front of him, hands on hips like some ageing superhero. Tillman had headed up The Group until it was disbanded six months ago and had recruited Lambert back into the NCA.

'Sir?'

'Sit,' said Tillman. 'Something important has come up.'

Lambert, who was already sitting, swivelled his chair around. 'I was just about to log in.'

Tillman pulled a second chair over. 'The drugs case? No, I want you to pass that over. Give your workload to Bryant. I need you on something else.'

He handed Lambert a piece of paper. Lambert turned it over and read an address in Dulwich.

'You know the journalist, Eustace Sackville?'

Lambert nodded. He'd met the man, a crime specialist on a national broadsheet, on a number of occasions.

'His wife's just been murdered and the case has been assigned to us. I want you to work with Kennedy. Get down there straight away and take the case over. The body was found three hours ago so you better be quick. An Inspector Wright is at the scene at the moment but knows it's passing to us.'

'That must have gone down well.'

Tillman shrugged.

'Why us?' asked Lambert, suspecting the truth.

'You know the sort of information Sackville has access to.

We want the best on this and your name came up as someone suitable to lead the case.'

Lambert nodded.

'One more thing,' said Tillman, handing Lambert an iPad. 'Moira Sackville,' he said, pointing to a picture of sixty-year-old woman bound to a chair.

Lambert flicked through to a second image. The lifeless figure of Moira Sackville, drained of colour, slash marks on each wrist, a puddle of blood by her ankles.

Tillman rubbed his chin. Lambert had known Tillman for ten years. In that time, the only sign of insecurity he'd ever seen in the man was the odd propensity of rubbing his chin in times of stress.

'It took some time for Mrs Sackville to bleed out...' said Tillman, lowering the volume of his voice as Lambert continued scrolling through the images until he reached a picture of a second chair, empty save for two binds hanging loose from the armrests. '... and her husband was made to watch every minute of it.'

Chapter 3

Detective Sergeant Matilda Kennedy was waiting for him at the crime scene, loitering outside the police cordon like an over-interested member of the public. She wore denim jeans, and a dark jacket over a t-shirt. Her red hair was hung loose on her shoulders, and Lambert wondered if she'd been on a night out when the call had come in.

'Sir,' she said, by means of greeting.

'You haven't been in yet?' asked Lambert.

'Thought I'd better wait for you. The SOCOs haven't cleared the scene yet, and I believe there is a pissed off inspector on the warpath.'

Lambert was sure he saw her eyes sparkle at the last comment. He hadn't worked directly with the young sergeant before but had heard only good reports. Apparently she was a sharp officer with a keen eye for detail. 'I better go speak to him now,' said Lambert, spotting DI Wright beyond the cordon. He showed the waiting uniformed officer his warrant card and scrambled beneath the tape.

'James,' said Lambert, offering his hand.

'Ah, DCI Lambert. I hear you're taking over my case,' said Wright, shaking the proffered hand.

'What can I say? Orders.'

'Orders,' mimicked Wright, resigned to the situation. 'You up to speed?'

'To a certain extent. Where is Sackville now?'

'He's been escorted to hospital for a check. Suffering from shock, unsurprisingly.'

It was the same hospital Sophie was staying in. 'How did he manage to call it in?' Lambert had listened to the 999 call on the way over. Sackville's haunted voice, matter-of-factly informing the operator that his wife had been murdered.

'We haven't managed to get any details from him. You'll see the set-up when you're let upstairs. He had marks to his wrists consistent with being handcuffed and tied. He mumbled something about being untied. It's possible the killer let him go so he could call it in.'

It was another hour before the SOCOs released the flat. Lambert had a sense of déjà vu as he viewed the scene, having seen the images on Tillman's phone. The incident had taken place in the Sackville's dining room. Lambert studied the two chairs, facing each other, and imagined the horrific nature of what had taken place. He pictured Eustace Sackville begging for mercy from the killer, offering himself in place of his wife; the look of terror on Moira Sackville's face, seeing her husband's pleading eyes. The despair and loss on both their faces as her life faded away.

'Any sign of a break in?' asked Lambert.

Wright shook his head. We've checked the locks on the door, the windows, even the loft. The killer was either invited in, or was already in the house.

The dining room was humid and stuffy, yet Lambert still felt a chill as he looked around. 'She bled out from her wrists,' he said, thinking aloud rather than asking for clarity.

'No other noticeable marks on her so far. The pathologist is pretty sure the wounds to her wrists are the cause of death. Obviously we'll know more after the autopsy,' said Wright.

'Have we ruled out suicide?' said Kennedy.

'I haven't ruled anything out so far,' said Lambert. He pushed the chair where Moira had sat, noting it was lighter than he'd imagined from the pictures on the iPad. He tested the chair where Eustace had supposedly sat. Unless his legs had been tied, the man should have been able to force himself up from the sitting position. Whether this meant anything was yet to be determined. 'I take it we've requested CCTV footage from the surrounding areas.'

'Yes, I've done most of your job for you,' said Wright, adding a mischievous, 'sir,' as Lambert fixed him with a hard stare.

'Thanks for your help, James. I'll call if we need anything else.'

They shook hands and Wright left.

'He seems happy about this,' said Kennedy, deadpan.

'Had any dealing with Eustace Sackville before?' asked Lambert.

'No. I did a quick check on the way over. He's been a bit quiet recently. No articles that I can find in the last nine months. I checked with the paper and he's still on staff,' said Kennedy, brushing a loose strand of red hair from her face.

'Initial thoughts?' asked Lambert.

'Presumptuous to look beyond Mr Sackville at the moment. No sign of a break in. I'd be interested to see the insurance policy on his wife. Could have been a poor attempt at suicide, could have been an elaborate set-up by Mr Sackville. Too many unknowns, as Tillman would say.'

Lambert was impressed by Kennedy's quick thinking. Although she was an experienced officer, most of her previous work had been organised crime. She would have seen murder scenes before, but nothing like this. Tillman's team didn't generally get involved in crimes of this nature. Normally something like this would be left to the Met's murder squads, or major incident teams. The Group had been formed to work on more covert operations, and since its disbandment Lambert had noticed their work was becoming more streamlined. Despite what Tillman had said about him being requested from above, it was hard not to feel that working on the case was some sort of demotion or, if not that, possibly a test to see if he was truly ready to return to work.

'I'm going to see Sackville. Tillman is setting up an incident room. Get the team together for a seven a.m. meet, and liaise with DI Wright over the CCTV footage. I want to know about everyone who set foot in this building in the last twenty-four hours.'

Lambert caught a taxi back to the hospital. He sat in the back and listened to Eustace Sackville's 999 call on his headphones again, searching for evidence that the man had been lying. His voice was whispered, but deep in tone. Lambert remembered Sackville as a smoker, and the years of nicotine had affected his vocal chords. 'It's my wife, she's been murdered.' The words were hauntingly simple, Sackville's voice drained of emotion – as if the fight had left him.

The operator went through the preliminaries, ascertaining location and if the intruder was still there.

'I watched her die,' added Sackville. 'He tied me up and made me watch her die. There was nothing I could do.'

The rest of the conversation, broken with sobs and a deep guttural coughing from Sackville, was unintelligible.

The hospital was even more desolate than before. Lambert wandered the labyrinthine corridors, trying not to think about Sophie who was asleep several floors above. He flashed his warrant card to the two uniformed police officers sitting outside Sackville's room.

'We've been told he can't be interviewed until morning, sir,' said one of the pair, a nervous looking officer who looked barely old enough to have completed his GCSEs.

'No one's spoken to him?'

'A member of Inspector Wright's team did, sir, but by all accounts he wasn't making any sense.'

'Who's the doctor in charge?'

'Dr Nitesh Patel. I'm afraid he's gone home,' said the constable, surprising Lambert by blushing.

'He's been sedated,' added the other constable.

'Great.' It was five a.m. and the only witness to Moira Sackville's death was comatose. 'I need to know the exact second he wakes or the doctor makes an appearance. Do not let anyone other than medical staff into that room. Clear?'

'Sir.'

Lambert walked the streets looking for somewhere to buy coffee. He found a petrol station with one of the newer coffee machines which used real beans. He called Kennedy, wincing as he sipped the bitter liquid.

'Everyone is ready at the incident room,' she said.

'Ok, I'm going to delay the meeting until Sackville is lucid. Any news on the CCTV?'

'There are two cameras on the front of the Sackvilles'

building, and more along the street. We're going through the footage now but I'm afraid it's a busy place. Lots of people coming and going.'

'You don't need to be told to search for anything unusual. Focus on people who have to be buzzed into the building rather than those who have keys, though don't rule anyone out. Hopefully we'll know more when I speak to Sackville.'

Chapter 4

Lambert returned to the hospital just as the coffee shop was opening and ordered his second Americano of the day. The place was coming alive with people, medical staff returning for the day shift, shop workers and ancillary staff, patients escaping the prison-like confines of their ward. Sophie was due to leave today and Lambert scanned the growing crowds, desperate to avoid bumping into Jeremy Taylor. He burnt his tongue on the coffee as he retraced his steps to where Sackville was currently residing. One of the uniformed constables had been replaced by a plain clothes officer. She was accompanied outside Sackville's door by the nervous sounding officer who had spoken to him last night. Both stood as Lambert walked towards them, Lambert shaking his hand free of the hot liquid he'd spilt.

'DC Shah,' said the woman, almost standing to attention.

'I remember you, Shah,' said Lambert. 'It's only been a few months, what do you take me for?' He'd worked briefly with the young detective during the Souljacker case. She'd assisted him in recreating the image of one of the suspects, a man known only as Campbell. Shah smiled, then, unsure if he was joking or not, cut the smile off abruptly.

'Dr Patel is in with Sackville now,' said the nervous sounding officer, who'd grown in confidence since the arrival of his co-worker. Fearing Lambert was about to reprimand him he continued, 'He's just gone in this second, we were about to call you.'

'Take a seat, both of you.' Lambert peered through a small rectangular window into Sackville's room, the large figure of the journalist momentarily obscured by the suited figure of the doctor currently examining him. 'Any other visitors?'

'No, sir.'

'What has Dr Patel told you?'

'Nothing, sir,' said Shah. 'He ignored us, didn't even acknowledge our presence.'

'Well don't let him hurt your feelings, Constable. What does he know about the incident?'

'He was informed about Mrs Sackville, last night,' said the nervous officer. 'There was no way of avoiding it. Mr Sackville was pretty incoherent at the time. After we told Dr Patel he decided to sedate him.'

The doctor left the room five minutes later. He didn't acknowledge Lambert's presence either and was about to walk off down the corridor when Lambert touched his shoulder.

'Dr Patel?'

'Yes?' said the man, turning to face Lambert, a look of distaste etched on his face.

'Detective Chief Inspector, Michael Lambert. I'm leading the case on Mrs Sackville's suspicious death.' The doctor shrugged his shoulders as if Lambert's position was of no interest to him. 'I need to speak to Mr Sackville.'

'Sorry, not possible.'

Lambert was experienced enough not to lose his temper. He'd come across jobsworths like Patel many times before. 'I'm afraid it's imperative I speak to Mr Sackville. He was the last person to see his wife alive. It is possible he witnessed a murder.'

'Mr Sackville has suffered serious mental and physical pain,' said Patel, walking away once more.

Lambert tried to placate the man. 'I understand completely, Doctor, but you must understand the urgency of the situation. If we are to have any chance of catching the person responsible for Mrs Sackville's death then we need to act as quickly as possible and we can't act at all until we hear what Mr Sackville has to say. I promise, five minutes at most. You can stop the interview at any time.'

The doctor nodded, considering what Lambert had said as if he was the person truly in charge of the situation.

'Five minutes,' he agreed, 'but you must stop if Mr Sackville becomes agitated in any way.'

'Thank you, Dr Patel. Before we go in, can you give me an update on Mr Sackville's condition?'

The doctor sighed, as if Lambert was asking him for an impossible favour. Lambert placed his hands inside his trouser pockets and clenched his fists.

'He was admitted with shock and severe trauma to his lower arms and wrists.'

'Can you give me some more detail on his wrist injuries?'

Patel moved his lips as if there was a bad smell in the room. 'We had to treat and strap his wrists. There were severe ligature marks and tissue damage on both sides. We've x-rayed him. There were no broken bones and I'm confident there will be no lasting damage. It's his mental state I'm most worried about. I've called in a clinical psychologist, who'll be here shortly.'

'I'm sure you don't like to hypothesise, Dr Patel, but if you were to guess, what would you say caused the injuries?'

'You're correct on that front, Mr Lambert. I'd say the marks are consistent with something being tied or strapped onto his wrists – but the pressure must have been immense considering the damage caused.'

'Could it have been rope, binds, handcuffs even?'

'Again I'm guessing, but the injuries are consistent with handcuffs of some sort. There were no burn marks which might result from the use of rope.'

'You've seen this sort of thing before?' asked Lambert.

'There's not much I haven't seen. Shall we?'

The doctor opened the door to Eustace Sackville's room. Lambert recognised the figure of the man lying in the bed, despite the unfamiliar context. He had come across Sackville on numerous occasions over the last couple of decades. Lambert remembered him as jovial, gregarious and with a respectful streak he hadn't always encountered with others of Sackville's profession. Now he looked like a pale, empty shell, years older than he should have been.

Then the man set his eyes on Lambert and something changed. There was still a sparkle there, a lightness to his piercing green eyes. 'DCI Lambert,' the man croaked, 'they're pulling out the big guns for me then.'

'Mr Sackville, it's good to see you again. I'm sorry it's in such awful circumstances.'

Sackville turned his head away in dismissal. 'None of this

formality bullshit, Lambert. Call me Eustace or Sackville, anything but Mr Sackville. Could you get me some water?'

Lambert picked up the glass jug to the side of Sackville's bed and filled two plastic beakers.

'Mr Lambert won't take up much of your time,' said Dr Patel.

Sackville waved the doctor away with a swipe of his hand. 'This needs to be done.' He took a sip of water, droplets spilling onto his chin which was decorated with specks of stubble. 'Sit then. Ask me what you have to.'

Lambert turned the chair to face him. He had to crane his neck to look up at the reclined figure. Dr Patel continued his sentry, arms folded at the edge of the bed.

'I understand what you're going through, Eustace. I know it won't be easy, but in your own words can you tell me everything that happened last night.'

Sackville nodded. 'I guess you actually do have some idea of what I'm going through,' he said. Sackville had reported on a number of Lambert's cases in the past and knew about the death of his daughter. Sackville took another sip of water. 'He was already in the house,' he said, the initial lightness Lambert had seen in his eyes disappearing, his face vacant as he recalled what had happened. 'At least I think he was. I came out of the bathroom and he was there. He had a knife, that's all it was, but it was pushed tight against Moira's throat.' The sound of grinding teeth filled the muted room. 'I hadn't heard a doorbell so I'm sure Moira hadn't buzzed anyone in – so he must have been there all along.'

'Can you describe him?' asked Lambert.

Sackville's eyes darted to the ceiling. 'Picture your clichéd version of a cat burglar and you've got him. Dressed head to toe in black. Mask instead of a balaclava. Leather I think. Even his eyes looked black through the slits in the mask.'

'Height? Build?'

'Six foot, six foot one. At one point he leant back on our bookcase, his head was level with the second from top shelf. You measure that, you'll get your height. It's funny what you think of in the circumstances, how your mind distracts you. He had a strong looking build, slim. When he cuffed me on the chair I could sense his strength.'

'Tell me what happened prior to that?'

'He told me to pull two chairs over,' Sackville hesitated, rubbing his neck. 'He told me to make sure they were facing, then he told me to sit.'

Lambert shuddered. Two months ago, he'd been in a similar position. Tied to a chair, a co-worker tied to a chair opposite. He'd thought he'd overcome the memories of that time, but now he wasn't sure.

'Mr Lambert, I'm not sure we should continue,' said Dr Patel.

Lambert shook himself from his reverie, and rounded on the man. 'We are continuing,' he said, turning back to Sackville. 'Continue, Eustace.'

'He told me to sit in the chair facing the window, to put my hands behind me. He said any movement towards him, however slight, would result in Moira's instant death followed by mine. I thought it was a simple house burglary, Michael. I thought the guy had messed up, got his timings wrong. I just thought he was going to tie us up, take whatever he wanted and then leave us alone. I couldn't see his face, so why…'

For the first time since Lambert had arrived, Sackville lost his composure. It was miraculous he'd kept it together so long.

'It's not your fault,' said Lambert. 'I'd have done exactly the same thing in your situation.'

'I doubt that. He pulled out a pair of cuffs. He manoeuvred Moira so she was behind me and he made her cuff me, my hands behind my back. He then told Moira to sit opposite me. As soon as I was secure he seemed to relax. He came over and pulled the cuffs tight to my wrists. He kept pushing them into my skin until he could push no more. Christ, I screamed like a bloody child.'

Sackville wiped his sleeve across his eyes. 'Moira screamed out for him to stop, and for some reason he did. Jesus.'

Lambert knew time was short. Recalling the incident was naturally having a great impact on Sackville, and Lambert feared he would break down again and that Patel would be forced to sedate him. 'Have some more water.'

'Thanks.' Sackville coughed. 'It's the not knowing. That fucking bastard paced the room, and refused to answer our questions about what he wanted. I think he was plucking up the courage to do what…'

'Tell me,' said Lambert.

Sackville swayed forwards and back on his pillow, his neck and facial muscles so tense they looked liable to snap at any moment. 'He stopped and looked at me, and I thought he was about to attack. He did, only it wasn't me.'

'This can't continue,' said Patel, almost as agitated as Sackville.

Lambert held up his hand. 'Please go on, Eustace.'

'He gagged her. It was fucking pitiful. I pulled at my cuffs, and they hurt even more, but I just kept fighting. The look in her eyes, Michael. You can't imagine. I saw everything. Fear, pain, loss, accusation. I saw our whole fucking life together disappearing and I was helpless to do anything about it. She was pleading to me, Michael. She wanted me to help her.' Sackville shook his head. 'You'll never fucking know.' He began sobbing, and Lambert had to look away as Patel went to intervene.

'Please, Eustace, just tell me,' said Lambert, staring at the hospital-white wall of Sackville's room.

'This is finished,' said Patel.

Lambert turned and looked back at Sackville, knowing he'd already pushed the man too far.

'It's okay,' said Sackville, trying to compose himself. 'He cut her, left wrist then right. It was almost tender, that sick bastard. Moira saw the blood and she disappeared. She didn't look at me any more. I kept asking him, why, fucking why? I told him to kill me instead but he just sat on one of the other chairs staring at me, ignoring my screams. Watching.'

Sackville's heart monitor began beeping rapidly, his heartbeat rocketing to one hundred and ten.

'Enough,' shouted Patel, pressing an alarm button.

As two nurses entered the room, Lambert called out. 'Who was he, Eustace?'

'I don't know, Lambert. You need to tell Prue. Prue McKenzie,' said Sackville, his voice a whisper as one of the nurses pulled a mask over his mouth and Lambert reluctantly left the room.

Chapter 5

'You must be doing something right. I've just received my first complaint about you.'

Lambert was sitting in Tillman's office, the blinds pulled down. 'Let me guess, Dr Patel?'

Tillman nodded. 'Was it worth it?'

'Unless he's an Oscar level actor, then we can rule out Eustace Sackville. Directly, at least.'

Tillman, who was leaning back on his swivel chair, raised his eyebrows.

'But I do think there was something he wasn't telling me.'

Tillman's chair groaned as he pulled himself upright. 'You think he arranged it somehow?'

'No, but I'm not ruling anything out yet. Why are we working on this, sir? Even if it's not a routine murder it's not really our department.'

'I told you, lots of interested parties on this one. You were requested. It seems your work on the Souljacker business has made you something of a celebrity. It needs to be contained though. I don't want it leaking to the press.'

'Really? Have you informed the uniforms guarding his room?'

'Yes, and the friends you've been making at the hospital.'

'Sackville's a journalist.'

'No press,' interrupted Tillman.

'Whatever you say. What is my team on this?'

'You'll be the SIO and head our team. We'll use outside help where necessary. You'll be needing this.' Tillman handed him a policy book.

Lambert smirked. Tillman was not renowned for following the rules. When they'd been part of The Group, the majority of the investigations had been so secretive that there was little or no record of them.

'You can laugh, but there is a lot of attention on this so do it right.'

Lambert left the room, still confused as to the importance given to the case. His team were assembled in the office, studying their laptops and case notes. Kennedy approached. 'How did it go with Mr Sackville?'

He relayed the conversation, noticing how intently Kennedy listened, her wide green eyes rarely diverting from his. 'Shall I get everyone together?' she asked.

Lambert nodded.

It was strange to head up a team after so long. Lambert stood in front of the six-strong team and called for silence. The team stared back at him, their faces a mixture of apathy and curiosity. He told them about his meeting with Sackville.

'What do we have in the way of family members?' he asked the room in general.

'It's a weird one, sir,' said Kennedy. 'There doesn't seem to be anyone in the way of immediate family. Both sets of parents have long since passed away. Both Mr and Mrs Sackville are only children. They married twenty-five years ago but are childless.'

Lambert paused. 'That might be relevant. Close friends, colleagues?'

'I've arranged a meeting with the editor of Sackville's paper for this morning,' said Kennedy.

'Good. Let's find out what he was working on. Get to know his colleagues. What about our victim?'

A young DC, the newest member of the team, Steve Devlin got to his feet. 'Mrs Sackville worked as a librarian,' he said. 'Dulwich Library. I'm planning to head over there after this, sir.'

'Give that to Kennedy,' said Lambert, noting the look of disappointment on Devlin's face. 'Sackville gave me the name "Prue McKenzie" when we talked. Kennedy, find out who she is. Get her thoughts on what happened. If Sackville's recollection is correct then we seem to have a killer who's not scared to take his time. Why did he make Eustace watch?' asked Lambert, thinking aloud.

'It's not that uncommon,' said Kennedy. 'Could be a power thing. Gets off on having his handiwork observed.'

'Let's check on The System for any similar cases where someone was forced to witness another's murder.'

'Why the wrists?' asked Devlin.

'Good point. The cause of death was two vertical incisions, one to each wrist. The autopsy may give us more. It was a long, slow death. Sackville seemed to think that was the killer's intention. Again, that might be significant.'

'It's reminiscent of suicide obviously,' said Kennedy.

'Yes,' agreed Lambert. 'But the most important thing for now is to find out as much detail about Mr and Mrs Sackville. It's imperative we have some idea of motive.'

'What are you thinking, sir?' asked Kennedy.

'From what Eustace Sackville told me, we are looking at someone professional. A killer who gained entry into the flat undetected, who had the patience and confidence to stay at the scene as Moira died. This was planned in advanced and Moira wasn't a random target.'

Chapter 6

'Kennedy, a word,' Tillman summoned her in just as the briefing ended. 'Shut the door.'

'Yes, sir,' said Matilda.

'Sit down.'

Matilda took a seat opposite her superior. He'd taken his jacket off and his pale blue shirt was tight against his body, as if constraining the flesh within. His head stood atop the widest shoulders she'd ever seen. He was like a prop-forward of a rugby team. Conspicuous muscle covered by a layer of fat.

'Update.'

'Shouldn't you be speaking to Lambert about that, sir?' She tilted her head, toying with him, wondering how far she could push.

Tillman stared straight ahead. 'As we discussed before, I want you to keep an eye on him. This is the first major case he's headed since he came back to us. You know his past.'

Matilda knew some of it. Lambert had been out of the force for the last two years. A few months ago he'd captured a serial killer who'd been active for over twenty years, by all accounts almost single-handed.

'I'm not going to spy on him Glenn, if that's what you want. Jesus, is that why...'

Tillman cut her off with a wave of his hand. 'Don't be so

ridiculous, Kennedy.' He looked genuinely aggrieved by her comment. They sat opposite each other in awkward silence, Matilda recalling the other evening where they'd both stayed on late at the local bar. Her ludicrous invitation for him to come back to her flat, and his even more ludicrous acceptance.

'I just want you to be mindful,' he said, breaking the silence. 'Let me know if he does anything out of the ordinary. He has a habit of doing things his own way. Just keep me updated.'

'Is there anything else, sir?' said Matilda, standing.

Tillman rubbed his chin, a bead of sweat dripping from his brow. She wanted to ask him about the other night but it wasn't the right place or time.

'Shall we save that for another time, Matilda?'

Matilda nodded and left his office, leaving the door ajar.

Lambert was still in the office, sitting alone, staring intently at his computer screen, but she knew he'd clocked her leaving Tillman's office. She walked over, noticing with surprise how fresh he looked despite being up all night waiting for Sackville to come round.

'Kennedy,' he said.

'Sir?'

'Anything new to tell me?'

'No.'

'What's your next move?'

'I have an address for Prue McKenzie. I'm off to see her. I'm afraid it'll be one of those visits. She doesn't know about Moira's death.'

Lambert returned his focus to his laptop. 'Okay, find out as much as you can.'

'Potential enemies, nemesis, that sort of thing. Somebody who'd just been fined for an overdue library book...' said Matilda, raising an eyebrow.

'Anything like that,' said Lambert, not looking away from his screen.

She thought about Lambert as she drove to Dulwich. The rumours and whispers about him were legendary within the department, though he seemed to have an uneasy relationship with Tillman. They'd worked an old case together, Lambert rescuing Tillman from a hostage situation which resulted in one of the captors dying. Then there was the Souljacker case where for a time Lambert had been a suspect in a string of killings spanning twenty years.

More than any of that, there was Lambert's daughter. Chloe Lambert had died age nine following a road accident when Lambert had been driving. The incident had taken place three years ago and resulted in Lambert being hospitalised, forced into an induced coma. He'd never been prosecuted for his role in the accident but the unkind whispers remained that somehow he was to blame.

Prue McKenzie lived in a semi-detached house close to Dulwich Park. Matilda pulled the car over two houses down. She knew nothing about the woman she was about to meet. As Moira Sackville had no immediate family, except for her husband, McKenzie would be the first person aside from the assigned professionals to learn of her death.

Matilda's shoes crunched on the loose stones of McKenzie's driveway. A light blue BMW with this year's licence plate took centre stage, polished to perfection. Matilda stood by the front door, took in a deep breath and rang the doorbell. She hated these types of visits, the reaction she would receive was unpredictable but never pleasant.

A thin, wiry woman in her mid-sixties opened the door and smiled at Matilda.

'Prue McKenzie?'

'Yes,' said the woman, surprising Matilda with the deepness of her voice.

'Detective Sergeant Matilda Kennedy, please may I come in?'

The initial jovial welcome vanished in an instant, the woman's calm appearance fading into a look of panic and dismay.

'Is it Jeffrey? Dear God, tell me what's happened. It's not one of the children?' The woman's deep voice had been replaced by a high pitched squeal close to hysteria.

'Let's go inside Mrs McKenzie. It's about your friend Moira Sackville.' Matilda put her hand on the woman, whose body trembled.

'Moira? What's happened?'

'Let's go in.' She followed the woman into the immaculate space of her house. All gleaming polished wood floors, and white walls adorned with original paintings. Mrs McKenzie led her through to a large living room. Two patterned sofas sat next to each other, creating an L shape.

'Please take a seat, Mrs McKenzie.'

The woman slumped in a chair like an unruly teenager.

'I'm afraid Mrs Sackville died last night in her apartment.'

McKenzie's face drained of colour. 'Died,' she said, her voice a whisper. 'How? You wouldn't be here if it wasn't serious.'

'I'm afraid we're treating her death as suspicious,' said Matilda, sitting down next to the woman.

'Eustace?'

'Mr Sackville is fine, though he has received some injuries.'

The woman murmured, placing her hand to her mouth. 'Injuries? Oh my God, she was murdered?' Her shaking intensified.

Matilda placed her hands on the woman's shoulders, trying to calm her.

'Can I get you a drink of water?'

The woman shook her head. 'Please, tell me what happened.'

'I'm afraid I can't go into too much detail,' said Matilda, remembering the strict instructions she'd received from Tillman about not disclosing the nature of the murder.

'In other words, she's been murdered,' said McKenzie.

'I'm sorry,' said Matilda. 'Please let me get you a drink.'

The woman nodded towards a door. Matilda found a glass beaker in a kitchen twice the size of her flat. She let the tap run, trying to calm her own trembling hands. She returned to the woman. 'Here you go, drink this. May I call you Prue?'

The woman, drinking in large gulping noises, nodded.

'Thanks, Prue. I need to ask you some questions. I'll try not to take too long. I understand you were very close to Mrs Sackville.'

The woman smiled. 'We were like sisters,' she said. 'Didn't have any other family, you see. It was just her and Eustace. They called each other orphans. Both sets of parents had died before they met each other at university. They found each other and have been together ever since. She couldn't have children so it's just been them, and me.'

'You met Mrs Sackville at university?'

'Yes, we were both studying English together. She's a

librarian.' She went to correct the tense and Matilda placed her hand on her shoulder again.

'Is there anyone I can call for you?' asked Matilda.

'It's okay, I'll call Jeffrey in a minute. What else do you need to know?' Matilda was impressed by the woman's change of tone, how she attempted to delay her own grief so she could help.

'I just need to know some more details about Mrs Sackville... Moira. We don't know much about her at the moment. Her husband is still in hospital.'

'My God, is it serious?'

'No, he will be okay.'

'I need to visit him, is that possible?'

Matilda wrote down the address and ward number where Eustace was staying. 'You may want to leave it until this evening as he's still a bit drowsy.'

'Thank you.'

'What can you tell me about Moira? What sort of person was she?'

'She was such a lovely woman. She'd do anything for you. I do a lot of charity work and Moira was always there to help, baking cakes, attending functions, always giving me as much support as possible. She was one of those people, you know, you could tell anything to.'

'I imagine it sounds a crazy question, but did she have any enemies? Anyone who'd want to hurt her?'

Prue laughed – a short, sharp snort, a mirthless sound. 'She was a librarian, enemies didn't normally come with the territory. Though even in small places like that there's politics, hierarchies, that sort of thing. She used to tell me about the pedantic people who worked there. Not all of them, mind you, just one or two. Some of the council staff who paid visits, the mad bureaucracy. She hated all those aspects. All she cared about were the books. I think that's why she got on so well with Eustace. They both loved words.'

'So she never told you of any trouble? Where she felt under physical threat?'

'God no. Just petty things. No one would want to harm her, why would they?'

'What about Eustace? Did you get on well with him?'

'He's a nice enough guy. I haven't really been able to socialise much with him despite him being married to my best friend. He was, he is, how should I put it … awkward in the sort of social situations we move in.'

The comment was meant to be harmless, throwaway, but Matilda saw a glimpse of the real Prue McKenzie in her words.

'In what way, awkward?' she asked.

'My husband is a QC, you know, a barrister.'

Matilda nodded.

'So a lot of our friends are, how shall we say, from the higher echelons of society. Moira could deal with that side of things, her family were well-to-do and she was left a lot of money. Eustace doesn't come from that sort of world and he didn't really try to blend in.'

'In what way? Was he just quiet during functions, that sort of thing?'

'Yes that and, it's sounds ludicrous, but he never put any effort into his appearance. Moira was fed up with it but she was sort of resigned.'

'Would you say they had a happy marriage?'

'I suppose so, but dynamics change over the years. You'll find that when you reach our age.'

Matilda didn't need to reach any age to understand that. 'Do you think Eustace could have had any enemies?'

'It's possible, given the sort of world he moved in – investigating criminals and whatnot. I didn't really know much about his work and Moira didn't like to share. Why do you ask?'

'It's only our first day of our investigation, we're just looking at all avenues at the moment.'

The woman seemed to have regained full composure, as if the death of her closest friend was a mere shock to the system which she'd already overcome. Matilda could tell she had something further to say, but rather than ask, she waited. The painful silence was alleviated by the ticking of the antique grandfather clock and the distant sounds of builders working on the nearest loft conversion.

'There was one thing,' said McKenzie, with false reluctance, like a classic gossip. 'I can't believe I'm telling you this but it will come out at some point. Moira was seeing somebody. You didn't get this information from me but it was one of the barristers at my husband's chambers, Charles Robinson. He's quite dashing and they met at one of my get-togethers.'

'How long was this going on?'

'Five years.'

Matilda sat back in the sofa, trying to control the wave of adrenaline that had come over her.

'Charles wouldn't hurt anybody, though'

Matilda sensed there was more. 'Tell me about them.'

Prue made a strange face as if sucking on a sour sweet.

Matilda knew the woman couldn't help herself. 'Moira told me some things about him, you know, sexual things.'

Matilda's heart raced, desperate for the information, thinking she may have made a breakthrough so early in the case. 'What sort of things?' she asked, keeping her tone neutral.

'Let's just say he did things Eustace wouldn't do. I don't know what the term is… S and M? I asked her to stop telling me after a time, I couldn't look Charles in the face.'

Matilda tried not to snigger at the sourness spreading across the woman's face. 'It would be helpful if you can give me some more details,' she said, gently. 'It could really help us.'

'I used to drown her out when she'd tell me things but he used to tie her up. I don't think it was anything too serious but she was always on about ropes and ties and what have you. Once she even mentioned he'd bought a pair of handcuffs.'

Chapter 7

Lambert alighted from the DLR at Canary Wharf station. Towering glass structures surrounded him on every side as he walked by the river. Kennedy had called him whilst he'd been on the train but he'd yet to check his voicemail. He was still suspicious of her earlier meeting with Tillman. There was something in the way she'd left Tillman's office which had annoyed him. If the meeting had to do with anything about the case then Lambert should have been informed. It wasn't proper protocol and Lambert had a distinct feeling that he wasn't yet fully trusted by his old colleague and superior, Tillman.

There had been a number of discrepancies Tillman had helped him with on the Souljacker case, not least a dead body found in Lambert's house. Tillman had questioned him extensively before allowing him to rejoin the NCA. He'd told Lambert it was the right time to return, but Lambert knew the man well enough not to take everything he said at face value.

The midday sun bounced off the glass panels and a drip of sweat tumbled down Lambert's forehead. He wiped it away with a brush of his hand, for a moment feeling completely isolated. Work had helped divert his attention but still his thoughts returned to his wife and her newborn child. The thought of Chloe's sister made him feel even more alone. He tried to shake the sense that Sophie would start a new life away from him and he would be left with his desolate bedsit and what remained of his career.

He walked through the revolving doors to the press building and after signing in took the lift to the fortieth floor. The doors pinged open to a hive of activity. A vast, open-plan workspace, filled with journalists working at their laptops and PCs. It was a stark contrast to the press rooms of old – the smoky, booze-fuelled workplaces where the hacks used to scratch out stories amongst the background of expletive banter. No one paid any attention as he walked across the office floor. He smirked as he passed a row of journalists working at stand-up desks, and knocked on an office door at the other end of the room.

A young woman, late twenties at most, opened the door and appraised him, assessing him in one quick glance as if she could see directly into his soul. 'DCI Lambert?' she said, holding out her hand.

Lambert shook hands, trying hard to hide his confusion.

'Mia Helmer. You look surprised, Mr Lambert.'

'Sorry, old habit. I'm ashamed to say I was expecting some-one…'

'More male?' said the woman, showing him into her office.

'Actually no. I was going to say, older, but I guess that's not appropriate either.'

The woman took a seat behind a vast glass desk, adorned only by a laptop. Her face broke into a smile for the briefest of seconds before returning to her default look, which was an unreadable mask. 'You wanted to speak to me about Eustace?' she said pointing to a seat opposite.

'Yes, thank you for seeing me at such short notice. I'm afraid it is really crucial that this conversation is off the record for the time being.'

Mia raised her eyebrows. Helmer was the crime editor for the paper, Sackville's direct line manager. 'So what do you have to tell me?' she said, noncommittal.

'I'm afraid Mr Sackville's wife was found dead in her apartment yesterday evening.'

If the woman was surprised she hid it well. Lambert had met professional poker players who gave away more signs of emotion. She didn't reply so he continued talking. 'At the moment we're treating the death as suspicious,' he said, unable to blank out the images of Moira Sackville tied to a chair, her pale body leaking blood into the pool of black liquid by her ankles.

'Well okay, this is the first I've heard of it so you must be doing something right. I imagine you think Eustace is involved somehow or you wouldn't be here. Am I correct?'

Lambert was stunned by the woman's coldness. 'Yes and no. We don't want this being publicised at the moment so I do have to insist it stays off record before I tell you any more details.'

'So you're offering me an exclusive?'

'Something like that, but I need you to wait before you run the story.' Lambert had only been in the office for five minutes but already he could understand how the woman had reached her senior position in such a short space of time. She had a natural authority about her. A cool charisma which he imagined helped her control even the most hardened of hacks.

'Give me all the details and we can decide on a time for release. But I'll tell you now, I won't wait any longer than twenty-four hours – especially seeing as one of my journalists is involved.'

'Fine,' said Lambert. He was surprised that the story had yet to leak anyway. He told her all the details about Moira Sackville's murder. How Eustace had been present, cuffed to one of the chairs and made to watch.

'Christ,' said Mia, losing her composure for a split second. 'Where is he now?'

'He's in hospital. We have a police officer with him.'

'You don't think he…'

Lambert shook his head. 'No, but obviously we can't rule anything out completely yet.'

'Who else knows?'

'No one, apart from the professionals involved,' said Lambert, doubting his own words. Matilda Kennedy had interviewed one of Moira's friends so the chances were that the word was out already.

'I need to run this,' said Mia.

It was inevitable the story would be public in a matter of hours. 'Not yet. Answer my questions and we'll see what we can do.'

'I'll need to speak to Eustace as well.'

'That's not possible.'

'Is he under arrest?'

'No, but he's under strict medical supervision. You wouldn't be allowed. But work with me and I'll let you know when he's free to talk.'

'What do you need to know?'

'Everything you can give me on Eustace. What's he been working on recently?'

'Not much. Look, Eustace is a special guy. He's very much respected here.'

'But?' said Lambert.

'He hasn't been submitting much copy of late. He'd told me he was working on a long term project. People trafficking in and out of London. He had a bee in his bonnet about some local businessman who he believed was working with a group from Croatia. All well and good, but he hasn't submitted anything for us in nine months and yet we still pay him.'

'Who was the local guy?'

Helmer looked at her laptop. It was clear she knew the answer and was debating whether to share the information with Lambert.

'He was investigating a local businessman called Curtis Blake. From what I can ascertain, he is legit. That's all I can tell you. If you want more details you'll have to speak to him yourself.'

'Anything else you can tell me about him? Is he particularly friendly with anyone in the office?'

'We hardly ever saw him. I had the odd report of people seeing him in local bars but other than that he kept himself to himself over the last few years. There were rumours – rumours, mind you – about marriage problems. But people like to create stories about people they don't regularly see, especially here.'

Lambert handed her his card. He didn't believe her. He was sure Mia knew exactly what Eustace was up to, and the truth of any rumours. 'Please let me know if you remember anything else.'

The editor nodded, dropping the card onto her desk. 'Perhaps we can work together on this,' she said. 'I can send someone around to meet you.'

'Once you're ready to be more forthcoming, let me know,'

said Lambert. 'Until then, I suggest you speak to our press office.'

He called Kennedy outside the newspaper offices. Her meeting with Prue McKenzie had been more of a success. She'd already arranged a meeting with Charles Robinson, a criminal barrister, at his chambers in Holborn.

Lambert caught the tube and arrived in Holborn before Kennedy. He waited for her in a coffee shop chain close to Holborn station.

He was halfway through his drink when she arrived. She nodded over and gestured with her hand, enquiring if he wanted another drink.

'You looked pleased with yourself,' he said, noting the spring in her walk as she approached.

'It happens occasionally. How was your meeting with the editor?'

'Unproductive. I think we can safely say the case is newsworthy now.'

Kennedy swept a loose strand of hair from her face. 'That'll please Tillman,' she said.

'Can't be helped.' The idea that they withhold details of the case from the press was ludicrous, considering the profession of Moira's husband. 'What do we know about this Charles Robinson?'

'I've done a bit of research. Criminal defence work mainly, started his career working for the CPS.'

'What do we know of his extracurricular appetites, other than those described by Mrs McKenzie?

'Nothing yet. Devlin's working on it, but I thought it best we go to the horse's mouth first.' Kennedy took a sip of her cappuccino. Lambert realised he didn't know much about his colleague other than what he'd been told second-hand. She was clearly highly intelligent, and he'd already noticed a dry sense of humour. She was attractive in an unconventional way. Tall and wiry, she had pointed prominent features with deep-set hazel eyes. It was the hair which distinguished her. It was tied back now – lines of fiery red pulled tight, making her pale forehead more prominent.

'Sip up,' said Lambert, getting to his feet.

It was a short walk to Robinson's chambers. Lunchtime was ending, reluctant workers returning to their offices bereft at having to leave the blazing sunshine. Kennedy followed a pace behind as they made the short walk. An immaculately attired man, mid-forties with short brown hair, greeted them as they entered the chambers. The man stood, and assessed them in one curious glance. 'How may I help?' he asked, his voice a resonant baritone.

'DCI Lambert, DS Kennedy. We have an appointment with Charles Robinson.'

'James Latchford, head clerk,' said the man, surprising Lambert who had mistaken him for one of the barristers. Latchford glanced down at the folio on his desk and beamed a smile at them. 'Yes, please take a seat and Mr Robinson will be with you shortly.'

Lambert paced the small reception area, admiring the bookcases lined with ancient legal texts, common law and statute books. He doubted the leather-backed tomes ever left their shelves, given that the printed words had all been codified and were available online. Still, they provided a decorative air of authority.

His concentration was diverted by a booming Welsh voice. 'DCI Lambert?'

Lambert turned to face Charles Robinson. Dressed in a three piece suit, a silk tie pressed so tight into his neck it almost choked him, the man looked little over fifty. He had a mane of silver hair, and the type of smile you would expect to see in a glossy magazine.

'And you must be DS Kennedy,' said Robinson, turning his attention to Matilda.

'Mr Robinson.'

'Please, call me Charles. Shall we?' He ushered them through a set of oak panelled doors towards his office. 'Please sit, may I get you coffee, tea?'

'No, thank you, Charles,' said Lambert.

'So, how may I help?'

'I'm afraid we have some bad news,' said Matilda. They had agreed on the walk over that she would speak first.

'Oh yes?' said Robinson, the smile remaining, his eyes narrowing.

'I'm afraid the body of Moira Sackville was found in her flat yesterday evening. She has been the victim of a suspected murder.'

Robinson's face collapsed, and Lambert saw another side to the man. An older, scared Robinson, the façade of his professional self vanishing. 'Moira? How? Why?' he said, his voice whisper quiet. He turned away from them in his swivel chair, facing a bookcase which mirrored the one in the reception area.

Lambert gave him a moment. 'How well did you know Mrs Sackville?' he asked.

Robinson didn't answer. He remained facing the bookcase.

Lambert was about to ask again when the man dragged his hand across his face and turned back in their direction. 'Sorry about that. This is quite a shock.' His bright red face highlighted the faint creases in his complexion, ageing him by ten years. 'How well did I know her? I knew her well. She is a good friend of Prue. Prue McKenzie. Sorry, Prue is a friend of the chambers, does a lot of work for charity. I met Moira through her at one of the functions. And her husband, Eustace,' he added as an afterthought. 'How is Eustace?'

'As well as can be expected,' said Lambert, not willing to divulge any more details at present.

'How close were you to Moira, Mr Robinson?' asked Kennedy.

Robinson linked his hands together, and stared at Kennedy. 'I suppose you know something or you wouldn't be here,' he said. 'I would sincerely hope this doesn't get out, for Eustace's sake, but yes, Moira and I were lovers for a time.'

Lambert doubted the man's concern was for Moira's widower. 'How long?'

'Five years, on and off.'

'How often did you see her?' asked Kennedy, a coldness in her tone.

'Listen, it was her choice. I never instigated anything, and would never contact her. I would only see her when she contacted me. That was the way it worked and I respected it.'

'Do you mind me asking if you have a significant partner?' asked Lambert.

Robinson frowned. 'No. My wife died fifteen years ago and there has been no one serious since.' He ran his hands through his hair, leaving a loose tuft sticking up from his scalp. 'I don't feel great about what happened. I don't prey on other people's wives as a rule. I'm afraid Moira wasn't that happy with Eustace, and that was long before I came along. I didn't steal her. She was obviously missing something in her life which I provided.'

'When was the last time you saw her?' said Kennedy.

Robinson clenched his hands together, his eyes darting upwards. 'About a year ago.'

'A year? You're sure?'

'Approximately, yes. I decided to end it. I'm afraid it had started to become quite tiresome.'

'And how did Mrs Sackville respond to this news?' asked Lambert.

'She was distraught. I received the odd phone call. Tears, that sort of thing, but I am sure she got over it.'

Lambert thought about what Kennedy had told him. The S and M Prue McKenzie had reluctantly detailed. 'No one is morally judging you, Mr Robinson. Our concern is to track Moira's killer. I'm afraid the crime scene was not a pleasant one.'

Robinson took in a number of shallow breaths. 'Do I really need to hear this?'

'I'll only go into as much details as necessary. There was a home invasion. Mrs Sackville was handcuffed to a chair,' said Lambert.

Robinson put his hand to his mouth. As a criminal barrister he would have heard much worse, as a defence barrister would have defended those accused of such acts. Either it was a show, or he was genuinely distressed by his lover's death. 'We believe the intruder cut open her wrists and that Mrs Sackville slowly bled to death.'

'Slowly?' said Robinson, his voice a squawk of anguish.

Lambert stared at the man, searching for any clues that he was play acting.

'Eustace?' said Robinson.

Lambert glanced at Matilda, her face impassive. 'He was made to watch.'

'He wasn't hurt?'

'He was cuffed to a chair as well.'

Robinson turned his attention towards the ceiling, seemingly picturing the scene. 'They let him go?'

'They?' said Matilda.

'Him, her, them?'

'Mr Sackville confirmed there was just the one intruder,' said Lambert.

'Why did they hurt Moira, and not Eustace?' Robinson was more focused, quizzing them as if they were on trial.

'That's what we need to find out. Mr Robinson, this is a delicate matter but can you elaborate on your relationship with Moira Sackville?'

'Elaborate?'

Lambert hesitated, thinking how best to broach the subject, when Matilda interjected. 'Did you and Mrs Sackville engage in any unusual sexual practices?'

Robinson flushed red. Lambert initially thought he was embarrassed but soon realised it was something else.

'And how the hell is that any of your business?' he asked, his booming voice heavily accented.

'It links in with our investigation,' said Matilda, unmoved by the barrister's protestations.

'Links in with your investigation? Why, because she was tied to a chair?'

'Cuffed,' said Lambert.

'What a tenuous, flimsy link! Who told you this?' said Robinson, the answer dawning on him. 'Prue McKenzie, what a surprise. I knew Moira would tell her, though I warned her not to, judgemental and no discretion.'

'I thought you were good friends with Mrs McKenzie?' said Kennedy.

Lambert was struck at how quickly Robinson had unravelled. He'd revealed more of himself in the last thirty seconds than he had throughout the rest of the interview.

'No one is good friends with her, except maybe Moira.' He shook his head, as if he'd forgotten about the death of his lover. 'You think she does all that charity work for the good causes? Don't make me laugh. It's all a show, a way to ingratiate herself. I bet she never puts a penny in out of her own pocket, just uses the money raised to buy the fancy caterers and party planners so she can look good amongst her friends.'

'But she introduced you?' said Lambert, keen to exploit Robinson in his emotional state.

'Not really. We were both at one of her parties and we met. We introduced ourselves.' His face was still red, his breathing laboured. He sat back in his chair, the colour draining from his face. 'I'm not going to discuss what we did. I won't let you sully her memory.'

Lambert nodded. 'I will need a note of your whereabouts last night.'

Robinson's eyes widened as he adopted a sardonic tone. 'It's always a pleasure helping you guys out. I was at an Inn's dinner. I was there till gone midnight. I ordered a taxi. Latchford will give you the number of the firm we use so you can check with the driver.'

Robinson stood, giving Lambert and Kennedy their cue to do the same. 'Listen, I'm sorry if I lost my temper,' said Robinson, to Kennedy in particular. 'I will assist in any way I can.' Lambert was intrigued by the barrister's sudden changes in behaviour. The news of Moira's death had clearly affected him.

It was raining as they left the chambers; a sudden downpour had reached the drains, leaving a faint sulphurous odour in the air. 'Verify what he told us,' said Lambert, as he heard a shout from behind him.

The figure of Charles Robinson jogged towards them, his face flushed from the exertion. 'I remembered something,' he said, his breath coming in rapid bursts between words. 'I'm sure it's nothing but thought you should know. A former client of mine used the same MO, similar at least, to what you've just told me.'

Lambert didn't respond. He took out his notebook, waited for Robinson to reveal himself.

'Obviously, I can't tell you anything confidential but it reached the court. May I?' he said, looking at Lambert's notepad.

Lambert handed it over and Robinson scribbled some words onto the paper. 'You'll find everything there,' said Robinson, writing R v. Whitfield CJ (2008) on the piece of paper.

'You represented Whitfield?' asked Lambert.

Robinson nodded.

'Verdict?'

Robinson pursed his lips. 'Not guilty.'

Chapter 8

They watched Robinson walking back towards chambers.

'He looks worried,' said Kennedy.

'Perhaps. Go back and read through the case, and everything we have on it. Call me when you have some details and we can decide if it's worth pursuing.'

'You don't think it will be?'

'It would be convenient, but let's see. I'm going to visit Eustace again. I want to know if he knew about Robinson, and what he's been working on lately.'

'I have an appointment with the head librarian from Moira's library. I postponed the meeting after McKenzie's revelations about Charles Robinson.'

'Good. You should have time to check the case first, or get someone else on it so we at least have a summary.'

Lambert caught the tube back to the hospital. He rarely used cars if he could help it and in central London it was usually quicker getting about by public transport. He thought about Robinson's changing personalities. The sadness he'd expressed on learning of Moira's death, followed by the anger at the insinuation he'd read into Kennedy's questions. He saw the case opening up before him, strand after strand branching out into infinite possibilities. He wanted a working theory but so far it was evading him. He hoped that Moira's death was personal.

That way it would be easier to find the killer. If it was random, which seemed unlikely, they would have to rely on the killer having made a mistake.

For now, they had to find out more about Moira Sackville. He realised they knew very little apart from her friendship with Prue McKenzie, and relationship with the Welsh barrister. Hopefully, Kennedy's meeting with Moira's colleagues would shed some more light on the woman.

After eating lunch in a small Italian off Lordship Lane, he called Sarah.

'DCI May.'

'Very formal,' said Lambert.

'I just like the way it sounds. How are you, stranger?'

'I'm well. Thought I'd check in, see if you remember me, that sort of thing.' The lunch had energised him and despite the stress of the case he felt momentarily optimistic, sitting in the sunshine, nursing an espresso, speaking to Sarah.

DCI Sarah May had been the SIO on the Souljacker case and they had ended up working together, albeit unofficially. They had become close after the case, and Lambert had spent some time at her flat in Bristol before returning to London. He hadn't realised how much he'd missed hearing her voice.

'You can call me any time, Michael, you know that. You don't need an excuse.'

'So what are you working on?' said Lambert, changing the subject.

'Same. We keep finding bodies.' She was referring to the legacy of the Souljacker. Following his death, a book was published electronically releasing the details of a number of murders. May had been tasked with following up and had so far discovered four unmarked graves. 'What about you, still on the drugs case?'

'No, I've been promoted. I'm heading up a murder investigation.'

'Look at you, back to your old ways.'

Lambert outlined the case, keeping the detail confidential.

'Some promising leads,' said May. 'You think it's a one-off?'

'I suppose it comes down to motive. If he was after her for some reason then it might end here. Don't know yet.'

'Well, let me know if you need any help,' said May, a mischievous lilt to her voice.

They were skirting around the real issue. He'd returned to London to start work, and there had been no resolution about their relationship. They'd promised to keep in touch, to visit, but nothing more definite. He would have loved to see her, but they were both too busy.

There was also something else pressing on him, which he blurted out. 'Sophie's had the baby.'

Sarah didn't respond and he thought for a second the line had been cut. 'Ah,' she said, eventually. 'When?'

'Three days ago. They've had to keep her in for some checks. There were some difficulties but she should be going home today. Sorry, Sarah, I should have told you before.'

'Don't be silly. How is she? How are you?'

'She's fine. The baby is called Jane.' He couldn't bring himself to say the words, Jane Chloe.

'How are you, Michael?' said Sarah, insistent.

'I'm okay. It's a bit surreal. Look, I can't talk about it at the moment.'

'I'll come down,' said Sarah.

Lambert snorted, his pulse quickening. 'You're coming to rescue me?'

Sarah laughed down the line, the melodic sound sending waves of feeling through him. 'Yes. You're all alone, and Sophie has this new baby, and...'

He cut her off. 'I have the case. I'll be fine. When we have some more time we can get together. It would be good to see you.'

'Smooth talker.' She hesitated. 'You know I should come. But fine. Call me when you need to.'

'I know. Look, I'd better go. Duty calls.'

'Look after yourself.'

'You too.'

He braced himself for seeing Sophie and the baby as he entered the hospital. It was possible they were still both upstairs in the maternity ward but he couldn't bring himself to find out, unsure if it was his place any more.

The rush of adrenaline from speaking to Sarah had faded, and he realised how tired he was. He bought another coffee from the hospital outlet, and headed towards the secure area where Sackville was being treated.

Nervous guy had left, and a WPC had joined the young DC Shah. Lambert didn't bother with introductions. 'Update?'

'A few coming and goings,' said Shah, handing him a report sheet. 'Nurses, food, Dr Patel, and a psychiatrist, Dr Byatt. They want to discharge him, sir.'

Lambert entered the room. Sackville was sitting up in bed watching daytime television. 'You're feeling better I hear?'

Sackville lifted his head. He looked worse than yesterday, his pale skin mottled and blotchy, his eyes sunken and lifeless.

Lambert didn't envy the man. He had no family left, and his career was fading. The rest of his life would be haunted by memories of his wife's murder. All the counselling in the world wouldn't change that.

'You remember our conversation yesterday?'

'They called it an interrogation in the war,' said Sackville, a crack of a smile appearing on his face.

'May I?' said Lambert, taking a seat. 'Sorry about that, I needed as much information as possible.'

'Have you told Prue?'

'Yes. I've also spoken to your editor.'

'I know.' Sackville pointed to a bouquet in the corner of the room.

'Your editor's young.'

'Mia? Young in age maybe, but she has an old soul. An old, deathless soul.'

'Yes, she seemed happy go lucky,' said Lambert, sharing the joke. 'She mentioned you're working on something at the moment but wouldn't go into much detail.'

'Don't get her started on journalistic sources, though I have to say I agree with her. Why did you want to know?'

'We have to look at all angles, obviously. Mia mentioned you've been investigating the Blake family.'

Sackville's face dropped. 'What did you give her for that, an exclusive?'

'She didn't reveal anything. Told me to speak to you directly if I wanted any details.'

'I've been investigating Curtis Blake on and off all my life.'

'Mia mentioned something about people trafficking. Blake updating his empire?'

'She hasn't quite grasped it, and I'm afraid there isn't much of a story.'

'Who is he working with?'

'Listen, I don't like Curtis Blake, and I don't respect him. In fact, I despise what he does and what he's done.'

'But?'

'Some of these new guys. They have no boundaries. You must know that?'

Lambert had seen many things he wished he hadn't over the years. As far as he was concerned, there had never been any boundaries for the majority of people he'd dealt with. The notion of the idealistic British criminal was the stuff of fiction. He was sure Eustace knew that as well as he did. 'Justice is blind, Eustace. If they're wrong, they're wrong.'

'There are degrees of wrongness, as you well know.'

'You're going to have to be more specific.'

Sackville adjusted the pillows on his bed. 'I need to get out of here. You name it – the people smuggling, trafficking, the mindless violence. The more I see, the worse it is.'

'It's always been that way, Eustace. Tell me what you know. Who do you have details on, who would want to do this to Moira?'

'You don't bloody get it, do you?'

Lambert lifted his palms. 'Enlighten me.'

'I've stopped working. Blake is just an excuse. I had a few meetings, took some notes and that's it. Just enough work to convince Mia to keep paying me until I retire. I'm done, no stomach left.'

Lambert stood. 'Want some water?'

Sackville shook his head, a look of disdain on his face.

'So you have no idea who would do this?'

'Listen, Lambert.'

Lambert paced the room, reluctant to say what had to be said. 'What about Moira?'

Sackville tensed, colour spreading to his cheeks.

'I need to ask. Did she have any enemies, Eustace?'

'Don't be bloody ridiculous.'

'I need something, Eustace. If there isn't a reason for this attack, if it was completely random, then we will never find out who did this to Moira. I need a motive.'

'She was a bloody librarian.'

The man wasn't listening. 'Look, I'm sorry to ask this Eustace but do you know Charles Robinson?'

Sackville tensed again, and for one absurd moment Lambert thought he was about to spring at him. 'That's long finished,' said Sackville, through gritted teeth.

'So you know about him and Moira.'

'Yes, I fucking know. She couldn't hide her guilty conscience.'

'When did it end?'

'A couple of years ago.'

Lambert hid his surprise, remembering that Robinson had said it had ended a year ago. 'Did you ever confront him?'

'No, but then we were never in the same room together after I found out.' Sackville took a swig of water. 'Could do with something stronger,' he said, wiping a drip from his face.

'Does he know that you know?'

'I imagine he fucking does, yes.' Eustace scrunched his face, the memory of his wife's infidelity somehow animating him more than her death. Something changed in his face, and he began pulling the covers from his bed. 'Is that bastard a suspect?' he said, trying to get to his feet, flailing on his back.

Lambert placed his hand on his shoulder. 'Come on, get back to bed. Robinson has an alibi for the evening of the attack.'

Sackville pulled the covers back over, making an angry swipe of his hand across his tear filled eyes.

'Let's leave it for now, Eustace. Get some rest. Is there anyone I can contact for you?'

Sackville shook his head. 'There's no one,' he said.

Chapter 9

Devlin stopped her as she returned to the office. 'You seen Lambert today?'

'Just left him, why?'

'I wanted to go through the CCTV footage with him.'

'Well, you can go through it with me first,' said Matilda. She liked the new DC, but on occasions he was a little too keen to show off his worth.

'Not much to show unfortunately. No cameras face the front of the building. There is a camera in the apartment's foyer. I edited all the frames which I thought of interest, and went through them with the concierge. Everyone is accounted for during the twenty-four hour period.'

Matilda frowned. They hadn't expected anything but it was still a disappointment. 'I don't think you need to bother DCI Lambert with no news, do you?'

Devlin looked momentarily crestfallen. 'No, Sarge.'

She took pity on him. 'I need a name checked. Noel Whitfield.' She handed him the piece of paper with the case name on it. 'I need all details on this case. Thirty minutes?'

Devlin nodded as he rushed back to his desk.

She updated the file as she waited for Devlin. She thought about the adulterous barrister, and his panicked response to their investigation. She would have liked it to have been a sign of a guilty conscience, a way of distracting them from their investigation, but feared it was just a sign of the kind of man he was. They'd just informed him that his long-term lover had been brutally murdered, and his main concern was protecting himself.

'Interesting case,' said Devlin, returning with a case file twenty minutes later. 'Serious cock-up by CPS in my opinion.'

'Give me the highlights,' said Matilda.

'Whitfield, aged thirty, was charged with attempted murder. He'd broken in, and had been waiting in the residence of the alleged victim, Andrew Haynes. Haynes' girlfriend, Rebecca Pritty, was present at the time. Whitfield was alleged to have tied both victims to two separate radiators in Haynes' bedroom. He made the girlfriend watch as he tortured Haynes, and left him to die after repeatedly stabbing him in the torso.'

'He survived?'

'If you can call it surviving. Permanently disabled.'

'And the girlfriend watched all this.'

'She was Whitfield's ex. He made her watch, no disguise, quite clear motive. He left her at the scene. Fortunately, a neighbour heard their screams early on and they got Haynes to hospital in time.'

'What happened in court?' asked Matilda, thinking she already knew the answer.

'Whitfield was represented by a Mr...' Devlin looked at his notes.

'Charles Robinson?'

Devlin tilted his head. 'Yes. Robinson found a number of discrepancies in the evidence gathering. The judge reluctantly declared there was no case to answer. Gave CPS a complete dressing down.'

'What about Whitfield since?'

'He was sectioned for a time but was released. He's been clean since. Last known address is over in Finchley.'

'And Haynes?'

'He went into psychiatric care for a time. Girlfriend left him. Last we know of him he's living with his brother in an estate in Tottenham.'

'Good summary, Devlin.'

Devlin couldn't hide his pleasure, a broad smile filling his face. 'Is it worth pursuing?'

'We'll have to tick the boxes now just in case. Sounds like an isolated incident to me. Try to locate Whitfield but don't approach him without speaking to me. I'll run it past Lambert.'

She read through the files Devlin had printed, looking for any discrepancies he may have missed, but came up blank. It took a great leap to link the Whitfield case with Sackville. Unless there was a clear link between him and either of the Sackvilles then it was difficult to see the cases being related unless it was pure coincidence.

She logged into The System, and ran differing routines matching the Sackvilles, Whitfield and Haynes, but no link was evident. She decided to wait until Devlin located Whitfield. It was too tenuous a link to bother pursuing at present.

She took lunch in the canteen, finding a small spot which overlooked the river. She glanced at the newspaper in front of her as she took mouthfuls of jacket potato but couldn't concentrate on the text. She kept replaying the case in her head. She'd thought so much about it in the last few hours, that it was as if she'd witnessed the incident. She had her own video of what happened in her head, and it followed what Eustace Sackville had told Lambert. A lone intruder, forcing the woman to cuff her husband then being cuffed herself. She pictured the man cutting Moira Sackville, could hear the sound of the knife tearing at her flesh.

Matilda understood this way of thinking was dangerous. For all they knew at present, Eustace's description of events could have been a fabrication. They had yet to rule him out as a suspect. It was feasible that he was the one responsible for Moira's death. That he had tied her up and had somehow managed to inflict the cuff marks on his own wrists as a defence. It was possible the scene Matilda was replaying in her mind was a lie.

She thought about the lawyer, Charles Robinson and his affair with Moira Sackville. Again, images played in her head like memories. Secret rendezvous, the bedroom games which had so appalled Prue McKenzie. She tried to picture Robinson as the intruder but couldn't visualise it. He'd left a poor first impression on her but he was too much of a coward to have killed Moira. The way he'd tried to distance himself from her murder, offering a former client to distract them from him. Even the way he talked, the practised confidence, the silky charisma. He was like a chimera, – but again, they couldn't rule him out. She had to shake the images of the murder from her head, and follow the facts.

'Don't mind, do you?' DC Donald Walker took a seat opposite her. 'How goes it Sergeant?'

Walker had been a member of her team for over two years. Last year they had both competed for a vacant sergeant position. Matilda was sure Walker had never forgiven her for winning.

'What do you want, Walker?'

'Just checking how your work with Lambert is going. Is he treating you right?'

Matilda sighed, deciding to get straight to the point. 'Is this to do with the sergeant test again?'

Walker fidgeted in his chair, picked at his infuriatingly manicured beard. 'We all know how you got that position, Kennedy.'

Matilda smiled. She'd attained the position through sheer hard work and results. Walker's tendency to open his mouth before thinking was one of the reasons he'd yet to be promoted. She adopted her most patronising tone, knowing it would get to Walker. 'Look, Don, I can't help it that I was deemed to be the most suitable for the position. Maybe next time, yeah?' She rolled her eyes upwards, enjoying Walker's discomfort.

Walker nodded his head a few times. 'You should have taken me up on my offer that time, you wouldn't be speaking to me like that if you had.'

Matilda stared hard at the man. He was referring to the last Christmas party where he'd had too many mulled wines and had made a fumbled pass at her. 'You were lucky I didn't report you then. I'd watch what I said, if I were you.'

'Oh, fuck off, Kennedy,' he whispered through gritted teeth.

Matilda took a bite of her congealed jacket potato, and looked down at her paper.

Walked waited a beat and eventually took the hint.

She watched him leave in her peripheral vision, not lifting her head until she was sure he'd left the canteen. She tensed her arm, noting her hand was trembling. She should report him. She'd heard whispers from a couple of other female officers that the Christmas party was not an isolated incident, but she had to be careful. However progressive the Met presented itself, it was still male dominated. Complaints of sexual harassment were treated seriously, but there was always the risk of being ostracised. The worst he'd done to her was make a silly pass, which hadn't bothered her that much. It was not enough to take it further, but she couldn't help thinking that his behaviour might escalate, if not with her then with someone else.

Lambert called, distracting her. They agreed to meet at Lordship Lane in two hours. She returned to the office, and was about to start researching Charles Robinson when a booming voice called to her from the other end of the room.

'Sergeant Kennedy. My office. Now,' said Tillman.

Chapter 10

Lambert stopped at a newsagent on Lordship Lane and purchased a bottle of water. The weather was relentless. The brief rainstorm earlier had done little to dampen the heat. His cotton shirt stuck to his body like a second skin. He downed the water in one and headed to the library. He kept getting the sense that the case was splintering in numerous directions, none of which were helping him. In cases like this, immediate family were normally where a case began and ended. Moira's only family was Eustace and at the moment, Lambert couldn't see him being involved. It was too complicated a set-up. If he'd wanted to eliminate his wife, for whatever reason, then it could have been done more easily. As a crime journalist, Eustace would have arranged things differently.

Not that they could eliminate him completely. Eustace knew about his wife's adultery so there was a potential motive. It was possible that he could have paid someone to commit the crime, and paid extra to be able to watch. Lambert had encountered similar scenarios before. Eustace was full of grief but Lambert had seen plenty of guilty men grieve for their actions.

Kennedy had changed clothing since this morning. Gone was the plain trouser suit, in its place a green summer dress. Her red hair was still tied neatly in a bun, and when she greeted him he noticed she wore more make up than usual.

'Something I should know?'

She screwed up her face, confused.

'I didn't realise we were dressing up,' said Lambert.

'Oh.' A flash of colour spread over her cheeks and faded.

Lambert held up his hands. 'I'm making no comment, Sergeant,' he said, smiling.

'Off to see a friend afterwards. Unless we have more work,' she added, as a reluctant afterthought.

'I'm sure we can spare you for one evening,' he said, moving past her into the entrance of the library trying to ignore the faint scent of her perfume.

He was surprised to find the library full of people. The atmosphere inside was stifled. People sat at desks battling away at their laptops or reading newspapers and periodicals. Lambert made his way over to the enquiries desk, trying to ignore the stench of body odour emanating from an elderly man who was reading an oversized print hardback. 'I'm here to see Sandra Levinson,' he said to the spectacle-wearing man behind the desk.

The man squeezed the bridge of his nose, as if Lambert's presence was an unwelcome distraction. 'I believe she's in her office. Up the stairs, through the door marked "do not enter". Is she expecting you?'

'Yes, thank you.'

Kennedy had called earlier, informing the head librarian about Moira Sackville. It seemed the woman had yet to tell her staff about their colleague's tragic, and violent, death. Either that or Moira's death had failed to touch the man behind the desk in anyway.

'You lead,' he told Kennedy as they knocked on the door.

A striking woman with large opal eyes opened the door. 'Hello?' she said, her smile warm and compassionate, only the few fine lines under her eyes betraying her age.

'Mrs Levinson? Sergeant Matilda Kennedy, we spoke on the phone earlier. This is DCI Michael Lambert.'

The smile vanished, as Levinson realised why they were there. 'Do come through,' she said.

The woman led them to a small office, little bigger than a broom cupboard, and asked them to sit. 'I'm afraid I'm still coming to terms with what you told me this morning, Sergeant Kennedy. I've lived in London all my life and it's the first time I've ever known someone…' Her words drifted off, as if she'd finished the sentence in her mind.

'Our sincere condolences, Mrs Levinson. Something like this is always a huge shock. There are people we can put you and your colleagues in touch with to help you through this time.'

'Thank you.'

'Did you know Moira well?' asked Lambert.

'Yes,' said Levinson, looking intently at him. 'I've been working here for five years. Moira was here when I started. In fact, I was surprised at the time that she'd not been offered my position. She had a wealth of experience, and a passion for the place which has been unequalled since. She later confided that she hadn't applied for the role, that she didn't want the added burden of such responsibility. She will be sorely missed.'

'Could you tell me a bit more about the person she was?' asked Kennedy.

Levinson turned to face Kennedy. Her look was intense. She focused on Matilda as if she was the only person in the room. If Kennedy was intimidated by the look, she didn't show it.

'As I mentioned, she was very passionate about the library. She was an avid reader, most of us are, as you can probably imagine. She loved helping people. There was a small band of elderly women who used to come see her every week for advice on what to read next.'

'How did she get on with other members of staff?' asked Lambert.

Levinson turned her focus, her eyes boring into him. 'Very well. We're quite a close knit team.'

'No animosity? Trouble with any of the library's patrons?' asked Kennedy.

'Moira? You couldn't wish to meet a lovelier person. In all my time here, I never heard a bad word said about her, or by her.' Levinson had raised her tone, and sounded defensive.

'Did you ever meet with her away from work?' asked Lambert.

'Not really. We have the occasional social get-together, at Christmas, that sort of thing.'

'Did you ever meet her friends, or family?'

'I met her husband once. Very jolly chap. He's a journalist. I helped him with some research on local history.'

'Did she ever confide in you?' asked Kennedy.

'About what?'

'Anything.'

'We didn't really have that sort of relationship, I'm afraid. We were colleagues first, friends second. I wish I could help you, I really do. I can't believe anyone would do this purposely to Moira. I mean, no one would single her out. I can only imagine it was random.'

Lambert stood, uninterested as to the woman's opinions on

motive. 'Thank you, Mrs Levinson, you've been a great help. We'll be in contact tomorrow. Some officers will be over to speak to the members of your team. In the meantime, please let me know if you think of anything which may be of help,' he said, handing over his card.

'Well, that was a waste of time,' said Kennedy, outside.

'Nothing is a waste of time. We know now she didn't socialise much with her colleagues. She loved books. Eustace was researching the local area. Any of those points may become relevant.'

'Let's hope so,' said Kennedy, who was almost hopping on the spot with eagerness to get away.

Lambert paused. 'Well, don't let me keep you.'

Kennedy opened her mouth then shut it.

'See you seven a.m. tomorrow morning.'

Kennedy frowned. 'Sir,' she said, sticking her hand out for a passing taxi.

Lambert caught a taxi home, too tired for public transport. Home was currently a bedsit in Lewisham. Sophie was keeping the house for the time being until they had formalised details of the separation. A wave of dampness and festering mould overcame him as he opened the communal front door. He could almost see the trapped hot air escape through the front door. He hauled his tired body up the stairs to his room, telling himself that it was only temporary.

His room was oppressive. Although he'd left his window on the latch, his room was still stifling. He opened the window fully and allowed the minuscule breeze to cool him. A thousand thoughts played in his mind. He needed time to collate, analyse, and organise them as was his way, but first he needed to rest.

His sleep pattern had never been normal, but now it was destroyed. He'd last slept late yesterday evening on the cold bench at the hospital. The lights had appeared then but despite his tiredness he didn't think he would hallucinate tonight.

He made a red bush tea, sat on the room's sole chair and listened to Andy Shauf singing about falling asleep. He tried to attack each raging thought one at a time, but the images of the last twenty-four hours swam in his head in a grotesque collage: Moira Sackville's crime scene, Eustace Sackville alone and distraught in a hospital bed, Sophie and the new baby, Matilda Kennedy setting off for an evening out. He imagined Sarah May was in London, wished that he could just call her and she would appear.

He undressed, and climbed into bed, his thoughts returning to Eustace Sackville. He thought about what the man had been through, the death of his only family, and tried to think about how he must be feeling alone in his hospital bed. Then his thoughts moved on to Sophie and the new baby; how Chloe's sister would never be part of his life, and he realised his and Eustace Sackville's situation were not that different.

Chapter 11

She realised it was a mistake. She realised every time she did it. She'd half hoped last night that Lambert would have asked her to work later so she could have avoided it.

She walked naked into the bathroom and switched on the shower. She searched through the cabinets but found only the most rudimentary of toiletries. It was unprofessional in more ways than one. She'd known from the moment she'd changed into the green dress, which had even received a note of assent from Lambert, that she would end up staying the night here. Yet she hadn't even brought a change of clothes. Now she would have to go home and change. She turned off the shower, returned to the bedroom and put on her clothes.

Tillman sat up in bed and looked at her. 'Leaving already?'

'Lambert's scheduled a meeting for seven and I can hardly turn up in last night's clothes.' Her tone was short, and summed up their relationship. The nights of passion, followed by the mornings of regret. Tillman was barely covered by a thin sheet. She surveyed him as she dressed, intrigued by the vastness of his pale body. His large figure at once overweight but muscled, far from her normal choice in men. She was sleeping with the boss, something she'd always secretly belittled other women for doing, but there was something about the man which drew her in.

Tillman rubbed his eyes. For a moment, she thought he was going to say something ridiculous, like she should leave some clothes at this place. 'I'll see you there,' he said, rolling over on his side. She fought a wave of desire and left.

She drove home, the evidence of last night's excesses seeping through her pores. She needed food and coffee. At home, she ran the coffee maker and showered again – dousing herself in shower gel and shampoo, scrubbing her teeth clean with an evangelical zeal. She toasted a bagel, and burnt her throat washing it down with the scalding coffee.

Devlin greeted her as she walked into the incident room five minutes early. 'Sarge, a Mrs Levinson called last night. She wants to speak to you. Something she forgot to mention yesterday, she said.'

Kennedy nodded, taking the note from him. She sat at her desk, glancing at Lambert who had seemingly not noticed her arrival.

'Right, let's get on with this,' said Lambert, getting to his feet. He was dressed in a suit she hadn't seen before. He looked surprisingly fresh, clean shaven, and bright eyed, as if he'd had a good night's rest. He handed out duties with almost military-like precision. He ordered a re-examination of the CCTV footage, checked that the Whitfield lead was being followed up, and instructed two of the team to start trawling through Eustace Sackville's past newspaper stories. 'Anything, however minor, that stands out – then notify me immediately,' he said.

The meeting lasted less than twenty minutes.

'Good night?' he said to Matilda, after everyone had left the conference room. His eyebrows arched high, giving him a comical look.

'It was fine, thank you,' she replied, deadpan. She told him she planned to see Levinson again that morning.

'Okay. I want you to visit Sackville after you've seen her. See if you can get anything from him. Maybe he'll open up to you. Try to find out some more about his article research and his relationship to the Blake family. I'm planning to see Blake today. And push him some more on Robinson.'

Matilda hesitated. 'You're going to see Blake alone?'

Lambert faltered. She thought she saw something in him she hadn't seen before. It was as if he'd let his guard slip for a second. 'I think I'll be safe. Keep me updated on what the librarian says.'

Sandra Levinson was prowling the non-fiction floor of the library when Matilda arrived. Matilda watched her from a distance, taken once more by the woman's beauty: the perfect symmetry of her face, and the elegant grace of her body. It was no exaggeration to suggest that the woman could have made a career in modelling.

As if she'd known Matilda had been watching her all this time, the librarian turned to face her in a slow drawn out movement. Her face broke into a smile on seeing Matilda, the faintest of lines appearing to the side of her eyes. 'Sergeant Kennedy, hello.' She carried an edition of A Room of One's Own, which she placed back on one of the bookshelves. 'Could I buy you a coffee? I'm dying for a hit of caffeine. There's a lovely little café down the road.'

'Sounds good,' said Matilda.

Matilda noticed the appreciative looks Levinson received as they walked down Lordship Lane, as if she was accompanying someone famous. The woman either didn't notice the stares, or was so used to them she didn't bother commenting. 'Let's sit outside, what can I get you?'

'Let me,' said Matilda.

'Don't be silly, I insist.'

Matilda ordered a black coffee, and enjoyed the sunshine as she waited for Levinson to return. She presumed the journey would be a wasted one as she couldn't imagine Levinson had the most devastating of news to tell her, but at least she could enjoy this one moment of pleasure.

'There you go. I bought us some pastries, hope you don't be mind.'

Matilda's mouth watered as she surveyed the crumbling flakes of the pains au chocolat. 'Thank you. I won't tell if you won't. How are things at the library, how has everyone taken the news?'

'It's a little surreal. Naturally, everyone was shocked but I think it's hard for them to accept the true extent of what has happened. Me included, I'm afraid. I keep looking at the entrance, somehow waiting for Moira to walk through.'

'I understand completely. These things take time.' Matilda took a bite of the pastry, a wave of guilt overcoming her as she savoured the melted chocolate within.

'I really hope I haven't wasted your time. It was when I told the team last night about Moira that I remembered something that happened a few months back. It was nothing really, but I thought it might help.'

'Anything you can tell us could help. However trivial it might seem.'

Levinson fell silent, her face taut in concentration. 'There was a man. I would have thought nothing of it, if it hadn't been for what he was wearing.'

Matilda placed a hand on the woman's arm, surprised by the feel of wiry muscle. 'Slow down. Where was this man?'

'He was hanging outside the library, nearly every morning when I came to work. Not directly outside but over the road.'

'When was this?'

'A couple of months ago. March, April maybe. He was there every morning for a week. I should have notified the police but he wasn't really doing anything except loitering. I would see him as I went into the library, and then I would check on him from my office window. He would sometimes just leave, but on one day he was there for a couple of hours.'

'And what did you notice about what he was wearing?'

'That was the thing,' said Levinson, a sparkle igniting her eyes. 'I'm a bit of a shoe snob and I'd noticed he was wearing a pair of shoes from Barker and Co. My husband likes their shoes. And he was wearing beautifully tailored trousers. Nothing unusual about that but he was wearing a hoodie over his shirt. This beaten old black thing and he had the hood up. It just didn't look right to me.'

'Did you tell any of the staff?'

'No, I didn't want to worry them unduly. You get a lot of strange folk coming in and out of here. They probably wouldn't have batted an eyelid anyway.'

'Could you give me more of a description? Did you get a good look at his face?'

'Only the once. He might have thought no one was looking but I peeked at him through the blinds in my office. He took his hood down for a moment and I saw him then. He was a lot older than I'd imagined, though he was quite good looking. He had a good head of hair, silvery grey. I'm afraid I must have touched the blinds as he glanced up at the window and put the hoodie back on. He hasn't appeared since.'

Matilda pulled her phone from her trouser pocket. 'Just bear with me a second, Sandra,' she said, searching on Google. She found the image she was looking for and handed the phone to Levinson.

'Yes, that's him. How did you know?'

Matilda sighed. 'It's a long story but thank you very much, that information could come in handy. She saved the image and texted it to Lambert. Underneath, she typed. 'We need to interview Charles Robinson again.'

Chapter 12

It had taken him fifteen minutes to get through the first gate. Now Lambert stood waiting outside the second. His jacket was damp beneath his suit jacket, the early morning sun already blistering hot.

'Who did you say you were again?' said the voice on the intercom.

He knew he was being mocked but played along anyway. There was sure to be more than one exit to the house and if he wasn't polite, he knew Curtis Blake would suddenly be unavailable. 'DCI Michael Lambert. I have an appointment with Mr Blake.'

'Please wait,' said the intercom voice.

Lambert waited another ten minutes before the front door opened. A slim muscular man dressed in a black suit walked down the stone pathway towards him, flanked on either side by two men almost twice his size wearing cheaper versions of the same suit. The man stopped, took off a pair of expensive looking sunglasses and assessed him with a stern glare. 'Will Atkinson, Mr Blake's head of security. May I see some ID, Mr Lambert,' he said, his voice strong and authoritative.

Lambert handed him his warrant card.

Atkinson looked harder than necessary. He was clearly ex-military. He nodded to one of his colleagues, and the steel gate opened.

'Quite the security set-up you have,' said Lambert.

Atkinson nodded. 'It's important to be safe,' he said.

Lambert held his arms out as one of the henchmen checked him for weapons.

'Thank you, please follow me,' said Atkinson.

The house, a detached property in Hampstead, would be worth millions. Blake owned a number of legitimate businesses, mainly property related, in the capital. It was feasible that he would make some enemies in such a line of work, but the level of security in the house was disproportionately high. The front door was made of steel. Atkinson had to punch in a six-digit pin to gain entry. Both the guards turned away as he entered the code, and Lambert was instructed to do the same. The door led to another gated area. Atkinson unlocked three locks to enter the main area of the house, leaving one of the guards to monitor the front door.

'You can't be too careful,' said Lambert, following Atkinson into a vast dining room where a man sat drinking coffee, talking on a mobile phone. The man looked up and pointed to a chair.

'Take a seat,' said Atkinson.

Lambert sat and waited for Curtis Blake to finish his call. The man was in his late fifties but looked older, his leathered face crisscrossed with deep grooves. He was wearing a white linen suit, a crisp shirt with the top button pushed into the loose flesh of his neck. He said something into the phone, before placing it on the dining table. 'DCI Lambert,' he said, more to himself than directly at Lambert. Leaning back in his chair, he continued. 'Yes, DCI Lambert. I know all about you. How is Glenn Tillman?'

Lambert had run through Blake's file on The System last night and knew that Tillman had investigated him a number of times over the years with no success.

'You'll have to ask him yourself. I am here on another issue.'

Blake lifted his coffee cup. 'Where are my manners? Can I get you something? Water, perhaps? You look like you ran here.'

'I'm fine.'

Lambert told him about Moira Sackville.

Blake drank his coffee, lost in contemplation. 'Poor Eustace. I never had the pleasure of meeting his wife.'

'You knew Eustace well.'

'Of course, of course. Eustace Sackville, reporter extraordinaire. That's why you wanted to speak to me?'

'I understand you and Eustace have a history?'

A smirk crossed Blake's lips but lent no humour to his face. 'I would hardly call it that.'

'You know he was investigating you?'

'You must have spoken to him already. Some preposterous idea he had. He still thinks I'm twenty, thinks I'm some sort of petty criminal. He even had the temerity to call me.'

'I don't think he believes you're a petty criminal,' said Lambert, looking around at the ostentatious decorations of the dining room.

Blake looked at his mobile. 'My point exactly. This has been hard won. I work fifteen, sixteen hours a day. I'm never off this bloody thing.'

'I understand that Eustace was looking at some competing groups?'

The smirk had disappeared from Blake's face. 'Some perceived competition. I told Sackville then, and I'm telling you now, that I have nothing to fear from Russians, Albanians, Kosovans, or whoever is the new flavour of the month. I have nothing to do with them, and they have nothing to do with me.'

'Why all the security?'

Blake shook his head as if he was talking to an imbecile. 'You don't become successful in this world without making enemies, Lambert, you must know that. This is all for precaution.' He took another sip of coffee. 'I know why you want to speak to me, Lambert. Let me see, you think Moira Sackville was killed, what, as a warning?'

Lambert sat stony-faced.

'No, not a warning. Why bother going to such lengths, may as well have bumped him off as well? You think Eustace was being punished for something. Something he knew, or something he did. Well, I'm sorry to disappoint you but I think you are barking up the wrong tree, as it were. At least, if it's concerning me. Why would I care about what that journalist was up to? Maybe he pissed off the wrong people somewhere. But really, it's all a bit, well, messy.'

'And it has nothing to do with you, I presume?'

Blake pursed his lips, his face cracking into a patchwork of lines like an uncharted map. 'Of course not. Now if you don't mind, Atkinson here will show you out. Please pass on my regards to your superior.'

Lambert felt a touch on his shoulder and turned to face Atkinson, who had crept up on him.

He allowed the head of security to escort him out. He couldn't argue with Blake's logic and he'd summed it up very well. The case was messy. Finding a motive was proving illusive and it was a possibility that the attack was a one-off, that there was no rhyme or reason, and that unless the killer struck again they would never find out who he was.

Lambert headed for the train station, thinking that the time may have come to start using a pool car. He'd avoided travelling by car as much as possible since the car accident which had taken his daughter but it was becoming unavoidable. Travelling by public transport may give him time to think but it also ate away at his time. As long as he didn't drive late at night, he was sure he would be okay.

He checked his phone. Kennedy had called and left a text message. It was something about Moira Sackville's ex-lover, the barrister Charles Robinson. Lambert was about to call her back when someone tapped him on the shoulder.

It was a firm tap, more a grab, and Lambert immediately went on the defensive. He turned in one swift moment, at the same time stepping back a few steps to avoid any contact from a would-be attacker.

'Steady there,' said the man who'd tapped his shoulder, lifting his hands in defence.

'Can I help you?' said Lambert, still poised for attack.

The man reached into the inside pocket of his threadbare jacket and showed Lambert a warrant card. 'DS Harrogate. We need to talk.'

Chapter 13

Harrogate led him to a small bar off the high street. The walls were decorated with television screens of various sizes showing different sports. The air conditioning was working full blast and was a welcome distraction from the outside heat. Harrogate ordered a pint of Guinness and a double vodka. 'Drink?' he asked.

'Water,' said Lambert.

They took a seat in a small booth at one corner of the bar, Lambert facing the bar's exit. Harrogate downed the vodka in one gulp and took a large swig of the Guinness. He wiped a line of white foam from his top lip, and took a second drink. His face was pitted with a few days' growth of stubble, his eyes tired-looking and bloodshot.

'What were you doing at Blake's place?' he asked.

Lambert tried not to bristle at the man's opening question. 'How do you know I was at the Blake residence, and what business is it of yours, Sergeant?'

Harrogate laughed, a deep rasping noise escaping his lips. 'Let's not be formal, Lambert. I know you were there because I've been working on Blake for the last five years and you may have just fucked up all that work.'

'I didn't see anything on his file.'

'You wouldn't, would you?' Blake downed the rest of the Guinness and pointed to the barman for a refill.

'If you're running some sort of covert operation then I apologise, but how could I possibly know? Now if you can get over yourself, we can perhaps swap information.'

The barman returned and Harrogate wordlessly gave him a ten pound note. 'Why were you there?'

Lambert relented and told him about Sackville.

'I'm surprised you got to see him,' said Harrogate.

'I had to clear security before I was granted an audience. Then he was as evasive as possible.'

'It sounds like a very tentative link between Blake and Sackville.'

'Pretty much what Blake said.'

'You treating it as a dead end?' Harrogate was halfway through the second pint, though the alcohol didn't seem to be having any notable effect. He had a similar body shape to Tillman, though where Tillman was muscle, Harrogate was flab.

'We'll have to see what Sackville comes back with, but I can't see Blake putting himself in such a position. So what about you?'

'Just trying to pull away the facade of the legitimate businessman. He protects himself through lines of red tape and lawyers. Naturally, he has a pyramid of lackeys doing all the dirty work for him.'

'Drugs?' asked Lambert, thinking about the case he'd been working on before Sackville.

'Probably, but we're looking at something else – people trafficking. We think his organisation has been working in line with an East European gang, Croatians, setting up houses throughout the city.'

'Why would they use Blake, they normally don't work with outsiders?' Lambert thought about the two bodyguards who had flanked Blake's head of security, Atkinson. He wondered if they'd been East European.

'Contacts. This is more than your normal street stuff. High money, all tastes… if you get my meaning.'

Lambert knew all too well. 'Have you spoken to Sackville before?'

Harrogate nodded. 'You know they go way back, don't you? Since he was a jobbing journo. I'd go so far as to say they were friends, if you can actually be friends with someone like Blake.'

Lambert stood, hiding his surprise about the last piece of information. 'I'll share any relevant information.'

Harrogate nodded, noncommittally, and looked over at the barman for a refill.

Back at the office Lambert met up with Kennedy. She explained what the librarian had told her. 'So Mr Robinson has been telling us lies?'

'Looks like it. Shall we get him in?'

'No, let's hold off. Try to find out some more about him. What cases he's been working on, who he's represented in the past. We need to find out some more personal details as well. Speak to his head clerk, Latchford. I want to know if he was seeing anyone else. What he knows about Moira.'

'I was thinking we should look into the death of his wife?' said Kennedy.

Lambert thought it was a dead end but nodded assent anyway. 'Where are you on the Whitfield case?'

'I'm still trying to track down Noel Whitfield. Devlin has

been to his last known address. We've arranged to meet the victim of the attack later today.'

Lambert updated her on Blake, and his meeting with DS Harrogate.

'We're to leave Blake alone then?' asked Kennedy.

Lambert frowned. 'I'll try not to ruin their investigation, but I'm not finished with Blake yet. Nor Eustace Sackville. There's something the pair of them are holding back. It seems they go way back. Someone's withholding information from me and I'm going to find out who and why.'

Tillman appeared as they were finishing. Lambert noticed Kennedy tensing at the arrival of their superior. 'Status report?'

Tillman's bulk was covered in a shirt at least a size too small for him. Lambert gave Tillman a brief status report, omitting his meeting with Harrogate, Kennedy remaining quiet throughout.

'So we're not focusing our energies in any one direction?' said Tillman, shaking his head.

'Too many loose ends at present.'

'I agree with you, Lambert. Get on it. People are expecting great things from you. In turn, that means they are relying on me. Kennedy, a word,' he said, strolling back to his office.

Lambert smiled to himself. He'd seen Tillman storm off so many times over the years that the sight of it had lost all its power. The smile faded as he remembered it was the second time in so many days that Kennedy had been summoned into his office without Lambert's presence. It wasn't unheard of, but it annoyed him that he wasn't privy to whatever they had to discuss. He tried not to dwell on the possibility that Tillman was asking for feedback about Lambert's performance.

It would be typical Tillman behaviour. Deliberately making it evident he was speaking to Kennedy. Putting doubts into Lambert's head, and not trying to hide the fact.

He'd agreed earlier to meet Sophie for lunch near their house in Beckenham and still had forty minutes before he had to leave. He opened The System and began searching on Curtis Blake and his team. Investigations into Blake stretched back over thirty years with little success. If he'd been successfully linked with a quarter of the crimes attributed to him then he would have spent the whole of his life inside. Everything was in his file: extortion, armed robbery, manslaughter, murder, even child abduction. Where the police had been successful in closing cases, it was always one of Blake's extended team which took the fall. Lambert thought back to what Harrogate had told him about the people trafficking and Blake working alongside the Croatians setting up brothels within the city. Although it couldn't be proved, it seemed this had always been a part of Blake's empire. A number of investigations over the years had included prostitution rings, often with minors.

Lambert spent his remaining time looking into the various members of Blake's team. He flicked through a list of Blake's known alliances; each had a hyperlink detailing personal histories. Everyone, from Blake's accountant to his chef, was listed. Lambert made a tentative search of Blake's security team. Harrogate had made a detailed report on each member – from Will Atkinson, the head of security, through to a number of bodyguards occasionally used by Blake. Lambert printed off a number of files before informing Devlin that he was heading out.

Sophie was sitting outside a café just down the road from

Beckenham Junction. She looked deathly pale, a large hat shading her from the sun. Lambert kissed her on the cheek, and sat down, taking a peek at the sleeping baby in the buggy next to her. Despite himself, he felt his heart racing.

'She's keeping you up?'

'How can you tell? Are you saying I'm not looking at my best?' Sophie glared at him hard, her face eventually softening as he realised she was teasing.

'I remember this phase,' said Lambert, pushing his luck. 'Are you on your own at the house?' he said, surprised by the jealous thought that the baby's father would be staying over.

'Mum's there now. She's driving me crazy, though she did offer to look after Jane.'

'Everything is okay, though?'

'Yes,' said Sophie, with a hint of impatience. 'She's sleeping well, and feeding is not a problem so I can't complain.'

'Is that your mother or the baby?' he said, trying to make her smile.

Sophie frowned. 'Shall we order?'

They ate grilled fish in the sunshine. Sophie relaxed, and for a brief time Lambert forgot about the Sackville case. He even managed to forget that the tiny, sleeping figure in the buggy was not his. It felt right – enjoying the heat, talking to the woman who was still his wife.

'So what about you?' asked Sophie.

'I'm fine.'

Sophie looked upwards and sighed. 'I expected nothing else. I know this must be weird for you. I'm sure it's upsetting. I've tried to put myself in your position but it's impossible. I'm struggling with it myself. Jeremy is offering to help but he's not going to be part of my life, although he will need to be part of Jane's. I don't know what to do, Michael. I never planned to be a single mum, and every time I look at Jane I think of Chloe, and…' She started to cry and forced herself to stop, wiping her hand across her eyes in defiance. 'Tell me how you're feeling, Michael.'

He didn't know what she wanted from him. He was never good in these circumstances. She'd always lamented the fact that at times he was unable to share, and there was nothing he could think of saying now that would make the situation between them any better. He could tell her he felt betrayed, and utterly alone. That Jane's birth somehow distanced him further from his dead daughter, and from Sophie herself. He could describe in detail his hatred for Jeremy Taylor, and what he'd done to his family. Everything made him sound self-absorbed so he just shrugged his shoulders. 'I'm doing fine. Work is busy. Look, Soph, I'll do whatever I can for you and her.' He looked at the buggy, at the still sleeping figure of the baby which looked so much like Chloe that it caused him physical discomfort.

'Okay, Michael, whatever you say,' said Sophie, standing up.

'Come on, Soph, don't be like that.'

'I need to get back, I told Mum we wouldn't be too long. Bye.'

As Sophie pushed the buggy down the hill, Lambert felt a sensation of déjà vu, as he remembered a time twelve years ago where he'd watched her wheel Chloe away. Then he'd felt the loneliness, having to return to a case when he would rather have spent time with his new-born child.

Now, he couldn't wait to return to work.

Chapter 14

The cold air of the flat was a welcome relief to the heat of the day. The shutters were pulled tight on each window, ensuring the cool air remained within. The man undressed and hung his suit on a hanger next to six identical garments. He placed his shirt in one of the white linen baskets in the room, his underwear in the second, and changed into a fresh set of clothes.

The main room had everything he needed. The bed he'd made that morning with the hospital corners, and the small immaculate kitchen area where he prepared the staples of his diet. The only furniture in the white walled room was a lone desk and chair where he ate his meals. To the side was a bathroom, scrubbed clean on a daily basis.

Things were moving faster than he'd expected. It could have been coincidental but he had waited too long to jeopardise things now. He made dinner – protein, vegetable, carbohydrate – washed the dishes and put them away. He scrubbed the table clean and switched off the light.

In the darkness, he moved to a third room.

He unlocked the door, and pulled it open a touch as his eyes adjusted to the glare. A bank of television screens blinked back at him, his gateway to the lives of others.

He'd taken down the cameras from the Sackville residence,

reluctantly accepting that it was too risky to witness at first hand Eustace Sackville's decline. There was still enough to keep him interested, the images from each residence changing every few seconds.

An alert flickered on screen two, as a woman entered the front door of her house. He checked the other cameras for the residence and noted with satisfaction that everyone was at home.

Chapter 15

They were almost too old to be kissed goodnight, especially the boy who was eight going on eighteen. Jake had an almost incessant rage, interspersed with occasional moments of compassion and tenderness which nowadays surprised and warmed her, and filled her with a dread that they would not continue for long.

'Can I go up?' she asked her husband, Sam, who was busying away in the kitchen coming up with one of his increasingly elaborate creations.

'Best not, they've been down an hour now and they were all tired. No point in waking them because you're late.'

She sighed. The last comment was unnecessary, but she decided not to respond. She poured a glass of red wine from the open bottle and topped up Sam's glass. He was five years her senior but had the energy and exuberance of a man half his age. He dashed through the kitchen like a professional, adding dashes of seasoning, and turning ingredients in the hot pans.

'Smells delicious,' she said.

He put his thumbs and forefinger to his mouth and blew out a kiss. 'Let's hope it tastes as good.'

'Did Hannah get her homework finished?' she asked, as they sat down for dinner. Hannah was ten, and would be entering her final year at primary school in September.

'I think so.'

'Oh come on, Sam. It's important.'

'I know, I know. I don't want to push her too much. It's nearly the summer holidays and she is absolutely knackered.' Sam rubbed his beard, a new affectation he'd told her he'd grown to keep up with the cool kids. Sam was a photographer, and ran a small studio in Covent Garden.

She sighed, and took a bite of the lamb Sam had prepared, her stress fading as she savoured the moistness of the pink flesh.

'How was your day?' said Sam.

'Fine. Same as any other, the sick and wounded. Mr Peartree finally went.'

'Went as in went?' said Sam, pulling his hand across his neck in a cutting motion.

She turned her head and pulled a face. 'Yes, as in went. It was very sad actually.'

'I'm sorry, how old was he?'

'Ninety-four.'

'Good innings then.'

'Yes, but he had no one, the poor man. The last people he ever saw were the resuscitation team. No one came to see him, apart from a bored lady at his care home.'

Sam pulled a second bottle of wine from the rack and moved his eyebrows up and down. 'It is a Wednesday,' he said.

'You should cut down at your age,' she said.

'My age,' he said, in mock outrage, moving towards her. He began tickling her, the fuzziness of his beard rubbing against her neck and sending tingles through her body. She reached up to kiss him when they were interrupted by the doorbell.

'Christ, what time is it?' said Sam, putting the wine bottle on the table. 'Whoever is there is going to receive the full force of my wrath,' he flashed his eyebrows up and down again before pretending to storm off.

She put the wine away, deciding she had other plans for the evening. She heard Sam exchanging words with someone as she started clearing the table. Sam returned, the jovial look she'd seen as he'd headed for the door had vanished. Her focus moved to the faceless man behind him, and the thick blade pressed against her husband's neck, and understood why.

Chapter 16

After meeting Sophie, Lambert had returned to the office only to be frustrated by the day's lack of progress. He left the office early, but spent the evening into the early morning on The System, and going through old newspaper articles written by Eustace Sackville. Eventually he'd gone to bed at three, his descent into sleep easy for a change, and woke at five-thirty. It was six forty-five now, and he was back at the incident room waiting for everyone to arrive for the seven a.m. briefing.

Kennedy appeared just in time, nursing a giant coffee. Her face was drawn, her unkempt hair tied back in a messy ponytail. The team gathered around him expectantly. Both the forensic and autopsy reports had been returned, not revealing anything they didn't know.

Moira Sackville had died from exsanguination, otherwise known as bleeding out. The best guess was that it had taken her three hours to die, though she was probably unconscious after the first hour, which corresponded with Eustace's testimony.

On the whiteboard, Lambert had listed a number of names. Eustace Sackville, Charles Robinson, Curtis Blake, Noel Whitfield. Below them, he added the names of Prue McKenzie, Moira's best friend, and the librarian, Sandra Levinson. He may as well have added the names of anyone else they'd talked to in the last two days, given how few real leads they had discovered.

'I've spent the evening going through Sackville's old press cuttings, which I'm afraid are numerous,' he told those gathered. 'Nothing springs out, but I think we could do with second pair of eyes on it. As you know, I visited Curtis Blake yesterday. Any further approach needs to be cleared with DS Harrogate, though come to me first if it's pressing.'

'Charles Robinson has agreed to see me again today,' said Kennedy.

'Okay. Go easy on him. If he was stalking Moira then I'm sure he'll come up with a bullshit reason. We should get the librarian in here to make a formal identification, even if it is just a photo at this stage.'

'Sir?' One of the team, DS Walker, lifted his finger. Lambert noticed that Kennedy bristled at the man's voice and wondered why. 'Don't want to sound out of turn, sir, but have we considered that this is motiveless? A motiveless murder by some nutcase off the street?'

Tillman had warned him about Walker. 'Ballsy and arrogant,' being the exact words he'd used.

Lambert had been considering the same thing ever since he'd been assigned the case. 'And what if we approached every case that way?' he said, knowing that sometimes it ended up being the only option, that some crimes would go unsolved, that certain people did terrible things for seemingly no coherent reason.

'Yes, sir, but...'

'Go with Kennedy to speak to Charles Robinson,' said Lambert, interrupting.

Kennedy looked over, her tired face animated with annoyance.

'See what you think of him.'

He was about to wrap things up when his mobile began beeping. The noise echoed around the room, as the rest of the team received notification. Lambert looked at Kennedy. 'What is it?'

'Jesus,' said Kennedy.

'Jesus indeed,' said Tillman, barging through the glass doors of the incident room.

Lambert signalled to Kennedy and they both followed Tillman to his office as nervous chatter spread through the room. 'You need to get over there now,' said Tillman. 'A team of uniforms is there, and the SOCOs have been called, but we can't afford for the crime scene to be contaminated.'

'It's definitely our man?'

'Looks like that way. All three victims have the same marks on their wrists according to the report. There's a survivor like last time. Laura Dempsey. She's still at the scene. She was still tied up when the cleaner arrived this morning. You better be quick as she's on her way to hospital. They haven't managed to get a coherent word from her. It's possible she's spent the last few hours alone looking at the damage this bastard has caused.'

The SOCOs beat them to it and had sealed off the scene. Lambert found the first officer at the scene, and was surprised to see it was the nervous looking constable who had been guarding Eustace Sackville's room the other day. 'You're having some busy days, officer,' said Lambert.

'You could say that, sir.'

'What can you tell me?'

'I was on patrol around the corner when the call came in.'

'The cleaner?'

'Yes, sir, she's over there.' He pointed to one of the ambulances where a woman was sitting, wrapped in a foil blanket despite the heat of the morning sun.

'She was waiting outside, shaking, and telling me to help Mrs Dempsey. She was in such a state that I went in alone. I thought she might need help. I made my way into the living room, and I saw it.' Sweat poured from the young man, his face a deathly pallor, his eyes low.

The constable shook himself, and impressed Lambert by continuing. 'At first I thought all four of them were dead. It was clear the husband and the two children were gone but I checked Mrs Dempsey and her pulse was healthy. I couldn't get any sense from her, and we had to wait until the fire service arrived before we could cut her out of the handcuffs. She was still in a state of shock when we put her in the ambulance. Hardly surprising considering what she must have gone through.'

Lambert was allowed to put on a SOCO uniform and attend the scene. The pathologist, Dr Rachel Walsh, spoke to him before he was allowed to enter the building. 'I don't need to tell you, but I will anyway. Don't move anything. Find a spot and keep it to it.'

He braced himself as he entered the house. The atmosphere always felt the same to him in murder cases. It was probably all in his mind, but he felt the coldness as he moved through the threshold of the house. The sense that something irrevocable had changed within the brick walls that no amount of scrubbing would ever eradicate.

If he'd seen a worse crime scene in his time on the force, then he couldn't recall it.

It wasn't necessarily the dead bodies which troubled him,

more the way they'd been arranged. Five chairs were placed in a makeshift circle. Two chairs, one where Laura Dempsey had sat, and one where the killer had presumably sat, were empty. The other three were occupied by Laura Dempsey's dead family. Lambert had read their names on the way over.

Samuel Dempsey sat between his two children, Jake and Hannah. All three victims had their wrists slashed in an identical manner to Moira Sackville.

The SOCOs were busy taking photos of every possible angle, examining the blood which pooled around each of the victims. Lambert knew they would be some time. Reluctantly he moved behind the chair where Laura would have sat. He tried to imagine how she would have felt as her family were murdered before her, but it was beyond his imagination. He scanned the room, looking for anything out of the ordinary which may have given them some clue as to what had occurred. The living room was a cluttered mess. Rows and rows of books filled every inch of space, a small television was placed in one corner of the room as an afterthought. Despite the coldness which spread through the room now, the many family photos of smiling faces suggested a happy home. Why would someone take that away, and in such a brutal manner?

Once out of the room, he had to resist the temptation to send a message to Sophie. She and the baby were not his family any more. He updated Kennedy outside. 'Exactly the same MO on the three victims. Only it looks like he's escalating his work.'

'We have two officers with Laura Dempsey,' said Kennedy. 'Are you going to see her?'

'Yes, but I don't think I'll be able to get anything worthwhile out of her at the moment. We need to find out everything we can about her and her family. Every minute detail about her and her husband's work, past and present. Check The System and search for any links, however tenuous, with the Sackvilles and anyone else we have under investigation. This can't be random.'

'What about Charles Robinson?' asked Kennedy.

'Leave him to me. Check the details on The System as I said. Then, if you have time, go with Walker and see Whitfield if you can track him down.'

Kennedy rolled her eyes and Lambert chose to ignore her protests. The Dempsey house had been cordoned off and the police tape had attracted a number of visitors, neighbours and the general public drawn to the scene by morbid curiosity. Lambert grimaced as they lifted their mobile phones, taking photos and videos of the building. Presumably the images would be all over social media within seconds. He hated this kind of voyeurism, couldn't understand what people achieved intruding on the hurt of others. He called Tillman and updated him.

'Trouble follows you around, Lambert,' said his boss.

'Seems that way.'

'We have absolutely nothing to go on at the moment, I take it?'

'Just the leads we mentioned this morning. We're looking for a link between Dempsey and Sackville. We're currently looking at a killer who's becoming more confident but, as yet, with no obvious agenda.'

'You'll find a link,' said Tillman. 'This was planned, orchestrated. He was clearly sending a message, otherwise why the marks on the wrists.'

'I agree, we just need to find out what that message is. There could be any number of reasons why he kills them this way.'

'Thanks for telling me that, Lambert. That's not something I'd considered after thirty years in police work. You can't imagine the grief I'm getting over this. Sort it out, sharpish.'

'Sir,' said Lambert, hanging up. Lambert was used to sarcasm from Tillman but was surprised to hear him sounding so stressed. It had been many years since he'd heard him voice any concerns about his superiors. Tillman was a force of nature. He didn't normally let his concerns for other people affect his decisions or actions. Lambert wondered again why Tillman was suffering such pressure on this particular case. The killings were certainly brutal and they'd now escalated by a considerable extent. But it still didn't explain the interest and demands that Tillman seemed to be experiencing from above.

Lambert summoned over the nervous looking constable. 'You've done a good job there,' he told the young man, noticing the beads of sweat which had formed on the man's forehead. 'Get back to the office and write up the report. Then go home, you may have some long days ahead of you.'

He instructed Devlin to stay at the scene. 'Call me if anything happens, however minor,' he said.

'Sir.'

Lambert headed towards the tube station. He loosened his tie, passing a huddle of sweaty tourists, lethargic and flushed in the heat. He was about to enter the station when his phone rang. It was an unknown number. He usually ignored them, it was most likely a sales call or an opportunistic journalist trying to find an unofficial route to him, but decided to take the call anyway.

He answered, stopping abruptly in the street, a woman pushing a pushchair had to swerve to avoid him. 'Sorry,' he mouthed silently to her as he answered the phone.

'Lambert.'

'Michael Lambert?' said the voice.

'That's correct.'

'I thought it time we were acquainted.'

'Who is this?' said Lambert.

'Who do you think?'

Lambert pulled the phone tight to his ear, focusing all his concentration on the voice. It was a male baritone. If he had to guess the age he'd say anywhere from thirty to fifty, well spoken. He didn't seem to be using any voice modifying software.

'I've no idea,' said Lambert.

'I think you do,' said the voice, giving him time for contemplation.

'Do you have any information on what just happened in...'

The voice interrupted him. 'You're standing outside East Finchley tube station. You look ruffled, Mr Lambert, you really should do your tie up.'

Lambert looked about him, his eyes darting from one high rise building to the other, searching for a pair of eyes on him. It was an impossible task but he kept looking as he spoke.

'Who are you? And what do you want?'

The voice chuckled. 'You're not going to find me,' he said. 'I can see you but you can't see me.'

'Tell me something worth hearing or I'm hanging up,' said Lambert, bluffing. He knew the man wanted an audience but the last thing he wanted to do was hang up. He needed to obtain as much information as possible. If this was the killer, as the voice on the other end of the line seemed to be suggesting, then this could be his only chance.

'Oh I don't think you want to do that, Mr Lambert. You need to listen carefully to me. First, no one is to know about this conversation. This is between you and me. Secondly, you need to know that you're not to blame.'

It was Lambert's turn to chuckle. 'And why the hell would I be to blame?'

'Well you did bring things forward, Lambert. This was always going to happen, but you accelerated my plans.'

'How? What have I done to speed up your process?' Lambert thought about the people he'd spoken to in the last couple of days. Eustace Sackville, Charles Robinson, the librarian, Sandra Levinson, Curtis Blake, even the officer who'd warned him to stay away, DS Harrogate. None of them sounded like the man he was speaking to now.

'You don't need to concern yourself as to how, you'll never work it out. What's going to happen is going to happen but there are things you could prevent. Laura and Eustace are all alone. I'm sure you feel the same way, but you are not as alone as they are.'

'What do you mean by that?'

'You and I are very similar, Lambert. You might not understand why yet but we are. But we could become identical.' Lambert heard a click on his phone, and the line went dead.

Chapter 17

Lambert looked about him at the commuters and tourists, the students with their oversized shorts and flip-flops, the office workers, escaping their confines for a cigarette break. He'd noticed a couple of people on their phones and searched for any sign that one of them had been speaking to him. He tried to memorise the conversation. The man had said they were similar. The words felt like a threat but he didn't yet fully understand how. He caught the tube, deciding for the time being to keep the call to himself.

He went home first. He checked his phone as he logged onto The System and was pleased to discover that an app the tech department installed had made a clear recording of the conversation. He loaded the file onto his laptop and encrypted it. He played it over and over, listening to the words of the man, the tone and cadence of his voice as he spoke to Lambert. At no point did he discuss the killings or allude to the fact that he was the killer. Everything was implied. Even if Lambert did bring this to Tillman's attention the caller would probably be laughed off as a hoax. They received calls like this all the time but Lambert was convinced this was different. He played the conversation one last time.

'You and I are similar,' said the voice, 'but we could become identical.'

He deleted the file from his phone and changed into a fresh set of clothes, the shirt he'd been wearing was sodden with sweat.

Kennedy called as he was about to leave his bedsit. 'Just to update you, sir. We've run a number of cross-checks on Laura Dempsey. No matches yet. Mrs Dempsey worked as a nurse practitioner. She was the assistant to the Head of Nursing at Watford General Hospital.'

'And the husband?' asked Lambert.

'He was an artist. Mainly photography work, but quite successful by all accounts. He ran a small studio off Covent Garden. He didn't have a record.'

'Have we spoken to the immediate family?'

'Mr Dempsey was survived by his father. Ninety-four, dementia sufferer. We've informed his retirement home. We haven't managed to reach Laura Dempsey's parents yet. One of her friends from the hospital has been informed. We've advised her against visiting just yet.'

'Okay, keep looking,' said Lambert. He knew he should tell Kennedy about the phone call he'd received but needed to keep the information to himself for the time being. He shut the door to his bedsit and walked down the stairs. He opened the front door of the building, stepping out into the blazing sunshine. Eustace Sackville had left his hospital by now and, with nowhere else to go, had returned to the flat where he'd witnessed his wife being murdered. Lambert hailed a black cab and told the driver the address.

Sackville answered the door in his dressing gown. He looked at Lambert wide-eyed as if he didn't recognise him.

'How are you holding up, Eustace?'

The man blinked. 'You'd better come in,' he said. Instead of walking to the living room Sackville led him to a small kitchenette area. The blinds were pulled down, the only illumination was from the lines of light escaping through the cracks in the plastic.

'Are you sure there's no one who can come and stay with you, Eustace?' asked Lambert. The kitchen was in disarray, the sink full of dirty washing. An empty whisky bottle sat alone on one of the sideboards, its replacement, a quarter drunk, sat on the small kitchen table.

'A couple of people from the paper have come by. They didn't want to stay. I see it in their eyes. I can't really blame them.'

'We have people watching the building.'

'If I'm under threat, so be it,' said Sackville. He went to pour himself a measure from the whisky bottle. 'Can I tempt you?'

Lambert shook his head, it was the middle of the day. 'Listen, Eustace, I have some news for you.'

'Oh yes?'

'This won't make for pleasant hearing, I'm afraid.'

'With what I've seen over the last few days, do you really think that matters?'

Lambert told him about the Dempsey family. How the mother, Laura Dempsey, had been the only survivor. How she'd been made to watch like Eustace had.

'Jesus Christ, that poor woman,' said Eustace, with shaking hands refilling his glass. Lambert wanted to stop him drinking but what could he tell him? That's there was nothing to be gained from drinking his life away?

'Mr Dempsey was an artist. Mrs Dempsey works as a nurse

in Watford. I know you don't want to answer any questions, Eustace, but this is important. Do you know either of them?'

Eustace shook his head.

'You're sure?'

'As sure as can be. I get to speak to a lot of people for my work, quite often a lot in the medical profession. Can't say I've come across any artists though. I can check through my records though, and let you know later.'

'And the name Laura Dempsey doesn't ring any bells?'

'None whatsoever. My mind, it's fragile at best at the moment.' He took another swig of whisky, his red eyes beginning to water.

'You need to get out of here, Eustace. I'll see if I can get you somewhere to stay, a B&B. Somewhere you can take your mind off this.'

'Thanks for the offer but this is my home, Michael. It wouldn't be fair on Moira to turn my back on it.'

Lambert left Sackville with his whisky bottle. He stopped outside the entrance to his flat and surveyed the area, wondering if he was under surveillance at that very moment. He called Devlin to confirm that the Sackville residence was being watched.

'I want you to check in on him every few hours,' said Lambert. 'Make sure he doesn't drink himself to death. I also want him to take a look at some photos of Laura Dempsey and her family. I'll email them over to you. Make sure he sees them, look for a reaction.'

Lambert called Charles Robinson's chambers. The barrister was due in court in the next couple of hours. He wanted to surprise him, to catch him off guard.

He hailed a black cab. He needed to speak to Laura Dempsey but knew he wouldn't be allowed to yet. He wondered again what seeing her children and husband murdered would have done to the woman's sanity. It was possible she would never properly recover. It was also unlikely that the killer had been foolish enough to show his face. No doubt he would have followed his MO from the Sackville killing and kept his mask on throughout.

It took the cab an hour to reach the court house, the Old Bailey in the heart of the city. Lambert walked the corridors of the old building. He knew many of the faces. Solicitors, barrister, care workers, even the occasional villain he'd passed during the years. He walked to the canteen where he found Charles Robinson nursing a drink, studying a file. Lambert ordered himself a coffee and took a seat some distance away, waiting for a time when Robinson was less relaxed. He sat facing Robinson's back, his eyes boring into the man, waiting. Eventually Robinson stood up to leave. Lambert followed at a distance. He was heading to the robing area where the barristers changed into their paraphernalia. He let the man walk through the door, secure in the knowledge that he was where he wanted him. He was about to follow through the door when a security guard stopped him.

'Sorry, sir, you can't go through there.'

Lambert showed him his warrant card.

'I'm sorry, sir, it's still off limits. You'll have to wait for whoever you need to see to come back out.'

Lambert smiled. 'You want to try to stop me, go ahead, but I'm going through that door.'

The security guard lifted his hand radio and called for

assistance. Lambert ignored him and walked through the doors. He found Robinson deep in conversation with a fellow barrister. A traditional white wig adorned his head. It altered his appearance, framed his face. He looked over at Lambert. He initially smiled but soon his face turned as he began to panic. 'Are you here to see me, DCI Lambert?' he said frowning.

His colleague moved away, retrieved something from one of the lockers and left the room. 'You really shouldn't be in here,' continued Robinson.

'We need to talk,' said Lambert.

'No time I'm afraid. I have a client meeting now and I'm due in court shortly.'

'This won't take a moment,' said Lambert.

'Really, I must insist,' said Robinson, 'it's a very important case and I must give my client my full attention.'

'You're defending?'

Robinson nodded.

'Maybe afterwards?'

'I could be some time.'

'I'm afraid I must insist,' said Lambert.

Robinson sighed. 'Fine. There'll be a recess, though I don't know for sure when that will be, so by all means wait for me. We can speak then if it really is that important.'

The door opened. The guard who'd stopped Lambert outside entered the room, flanked by three others.

'Bit of overkill?' said Lambert.

'You need to leave,' said the guard.

'I was leaving anyway. Oh, Charles, just before I go. You may not have heard but it seems Mrs Sackville's friend has struck again.'

The colour drained from Robinson's face, his skin the same colour as his wig.

'What do you mean?'

'Three more last night. A fourth witnessed it.'

'Why are you telling me now?' asked Robinson.

'Just thought you should know,' said Lambert, turning his back. 'I'll see you at recess.'

He would probably get in trouble but it had been worth it. He'd wanted Robinson upset and on edge, and by the man's reaction he'd succeeded. Robinson had looked surprised by the coded message concerning Laura Dempsey's family, but Lambert had seen Oscar-worthy performances before from suspects and some of the most accomplished actors he'd ever met shared Robinson's profession. He'd planted a seed in Robinson's brain. When his case broke for recess, Lambert planned to ask the barrister about his stalking activity outside Moira Sackville's library.

'I need you to leave the building,' said the guard.

'My pleasure,' said Lambert, making a note of the listed cases on the noticeboard.

Although the building was air-conditioned, the heat wave had everyone on edge. He pitied Robinson's client, knowing the barrister's attention would be elsewhere during the trial. At a local coffee shop, he found a seat by the window and called a contact of his who worked at the Old Bailey and asked him to keep an eye on Robinson's case. As he waited, he uploaded The System on his laptop, using his secured 4G dongle and began searching through the data his team had already compiled.

The pages already numbered in the hundreds. All of Eustace Sackville's cases which were discoverable online had been added, as had details of criminal cases involving Charles Robinson. Lambert tried running some subroutines, looking for matches between the pair. Unfortunately, Sackville had spent much of his career working out of the Old Bailey so there were well over fifty cases he'd reported which had featured Robinson as a defending barrister. Now all it needed was someone to read them. He called Devlin and gave him the bad news.

Lambert worked until he felt as if he'd mined The System of all possible information. The System was only as good as the information supplied to it, and at the moment everything was unspecific. As a result, the information returned from the searches was too general to be of use.

His contact from the Old Bailey called moments later. Lambert bought a pain au raisin and devoured it as he made his way back to the courthouse. He'd had the constant feeling of being watched ever since the unknown call from that morning. He glanced at everyone he passed, looking for a hint of recognition. Most people looked away from his gaze, the occasional person meeting his look as if they'd been offered a challenge.

Inside the building, he joined a throng of people and slipped past the security guards. He found Robinson in the canteen talking to a beanpole-like figure, who by the look of his acne-ridden skin was only a teenager. Lambert was about to approach the pair, when a thought struck him about Mr Dempsey senior, all alone with his dementia in the care home. He remembered what Kennedy had told him about Laura Dempsey's parents, how she hadn't managed to make contact with them since the incident. He pictured them somewhere in the city, getting on with daily life oblivious to the fact that their grandchildren and son-in-law had been murdered in front of their daughter's eyes. It didn't make sense. In this day and age they should have been located. They would have checked their phones, or emails.

Lambert thought about Eustace Sackville all alone in the flat he'd once shared with his wife. He forgot all about Robinson and fled the building.

Chapter 18

The road was littered with cars but there was not a taxi in sight. Lambert scanned up and down the road, desperate for the sight of a black cab. As he waited he called Devlin and found the address. He told Devlin to arrange for backup and to let Kennedy know if she was in the vicinity. A hundred yards down the street a black cab was dropping off two occupants. Lambert sprinted across the road, narrowly missing an oncoming cyclist. As he approached the taxi he watched in dismay as a young couple climbed in the back. He upped his pace and reached the cab before it pulled away. He yanked open the passenger door and, breathless, took out his warrant card. The couple looked at him as if he were insane.

'Let's have a look at that, mate,' said the man, a spiky-haired youth dressed in shorts and a pink t-shirt, well-worn flip-flops dangling off his feet.

'Get out of the cab,' said Lambert.

'Can't we come along too?' asked Flip-flop's companion.

'No. Out, be quick about it.'

'Bloody disgrace,' said Flip-flop, as they both clambered out the door. The spiky-haired youth gave Lambert a glare he thought was menacing and stood next to his girlfriend holding hands as Lambert climbed in.

'You know I don't have to take you anywhere,' said the driver, glaring at Lambert from his rear-view mirror.

'I'd appreciate your help on this,' said Lambert, inwardly sighing at the loops he was going through just to start the journey. 'I'm on a murder investigation and I need to get somewhere urgently.'

The driver screwed his face up and made an elaborate show of turning on the counter. Lambert told him the address and they set off.

'Don't they supply you guys with cars any more?'

'Take any route you want,' said Lambert, ignoring the question. 'You can go through red lights as long as you're safe. Just get me there as quick as you can.'

'Yeah right, you say that now, but when the tickets come in you'll be nowhere to be seen.'

'For pity's sake, just drive,' said Lambert.

The driver rushed through a yellow light but was soon caught up in traffic. Lambert leant back, his jacket sticking to the faux leather seat. He was sure they had been going about it all wrong. He thought back to what the killer had said to him on the phone, about Eustace and Laura being alone, and sighed at the amount of time that had been wasted. Eventually the car pulled up outside the residence. Two squad cars were waiting and Lambert was surprised to see Matilda Kennedy already at the scene with Walker and Devlin. The driver tapped at the figure on the counter. Lambert pulled out some cash and gave the driver a generous tip.

'Where we at?' he shouted over to Kennedy as he exited the car.

'We haven't tried the door on your orders. We made several phone calls to both their mobiles but it goes to voicemail each time.' Kennedy edged close to him as they walked up the stone steps to the house. Her face was flushed, the heat radiating off her.

'Do you mind me asking what we're doing here, sir?' she said.

'It's just a thought. It came to me after you told me about Mr Dempsey's father. I just hope they're on holiday or out for the day.'

He rang the doorbell. They were at the home of Laura Dempsey's parents, Mr and Mrs Patchett. Lambert opened the letterbox and called their names. He squinted through the narrow gap for any sign of disturbance. He rang the doorbell and banged on the door again. No answer.

'Devlin, around the back. Take one of the uniforms with you.'

Devlin nodded, and summoned one of the uniformed team.

'Right, let's get this door open.'

Lambert nodded over to one of the uniforms who held a weighted battering ram. The man walked over at an eager pace, seemingly revelling in his job. He felt the door for the lock and told everyone to stand back. It took only one hit and the door flew open, a wave of stale air rushing out at them.

'Check upstairs,' he told Kennedy. 'You, with me,' he said to a uniformed officer.

'What are we expecting to find, sir?' asked the constable.

'Just be prepared.'

The house was immaculate. The pristine white walls of the hallway were adorned with family photos. In one picture, two figures he presumed were Mr and Mrs Patchett were surrounded by the Dempsey clan. Laura, and her now dead husband and children looked back at him smiling, forever caught in a happy memory.

The first door they came to led to an open space. It looked as if two rooms had been knocked into one. A large kitchen area with dark granite surfaces led to a beautiful oak dining table. Lambert pictured the Sunday lunches and Christmas meals, the happy times the family would never see again. There was no sign of a disturbance and for a moment Lambert's mood lightened. It was possible that his hunch had been wrong, that both parents were away, oblivious to the tragic news which awaited them. The uniformed constable moved through to a side door which led to an oval shaped living room. At the end of the room, sliding glass doors looked out onto a surprisingly large garden area. Lambert was about to open the doors to see what awaited them in the garden when the sound of Matilda Kennedy's voice called to him from upstairs.

Chapter 19

The familiar stench of blood drifted towards him as he rushed the stairs. He thought about the first crime scene he'd ever experienced, that of his university friend Billy Nolan, and the litany of dead bodies he'd seen since then, and realised the smell had never left him.

Kennedy stood on the upstairs landing, a pale-looking DC Walker next to her. 'Through there,' she said. 'We haven't gone in yet.'

Lambert peered through into a room thirty years out of date. Thick, flowery wallpaper adorned the walls, pink velvet curtains trapping the semi-darkness in the room. Lambert pulled on a latex glove, and switched on the light. A queen-sized bed took up most of the floor area. Beneath an ancient-looking duvet, soaked in blood, sat two figures. The lifeless corpses of Laura Dempsey's parents, Mr and Mrs Patchett, slumped against the headboard as if they were relaxing on a Sunday morning. The figure of Mrs Patchett was collapsed against her husband. Careful not to disturb the crime scene, Lambert didn't enter the room. One look at Mr Patchett's wrists was enough to confirm his fear.

At the end of the bed a curved wooden chair faced the murdered pair, as if they were being surveyed by a ghost.

'You were expecting this?' asked Kennedy. She stood behind him, her breathing a beat more rapid than normal. 'How?'

Lambert retreated from the scene. 'Walker, secure the house and call the SOCOs. Start organising house-to-house interviews. I want to know everyone who came and went in the last forty-eight hours.'

Walker went to protest but one look at Lambert convinced him otherwise.

Lambert waited until Walker had left before speaking. 'After you told me about Mr Dempsey senior, it got me thinking. Laura doesn't have any siblings. Her only living relatives were her parents. I thought about Sackville, how with his wife dead and he had no family left. Laura still had someone, or so we thought.'

Kennedy let the information sink in. He wished he could tell her about the conversation with the killer, but he'd understood the hidden threat in the killer's words.

'So you think the killer's objective was to kill the families of Sackville and Dempsey?'

Lambert nodded. 'He wants them to be alone. They both have no one left.'

'Jesus. Why?'

Although he was sure it was a rhetorical question, Lambert thought the question highlighted a sense of naivety in Kennedy. It came with age. She was only in her mid-twenties and despite the things she'd no doubt seen in her time, she still clung onto a level of innocence. It wouldn't be long before that had been completely destroyed. He would have told her to cling onto it for as long as possible, but it was not for him to comment.

'It may or may not be significant. He might have some sort of grudge against them both, or he might just like the power he feels from wiping out a family line. It's what we need to find out.'

Kennedy shivered as if dragging herself back into reality. The naïve girl disappeared, and the professional police officer returned. The SOCOs arrived and they left the house. Walker had organised the uniforms well and the area was full of activity.

'I've also called the team looking after Laura. She's still out of it,' said Kennedy, a few minutes later.

'We'll need to speak to her, sooner rather than later, before we tell her about her parents. She may not be able to give us anything meaningful, but we need her to try.'

'I'm trying to get my head round the motive on this. Could it just be coincidence? Maybe he kept Eustace and Laura alive as a witness to his work?'

Lambert shrugged. 'I don't think so. There would be no real reason to kill her parents. No one was there to witness the parents' deaths. I think it is the ultimate punishment. A very specific, calculated punishment. Murder is final, but this... Just think what Eustace and Laura will have to live with. Not only the death of their immediate family. She had to watch her children be murdered in front of her for Christ's sake. That is the last memory of her children and her husband.'

Kennedy's face was flushed, droplets of sweat fell from her brow onto her cheeks like tears.

'Sackville and Dempsey must be linked somehow. We need to get them together,' said Lambert.

Kennedy swayed on the spot, hesitating as if she wanted to say something.

'Everything okay?' asked Lambert.

'Yes, I'll go assist Walker.'

Lambert noted the way Kennedy almost spat out her

colleague's name. 'Good. Oh, and Kennedy, could I have your car keys?'

It was strange being back at the driving wheel of a car again. The last time he'd driven, he'd rolled the car and had awoken in a ditch. Two years before that he'd crashed his car whilst driving Chloe. He told himself that if he experienced any sign of tiredness, he would pull the car over. He wouldn't take the risk again.

The A/C was on full blast. Lambert gripped the steering wheel and tried to organise the random thoughts swarming his mind. It was a horrendous way to think of it, but the murder of Mr and Mrs Patchett would enable him to eliminate some suspects, and would narrow down the search. It was vital now that he speak to Laura Dempsey.

London did not respond well to heatwaves. It was such a rarity that people never modified their behaviour to account for the heat, save for the shedding of clothes. Cars jammed the roads, and pink bodies swarmed the pavements making the most of the blistering sun. Lambert stopped at a set of traffic lights. His phone rang, and he fiddled in his pockets until he located it. The screen told him it was an unknown caller. Lambert took a deep breath and accepted the call. A beat cop crossed the road in front of him. He looked at Lambert on his phone, and looked away pretending he hadn't seen anything. Lambert put the phone on speaker and stuck it on the dashboard.

'Lambert.'

'I'm impressed. Much quicker than I'd anticipated.'

'Did we disrupt you?'

'You weren't that quick,' said the voice.

Lambert concentrated on the sound of the voice, searching for any clue to its source. The man was well spoken with no discernible trace of an accent.

'I just ask as there was no witness this time.'

'There was a witness.'

The lights turned green, and Lambert edged the car forward. 'I guess it would be too easy to ask what your motive is?'

'I think you know, Mr Lambert. I've been reading up on you. As I said before, I think we are more similar than you can imagine. Even more so now.'

'Now? We're nothing alike, you sick fuck,' said Lambert, regretting losing his temper.

'I'm not sure your victims would feel the same way.'

Lambert gripped the steering wheel tighter, and swung the car into a left-hand turn. 'I don't have any victims.'

'You've killed before.'

Lambert couldn't contain the adrenaline which peppered his bloodstream. He knew where the conversation was leading. It would make sense to hang up but he wanted the killer to let slip. 'I have only killed in the line of duty.'

'Sanctioned murder.'

'This isn't going anywhere.'

'You don't deny it.'

'I have never murdered anyone,' said Lambert, hating himself for getting into an argument.

'Technically you have. You purposefully set out to kill someone, and you succeeded.'

Lambert had killed two people on duty. 'I'm not sure where you think you're getting your information, but I have only killed in the line of duty in self-defence. As I recall, I haven't tied anyone up and bled them out over a number of hours whilst a loving family member was made to look on.'

'Semantics. You had your reasons, and I have mine.'

'I take it by what you say that you're not finished?'

'Why stop, when there's so much to be done?'

The road had cleared, and Lambert put his foot down as if he were in pursuit. 'I'll stop you, you...'

'Michael you've already lost one daughter. Don't risk losing another.'

Lambert threw the phone on the car floor as the killer hung up. The threat could not have been any clearer. He thought of nothing else as he drove the rest of the journey to the hospital.

Laura Dempsey was staying at the Royal Free Hospital in North London. As with Eustace Sackville, she'd been kept under guard by two officers, though Lambert was sure she wasn't in imminent danger. Everything that could have been done to her had already happened. He imagined that in her current state death would be a welcome diversion.

The air conditioning of the hospital was a welcome respite to the heat outside. Lambert felt the sweat drying as his skin cooled. Laura was being kept in a secure room on the eighth floor. Lambert was pleased to find one of the officers guarding the entrance to the ward, the second positioned outside Dempsey's room. 'DC Shah, we meet again.'

'Sir,' said Shah getting to her feet.

'Take a load off, Constable. Where are we with Mrs Dempsey?'

'She's not in a great way, as you can imagine. They keep sedating her. Every time she comes round, she freaks out, pulls at the drip and has to be held down. It's not pretty.'

'It can't happen again. I need to speak to her. Who's in charge?'

'Sister Reece administered the shot last time. Dr Hughes is in overall charge. I believe she's left for the day.'

'Already?'

'She had to consult at another hospital. Sister Reece's office is down the hallway.'

He found Reece sitting behind a counter with two nurses. They were reading through a number of medical files and from the snippets Lambert overheard, were working out the timetable for the next day. None of them paid Lambert any heed.

Lambert withdrew his warrant card and laid it on the counter. 'Sister Reece?'

The nurse finished her conversation before looking up at Lambert. 'Yes,' she said, speaking with the confidence of someone who knew her own importance.

'DCI Lambert. May I speak to you about Laura Dempsey?'

Reece sighed. She had a round face framed by a straight black fringe. Her small, narrow eyes were set deep into her face. 'We are having a meeting,' she said.

'And I'm trying to conduct a murder investigation.'

She shook her head as if he was being unreasonable. 'Sally, take over please. Follow me,' she said to Lambert, walking to the back office. 'Close the door behind you and take a seat.'

'Laura Dempsey,' said Lambert.

'Yes.'

'What can you tell me about her current situation?' Lambert was struggling to keep his temper in check. He couldn't understand what the woman was trying to achieve by being so obtuse.

'You'll need to speak to Dr Hughes, I'm afraid.'

Lambert had been around hospitals long enough to know just how important the nurses were to the successful running of the wards. How at times they wielded as much power, and knowledge, as some of their more qualified colleagues. 'She's under sedation?'

'That's correct.'

'Do you have any idea when she is likely to come round?'

'When we take her off the meds,' said Reece, as if she was talking to a simpleton.

'It is imperative that I speak to Mrs Dempsey today,' said Lambert, ignoring the jibe.

'Not going to happen today.'

Lambert involuntarily clenched his fingers. It would happen today, he thought, even if he had to take the drip out of Dempsey himself. 'It needs to happen today. There have been some developments.'

The woman relented. 'Look, I understand the situation but you'll have to speak to Dr Hughes. I don't have the authority, and I can't risk Mrs Dempsey's health. I'm afraid Dr Hughes won't be back until tomorrow.'

Over the years, Lambert had normally found the medical profession to be helpful. They always had their own agenda, which he could respect, but generally they would assist as far as they were able. 'You know why she is under guard?'

'None of my business.'

'I'll take that as yes. What you didn't know is that we have just found Mrs Dempsey's parents. They were also murdered, in the same way as Mrs Dempsey's husband and children. There is a very real danger that this killer will strike again and Laura may have information that would prove vital to apprehending this killer. Now, are you happy living with the fact that another murder might be down to your unwillingness to let Mrs Dempsey help us? Are you happy being complicit in the murder of another family, of more children?' It was excessive, but Lambert had reached breaking point.

Reece rubbed her face. 'I'll need to get it signed off.'

'I'll be waiting outside her room.'

Dr Hughes had clearly attended a different public relations class to Sister Reece. Twenty years the nurse's junior, she welcomed Lambert with a smile. It was over an hour later. 'I understand the situation, DCI Lambert, but I must stress that Mrs Dempsey is not in a fit state to deal with these questions.' Hughes had a soft voice, lilted with an almost melodic Geordie accent.

'I wouldn't be here if it wasn't necessary. People's lives are at risk, and Mrs Dempsey may help us prevent further deaths. I'm sure she wouldn't want this to happen to anyone else.'

'Let me check on her, and I'll let you know.'

Lambert peered through the door, surprised to see Laura Dempsey sitting up in her bed.

Hughes returned ten minutes later. 'I've spoken to Mrs Dempsey. The rest has done her some good but she is groggy. I can give you a few minutes.'

'Can I tell her about her parents?'

Hughes pinched her nose. 'I think we should leave it for now. I'm taking her off the tranquilisers. Let's see if she rests, and then we can tell her. She's had no visitors. Is there anyone you can contact for her?'

That was the whole point, thought Lambert. 'We will speak to her friends. We've had to keep this very low key.'

Hughes nodded. 'Five minutes.'

Lambert signalled to Shah to accompany him. Dempsey was still sat up in bed, her vacant eyes staring at the wall. The room was claustrophobic, a low ceiling with a small rectangular window covered by a beige set of blinds, the whistle of air conditioning the only sound in the confined room.

'Mrs Dempsey. My name is DCI Michael Lambert. This is DC Shah. I am very sorry for your loss. Please rest assured that we are doing everything possible to catch the person who did this.'

Laura's head moved an inch, a rush of air escaping from her nose.

'I'm so sorry to have to ask you this, but please could you tell me what happened.' Even as he said it, he realised how absurd the words sounded. He was asking a mother, and a wife, to describe the slaughter of her family.

Laura visibly recoiled at his words, as if the memory of that evening was being replayed in her mind. 'He killed them all. One by one,' she said, her voice a dry rasp. 'He made me watch.'

'Did you see his face?' asked Lambert, remembering his training, trying to rid the situation of emotion.

'Mask.'

'I know this is a dreadful question, but can you think of why someone would do this to your family?'

She recoiled again, her body starting to tremble. Shah moved over to the woman and held her arm. Laura looked at her as if she was a mirage. 'No,' said Dempsey.

Lambert could only imagine how excruciating his questions were for her but knew he had to continue. 'May I ask, has your husband had any trouble recently? From customers perhaps, or business contacts?'

'Everyone loves Sam.'

'And you? Would anyone have a grudge against you, Mrs Dempsey?'

Laura turned her head an inch, her eyes darting upwards then at Lambert. She didn't answer. Lambert was desperate to know what she was thinking. Her eyes started to water, and he imagined the idea that she was to blame may never have occurred to her.

'Do you know someone called Moira Sackville?' he asked.

She shook her head, her eyes filling with tears.

'How about Eustace Sackville?'

A less experienced observer would have missed it, but Lambert saw a flicker of recognition before she shook her head again. He was about to ask again when Dr Hughes returned. 'Right, that's enough,' she said, in her Geordie lilt.

Chapter 20

Walker didn't have to say anything but she was reminded every second of the journey that she was in his car. She could barely breathe without him looking at her. The interior was spotlessly clean, as if it had just come out of the showroom. Walker ignored the directions from the satnav as if showing off his superior road knowledge.

Matilda didn't want to complain about being partnered with him but she wasn't sure how long she could last. Just looking at him made her skin crawl. He had a permanent smug look on his face, as if he knew something she didn't. She thought back to the conversation at the canteen at headquarters and wished she'd somehow taped it or that someone had overheard. She knew that sooner or later he would slip up again and this time she would be ready.

They drove for another thirty minutes in painful silence, Walker breaking the monotony every now and again by smiling to himself at some internal quip.

The hospital where Laura Dempsey worked had been informed of her family's murder but had yet to be informed about the death of Laura's parents.

A nurse was waiting for them in the hospital reception. Walker perked up on seeing her. Although she was fifteen years his senior, she was a typical male fantasy – tall, slim, blonde hair, blue-eyes She introduced herself as Lucy Marshall. She beamed at Walker but barely made eye contact with Matilda.

'It's unbelievable news,' she said, her face impassive. 'I haven't been able to speak to Laura. How is she?'

'She's physically unhurt,' said Matilda. 'We have her under guard at the moment. We'll let you know as soon as she's able to speak.'

'Under guard? Why? Is she in danger?'

'It's just precautions. Shall we get a coffee and we can talk in more detail.'

It was the end of lunchtime and the coffee shop within the hospital was nearly empty. They took a seat near the rear and Walker went to order the drinks.

'How long have you known Laura?' asked Matilda.

'We've worked here together for the last fifteen years.'

Walker returned with the coffees, Marshall's face lighting up.

'So Laura's worked here for some time?' confirmed Matilda.

Marshall nodded, her eyes focused solely on Walker. 'I think she worked somewhere before here. A care home or something. Decided she'd had enough and wanted to study for her professional qualifications. She's a bit older than me,' she said dragging her hand through her long hair.

'What can you tell us about Laura?' asked Walker.

Matilda was amazed her colleague's acting ability, the look of care and concern in his eyes as he spoke to the nurse.

'Laura's great. As I've said we've been friends since we started here. She's a wonderful woman, very hard working. Conscientious. She's a great laugh as well, or at least she used to be.'

'Used to be?' asked Matilda. The woman frowned and took a drink from her coffee.

'Don't get me wrong, she's still fun but, well, things changed a bit when she got married, as you'd expect.'

'In what way?'

'Well obviously she stopped coming out so much and she was soon pregnant. She used to be wild back in the day. Not for me this settling down business,' she said, looking coyly at Walker.

'How wild was she before?' asked Walker, fiddling with his beard, flirting with the nurse who was technically old enough to be his mother.

'Let's just say she was a popular girl,' said Marshall.

'And what about now? Did she have any enemies? Any male interest?'

'Enemies? No. Obviously there's the normal politics bullshit we all have to endure. And the patients.' The nurse stopped and looked around the coffee shop, checking no one could overhear. 'The patients are what make this job a nightmare. She's had a few complaints against her, we all have, but no disciplinary issues as far as I'm aware.'

'And men?' asked Walker.

Marshall smiled, sipping her coffee. 'She's a happily married… Oh,' The woman's face paled, as she remembered the reason they were there – the brutal slaughter of Laura's family. 'God I'm sorry, I forgot.'

'No, that's fine,' said Walker, placing his hand on the nurse's arm.

It was all Matilda could do not to snatch it away. 'Did she have any male interest?' asked Matilda, desperate now for the interview to be finished.

Marshall smiled and looked at Matilda, her focus on her

for the first time since they'd met. Walker's hand was still on her arm.

'Well Laura is a bit of a looker and you know how these places are. She wasn't short of offers, but there was nothing going on if that's what you're getting at.' The woman held her gaze as if she was somehow challenging her.

Matilda stood up, ending the meeting. 'Thank you for your time. Please let me know if you can think of anything else which could help us, and Laura.'

'Did you get her number?' asked Matilda, when they were back in the car.

'Don't be like that, Kennedy. Jealousy is such a terrible affliction.'

'The only terrible affliction is your propensity for bullshit and you were way too familiar with that nurse.'

'I was just comforting her. Her best friend has just suffered a traumatic experience. I wouldn't have had to if you hadn't been so cold.'

'If you're that interested you can check up on Laura when we get back to the office. You can also run a search using her maiden name.'

Walker glared at her through the rear-view mirror. She could see it was eating away at him taking an order from her. They sat in silence until it became too much for Walker.

'Okay, boss,' he said eventually, throwing his arms up in the air in mock outrage. 'I'll get straight on it.'

Chapter 21

He found Kennedy in the coffee shop two streets down from the station, staring into space.

'Where's Walker?' asked Lambert.

'In the office. I've got him searching The System.'

Lambert sat opposite her, Kennedy's back straightening in response. 'How are things working out with Walker?'

'It's only been a day.'

'I know, but you've dealt with him before.'

Kennedy lowered her eyelids as a blast of sunshine filtered in through the window. 'You could say that. How long is he going to be on the team?'

It was clear she was not ready to discuss her true feelings about her colleague. 'For this case at least. Or as long as Tillman wants him.'

'Tillman?' The word came out as a squeak, and Lambert noticed a subtle change in her body positioning.

His phone rang, an unknown number.

Lambert gripped the phone, and looked outside the window. Across the street, a man wearing a t-shirt and high-vis jacket held a phone to his ear. He stared through the glass at Lambert, and began to talk. A group of students walked by. Two of them, young girls wearing summer dresses and Doc Martens, held phones to their ears. Kennedy shot him a puzzled look as the phone continued to ring.

'Speak later,' he said, leaving the table. He pressed the green button on his phone's screen as he left the coffee shop. 'Lambert.'

'I'm not there,' said the voice.

'Where are you then?'

The voice laughed. 'How are your investigations developing?'

'What do you care?'

'I care a great deal. I haven't finished yet.'

'There's a finishing point?' asked Lambert.

'That's up to you.'

It was a brittle comfort knowing that the man planned to finish whatever quest he was on. It also meant there would be more victims. 'What's next?'

'Let's not spoil things by asking stupid questions. What does Matilda Kennedy think about all this?'

Lambert paused, unsure what to say. He opened his car, which was parked on the side street next to the shop, and sat in the driver's seat. He began picturing everyone he'd seen inside. It had been busy, but he recalled the faces. A group of four businessmen, with their suit jackets and ties. Two mothers, their newborns in oversized prams to their side. He recalled five people sitting alone. Three men, two reading newspapers, one on his iPad. Two female students, working on laptops. 'She thinks the same as me. That you're desperate for attention.'

'I hope she thinks a bit deeper than that, Lambert. With her roots, I'm sure she will.'

'Roots?' asked Lambert, despite himself.

'You must know Daddy Kennedy, no?'

'Enlighten me.'

'Assistant Chief Constable Kennedy. North Shields. Quite a family. Probably explains her fixation with authority.'

Each word from the man was perfectly measured, as if he'd planned the conversation and learnt his lines like an actor. 'Tell me what you want, or hang up,' said Lambert.

'I've told you before, Lambert. We're alike, you and I. Not completely but almost.'

'I'm nothing like you.'

'Perhaps. Anyway, must dash. You should really take a break, Lambert. Make the most of the sunshine, pop to the seaside perhaps. Say hello to Eustace when you get there.'

The line was cut.

Lambert started the car, and rushed into the traffic. He hated himself for reacting to the call but he had to see Eustace Sackville. He slammed his fist onto the dashboard as he became caught at temporary traffic lights a mile from Sackville's flat. 'Come on,' he screamed, pulling the magnetic siren onto his roof. The vehicles in front pulled over, and Lambert cursed, knowing he would have to report his actions.

There was no answer to the bell outside Sackville's flat. He knocked on the glass panelled doors, and the concierge made his way over at the pace of a snail. Lambert displayed his warrant card, and seconds later was in the lift. He sprinted the short distance to Sackville's front door and noticed it was open, the lock smashed.

He took the expandable baton from his belt and pushed the door open. A woman was looking through the drawers in the living room sideboard. She looked over at Lambert as if she had every right to be in the room. 'Shit,' she said.

'You alone?'

'Yes, I'm alone, DCI Lambert. Why not join me?'

The woman was Mia Helmer, the editor from Sackville's newspaper.

'I'll be arresting you if you don't clarify the situation to my liking,' said Lambert, edging through the door. He glanced around the room, verifying that Helmer was alone. 'And drop whatever you have there.'

Helmer glanced at a set of papers in her hand as if she'd just seen them for the first time. 'The door was broken when I got here.'

'Why are you here in the first place?'

'I wanted to see Eustace. I hadn't heard from him since the incident. I thought he could do with seeing a friendly face.'

Lambert remembered the journalist's emotionless reaction to Moira Sackville's murder, her only real interest being the story.

'Take a seat, Mia. Start from the beginning.'

She still held the file in her hands. She carried it to the sofa and sat down. Lambert took it from her. 'How long have you been here?'

'Fifteen minutes. I saw the door was broken so I went in to check everything was okay.'

'You called the police?'

She clenched her face muscles. 'Not yet. Sorry, I got side tracked.'

'You expect me to believe this is a coincidence. Look at the place, it doesn't look as if someone else has been here first. What are you here for?'

Mia lifted her hands in the air. 'I'm being deadly serious. The door was broken when I arrived, check for prints or whatever it is you do. I haven't been near the lock. Anyway, why are you here?'

Lambert thought back to what the killer had said. 'Does Eustace have another place?'

'To live?' asked Mia, surprised by Lambert's change of direction.

'Somewhere by the sea?'

'Not that I'm aware of, why?'

Lambert was sure the killer had been here, had broken the lock. 'Why did you come here?

Mia paused, about to go in defence mode. 'Anonymous tip, would you believe. Told me to go here alone.'

'And you did?'

'I told my assistant to call you lot if she hadn't heard from me in an hour.'

'And what did you hope to find?'

'A story.'

'Well, you're in one now.' Lambert took out his mobile.

'Wait, we're about to go public with the Dempsey murders. We know about Laura Dempsey's parents as well. You don't want us going public with these revelations.'

'If you know, then the others will.'

Mia paused. She took in a deep breath. 'I'm not so sure.'

'Why, who spoke to you?

Mia didn't answer. She stared blankly at Lambert.

'The killer?'

Mia paused then nodded.

'What else did he say?'

'He told me to listen, and listed all the murders from Moira onwards. He told me to go public.'

If she was shaken up by the revelations, she was hiding it well. She stared back at Lambert with the same icy composure she'd shown the first time he'd met her at her office. If it was all a show then she was an assured actress.

'Did he give a reason?'

Mia shook her head. 'He just told me to go here, to find out what Eustace knows.'

'So what are you offering?'

'We won't print anything yet, but time is running out.'

It wasn't the greatest of deals but he didn't want the news getting out yet, and was sure Tillman didn't either. 'Okay, but I want a full statement. I need to know everything the killer said to you.'

He called it in.

'Right, empty all your pockets and everything from your bag onto the table.'

He confiscated the journalist's phone. 'Did he tell you to look for anything specific?'

Mia pursed her lips, an unruly child sitting on time out. 'No.'

'And have you found it?'

'You want to strip search me?' Mia tilted her head.

'I'm not ruling it out.'

He began searching where Mia had left off. The sideboard drawers were chaotic. He flicked through piles of bills and statements which stretched back for years, obsolete instruction manuals, tickets stubs, loose batteries and coins. If there was important information in the flat then he doubted Eustace would have hidden it somewhere so open.

Kennedy, Walker and Devlin arrived twenty minutes later. Lambert pointed to Devlin. 'Arrest this woman for breaking and entering,' he said.

For the first time in the brief time he'd known her, Mia showed some emotion. 'We had a deal.'

'I don't remember agreeing to anything. You got me thinking, Mia. Why would the killer break in here then tell you about it? He would have taken whatever he needed.'

'You must be fucking joking. This will be on the front page as soon as I get out.'

'Tell my team all you know and we'll go from there.'

Devlin lifted the journalist from the sofa and received a slap in the face.

'You can't touch me,' said Mia, her neck tendons at breaking point.

Devlin cuffed the woman.

'Add assault to the charges,' said Lambert, as Devlin led the journalist away.

'Okay, okay,' said Mia. 'Take these fucking things off and I'll show you.'

Devlin looked over and Lambert nodded.

'Do you mind?' said Mia, opening her blouse.

'Kennedy,' said Lambert, turning his back.

'You can open your eyes,' said Kennedy, seconds later, smirking. In her hand she held a micro USB stick, wrapped in some sort of plastic covering,

Lambert shook his head. 'He told you?' he asked Mia.

Kennedy stared at him confused. 'Eustace?'

Mia smiled. 'Not the brightest, is she? He couldn't find it, that's why he called me.'

'Can someone tell me what is going on?' said Kennedy.

'Hang on. Where did you find it?'

'Why do you think it's wrapped in polythene?'

Lambert put the stick to his nose. 'Whisky.'

'Always at the bottom of a bottle.'

'Devlin, take Miss Helmer in for a statement. The agreement stands for now, Mia. If the story goes public in the next twenty-four hours you'll be arrested and charged.'

'I want every inch of this place searched,' he said, once Devlin had led Mia away. 'We need to know where Eustace is hiding and why.' He thought back to what the killer had told him. 'Eustace mentioned something to me about the seaside. Let me know if you find anything relevant.'

Sackville's office was even more cluttered than the living room. Lambert counted five glass tumblers, each reeking of single malt. Piles of books and papers were strewn on the shelves about Sackville's desk. He switched on the man's PC, surprised to be able to go straight through to his desktop. He plugged in the USB stick, hoping his luck would continue. The PC was ancient, the fan struggling as the computer accessed the files on the drive.

A list of over one hundred files appeared on the screen. Lambert double clicked the first file and was dismayed to find a request to enter a password. He tried ten more random files, receiving the same message each time. He was about to give in, when he noticed the last seven files. The first letter of each file were arranged to make an acronym scrolling down the page in a vertical line. The acronym read: BLAKE.

Chapter 22

Lambert handed the USB stick to Kennedy. 'Get this to the tech guys, priority. I need every file examined. Let me know when you're finished here.'

'Where are you going?'

'Best you don't know.'

Kennedy paused. 'Was that call anything to do with this?' she asked.

'What?'

'The call. At the coffee shop. One second we're talking, the next you've received a call and you've made your way here.'

'Coincidence,' said Lambert, leaving the flat.

Lambert drove through the rush hour traffic, under the Rotherhithe tunnel to Blackheath. He already knew Sackville was investigating Blake, and was sure the journalist had left the acronym on the files for a reason. Sackville, Dempsey and Blake were linked somehow. He needed to speak to Laura Dempsey again, to see what she knew about Blake.

It was an hour before he pulled up outside Blake's house, adrenaline surging through him. He went to push the doorbell when he was shoved in the back.

He stumbled forward, losing his balance and having to soften his fall with his hands. He reached for the pepper spray from his belt. He turned to face his attacker, bracing himself for a further blow. 'What the hell do you think you are doing, Sergeant?' he asked the man standing over him, blocking the sun.

DS Harrogate reached out his hand. Lambert took it, fighting the urge to use the pepper spray, and let Harrogate pull him to his feet. 'Sorry about that, sir, but I can't have you speaking to Blake. I believe your superior has instructed you to leave him alone.'

The two officers stood inches apart. Harrogate was tensed, ready for confrontation. Lambert was surprised by the man's nerve. He had confronted his superior, not to mention the way he blindsided him and pushed him to the ground.

'I'm investigating Blake in conjunction with a murder enquiry,' he told the junior officer.

'That's all fine and good, sir, but you're still not speaking to him without my say so,' said Harrogate, sneering as he said, 'sir.'

Lambert was seconds away from knocking the look off the man's face. 'I'm two ranks above you'

Harrogate shrugged. 'Well my boss is another two above you and that's where I take my orders.'

'What's so important about Blake that you want to stop me going in?'

'I'm not at liberty to say.'

Harrogate's insolence was starting to become tiresome. Lambert knew it could go one of two ways. 'So let's get this straight. If I decide to press that bell again you're going to try and stop me?'

Harrogate stood defiantly, his eyes not leaving Lambert's. He was out of breath, his chest rising and falling rapidly. 'Before you do,' said Harrogate, betraying the slightest trace of fear, 'you may want to speak to Chief Superintendent Tillman.'

'And why's that?'

'He knows all about the situation here and why you can't speak to Blake.'

Lambert shook his head and cursed under his breath. It was one thing going against the DS and whoever he reported to, another thing entirely going against Tillman.

'We're going to get to the bottom of this, Sergeant.'

Harrogate shrugged and Lambert returned to his car, deciding confronting Blake again could wait.

Lambert drove back towards his bedsit, still reeling from his confrontation with Harrogate. It was typical Tillman behaviour, causing issues for him from behind the scenes.

He showered and changed, deciding to log into The System before heading out for a drink. Tillman was the only officer who had the authority to monitor his searches, but still he felt reluctant searching on Kennedy's father. Whatever limitations Tillman had as an officer, diligence was not one of them. Lambert knew the man was monitoring everything. He would see that Lambert had run the search, and would probably demand an explanation. Lambert could try and pass it off as mere curiosity, but Tillman was a hard man to fool. There was also the possibility that whatever was happening with Tillman and Kennedy would prevent Tillman approaching him.

Deciding it was a future problem, he entered the search. Although The Group no longer existed, it seemed the limitations had not been placed on The System. Full details on Assistant Chief Constable Kennedy appeared in seconds. Such details would not normally be readily accessible to someone of his rank without going through innumerable obstacles.

As the killer had suggested, the assistant chief was still active in North Shields. A former member of the Met, he'd moved north some thirty years ago. The System's file was detailed, numbering in the hundreds of pages. It listed Kennedy's rise through the ranks, and every case he had reported since being a beat cop thirty plus years ago.

Lambert was in a position to run a search on the man, and cross reference that search with everyone currently being investigated on the Sackville and Dempsey case. Despite being an assistant chief constable, Kennedy would not be aware of the search. Only Tillman and one or two nameless superiors would have such access.

He saved the searches without sending the request and logged out of The System.

It had been over two months since he'd last gone for a drink, having put himself on a self-imposed abstinence kick. Now he could think of nothing better than sitting outside in the sunshine drinking some ice-cold lager.

'Now, how did I know I'd find you here?' said a voice as he was about to enter the bar.

For the first time in days, Lambert smiled. 'Sarah,' he said.

DCI Sarah May smiled back at him. She was out of her normal work outfit, dressed in a pale summer dress which rose above her knees. Her dark hair was loose on her shoulders. With the sun shining behind her Lambert thought he hadn't seen such a splendid sight in months.

'I see your investigative skills are still top notch,' he said.

'This is people-finding 101,' said May. 'Once I knew your

address, the next step was to find the nearest bar. It's hardly rocket science. Are you going to buy me a drink then?'

They walked inside, the place overflowing with customers. 'You realise this is pure coincidence,' he said. 'I haven't drunk in months.'

'Save it and get me a white wine. See you outside.'

Lambert took a heavy drink from his pint at the bar and ordered a second as he waited for May's wine to arrive. He felt an instant hit from the drink, the built up tension beginning to escape from his body.

'Why didn't you tell me you were coming?' he said to May, who had found a spot in the beer garden under the shade of an overhanging tree.

'What, and spoil the surprise? I'm down here on work actually, decided to give myself the afternoon off. So, tell me about this new case?' she said.

Lambert took another drink, the problems of the case fading further away. May edged close to him, her thigh pressing lightly against his. She already knew about Eustace Sackville. He updated her on Laura Dempsey and the woman's parents.

'Sounds like a doozy,' she said. 'You do pick them.'

'A doozy?' he said, revelling in the humour he saw in May's eyes. 'Feels like they pick me sometimes.' He told her about Mia Helmer and the USB stick that was with the tech guys as they spoke. He decided to omit the details of his conversation with the killer for the time being.

'So Sackville's missing?'

'Perhaps. He's not answering his calls.'

'But you think this Blake is involved?'

'He's involved somehow. As normal I'm not privy to all the

information. I've been told not to speak to him again unless I have some actual evidence.' He hadn't seen Sarah in over a month but it was like they'd never been apart. He was totally relaxed in her company. He only wished he knew how to tell her.

'So are you going to show me this new flat of yours?' she asked.

Lambert downed the rest of his drink in one go. 'It is pretty awful' he said, as he led her away.

Lambert forgot about everything for the next few hours.

'This reminds me of being a student,' said May. They lay together on the queen size bed on top of the sheets. He felt the heat from her body, the air within the room sticky with moisture.

'You mean lounging about in the afternoon?' asked Lambert.

'Yes that, and my surroundings.'

'It's only temporary,' said Lambert, playfully pushing her away and stepping out of bed. He moved to a window and pulled the curtains open, trying in vain to get some cool air into the room from the small window.

'How are things with Sophie?' asked Sarah, wrapping herself in the top sheet.

'She's back home now. And the baby's fine by all accounts.'

'Has she said anything about you two?'

'Us two?' said Lambert.

'Come on, Michael, you know she stills wants you as part of her life.'

'I'm not sure about that,' said Lambert.

'Why else would she have invited you to the hospital?'

'It's not my child, Sarah.'

'I know but she is Chloe's sister. There's still a life there for you if you want it.'

Lambert felt all the tension return to his body. He wasn't sure what Sarah wanted from him or how best to answer what she'd said. It wasn't like her to seek assurance, but maybe that's what she'd wanted all along.

As if reading his thoughts she moved over to him. She placed her hand on his chin and lifted his head up. 'I'm not trying to get rid of you, you fool. The last thing I want to do is push you back to her but there are more important things to consider.'

He kissed her, her lips wet and salty with sweat.

'Shower?' he suggested.

'You go ahead. I'm going to have a drink.'

Lambert turned the shower on to its lowest setting until the ancient faucet began spewing drips of cold water. Minutes later, the doorbell rang and he turned the shower off and dried. He pulled on his dressing gown and returned to the living area in time to see Sarah dressed in his underwear and t-shirt leading a bemused and smirking Matilda Kennedy into the room.

Lambert stood in the main room and pulled his dressing gown tighter.

'I see you've met DCI Sarah May,' he said to Kennedy, who still wore a slightly bemused look. The two women looked at each other and exchanged smiles.

'Sorry to interrupt, I did try to call, sir.'

'What is it?'

'We've managed to crack the files. The tech team's working through them as we speak but I've found some information that may be useful for tracking Eustace Sackville down.'

'Okay, give me ten minutes to get changed.'

'Tea?' said Sarah May to Kennedy.

'I'm fine, thank you. I think I'll wait downstairs. It was lovely to meet you.'

'Likewise,' said Sarah.

'She's nice,' said Sarah after Kennedy had left.

Lambert didn't reply and began getting changed.

'Much prettier than you'd let on.'

'I haven't said anything about how she looks,' said Lambert.

'And rather young.'

'I didn't say anything,' protested Lambert.

'I'm only teasing.'

Lambert pulled on his jacket. 'Can you stay?' he asked.

'Sorry,' said May leaning towards him and kissing him on the cheek. 'Duty calls. I'll be in London for the next few days. I'll let you know when I leave for Bristol.'

'Fair enough.'

'Don't look so forlorn,' said May, placing her hand on his cheek. 'Give me a call when things have settled down a bit.'

'Okay,' said Lambert. 'You can let yourself out I take it.'

'Of course. I'm not a DCI for nothing, you know.'

Kennedy was waiting for him outside his building, leaning against her new car.

'Wipe that smirk off your face,' he warned her.

She lifted her hands up in mock surrender. 'I'm saying nothing.'

'You're still smiling though.'

She moved her hand slowly across her mouth and the smile disappeared.

'One of the files had some photos. Old ones, I think, of Mr and Mrs Sackville's honeymoon. I recognised the place,

Broadstairs in Kent. I did some research and found a caravan site. Apparently the Sackvilles have been there every summer for the last thirty years. I thought we could go and take a look now. It's only an hour or so away.'

'You just want to try out your new car, don't you?' said Lambert climbing into the passenger seat.

'I gave the keys to my last car to someone and never saw it again.'

'Enough talk, let's go.'

The sun had set by the time they reached Broadstairs. 'We should probably have waited until tomorrow,' said Kennedy, as they drove through the back roads to the caravan site. It was a clear night, and away from the pollution of the city the sky was blanketed by stars.

'We're here now.'

The caravan site Sackville used was on private ground, reserved for owners of the static caravans. There was no reception area so they had been unable to call ahead. Kennedy drove the car up a dirt track and parked in a makeshift carpark. The site wasn't illuminated so Lambert used his flashlight to see where he was going. 'Which number?'

'Fifty-eight,' said Kennedy.

A haze of insects followed the gaze of the torchlight. The caravans had seen better days. The harsh glare of the light revealed rusting structures in need of paint. Lambert heard the gentle lap of the sea, a background noise competing with the incessant chatter of the grasshoppers.

'Here,' said Kennedy, pointing to a rectangular static caravan perched surprisingly close to a cliff edge.

Lambert ran his torchlight up and down the structure. Four

horizontal hoops adorned the caravan, alternative lines of brown and dirty white. Lambert shone the torch beneath the caravan, and jumped back as something darted out of the shaded area and scampered into the undergrowth by the cliff edge. 'What the hell was that?'

Kennedy shrugged. 'Fox?'

Lambert knocked on the front door, his hand yielding into the soft plastic. No one answered so he shone the torch through a side window. 'Someone's using the place. I can see some takeaway cartons.' He peered closer. 'Looks like a copy of today's paper.'

'Which one?'

'Sackville's'

'What should we do?'

'What time is it?' asked Lambert.

'Ten forty-five.'

'We wait till the pubs close.'

Lambert switched off the flashlight. They both sat on the cliff edge, moonlight bouncing off the sea. 'Romantic,' said Kennedy. 'Speaking of which...'

'I'm not sure we should be pursuing this line of conversation,' said Lambert.

'Come on, sir, spill the beans.'

'Nothing to tell.'

Kennedy fell briefly silent. 'She's the DI you worked with on the Souljacker thing?'

'DCI now.'

A sound startled them, someone stumbling up the path. The figure appeared to be singing, a tuneless noise which sounded to Lambert like a poor interpretation of Danny Boy.

'Sackville?' whispered Kennedy.

'Let's not startle him.'

They got to their feet, Lambert reaching for his flashlight but not switching it on. The figure came into sight. It had to be Sackville. Lambert recognised the man's body shape. Short, stocky, with an increasingly protruding stomach. They both had to stifle a laugh as Sackville stumbled and fell to the ground, releasing a line of expletives into the night air.

'He's carrying a bottle,' said Kennedy.

Sackville took a swig from the bottle, and fumbled in his pocket for a key to the caravan. Lambert knew there was no easy way to announce their presence. He switched on the flashlight. 'Eustace, don't be alarmed, it's Michael Lambert.'

The tactic didn't work. Sackville was momentarily caught in the glare of the light as he weighed up his options. Making a decision, he dropped the bottle, letting out a cry of despair as it smashed on the stone steps, and began running down the path.

'Eustace,' said Lambert, amused and exasperated. He jogged down the path after him, the journalist's footing slipping with every other step. Lambert reached out and pulled on Sackville's shoulder, avoiding a clumsy attempt at a punch. 'Jesus, will you calm down. It's Lambert.'

Sackville bent over, his hands on his knees, and vomited.

Lambert took a few steps back, the acrid smell overpowering. 'That's not nice, Eustace.'

Sackville stood up, a line of sick dripping from his mouth. He used the sleeve of his jacket to wipe it away. 'You're a surprise I could do without,' he said.

Sackville led them to the caravan where Lambert attempted to make them all coffee. 'You know my colleague, DS Kennedy.'

'Charmed, excuse the mess.'

Lambert found three plastic beakers and filled them with instant coffee. 'Get that down you, Eustace.'

'How did you track me here?' Sackville looked genuinely concerned. The implication was clear. If they could find him, then other people could.

'Who are you hiding from, Eustace?'

'I think you know.'

'Blake.'

Sackville winced as he drank the coffee. 'Could you Irish this up for me?'

'Not yet, you're borderline incoherent as it is.'

Lambert told him about the files they'd found at his flat.

'Mia broke in?'

'We believe so.'

'She hasn't got the files though?'

'No, we have them. We're going through them now. Tell me, what do you have on Blake?'

'Nothing I can prove. I told Mia a cover story. The so-called rivals of his are actually his colleagues. At least, he thinks they are. Croatians.'

'Trafficking?' asked Kennedy.

Sackville nodded. 'Every time I get near, someone disappears. And then Moira…' He began sobbing. Great, heaving cries, the sound of days of anguish being released.

'You know DS Harrogate?' asked Lambert, noticing the look of surprise from Kennedy.

'I know of him. I know he is investigating Blake somehow.'

'How much do you have on Blake, Eustace? Enough for him to take Moira's life?'

'I could write a book on Blake, but couldn't prove a thing.'

'Is there anything new? Something which could have provoked him?' said Kennedy

'No, but if there was why the fuck didn't he just kill me?'

Lambert touched Sackville's shoulder. 'It could have been someone from the other side, his so-called colleagues, the Croatians. The message could be for everyone else's benefit. Mess with us, and your family is at risk.'

'Could be. I wouldn't put anything past those sick bastards.'

'And what about Laura Dempsey?' said Kennedy.

'You're sure you don't know anything about her, Eustace?'

Sackville shook his head. 'Send me over everything you have on her, and I'll do some research. See if she links in somehow. Seems unlikely.'

'Thanks, Eustace. Are you sure you want to stay here? As I said before, we could put you somewhere safe.'

Eustace Sackville looked around the mess of the caravan. 'Perhaps that wouldn't be such a bad idea.'

Chapter 23

Sarah was gone by the time he returned to his bedsit. After dropping him off, Kennedy was taking Sackville to the station where they would arrange for secure housing for the journalist.

Locating Sackville had created more questions than it had solved. Lambert ran another search on The System, trying to find out Harrogate's interest in Blake, but no active investigations were displayed. Whatever Harrogate was up to was undercover, though not so much so that a journalist hadn't worked it out.

Lambert took a bottle of vodka from the mini fridge in the kitchen area and poured himself a measure. The first sip stung the back of his throat, the acid-like liquid tasting of nothing but sending a wave of relaxation through him. He poured a second helping and sat on the bed where only that afternoon Sarah May had slept, the crinkled sheets forming an approximation of her sleeping form.

He realised he hadn't checked in with Sophie for some time. He remembered the trauma of the first few days with Chloe, the radical shift in their routine and sleeping habits, and wondered how Sophie was dealing with everything. She had her mother for company, but that wasn't quite the same. He decided he would visit first thing, however difficult it would be seeing the new baby in the house, sleeping where Chloe had once slept.

He downed a third drink and switched off the light. The vodka had been a mistake. It was keeping him awake. He was caught halfway between sleep and consciousness. Images from the last few days played in his head, a random collage of distortion. His wife's new baby, Eustace Sackville stumbling up the path to his caravan, Kennedy at the coffee shop, Laura Dempsey's parents alone in their flat, DS Harrogate attacking him outside Blake's house. His mind danced with scenarios and thoughts, as he tried to fall asleep. Did Mr and Mrs Patchett know their grandchildren and son-in-law had been murdered, that their daughter was now effectively alone in the world? He thought about the killer, surely not Curtis Blake unless he was disguising his voice or, more likely, using a proxy, calling him at the most important of times, as if he was somehow tracking him.

The thoughts and questions appeared and disappeared, his mind too tired to hold onto any one thought long enough for him to fully analyse it.

At some point he must have fallen asleep. The incessant bleep of his phone tore him from his rest. In a daze, he patted the bed searching for it, his body drenched in sweat. He found it on the bedside table, knocking over the glass from earlier that night. 'Yes,' he screamed into the receiver, only to realise that he must have set his alarm at some point.

It was six a.m. He showered and changed, called Kennedy and told her to take the morning's debrief from the night team.

After a short drive, he sat outside his old house and waited. The city workers were already up, dropping their children off to school, boys in grey shirts, girls in checked dresses, to their breakfast clubs before catching their trains into town. Sophie had stayed at home until Chloe started pre-school, had gone back part-time at the solicitors' firm when Chloe was three, and gone full time when Chloe started school. Sophie made partner before Chloe had left infant school.

A father held hands with a young girl who skipped along, book bag over her shoulder, and Lambert had to stifle a cry as he remembered holding hands with Chloe, walking her down the same road to the same school.

The front door opened and Sophie poked her head around the door, checking the road was clear, and stepped out in her dressing gown to pick up the milk and bread on the doorstep.

Lambert took the bag of pastries he'd purchased from the local bakery, and made his way over to his old house. He knocked on the door, absurdly nervous.

'Oh,' said Sophie, opening the door, only her head visible. 'Michael.'

'Sorry, I can come back. I was just passing and thought…'

'No, don't be ridiculous. It's just a surprise, come in, come in.'

Lambert followed her down the hallway to the kitchen area. He'd been living here a few months ago, but now the place had the feel of somewhere he didn't know or belong. They'd had a kitchen extension built following Chloe's arrival. Large, glass panelled concertina doors were already opened, leading through to a wood slatted garden area where Sophie's mother enjoyed the morning sunshine. In the shade of the dining area, the baby slept in a brand new carrycot.

'Oh, Michael,' she said, mirroring her daughter.

'Glenda.'

'Coffee?'

'Thanks. I've bought some treats,' he said, lifting up the bag of pastries.

'Great,' said Sophie, taking the bag off him and returning to the kitchen.

'Nice of you to make an appearance,' said Glenda, once Sophie had left. They'd never had the best of relationships. Glenda, like her daughter a high level solicitor, had never approved of his work. Sophie had told him, early on in their relationship, that she'd gone so far as to tell Sophie to leave him. Supposedly, a policeman's wife was no life for her daughter. The relationship had soured beyond recognition following Chloe's death, for which she still blamed Lambert.

He chose to ignore the latent slur. 'Good to see you too, Glenda. How's William?'

'Fine. Having to fend for himself. I imagine he's enjoying his freedom.'

I bet he is, thought Lambert. Sophie's father had always been a bit more amenable to Lambert's line of work. He used to run a small accountancy firm and had managed to retire early. He spent most of his time between the local tennis and sailing clubs. Lambert had often teased Sophie that anywhere would have been preferable to spending time at home.

Glenda smiled at him. She'd hadn't looked away from him since he'd arrived. It was her way with people, a passive aggressive way of sizing people up and putting them in their place. Her distaste was all too evident. 'Why are you here, Michael?'

'I'm checking on Sophie, and…'

'Jane.'

'I know the child's name, Glenda. Sophie has asked me to keep in contact, so I am.'

'Sophie doesn't know what she wants,' she replied, through gritted teeth.

'Right, coffee and pastries. A glorious morning and a sleeping child. Heaven.' Sophie placed a steaming cup of oily coffee in from of him, and the plate of pastries in the middle of the table.

Glenda leant back in her chair, and smiled. 'How are things back at work?' she asked, as if the last conversation hadn't occurred. 'Must be strange after all that time away?'

'It's like I've never been away.'

'Is that a good thing?' asked Sophie.

Lambert thought about how easily he'd settled into the makeshift routine, the late and unpredictable hours. He thought about the things he'd witnessed and how quickly his mind was able to accept the atrocities. 'Good question.' He leant over the table and took an apple turnover off the plate. He was about to take a bite when Glenda handed him a napkin.

'How are you keeping, more importantly?' he asked Sophie.

'Fine. Jane is a heavy sleeper. For the time being.' Sophie touched the wooden table.

Lambert couldn't bring himself to ask about Jeremy Taylor. 'How have work been?'

'Sent me those,' said Sophie, pointing to large bouquet on the dining table. 'They're great as always.'

Lambert pictured Taylor arranging a collection at work, choosing the flowers for his wife. 'This is all a bit strange,' he said.

Glenda sighed, and he ignored the woman as she rolled her eyes.

'Mum, perhaps you could check on Jane.'

'But she's asleep.'

Sophie turned and fixed her mother with a glare only she could get away with.

'Fine. I'll make myself scarce, why not?'

'A joy as always,' said Lambert once his mother-in-law was out of earshot.

'Don't, Michael, she's been wonderful. I don't know what I would have done without her.'

'Is that a dig at me?'

'What? No. Of course it bloody isn't.'

'Sorry, I didn't mean it...'

'Look, I can only imagine how difficult this is, but there are stranger things in the world.'

Lambert pictured Laura Dempsey's family, immediate and extended, wrists cut open. 'Don't I know it. What about... him...'

'Jeremy?'

Lambert nodded. He knew he was behaving like a love-scorned teenager, and worse, knew how hypocritical he was having not told Sophie about Sarah May. 'Yes, Jeremy,' he said, as if swearing in a church.

'He's been here every day. He's due at lunchtime. The firm have given him paternity leave which he'll be starting soon.'

The words stung. It was too difficult. Sitting in what was once was his home, with a woman who was still technically his wife, discussing another man's paternity leave.

'Sit, Michael. I didn't mean to upset you.' Sophie placed her hand on his arm. He pulled away, as gently as possible.

'You haven't. I need to get back to work. I'm waiting on a debrief on a case we're working on.'

Sophie followed him into the dining area. 'You haven't even asked to hold her,' she said, gazing over to the carrycot where the baby slept.

Sophie had told him he was a natural with Chloe. He'd loved holding her as a baby. He'd had a knack of getting her to sleep which had confounded and amazed Sophie in equal measures.

'She's not mine, Soph.'

'She's Chloe's sister,' said Sophie, her eyes watering.

'But she's not mine.'

Chapter 24

Matilda started the morning debrief, updating the team about Eustace Sackville, who was currently in protection. She could only imagine the expense.

She'd dropped Eustace Sackville off at the safe house, a terraced property in North London, and left strict instructions with the two officers responsible for guarding the place. As there didn't seem to be any imminent danger to the journalist, she wondered how the costs would be justified. Tillman had called her as she drove home. He'd wanted to see her but she'd declined his invitation, knowing she had to run the debrief session.

It was all she could do now to stay awake. The night team had little to add, and she gave out instructions for the day which included her going to see Noel Whitfield along with Walker.

'What is our main line of enquiry at the moment?' asked Devlin.

It was a reasonable enough question. 'DCI Lambert wants us to consider that Dempsey and Sackville are linked somehow. Our focus is finding what links Eustace and Laura, rather than what links the actual victims.'

'And what if they're not linked? What if the victims are random?' Walker couldn't resist getting involved.

'Then we're stuffed,' said Matilda, receiving a wave of supportive laughs from the exiting members of the team. 'Now, we all know our roles for today. Back here at six for the debrief.'

Everyone dispersed, Matilda pleased to see the sense of urgency and excitement. Although everything was tentative at the moment, there was a feeling that they were getting closer.

The last known location of Noel Whitfield was a flat in Finchley. 'Why exactly are we here again?' asked Walker, once they'd parked by a set of tall metal bins overflowing with garbage. The flat was located in a high rise building. Like Walker, Matilda knew the area was not overly welcoming to the police. Officers were told to approach the building in a minimum of pairs, but ideally in larger groups.

'I told you. We need to rule Whitfield out.' Kennedy had explained the finer points of the Whitfield case. How the man, represented by Moira Sackville's former lover, Charles Robinson, had been acquitted of the attempted murder of Andrew Haynes. How he had supposedly left Haynes permanently disabled, and made Rebecca Pritty watch as he'd tortured and repeatedly stabbed the man.

'I can't believe he's not institutionalised. It was just a technicality, after all,' said Walker.

Matilda had met with Whitfield's case worker. He was considered a risk but they didn't have the powers, or as the man had alluded, the money, to take him into care.

Whitfield lived on the twelfth floor. Both the building's lifts were out of order, and they were forced to make the long trek up the stairs. 'Imagine having to climb these every day,' said Walker, more to himself than to Matilda.

'Think about those on the higher floors.'

The stairwells smelt like one continuous, never ending urinal, the trapped heat in the building intensifying the stench. Chipped paint fell from the graffiti covered walls. Think about living here at all, she thought.

Matilda took a deep breath of fresh air as she opened the doorway to Whitfield's floor, a welcome 0breeze billowed around the floor which, like the stairwell, had been used as a makeshift toilet. The light brick walls were stained, and Matilda was forced to step over an unpleasant looking puddle of liquid to access Whitfield's front door. 'Ready?' she said to Walker, rapping her knuckles against the wooden door.

Walker peered through the door. 'TV's on.'

Matilda knocked again. 'Wait,' she whispered, pressing her ear to the door.

Walker reached for his belt, hand posed on the expandable truncheon. He relaxed once the door creaked open. An overweight black lady, wrapped in what appeared to be little more than a brightly coloured sheet, stood in the doorway, one hand on her hip.

Matilda flashed her warrant badge. 'May we speak to Noel Whitfield, please?'

The woman sighed. She looked Matilda up and down twice. 'Noel,' she screamed, not looking away.

'What?' Whitfield's voice drifted towards them, weak and effeminate.

'Someone for you.'

Matilda looked behind the woman, and made out a figure walking up the hallway. The woman moved back, and Whitfield came into sight. He was wearing only his boxer shorts, his face and body so emaciated that Matilda could easily see the shape of his rib cage, the contours of his eye sockets. 'Noel Whitfield?'

'Who's asking?' said the man, his voice so soft it was almost inaudible.

Matilda only introduced herself. Walker leant over the wall, checking the car was still there. By the looks of it he had come to the same conclusion as Matilda. Whitfield was not capable of the crimes which had befallen Moira Sackville, and the Dempsey family. He looked in desperate need of nutrition. 'When was the last time you left the flat?' asked Kennedy.

'I'm out of it now, aren't I?'

'I mean, actually left it. Went for a walk, or to the shops?'

'I do all his shopping for him,' said the woman, still standing in a defensive pose.

'Yes, Sally does all my shopping. I don't like going out much.'

'When was the last time, Noel?'

'Don't know, three, four years ago.'

They drove back to the station in silence. Matilda imagined that Walker had been as shocked as she was when Lambert had put them together. He'd eased off with the macho bullshit since the posting but Matilda sensed a tension in the man every time she was with him. She'd sensed it before in other people. Walker was a time bomb. It was eating him up holding his tongue, and she knew he would eventually snap. He rubbed his manicured beard. 'What a waste of time and effort.'

'At least we can take one suspect off the list.'

'Yeah, right. If it wasn't such a ridiculous idea, I would say Lambert sent us on this wild goose chase on purpose.'

'Lambert?'

'Yes, Lambert.'

'Why would he do that?'

'Maybe he wants you out the way. It's his first big case since he returned. He could be onto something, and wants to take the glory himself.'

She thought back to last night, the way Lambert had been with Sackville. 'You don't know what you're talking about.'

'Oh yeah, look at the shit storm he caused on the Souljacker case. Going offline like that.'

Kennedy knew he was trying to get her onside. It was so obvious as to be painful. 'I would keep your opinions to yourself, Walker.'

'Sorry for having an opinion.'

'Opinions are okay, but you're being disloyal.'

Walker smirked. 'Can't be disloyal to the team, can we?'

'What the hell does that mean?'

'Same rules apply to everyone,' said Walker. He wound down the passenger side window and gazed out, signalling he'd finished talking.

Matilda shook her head and switched on the radio.

The incident room was full by the time they returned. Even Tillman was there, effortlessly ignoring her. He was deep in conversation with Lambert, who'd at least looked up once she'd arrived. They were talking to another officer whom she didn't recognise. There was a buzz to the room but also a palpable tension. She'd been in this position in a case before. Everyone realised they were close to something but it was intangible at the moment. Matilda knew there was a danger they could lose focus at this stage. There were too many possibilities, too many different avenues they could take. Now was the time to focus on one or two lines of enquiry but such a decision was beyond her pay scale at present. Lambert stopped talking to Tillman, and nodded over to her.

'This is DS Harrogate from Organised Crime.'

Harrogate nodded.

'You're investigating Blake?' said Matilda.

'That's right.'

'We'll go into more details during the briefing,' said Lambert. He gently pressed his hand against her back and led her away from Harrogate. 'How did it go with Whitfield?'

'Dead end. He's been holed up in his flat the last few years. Nothing but skin and bones. What's he doing here?'

'Politics as normal. Someone's been on to Tillman. They're warning us off pursuing Blake for the time being.'

'So what Sackville said was true?' said Matilda.

'Looks that way.'

'But this is a murder enquiry.'

'They don't think it supersedes what he's working on. You know how things work, Kennedy. According to Harrogate this is just the tip of the iceberg. If they get what they want, hundreds of unsolved murders will be resolved.'

'It's bullshit,' said Matilda.

'Listen it's only guidelines. Let him have his say but I promise you nothing's going to stop us getting the person we want.'

Lambert looked around the room and the silence gradually descended. 'Thank you for all coming, I know you've a lot of work on. I wanted to call an untimed debrief to update you on a few new strands. As you know, DS Kennedy and I met with Eustace Sackville again last evening. We discussed his recent reports on Blake. It seems that Blake is already under investigation by Organised Crime. This is DS Harrogate. He'll explain more.'

Matilda smirked. Without even trying, Lambert had made evident his distaste for Harrogate.

Harrogate's explanation was less than brief. He told them that he was running a classified operation involving people trafficking. 'Nothing about this can leave this room,' he warned everyone.

Matilda looked around the room, noticing the man's tone had not gone down very well with the rest of the team.

As Harrogate sat down, Lambert looked at him puzzled.

'You heard it boys and girls. We've to ease back on Blake for the time being. Thank you DS Harrogate, that will be all.'

Harrogate grimaced and looked about him, clearly unhappy to be dismissed in front of everyone. He looked at Tillman for support but the chief superintendent just shrugged his shoulders. 'Be seeing you,' said Lambert as Harrogate left the room to a chorus of whispered laughs.

Lambert exchanged a look with Tillman who stood up. 'Unfortunately we're to do as Harrogate suggested for the time being. But we're definitely not ruling Blake out at this stage. If anything concrete comes in then I'm giving you permission to go in,' said Tillman, 'Right, I'll leave you all to it.'

An audible gasp of relief shook the room once Tillman had left.

'Devlin, what do we have on the Sackville files?' said Lambert.

'We started going through them last night, our focus on

the files mentioning Blake. Sackville's personal investigations back up what DS Harrogate just said, though to be fair they go into a little more detail.'

Everyone laughed at this and Devlin smiled, pleased with the solidarity in the room. 'The trouble is there are over four hundred thousand words in the document. We've run all the cross-searches we can think of linking everyone so far involved in the case. But we're just going to have to sit down and read them, old school.'

'I'll leave that with you,' said Lambert. 'Get as much help as you want. Divide it into small sections and get reading. Reconvene back here at seven p.m.'

'Sir we're supposed to attend the drinks with murder squad this evening. DS Sherwood is leaving,' shouted out one of the constables from the tech team.

'I think the six reported murders take precedence over a piss up,' said Lambert, before adding: 'That said, I'm not saying we're not going, but we're back here at seven first. There is a link between the Sackville and Dempsey families, I'm sure of it. Now we just have to find it. Back here at seven.'

The team dispersed. Matilda agreed with Lambert. She only wished she knew how to find the link.

Lambert moved to Kennedy's desk. 'We're going to have to get Dempsey and Sackville together at some point.'

'They're not going to release her from the hospital any time soon.'

'Then we might have to bring Sackville in. I want you to speak to Laura Dempsey. See if you can get any more from her, even if you have to tell her about Blake. About what Sackville's been working on.'

'What about DS Harrogate?'

'Ignore Harrogate. I'm just paying lip service to Tillman and the others. Speak to her and tell her whatever you need to jolt her memory. The more I think about it, the more there's no way this is coincidental. He's choosing his victims and there's a reason. Laura Dempsey and Eustace Sackville will have to tell us.'

Devlin stopped them as they left the incident room. 'Sir, someone in reception wants to speak to you.'

Chapter 25

Charles Robinson was waiting in reception. 'DCI Lambert, DS Kennedy. This is my colleague, Giles Lansdowne.'

'What can I do for you, Mr Robinson?' Lambert had put Robinson to the back of his mind since discovering the bodies of Laura Dempsey's parents. The ensuing silence had obviously bothered the barrister.

'I thought it prudent to clear up any questions you may have for me. The last I saw of you…'

'Is there something you wish to tell us, Mr Robinson?'

Robinson looked at his colleague. 'Nothing specific, but if you have anything to ask me?'

Lambert exchanged a glance with Kennedy, noticing the hint of amusement in her eyes. 'We have nothing to ask you at present, but thanks for making the journey.'

Robinson grimaced. 'I must say, I am finding this most inconvenient. I know how you work these things, and I would have really hoped for some better treatment.'

'Work these things?' asked Kennedy.

'Better treatment?' added Lambert.

'You are trying to make me uncomfortable, for whatever reason. I know you want to ask me some more questions, why else did you approach me at the Bailey?'

'Things move on, Mr Robinson. We'll be in contact if necessary.'

'May I suggest that you call me if you want to speak to my client any further?' Giles Lansdowne handed Lambert a gold embossed business card.

'You think you need legal representation, Mr Robinson?'

'Let's go, Giles. I'm not playing silly buggers any more.'

'What was that all about?' asked Kennedy, as the two lawyers left the building.

'I was about to question Robinson at the Old Bailey when I thought about Laura's parents. He's just protecting himself, doesn't want his name dragged through the mud.'

'Why don't we question him?'

'Let him sweat for the time being. I'll speak to him on my own terms. He hasn't been forthcoming with us so I don't think he deserves special treatment.'

'I take it Giles Lansdowne won't be present,' said Kennedy, that look of amusement on her face again.

'Highly unlikely. Right, I'll see you at the debrief.'

'Sir.'

'Matilda, before you go.'

Kennedy raised her eyebrows at him using her first name.

'If there is anything you need to tell me, at any time, you know where to find me.'

'Yes, sir.'

'I mean it. If there is anything you need to tell me, related to the case, or not, then you can tell me in full confidence.'

'Good to know. Thank you, sir.'

Back in his office, he logged on to The System. He searched through Eustace Sackville's social media posting using the back end access. He did the same for Laura Dempsey, and cross-checked the searches. He added in Curtis Blake, and broadened the search to include internet searches, and news stories. If The System had a downside, it was its effectiveness. The searches on the individuals provided hundreds of results, too numerous to tackle without hours of manpower. Lambert tried limiting the search, but was hampered by not knowing exactly what he was looking for. In one of his folders, the searches on Kennedy's father waited for him. He wasn't convinced anything relevant was in the files, thought it was possible that the killer was trying to divert his attention.

He called the tech department to check if there was any way of tracking unknown calls on his phone. 'If you bring the phone in we can see what we can do,' said a female voice.

'What are the chances of tracking it if the caller doesn't want us to?'

'If they are moderately competent then it could prove to be very difficult. They could call via Wi-Fi and bounce the IP addresses all over the place.'

Lambert hung up and drummed his fingers on the desk, frustrated at how close they were. He hoped Kennedy's interview with Laura Dempsey would reap some reward. If that failed, then he would have to get Dempsey and Sackville together soon. He was adamant they were both withholding something.

He drove the short distance to Sackville's safe house, and showed his warrant card to the two plain clothes officers.

'How you liking your new surroundings, Eustace?'

'Can't complain, though we're running low on single malt.'

'It's barely past noon,' said Lambert, boiling the kettle.

'Don't I know it.'

'It's Blake's sixtieth in a couple of days. You going?'

Sackville snorted, accepting the mug of instant coffee. 'It's officially a surprise party, from what I've heard. Blake is going to make a grand entrance once the guests arrive.'

'Who's going to be there?'

'Apart from family, everyone. You should take all your outstanding arrest warrants, you'd have a field day.'

Lambert thought about DS Harrogate's case, and wondered if he had plans for the day. Whatever Harrogate thought, and the orders he'd received from Tillman, the only reason he hadn't visited Blake again was due to the phone calls he kept receiving. It was possible they were a diversion tactic set by Blake, but Lambert was happy to wait until he knew more.

'So, we've started reading through your files.'

'Right. Not sure I've given you permission, but anyway.'

'A lot of prose, Eustace. Could you help by narrowing down our search?'

'The files about Blake are all there. Not much more I can do, and by the sounds of it your boy Harrogate has all that business sorted out.'

'What do you know about Blake's staff?'

'Staff? That is a very loose term. Why, what are you angling at?'

'Anyone you could think of who would be disloyal?'

'To Curtis Blake? Not if they have any sense. Some of the stories I've heard.'

Lambert had heard them all, had seen the fallout on occasions. Betraying people like Curtis Blake resulted in more than death. From what Lambert had seen, death was the last, merciful act.

'Anyone new, anyone you're not sure of?'

Sackville looked distastefully at his instant coffee.

'Tell me what you know and I'll order some supplies. This could be for your own benefit, Eustace.'

'His team are pretty well established. Your buddy Harrogate knows all this, by the way. His inner sanctum are mainly family, even his accountant is a nephew. There are outsiders who work for him but they are accounted for. The only senior people not family would be the lawyer, and the security guy. In fact, all the security are outsiders. He prefers ex-military. Head guy is Atkinson, then Wallace and Richards. There are at least seven or eight or more ex-service personnel who work below Atkinson. The whole team were together in the Gulf. They're all ex-special ops of one sort or another. Below that team, they have a subset who do some of the more unsavoury work.'

'The lawyer?'

'He uses a firm. Price and Barker.'

Lambert closed his eyes for a second, and looked away.

'Your wife works there, doesn't she?'

Lambert stared at him, thinking hard.

'I'm sure it's a coincidence. What department is she in?'

'Family law.' Lambert thought about his anonymous caller, all the information he had.

'Blake has his own team. It's not what you'd expect. Blake is under the impression that he's legit, so they're all commercial solicitors. I think they ship the criminal work out.'

'I guess he uses the senior guys, the partners?'

'Yes, the main guy is…'

'Don't tell me,' said Lambert. 'Jeremy Taylor.'

Chapter 26

He called Sophie as soon as he reached the car.

'Everything okay?' she asked.

'Just checking in. Nothing out of the ordinary happened recently?'

'No. Oh hang on, I did push a small child out of me a few days ago but apart from that...'

'Very droll.'

'You sound worried, is there something wrong?'

It was pointless worrying her for no due reason. Taylor being involved had to be a coincidence. By all accounts, he'd been overseeing Blake's legal work for a number of years, long before Sophie had been on the scene. 'No, I just felt bad about earlier. How's Glenda?'

'Fine. What is it, Michael? You can tell me.'

'Nothing, honest. I'll speak to you later.'

The phone rang as soon as he ended the call. 'Yep,' said Lambert, having not looked at the number.

'Lambert.'

Lambert pressed the brake pedal a little harder than planned, receiving a horn blast from the car behind him. He lifted his hand in apology.

Lambert sensed the change in the man's voice immediately.

It was a subtle shift in tone, almost indecipherable. The killer sounded stressed.

'It's not going to work,' said the voice. 'You're not going to turn me into some sort of joke.'

Lambert tried to pull over, blasting his horn at the stalled car in front of him.

'Slow down. What are you talking about?' he shouted into the speakerphone. The stalled car pulled away and Lambert parked on a double yellow line and switched on his hazards, receiving a line of angry horn blasts and shouts from his fellow drivers.

'Don't play dumb with me, Lambert, I know too much about you. I know you've met with Mia Helmer on more than one occasion. You met with her only the other day at Eustace's flat.'

Lambert thought back to catching the journalist going through Sackville's belongings and the ensuing file he'd discovered listing Curtis Blake's involvement in trafficking. He could only presume that Helmer had leaked the story despite the promises she'd made.

'I've met with Helmer but I haven't told her to run any story,' he said, gambling. 'From what I understand, you guided her to the flat in the first place.'

The killer paused and it took all Lambert's will for him not to speak again. He sat still, each passing car which had to manoeuvre around him breaking the silence with obscenities.

Eventually the killer spoke, the stressed tone from seconds before had vanished. The man sounded back in control.

'What does it matter?' he said. 'We're entering end time now. Party time is coming. Such ridiculous tactics won't stop me.'

'Why don't you tell me the truth?' said Lambert. 'Tell me

where Helmer went wrong. Tell me what this is all about and we can put your side of the story to the public. Surely you don't want them to hear these lies about you.' He could only guess at what Helmer had printed. 'Just tell me what this is all about.' Lambert hesitated, and decided to gamble. 'Tell me what Eustace Sackville and Laura Dempsey did to you. Tell me what they did to deserve this punishment.' Lambert sensed rather than heard the intake of breath on the other side of the line.

'You truly don't know anything, do you?'

'What about Curtis Blake?' continued Lambert, undeterred.

'What about him?' said the killer laughing, as if the question was ridiculous. 'You're grasping at straws, Mr Lambert. Have you asked your partner about her father yet? She really does have issues with authority you know. But her latest issue is going to get her into grave trouble.'

'Don't change the subject. What have you got to hide? If end times are coming, as you said, why can't you let me know?'

'That would be spoiling all the fun, Mr Lambert,' said the killer. 'Be watching you,' he said, hanging up.

'Hello? Hello?' screamed Lambert into the handset, receiving a low monotone noise in return. He slammed his fist against the dashboard before taking out his notebook and recording the conversation as best he could. The killer had spoken in code. Lambert jotted down the crucial bits: End time is coming, it's party time. He noted what the killer had said about Matilda without directly mentioning her name. About her authority issues and how her latest dalliance had put her in grave danger. It seemed now he would have to find out who she was seeing, which would be awkward at best.

He opened the car door, a cyclist swerving to miss him.

Lambert held his hands up but the cyclist was not satisfied. He placed his bike on the pavement and moved towards him. He was a lean figure, dressed in black Lycra, at least six foot four. His rage was all too evident. He moved towards Lambert, ready to engage in violence, only to stop at the last second as Lambert stood his ground and stared the man down.

'I'm sorry,' said Lambert. 'I wasn't thinking.' He didn't flinch as the man took one step nearer. Lambert was about to reach his hand into his pocket to take out his warrant card then decided against it. Blood thundered through his body, laced with adrenaline. It was hard to accept but deep down he wanted the man to attack him, wanted a reason to unleash the pent up violence within him. As if sensing this, the cyclist stopped and backed away.

Lambert located a newsagent and found the newspaper Eustace Sackville sometimes worked for. He scanned through the paper looking for any mention of Sackville or Dempsey but couldn't find anything.

'When do your newspapers come in?' he asked the person behind the counter.

'First thing in the morning.'

'Do you not get another batch in at any time?'

The boy looked over to a woman who Lambert presumed was the boy's mother. She turned and smiled at Lambert. 'Can I help?' she said.

'Do you know if there are any later editions of this newspaper?'

'Not with us, I'm afraid. I think you may find later editions at the train station.'

'Thank you.'

Outside, Lambert began running. He supposed he may have been able to find the story online if it existed but he wanted to see the print edition. He sped past shocked onlookers, running along the embankment until he reached Charing Cross Station.

He found a second newsagent and immediately spotted the paper. The headline on the cover was a different front page to the one he'd just seen:

Dead Lucky ran the headline.

Family Killer Strikes Terror in Central London, Reported by Senior Crime Editor, Mia Helmer.

Lambert grabbed the paper and cursed, walking out of the newsagents without paying. The story listed the murders of Moira Sackville, Laura Dempsey's husband and children, and her parents, Mr and Mrs Pratchett. Apparently, Laura Dempsey was the lucky one for having escaped the killer. Lambert knew only too well that there were worse things than dying.

Helmer had gone back on her promise. Lambert skimmed through the three pages the paper had given over to the story. He absorbed the vague details and theories put forward by the journalist, until he reached the part he was sure had triggered the killer's indignation. It appeared Mia Helmer had approached a so-called serial killer expert from the USA. Graham Milestone was reported to be a former FBI profiler and given the imprecise details from Mia on the recent murders had formulated a profile of the killer. Milestone suggested the killer was male, middle-aged, desperately lonely and in need of attention. It was standard stuff, something any criminology graduate could have come up with.

The article continued to state that the killer enjoyed watching his victims die. The paper had even given the killer an uninspired nickname, the Watcher. The profiler had his theories on this as well. One line in particular captured Lambert's eye. 'It was possible the killer suffered abuse from a family member as a child.' Lambert scrunched the paper together and swore out loud, startling an elderly woman who'd been walking by him at the time.

'Sorry,' he said, understanding what had got the killer so agitated. He only hoped it hadn't prompted him into speeding up his process.

Chapter 27

Lambert looked more agitated than normal. He handed her a newspaper and said, 'Did you know about this?'

Matilda took the paper and unfolded it, Lambert having scrunched it into a ball. She saw the headline on the front and guessed the rest.

'Helmer?' she asked.

'I want to see her first thing tomorrow,' said Lambert. 'What do you know about this profiling guy?'

Matilda carried on reading, trying to catch up with Lambert. She read to the part about the profiler and his rather obvious observations about the killer, now nicknamed the Watcher. 'Never heard of him. I'll run some checks.'

Lambert ignored her and clapped his hands. A hush descended over the incident room. 'For those of you who haven't done so, read the article by Mia Helmer. Helmer is Eustace Sackville's editor. She's just released a puff piece on the killer.'

A muttering of confusion filled the air, which Lambert cut short. 'I'll be speaking to Helmer first thing in the morning. The gist of it is that Helmer has accused the killer of being a victim of abuse. What effect this will have on the killer is unknown but we need to be prepared. The assumption is possibly correct, but the killer may not like it being public knowledge.'

Matilda surveyed her colleagues, noting the occasional look of doubt on some of their faces. If Lambert noticed, as she was sure he had, he chose not to mention it.

'We can forget DC Harrogate's objection at the moment. I want a closer look at all Blake's employees, present and past. We can't quiz them yet but if you find any link between them and Sackville or Dempsey, however minor, flag it up immediately.'

Matilda saw how impatient Lambert was as everyone read back their reports. It was past eight o'clock and they were all due at the local bar where DS Sherwood was having his leaving drinks after thirty years on the force. Matilda knew Lambert didn't care about that. It was as if he was waiting for something else to happen on the case, something he could latch onto.

'Everyone back at seven a.m.,' he said, to a chorus of disapproval. 'And don't go crazy tonight,' he warned, like an overzealous parent.

'What's got into him?' said Walker, sidling over to her after Lambert had left.

'He's just keen for a breakthrough, as you should be,' said Matilda, packing her belongings and moving away.

The party was already in full swing by the time she arrived. She was surprised to see Lambert was already there. She'd presumed he'd gone home. He was at the bar sipping on a beaker of whisky, talking to Tillman who did his usual impeccable job of ignoring her.

She walked to the bar metres away from the pair of them and ordered herself a pint of lager.

'Oh get us one, Tilly.' It was Rebecca Shah, one of the DCs Matilda was friendly with.

'You made an effort,' she said, ordering Shah a drink. They found a corner of the bar and clinked glasses together.

Shah was in her civvies, her face made up. Matilda felt a bit frumpy in comparison. She was still in the same clothes she'd worn all day, decades old jeans, light blouse and cardigan. The closest her face had come to make up was a splash of cold water in the toilets before leaving.

'I'm on a bit of a promise,' said Shah, giggling into her pint.

'Who's the lucky lad?' said Matilda, nodding her head to a group of Shah's colleagues at the other end of the bar.

'You're kidding aren't you? I wouldn't touch anyone in here with your hands. No, I've gone upmarket this time. A lawyer no less.'

'Look at you,' said Matilda. 'Is he coming here?'

'Oh yeah, I'm really going to let him come here in a room full of coppers. I'm meeting him later. Have a few drinks with you guys then I'm going to head off.'

'I'm probably going to do the same,' said Matilda, feeling the tiredness seep through her.

'What about you? Seeing anyone at the moment?' said Shah.

'No time for such frivolities,' said Matilda, knowing the truth would not only shock the young constable but might result in her not speaking to her again.

'What can I get you ladies?' said Walker, approaching them.

Matilda couldn't help but display her distaste, and noticed Shah had picked up on it. 'Nothing for us, thanks,' said Shah.

'I think Matilda can answer for herself, Becky,' said Walker. He'd cleaned up since the incident room, changing into a new shirt, his hair gelled back, slick like a parody of an Italian gangster, his thick beard perfect as ever.

'Nothing for me,' said Matilda.

'Suit yourself,' said Walker and headed towards the bar.

'What was that about?' said Shah.

'Oh nothing.'

Shah hesitated. Looking sheepish she said, 'Have you two…?'

'God, no,' said Matilda.

Shah took a long drink. 'Does he want to?'

'He's only human,' said Matilda, laughing.

'I'm afraid I may have…' said Shah.

'You and Walker? When?'

'Couple of years back now, when I'd just joined. Naive and foolish. It was just a night.'

'Sorry, I didn't mean anything when I said…'

'No, you're right,' said Shah. 'You're best clear of him.'

'Let me get us some more drinks.'

'My round,' said Shah.

Walker approached her as Shah was at the bar. 'She's a pretty one.'

Matilda sighed. 'Don't you see enough of me in the daytime? The room is full of people, why don't you go and pester someone else?' From the corner of her eye Matilda saw Tillman glance over, quickly diverting his attention when he knew he'd been caught looking.

'Just being friendly, Tilly. Jesus.'

It was the first time he'd ever used that name for her. It was a name only her closest friends called her and she didn't like him using it. 'Kennedy will be fine.'

Shah returned with the drinks, placing her shoulder in between her and Walker. The three of them stood in silence for a second before Walker finally took the hint and moved off.

'He was like this with me. Just wouldn't take no for an answer,' said Shah. 'I was flattered at the time but now I know he's like this with lots of people.'

Matilda had heard the rumours.

'He's clever, mind you. Never quite steps over the line.'

Matilda took a sip of her drink. 'Enough talk about that twat. Tell me more about this mysterious lawyer of yours.'

She ended up staying longer than planned. Shah left for her date sometime around nine and Matilda spent the next two hours moving from conversation to conversation, most of the talk focusing on work and the retiring sergeant's notorious libido. At closing time she found herself deep in conversation with Devlin. She felt quite lightheaded, despite pacing herself through the evening.

'It's great being part of this team. I feel really lucky,' said Devlin. Matilda stared at the bar light above the constable's head as he talked, the bulb shining down on his hair, highlighting his prematurely balding scalp.

'Working under DCI Lambert is a real privilege,' continued Devlin.

'Oh I agree,' said Matilda. 'One for the road?'

Devlin shrugged and wobbled, and had to use the bar to regain his balance. 'We shouldn't really,' he said.

'Two G&Ts,' Matilda shouted to the barman.

'We're closed,' said the barman, a man of indecipherable age.

'Come on, George. It's for me,' said Matilda.

The barman shook his head but poured the drinks anyway. Devlin excused himself and stumbled to the bathrooms. Matilda scanned the thinning crowd and smiled as she saw that Tillman was still there talking to some senior busybody from the murder squad.

She wiped the smile off her face quickly and returned to her drink, downing the gin and tonic. It was a mistake. The alcohol was having a greater effect on her than normal.

'I think you've had enough, DS Kennedy,' said the barman.

'I think you've had enough,' replied Matilda, noticing her own slurred voice pattern.

George put both arms onto the bar and raised his eyebrows.

'I need some air,' said Matilda.

'Shall I order you a taxi?'

Matilda shook her head, too tired to speak any further. The next thing she knew, she was outside but couldn't remember getting there. Her arm was stuck out, hailing every passing car as if it was a taxi. This is not good, she thought to herself. She'd be back at work in a few hours and would be nursing the mother of all hangovers. Her head thumped. She bent over and found herself staring at her shoes. Looking to her right, she noticed another pair of shoes. Immaculate black shoes, shined to perfection.

'What do you want, Walker?' she said, lifting her shoulders, mustering every ounce of will she had to sober up.

'Just checking you're okay,' said Walker, sounding plausibly genuine. 'You look a bit wobbly.'

Matilda looked around her. The bar was shut, locked up, lights switched off. A couple of officers were leant up against the wall smoking. She sighed inwardly, relieved. Then Walker put his arm around her and the anger bubbled up. She shouldn't have to be relieved to see other police officers. She shouldn't have to be concerned about one of her colleagues' intentions. She darted her left shoulder backwards, shrugging off Walker's arm.

'Get off me,' she said, through gritted teeth.

'Steady, Tilly,' said Walker. 'I'm just checking you're okay.' He said the words softly so as not to draw attention to himself.

'Don't fucking touch me and don't call me Tilly.'

'Look, if you don't want my help just say so. I can get a taxi for you. Make sure you get home safely.'

She was amazed that he had the temerity to think this would work. Even in her drunken state she saw right through him, the fake concern, the soft words and gentle hand gestures. She looked around, dismayed to see the other officers had disappeared. 'Just go fuck yourself, Walker. Your little tricks won't work with me.'

It was enough for the real Walker to reveal himself. The concerned face was replaced by the snarling arrogance she'd always associated him with. 'What? I'm too low a pay grade for you?' he said.

Matilda turned her body to face him. 'What the hell does that mean?'

'I know things, Tilly,' he said, emphasising the word Tilly, his head poking forward to hers as if in challenge.

She resisted the bait. It was impossible that he knew about Tillman, they'd hidden their tracks too well.

'Okay, Walker, whatever. You carry on living in your little dream world. You may have fooled the others but I keep my eyes open and I won't be scared to let others know.'

'I've absolutely no idea what you're talking about, but that sounded like some sort of threat to me.'

Matilda was about to respond, was about to tell him everything she'd heard about him, when a voice rang out from nowhere.

'Evening troops,' came the familiar baritone.

Walker tensed at the voice, the arrogance vanishing in an instant.

'Sir,' she said.

Behind her stood Glenn Tillman, feet wide apart, ready for action.

Chapter 28

The incident room was sprinkled with broken bodies slouched on chairs. At least two officers sat with their heads in their hands, everyone's face was drawn, washed out, and the air conditioning, its gentle hum the only sound in the funeral-like atmosphere, did little to hide the fetid aroma in the room. Lambert slammed his work file on the desk. 'Who died?' he asked.

The team shuffled themselves into position, straightening backs, willing themselves out of their hangovers. Lambert didn't read the riot act. It was unprofessional, but they had been working full out for some time now and he couldn't blame them. 'Right, get over it everyone. We're back to work now. Save your hangovers for this evening. Where are we, Sergeant?'

Kennedy raised her head. From the effort, it looked as if it weighed a tonne. Her voice came out as a faint rasp. She took a swig of water and tried again. 'I have arranged to see Laura Dempsey this morning. As requested,' she added, with a hint of accusation.

Lambert nodded. He was battling his own private hangover, though he imagined it was half of what Kennedy was enduring. Lambert had his own plans for the morning which he decided not to share with the team yet. He handed out more duties to the team and finished the meeting before everyone lost interest. 'Anyone seen Walker?' he asked before wrapping up.

The faces were blank. Kennedy had returned her focus to her phone so he couldn't read her reaction. Lambert remained standing, wondering if something was being hidden from him. In the end he relented. 'Tell him to see me the second he arrives.'

Tillman looked little better than the rest of the team. He was sitting behind his desk, nursing a metallic beaker. 'Late night?' said Lambert.

Tillman screwed up his face, a patchwork of wrinkles appearing on his ample face. 'You could say that. What can I do for you, Lambert?'

'We haven't had time to talk about DS Harrogate yet, sir,' said Lambert, taking a seat opposite the man.

Tillman groaned and sipped the hot liquid in his beaker, letting out a satisfied sigh as he placed the drink on the desk. Lambert noticed a slight colouring on Tillman's knuckles. Tillman caught him looking, and pulled his hand away. 'What do you want to know about Harrogate?'

Lambert paused, thought about asking about the knuckle marks and decided against it. 'I want to know why he is impeding my investigation, and why you are allowing it.'

Tillman snorted, but Lambert could tell his comment had annoyed him. The old Tillman would never have let this happen. Things had changed since Lambert had left The Group for his enforced sabbatical. Tillman's powers had been curtailed, and Lambert wanted to press the point. Although it pained his superior, he hoped to provoke a reaction from him so he could get some answers.

'Why am I allowing it?'

Lambert shrugged his shoulders.

Tillman placed his elbows on the desk and linked his hands.

'You always were a manipulative sod, do you know that?' He rubbed his face, air snorting out of his nose. Lambert sensed an internal power struggle within the man. He'd obviously received orders, but Lambert knew Tillman's history – and orders were traditionally something which rarely troubled him. 'I told you when you returned, Lambert, The Group is no more. We don't have the same powers as before. Harrogate, and those many pay ranks about him have a long standing operation on Blake. It takes precedence.'

'This is you? Glenn Tillman?'

'Steady, Lambert.'

'Well, this is horseshit, sir. Blake's a major suspect on a series of murders, each more elaborate than the last, and I'm supposed to take a back seat.'

'Get over yourself, Lambert. No one is asking you to take a back seat. As soon as you have something concrete, then you will have my support. Until then, just modify your investigation.'

'Modify.' It was Lambert's turn to snort. They sat in silence, broken only by the sound of Tillman lifting his drink and gulping its contents. 'Does he have someone on the inside?'

Tillman's head bobbed up and down as he considered his response. Lambert had been undercover before and knew the drill. It was likely that Harrogate was the undercover officer's handler. Only a handful of senior officers would know about the officer's identity. 'I can't comment.'

Lambert took that as confirmation. 'Do you know who it is?'

Tillman stared back at him blankly. Lambert thought about Blake's team. His security personnel and the faces he'd glimpsed inside the house. It was some feat infiltrating Blake's world, and it was possible the operation had been going on for years. Lambert held his hands up. 'Okay,' he said. 'You going to tell me who you punched?' he added, as an afterthought.

'Get out,' said Tillman.

Kennedy was still at her desk when he returned to the main office. 'You look terrible,' he told her.

'Thanks, sir.'

'Well, you do.'

Kennedy laughed. 'Charmer. I may have had one drink too many last night. It won't affect my work.'

'It better not. When are you seeing Laura Dempsey?'

'I spoke to the ward sister, and we've arranged for me to visit at eleven a.m. Dr Hughes will be present. Dr Hughes took the decision to tell Laura about her parents' death last night. She has been placed under psychiatric care.'

'Jesus, I'm not surprised.' He could only imagine, and was scared to do so. He'd seen tragic loss in his time on the force but nothing like this. To lose your husband and children, only to be told your parents had died as well, all by the same killer, by the same gruesome hand. If it was a revenge killing, Lambert shuddered to think what Dempsey must have done to provoke such a reaction.

'Come on,' he said to Kennedy. 'You can come with me to see Mia Helmer and we can go together to see Dempsey.

Lambert drove. Kennedy's mood had not brightened. She stared out of the windscreen as if she was suffering tunnel vision. All the colour had left her face, even her red hair looked dank and lifeless. 'Have you eaten?'

Kennedy took a few seconds to answer. 'Sorry, what?'

'Have you eaten?'

'Dry toast.'

Lambert didn't answer, not wanting to lecture her. He'd been in her situation too many times to start pointing fingers. 'Anything you want to tell me about last night?'

He sensed a shift in Kennedy's breathing, as if he'd stumbled on something she wished to keep secret. 'Like what?' she said, her focus still on the oncoming road.

'You tell me. You're not your useful bubbly self.'

She tore her eyes from the road and looked at him. 'Bubbly?' she said, a hint of brightness in her tone.

'I don't know. Effervescent? Energetic? Still breathing?'

'I'm just hungover, sir. I'll be fine soon enough.'

Lambert nodded. 'You heard from Walker today?'

Although he was concentrating on driving, he noticed her body tense. He'd seen Walker approach her and Shah last night and the conversation had looked uneasy at best. He'd hoped partnering them would have helped resolve whatever differences they had, but feared it may have served only to have strained their relationship.

'Phone's on silent,' she said, her focus returning to the road – signalling the conversation was over.

The entrance to the newspaper's offices was full of hurrying people. The temperature had dropped significantly since yesterday, and Lambert zipped up his jacket. 'Mia Helmer,' he said to one of the receptionists, displaying his warrant card. 'We know the way.'

No one bothered them as they made the way across the open-plan area to Helmer's office. Heads were leant forwards, eyes straining on the copy in front of them, their presence nothing out of the ordinary.

Lambert didn't bother knocking. He opened Helmer's door and walked straight in. Helmer was in conversation with two suited men. Both were in their sixties and looked like identikit models of each other. Both had full heads of greying hair, and finely tailored suits which did a good job of masking the considerable girth of their stomachs. 'What is the meaning of this?' said one of the pair, getting to his feet.

Lambert didn't offer any explanation, simply waited for Helmer to dismiss the men. 'They're for me,' she said.

'Shall I call security?' said the man who'd got to his feet.

'No, it's fine, Lance. I'll get back to you shortly.'

Both men grimaced as they walked by, the talkative one looking Lambert up and down with a look of distaste.

'Now that wasn't very friendly, DCI Lambert,' said Helmer, once the men had left and Kennedy had shut the door.

'You're lucky I haven't dragged you out of this office,' said Lambert. 'Yet.'

Helmer rolled her eyes, ignoring Lambert's threat. 'DS Kennedy, how are you?'

Kennedy nodded her head an inch and took a seat. Lambert eased his breathing and sat next to her. 'Would you like to tell me what the hell is going on, Helmer?'

'Coffee?'

'Don't test me, Helmer. What were you thinking, printing that story?'

Helmer pushed the lid of her minute laptop shut. She had long fingers, her manicured nails painted a garish red. 'The last time I looked there was still something called freedom of the press.'

'The last time I saw you, you'd illegally gained entry into Eustace Sackville's flat.'

'Come now, Michael. As you are well aware, I was checking on Eustace's wellbeing. The door to his flat had been broken. What was I supposed to do?

'Not steal his flash drive.'

'Everything is so black and white with you. I was simply recovering company property.'

'Let's leave that for the time being,' said Kennedy, speaking for the first time since they'd entered the office. 'Why did you print the story about the killer without speaking to us first?'

'Why would I have done that?'

'The reason you would have done that, Helmer, is that it was the professional thing to do. Your amateur profiling could result in all sorts of unwelcome repercussions.'

Helmer drummed her fingers on her desk, the sound of bone on glass reverberating around the room. 'What sort of repercussions?' she asked.

Lambert heard the killer's words in his head, wondered again if he should share the information with someone. Helmer wouldn't have reached the position she was in by being so naïve. Lambert was convinced she was hiding something. 'Let's cut the crap. Why didn't you share your so-called expert's view with us first?'

Helmer looked incredulous. 'Since when do we have to run everything past you? If we did that, we'd never get anything published.'

'What do you know, Helmer? Was there a second file you smuggled out of Sackville's flat?'

'Is he always this paranoid?' said Helmer to Kennedy.

Lambert stood. 'If you are withholding something, Helmer, I will arrest you for obstruction. Think about what you're doing, for Christ's sake. You could be responsible for another killing.'

Helmer scratched her head. 'I don't know what you're getting at. Naturally, I would share any relevant information for you. I'll keep you updated, DCI Lambert.' She raised her eyebrows, taunting him.

'Come on, Kennedy,' said Lambert. 'We're wasting our time here.'

As Kennedy stood, Helmer surprised Lambert by getting to her feet. 'I'll tell you one thing, DCI Lambert. You'd probably find out anyway.'

'Go on.'

'Eustace Sackville has been suspended indefinitely from work, subject to an internal investigation.'

'What? You're kidding?' said Kennedy.

'I can't tell you any more than that at the moment.'

'Is it related to this case?' asked Lambert.

'It's all I can tell you at the moment,' repeated Helmer.

Chapter 29

'What the hell is that?'

'It's a breakfast bagel, what's it look like?' Lambert winced as he looked at the congealed mess he'd placed before Kennedy. 'Eat that and drink your black coffee and you'll be right as rain.'

They were at the hospital where Laura Dempsey was under psychiatric care. 'You don't have to be here, sir, I'm fine,' said Kennedy.

'I'm not here because of you. If I was concerned enough to accompany you, then I'd be concerned enough to take you off the case. Now Laura knows about the death of her parents, I think it prudent that we both go to see her. I can only imagine her mental state.'

Kennedy took a bite of her bagel, a line of yellow liquid dripping from the bagel onto her plate. She chewed diligently before speaking. 'I'd be surprised if she's coherent. I imagine she's on suicide watch.'

'That's one hell of a long term project for someone,' said Lambert. Again, he wondered if it was a revenge killing, and if so what Dempsey had done to illicit such a savage response. Not that revenge was always delivered in equal measure. He'd seen countless incidents of revenge killings. With the very rare exception, they were always disproportionate to the original offence.

Kennedy looked as if she was enjoying her meal. The colour was returning to her face, and she was becoming more agitated. 'She was some piece of work,' she said, wiping a line of ketchup from her upper lip.

'Helmer?'

Kennedy took a final bite, nodding. 'What do you think she meant about Sackville?'

'Christ, I don't know. I've only known her a couple of days but I can tell she likes her games. I'll speak to Eustace later and find out more.'

They met with Dr Hughes before they were allowed to see Dempsey. 'I don't really like this,' said Hughes, in her Geordie lilt. 'She's refused sedatives, so she's lucid, but she's obviously not in a good place. I don't want you speaking to her about her parents at the moment. I don't think she's fully come to terms with that yet. She saw what happened to her family, but the thought of her parents' deaths is abstract at the moment. She is almost definitely in denial, and for the time being I think that is the safest place for her.'

'We won't mention that. We need to ask her a couple of questions about her past.'

'You will stop as soon as I say,' said Hughes, the inflection in her voice suggesting the comment was final.

'Of course,' said Lambert, thinking back to Dr Patel's more abrasive approach, marvelling at the difference and the reaction it received.

Hughes knocked on the door and led them through. Laura Dempsey sat up, pulling her sheet over her shoulders so that the only part of her body visible was her neck and head. Ghost-white, her face looked devoid of emotion. Lambert saw a complete emptiness which was difficult to look at. The room had that cloying hospital smell Lambert was becoming over familiar with. Starch sheets, antiseptic, and Laura Dempsey's body odour, mixed together to create something which made Lambert close to nauseous. He placed his hand on the frame of Dempsey's bed, surprised by the coldness of the metal. He nodded at Kennedy, told himself to remember why they were there.

'Laura, my name is Matilda Kennedy. I am a detective sergeant working on your family's case.'

Dempsey turned her head to look at Kennedy. Eyes wide and vacant, she stared at Kennedy as if she hadn't realised she was in the room.

'I can't imagine how difficult this must be for you, Laura. I need to ask you a few questions if that's okay?'

Dempsey shrugged and pulled her sheet down. She was wearing a hospital gown. Lambert noticed a dark rash on her neck, and patches on her forearms.

Kennedy pulled out an iPad from her bag and opened the screen. 'I'm going to show you a picture, Laura.'

Dempsey's body tensed and she pulled the sheet back up above her shoulders.

'Please don't worry, Laura. It's just a picture of a man who has also suffered a loss. His name is Eustace Sackville. Do you recognise him?' Kennedy turned the iPad so Dempsey could see the screen. It was hard for Lambert to tell if she was looking or not. The same impassive look was stencilled onto her face. Her mouth hung open and her eyes looked as if they were staring into space. 'No,' she said.

'Please take a second to think. Mr Sackville is a journalist. Have you ever had any dealings with journalists?'

For the first time since entering the room, Lambert saw a flicker of recognition in Dempsey's eyes. 'We deal with journalists now and again at the hospital but I don't recognise him.'

'Thank you, Laura.' Kennedy displayed another picture. 'This is Mr Sackville's wife, Moira.'

'She's dead.' It wasn't a question, more a statement of fact. The words came out in monotone with a terrible finality.

Kennedy exchanged a look with Lambert. He nodded for her to continue, receiving confirmation from Dr Hughes.

'I'm afraid so, Laura.'

'Him?' said Dempsey, in the same monotone voice.

'We believe so, Laura. Do you recognise this woman?'

Dempsey pursed her lips and stared at Kennedy as if she was stupid. 'No,' she snapped.

'Sorry, Laura. One last photo.' Kennedy glanced again at Lambert for confirmation. It was a long shot but Lambert thought it was worth pursuing. 'Do you know this man?' asked Kennedy.

Lambert had studied enough suspects over the years to notice a look of recognition. Dempsey's eyes squinted and she asked to hold the iPad. Her hands were shaking. 'Who is this?'

'His name is Curtis Blake.'

Dempsey looked up at the ceiling, her porcelain skin shading with colour. Lambert tensed, and stopped himself from pushing the matter further. She would tell them when she was ready.

Laura began shaking her head. 'I'm sorry. There's something about his face, those eyes... but I can't quite place him.'

'I think that will do for now,' said Dr Hughes. Dempsey was becoming agitated and now seemed the right time to stop the questioning.

‘Thank you, Laura. You’ve been very helpful. As soon as you remember anything, please call us or speak to one of the officers outside your room.’

As they were leaving, Dempsey called out. ‘It’s not him, if that’s what you think.’ The words came out in a high pitched squeal. ‘He’s too old. He was young, unbelievably strong.’

‘That’s fine, Laura. Thank you, officers,’ said Dr Hughes, ushering them out and shutting the door.

‘She recognised Blake,’ said Kennedy.

Lambert had been thinking about the same thing ever since they’d left the hospital. The steering wheel felt sticky beneath his hands, and he noticed his palms were sweaty which was unusual for him. ‘She definitely recognised him. When we get back, I want you to try and dig out some other pictures of Blake. Perhaps look at older photos. She may have known him from the past, and didn’t recognise him as an older man. Check both their work histories. We need to find a time or place where the paths crossed.’

Kennedy’s head bobbed up and down in assent. She’d recovered from this morning’s hangover, and was full of energy.

‘It wasn’t appropriate, anyway. We’ll quiz her again later.’

Lambert dropped her at the station, parking the car in the underground carpark. He stopped when they reached the entrance to the lifts.

‘You not coming in, sir?’

‘No. Work on the photos. I’ll be back in an hour or so. We can go and see Sackville together. Let me know as soon as you uncover something.’

Kennedy nodded, clearly energised by the trust he was showing in her. He left the building, intending to catch the tube to

Holborn, when he was stopped by one of the team. 'Christ, what happened to you?'

DC Walker was dressed in his normal attire. Tailored suit, crisp shirt and tie, shoes polished within an inch of their life. Everything looked in place, except for the purple-black bruise which discoloured his eye.

Chapter 30

A number of things clicked into place at once. Lambert sighed, fearing what Walker was going to say. 'Been in the wars, Constable?'

'You could say that.'

'You missed the debrief this morning.'

'Sorry, I went to get this checked out,' said Walker, pointing to his eye. 'My vision is still a bit blurry.'

'Okay. Well, get back to it. We need everyone on top form for today.'

'Sir…'

Lambert interrupted him before he had time to finish his sentence. 'Look, before we go any further with this can you just take some time to think. I don't know what happened to you, or who was responsible, but I have my suspicions. If you are about to make an accusations then I would suggest you tread carefully. I take it this happened at the party last night.'

'Sir.'

Lambert pinched his nose. He could do without this at present. 'Look, Walker, I don't know you very well. You seem to be a diligent worker but I get a sense that you wind people up the wrong way.'

Walker went to interject but Lambert stopped him. 'I may be wrong, but either way I think you should think carefully before you report anything to me. I don't want you to hide anything, and if you feel strongly about this then I will help you pursue it. However, I still think you need some time to think. You'll have a long time to regret any hasty, emotional decision. Do you agree?'

'I'm not making an emotional response, sir, and it's not just this.' He touched his eye, wincing at the pain. 'I want to report unprofessional behaviour. I can go to you, or I can take it to elsewhere.'

Lambert wanted to tell the officer to pull himself together, that there were greater concerns at the moment, but realised if he did so his words could end up being used against him. 'Okay, Walker. As soon as you tell me what you want to tell me, then it's out there forever. There will be no turning back. I'll take a report from you now, or you can go home, wait twenty-four hours and we can revisit the situation then.'

Walked swayed on his feet, his lips were pursed, his face reddening. 'Fine, but I'm not going to change my mind.'

'Good. Go home, get some rest. We can meet tomorrow at lunchtime.'

'Sir.'

The tube was full of over-heated and underdressed people. When he should have been focused on the case, all he could think about was Walker's black eye, and the marks on Tillman's knuckles. He'd probably done Walker a favour by not taking the report yet. It would be a mistake, going up against Tillman. Unless there had been a witnesses, and Walker could prove the attack was unprovoked, then Tillman would escape punishment. He knew too many people, and knew too much about those people, for such an incident to have any detrimental effect on his career. If Walker made an official complaint then he would end up regretting it. There would be some sympathetic ears but Walker would struggle to regain any trust from his colleagues. It shouldn't be that way, but it was, and hopefully Walker would come to his senses in the next twenty-four hours.

Lambert's felt a rush of adrenaline as he entered the building of Price and Barker Solicitors. He couldn't remember the last time he'd been in the building. It was probably over three years ago, before Chloe's death, before everything had changed.

It probably wasn't his wisest move, but he wanted to see Taylor face to face. There was an obvious conflict in speaking to the solicitor, and he should have taken Kennedy with him, but no one in the force knew about the situation with Sophie and Taylor and he wasn't about to advertise it.

He approached the desk and asked to speak to Jeremy Taylor. The petite woman behind the desk smiled politely at him and asked him if he had an appointment.

'Just tell him Michael Lambert is here to see him.'

If the woman recognised his name, she hid it well. 'I'm afraid he won't see anyone without an appointment. Perhaps if you could tell me what it's about.'

Lambert showed her his warrant card.

'I'll try,' she said, after taking a couple of glances at his face to match the picture.

'Thank you,' said Lambert, taking a seat on one of the leather sofas in the reception area.

He was surprised when five minutes later, Jeremy Taylor appeared. He'd thought he would have sent his PA to collect him. Lambert stood, dismayed to find his heart was racing. Taylor was dressed immaculately in a dark suit. He looked as reticent as Lambert felt. He didn't offer a handshake, which didn't surprise Lambert after their last encounter. 'Michael,' he said. 'How may I help you?'

Lambert had hoped he would be able to put his feelings about Taylor and his relationship with Sophie to one side, but seeing him again in the flesh made him realise everything was still too raw. He fought the rising wave of adrenaline in his system, and the absurd desire to strike out at the man. 'I'm here on police business. I would like to speak to you about one of your clients, Curtis Blake.'

'Oh,' said Taylor, momentarily confused. 'Okay, please follow me.'

Lambert followed him to the lifts, and was relieved when a number of other people joined them inside. By the time they reached Taylor's floor, they were alone in the lift. 'Here we are,' said Taylor as the doors opened.

Lambert stepped out onto the plush carpet of the top floor, and realised he'd been holding his breath. He let the breath seep out of his mouth as he followed a pace behind Taylor.

'In here should be fine,' said Taylor, opening the door to a conference room. 'Please take a seat. May I get you anything to drink?'

The majority of space in the conference room was taken up by a giant oval shaped table, with over twenty chairs on the periphery. Lambert shook his head and pulled out one of the leather backed seats.

'So, this is regarding Curtis Blake? You realise I am bound by client confidentiality.'

Lambert tried to get the image of Taylor holding his wife's child out of his mind. He needed to focus. He ignored

Taylor's last statement. 'How long have you worked for Mr Blake?'

Taylor's eyes darted upwards. 'Personally, ten, maybe twelve years. I think he's been with the firm for a good time longer. He is one of our oldest clients.'

'And what exactly is it you do for him?'

Taylor frowned. 'I would have thought that was obvious.'

'I realise you are his solicitors but what specific area of legal expertise do you provide for him?'

'You realise this is highly inappropriate?'

'You want to talk to me about inappropriateness?'

Taylor flushed, and Lambert regretted the jibe. 'Mr Blake has a number of interests. When you have an organisation as large as his, there are a number of legal ramifications. We represent him across the board, everything from personnel to building contracts.'

Lambert pursed his lips and nodded in beat to his rapid heartbeat. 'And if anything... untoward is discovered, you would turn a blind eye?'

'I'm not sure what you are insinuating, but I can assure you this firm would never be involved in anything unethical or illegal.'

'You must know about Blake's reputation, Jeremy.'

Taylor bristled at the use of his first name. 'Please, tell me what this is about. Is Mr Blake under some form of investigation? If so, this meeting will need to be reconvened in a more appropriate setting.'

Lambert considered telling him about the killings. He wondered if it would shock Taylor, or if the man would maintain the façade of composure he liked to present. He wasn't really sure why he was here. Taylor wouldn't be allowed to divulge any specific details about Blake's business and lifestyle. Lambert had understood that before he'd arrived. Was he there for work, or to size up Taylor? To see what type of man would be parenting Chloe's sister.

He feared it was the latter. 'Okay, I see this is a waste of time.'

He stood, Taylor mirroring his actions.

'I didn't mean for any of this to happen,' said Taylor. The man looked nervous, his gaze not quite catching Lambert's.

It was hard for Lambert to admit but it wasn't Taylor's fault. Lambert had grown apart from Sophie following Chloe's death. They'd slept in separate rooms, had functioned as little more than flatmates for a long time. Albeit, flatmates with a shared tragedy. He couldn't blame Sophie for seeking comfort elsewhere, any more than he could blame the man before him.

'I realise that,' said Lambert. 'It will take a bit of getting used to. Thanks for your time, I can see myself to the lifts.'

Outside he considered entering the nearest pub and easing his growing tension with a few drinks. Instead he opted for a coffee shop, ordering an Americano and a multi-seed muffin which gave the illusion of being healthy.

Too many distractions, he thought as he logged onto The System. With Walker's black eye, and his own unwise meeting with Taylor, there was a danger the case could spiral out of his control. He took out his notebook, and started writing. Sometimes the old-fashioned ways were the best. He listed the victims, then crossed them out and wrote the names of the two surviving members. Eustace Sackville and Laura Dempsey, formerly Laura Patchett. He was positive they were the key.

He wrote another name, Curtis Blake. Dempsey had recognised Blake's picture. Dempsey, Sackville and Blake were linked. If he discovered the connection, he was sure everything would follow.

A message was waiting for him on The System. After Moira Sackville's death, he'd put out a nationwide search for suspicions deaths involving wrist injuries. The report had come back. It made for interesting reading. Most of the deaths were botched, or mistimed suicide attempts.

He read reports of four separate teenage girls who had taken their lives in the last month, each found in their bathtubs. The parents' statements were harrowing. The same phrases repeated over and over. 'We had no idea. It was a cry for help. She seemed so happy. We loved her so much. If only we'd got there earlier.'

Another case involved a woman who had accidently sliced her own wrist with a box cutter whilst at work, severing an artery and dying in front of bewildered co-workers.

Only one case was marked as a possible murder inquiry. Six months ago, a man by the name of Neil Lennox had died in his sleep in Gloucester. Lennox was retired and lived alone. Both his wrists had been severed, the vertical slash marks similar to those found on Moira Sackville and the Dempsey victims. His body hadn't been discovered for forty-eight hours, not until a care worker had been unable to gain access to the man's house for their weekly appointment. The pathologist report had suggested that it may have taken Lennox up to six hours to die. Although there was no sign of a break in, a thorough search of the house had failed to uncover anything which could have caused the injuries sustained by Lennox.

Lambert closed his eyes and pictured a frail old man dying.

In the vision was a second figure, the killer sitting opposite and watching the fruit of his first attempt. It was probably all a coincidence, wishful thinking on his part, but when he read further, Lambert couldn't hide a growing sense that what he was a reading was a breakthrough.

Not only had Lennox been a former police officer, but he'd worked in the Met for over thirty years. Lambert slammed his laptop shut.

Lambert headed back to the station, convinced that somehow Lennox was the missing link between Dempsey and Sackville.

Chapter 31

Matilda bought a sandwich from the canteen and returned to her desk. Her blood still thundered in her ears. She'd fooled Lambert into believing she was over her hangover, but it was still present. At least she could function now. When she'd left Tillman's apartment that morning, she'd struggled to put one foot in front of the other.

Christ, what had possessed her? She must have drunk much more than she'd thought. She remembered drinking a last gin and tonic just as the bar was closing, but she'd thought she'd been well behaved during the rest of the evening. The night had flipped in an instant. Her main memories were throwing up in Tillman's bathroom, Tillman showing a compassionate side she hadn't experienced before, and the confrontation prior to that.

It was as if they were on borrowed time. Walker had yet to turn up for work, but when he did everything would change. Walker had refused to leave her alone, and when Tillman arrived he'd freaked out. He'd told Tillman to mind his own business, and had pushed him in the chest. Tillman had stopped the argument by punching him squarely in the eye. Walker had crashed to the ground, and scampered away like a beaten dog.

Walker had attacked Tillman, she'd been in a lucid enough state to have witnessed that, but it was their word against his. The officers she'd seen moments before had disappeared.

Normally, that would be enough but as Walker left he'd snarled at them. 'I know about you two,' he'd said.

She looked through Blake's file once more. For a supposed crime lord, he'd had very few run-ins with the police. In the last thirty years there had been a number of investigations but Blake had only the one entry on his record, a conviction for possession from over twenty years ago. Blake had been carrying five ounces of marijuana when he'd been questioned by an officer over another case. She printed the file and searched the rest of the records. She tried to concentrate but her thoughts kept returning to last night. The more she thought about it, the more contrived the events seemed. Tillman's punch was justified to a certain extent, but there had been something about the way Walker had behaved which didn't quite add up. Matilda closed her eyes, and tried to latch onto the faded memory. She couldn't quite place it, but her feeling was that Walker had provoked Tillman on purpose. 'He wanted Tillman to hit him,' she whispered to herself.

Devlin appeared at her desk and handed her the report she'd printed up. 'Cold case?' he asked.

'Something like that. You seen Walker today?'

'No, haven't left my desk all day. Still a bit rough.'

'Aren't we all. What are you working on?'

'Still going through Sackville's old case reports. Some fascinating stuff.'

'That's great, Devlin, but does any of it link with our investigation?'

Devlin sucked in his cheeks. It was an unnecessary criticism but she couldn't take it back now.

'I'll get back to it then,' he said.

Matilda read the file, but was still distracted by last night.

'Kennedy, incident room.' Matilda looked up to see Lambert hovering over the desk. She grabbed the file and followed him into the room, wondering if Walker had already spoken to him.

She was relieved to see Devlin and the rest of the team also in the room. Lambert sat and asked them to do the same. He always looked so fresh, as if he'd had a peaceful night's rest. It was only his eyes which gave him away. They looked lost, haunted. She'd seen the look on countless officers over the years, but with Lambert it was something else. It wasn't just the stress of the case. She occasionally caught him staring into space. It was as if sometimes he forgot himself, that part of him was missing.

Lambert asked for a report from each of them before making his revelation. 'I asked for a report shortly after Moira Sackville's murder and it has just come in. I was looking for similar MOs, such as the Whitfield report so helpfully reported to us by Charles Robinson. However, I focused specifically on the injuries to Moira Sackville. Namely, the vertical cuts to her wrists. One is quite interesting.' Lambert clicked a switch and a case report appeared on the whiteboard at the end of the room.

The file was on a slideshow. Five pages in, and the picture of an elderly man appeared on the screen. Lambert paused the slideshow. Neil Lennox. A former DI with the Met. His body was discovered six months ago at his home in Gloucester.

He clicked a button. A picture of Lennox's frail arm appeared on the screen. The tanned, liver spotted limb was drained of colour. Lambert clicked again and a picture of Lennox's wrists appeared. Thick jagged welts zig-zagged across Lennox's arm as if someone had hacked at his flesh. 'He bled out, like the others. Was possibly alive for six hours. No murder weapon was found at the scene.'

'Was there a witness?' asked Matilda.

'No, at least none were forthcoming. The body was found forty-eight hours later. He was found in bed. He wasn't tied up. No sign of anyone witnessing the attack.'

'What are you thinking, sir?'

'I need to speak to the SIO on the case. But I think this man was possibly the first victim of the Watcher. Possibly his trial run.'

'And he was the witness?' said Kennedy.

'Yes.'

'I'll drive. You still look rough,' said Lambert, once they were outside.

Matilda was unable to argue. Lambert had made contact with the SIO on the Lennox case, and they'd agreed to meet at a service station on the M4, just outside Reading.

'Did you manage to find any other images of Blake we can use to jog Dempsey's memory?' he asked, as he pulled away.

She told him about Blake's case history. His one arrest for marijuana possession. 'I don't suppose Lennox was the arresting officer?' he asked.

'That would be nice, but no. A DS Garvey if memory serves.'

'Can't have it all, I suppose. So...'

Matilda tensed. It was turning into the worst hangover of her life, and she didn't understand why. She was lethargic, and could feel the alcohol in her system. She hoped Lambert couldn't smell it on her. She kept her focus ahead, the motion of the car making her nauseous.

'I saw DS Walker this morning.'

Adrenaline flooded her system. She felt her breath in her throat. 'Oh, yes?' she said, after what felt like minutes.

'Yes. He's looking a bit worse for wear.'

'He wouldn't be the only one today.'

'No, but he's the only one with a black eye.'

Matilda froze, then turned to look at Lambert, who kept his eyes on the road. 'I'm not going to ask for the truth now, Kennedy, but if you know anything about why he's got a black eye, and if you are involved in anyway, I want you to seriously consider your options.'

Matilda returned her gaze to the road.

'I'm seeing Walker tomorrow morning. If you have anything to tell me, I'd do so before then.'

DI Andrea Elwin was waiting for them at the service station. 'Thank you for agreeing to meet us halfway,' said Lambert.

Elwin nodded. She had a sharp, almost severe, bone structure to her face made worse by the short cut frame of her hair which extenuated the pointed shape of her nose and chin. She didn't smile. 'It's on my way home, anyway. You were interested in the Lennox case?'

'Yes. The MO of the murder fits in with a case we are working on at the moment.'

'I've heard. The Watcher. Even we get the news this far out of London.' It was possible the woman was making a humorous quip, but there was sign of humour in her look. 'It's not quite the same MO though, is it?' continued Elwin.

'The pathologist's report would suggest the injuries suffered by Mr Lennox were consistent with those on Moira Sackville and the Dempsey family,' said Kennedy.

'But there was a witness for those killings. The killer got

off on someone watching his handiwork. Plus he cuffed the other victims.'

'In the case of Sackville, and Laura Dempsey's immediate family, yes. But Dempsey's parents, the Patchetts, were killed without a witness. At least not one we know of, though as you mention they were cuffed.'

'Well, either way, this is the first inroad we've had on the Lennox case. It was a complete dead end. Lennox was survived by one son who hasn't spoken to him in twenty years and lives in Australia. Lennox had a couple of drinking buddies he met now and again but that's it. We looked at the care worker who rang the alarm. She admitted she had little time for him. I believe her words were, "an old, arrogant, sexist bastard," but she didn't kill him. No sign of a break in so we presumed he answered the door. No real sign of a struggle but he was a weak old man. We would have thought it was suicide but there was no sign of an instrument which would have caused his injuries.'

Lambert had read the report so she wasn't telling him anything new. 'To be honest, I was more interested in what you learnt about Lennox's background.'

Elwin pushed out her lower lip, giving her an almost cartoonish look. 'I see, specifically?'

'Did you check his work history?' asked Kennedy.

'Naturally. We contacted his former colleagues in the Met, though most are no longer with us.' Elwin picked up the case file she'd brought with her. She licked her index figure and flicked through her notes. 'We spoke to Doug Lindsay who was a DC at the time Lennox was working. He left the force twenty-five years ago but had a strong recollection about our man. Not fond memories. Seems Mr Lennox was a bit of a bully, and probably not the straightest of officers.'

'Anything significant?' asked Lambert.

'Suggestions of backhanders, turning a blind eye, that sort of a thing. Nothing more significant than that. At least not according to Mr Lindsay. He didn't have much good to say for the man.'

'You think there was a possible revenge motive?' asked Kennedy.

Elwin's eyes widened. She was clearly put out by the question. 'What do you think, Sergeant? There was nothing. No DNA, no fingerprints, just a bloody suicide with no weapon for the death. We looked at revenge. We started local, more recent, and spread our net, but it was like picking the proverbial needle from a haystack. Where would you begin?'

Lambert knew the predicament all too well. 'Well, thanks for your help.'

'You can have this,' said Elwin, handing him the file. 'You think this was your man?'

'We'll know soon enough.'

'You'll keep me informed?' Elwin still had hold of the file.

Lambert understood the words. 'Yes. Your help will be mentioned in the report,' he said.

Chapter 32

Back at the station, Lambert summoned everyone to the incident room, updating them on Lennox and making it the number one priority.

Even Tillman made the pilgrimage from his office. He stood at the rear of the room, arms folded, as Lambert wrote three names onto the whiteboard. Sackville, Dempsey, Lennox. 'The working theory is that all three are linked. I believe Lennox was the killer's first victim. The job was less neat than with the others,' he said, displaying the pictures of Lennox's fatal wound on the screen. 'We need to work out the link between these three. These are not random victims.'

'What about Curtis Blake?' asked Devlin, who'd grown in Lambert's estimation as the week had progressed.

'Cross-check everything with him in particular, since Sackville and Dempsey haven't been able to make any link explicit.'

He allocated roles for everyone but saved most of the work for himself. He had to speak to both Sackville and Dempsey again. He had a nagging feeling that one, or both of them, was hiding something from him. It was intangible at the moment. Neither had any obvious reason for lying to him, but still it troubled him.

Lambert dismissed everyone and returned to his desk. He

hadn't heard from the Watcher since the newspaper article had been released. He tried not to read too much into it and refused to dwell on the menace from the killer.

He was about to call for Kennedy when he noticed her enter Tillman's office. He'd grown to trust her over the duration of the case. It was still possible that Tillman had asked her to keep tabs on him, but that was down more to Tillman than her. What was more concerning to Lambert was that she was actually having some sort of affair with Tillman. Although both parties were single, the revelation of an affair could be devastating to both their careers, especially given the additional problem of Walker. Lambert had given her the opportunity to be honest with him. If she did, then he might be able to help her if Walker made an accusation. There would be no speaking to Tillman about the issue.

It was a frustrating diversion, and he decided to head to Sackville's safe house without her. Sophie called as he made his way through the rush hour traffic. A blast of rain came from nowhere, thick jets of water battering his windscreen. He put his wipers on their highest speed, the rubber blades squeaking against the glass, as he switched on the speakerphone system. 'Hi Soph, all okay?'

'Hi Michael. Have you got a sec?'

'What is it?' he said, sensing a hint of concern in her voice.

'It's nothing really. Well, maybe it is. I don't know...'

'It's okay, Sophie. Tell me from the beginning.'

Sophie paused. It sounded as if she was about to burst into tears.

'Is your mum still there?' he asked.

'She's on her way over.' The words were stunted, out of sync.

'Tell me, Sophie,' he said, as softly as possible.

'As I said, it's probably nothing. I just went to open the back door and noticed it was still open. I swore I locked last night. I checked it at least twice. You know how I am.'

In all the years he'd known her, she'd always been a stickler for security. She wasn't quite OCD about it, but was certainly borderline. 'Okay, let's not panic. You're sure it's not...'

'Michael, if you're about to say something about it being baby related, I can assure you I'm not losing my mind,' she said, control returning to her voice.

'No, I wasn't going to say that,' said Lambert, unsure as to what he was going to say.

'Anyway, when I tried to lock the door, I couldn't.'

'What do you mean, you couldn't?'

'Just what I said. The lock's broken. When I put the key in, there's nothing for it to latch onto. I hate the idea that someone was in our house.

The rain thundered harder onto the windscreen, Lambert unable to see more than a couple of metres in front. He took a deep breath. It was probably nothing, but he couldn't take the risk. 'Has anything been taken?'

'No. Nothing has been disturbed. The alarm wasn't activated either so I imagine it's just a problem with the lock.'

'Call a locksmith. Emergency if necessary. Make sure you get the locks checked on all the doors and windows. Don't worry about the cost. I've got an appointment now, but I'll come straight round afterwards.'

'I feel anxious, Michael'

'Don't worry. It's just one of those things. People get broken into. Make sure the alarm is working. Call the locksmith for now, and I'll be round as soon as possible.'

Sophie hung up, and Lambert immediately called Devlin. He told him to send a patrol car to Sophie's house and to wait for instruction.

Sackville was only semi-coherent by the time he reached the safe house. Lambert exchanged looks with one of the guarding officers who just shrugged his shoulders. 'It's all he does. Do you want us to stop him from now on?' asked the officer.

Sackville was slumped on the sofa watching an obscure detective show from the seventies. He held a full glass of single malt in one hand, the other hand busy scratching his ample stomach. 'We should, but considering what he's been through… Perhaps keep a bit of an eye on him, though?

'Sir,' mumbled the officer, leaving the room.

'What you drinking, Eustace?'

'Hey, Michael,' said Sackville, lifting his glass and spilling some of the contents onto his shirt. He tried to pull his body into a more respectable position but the effort proved too much. He lay there on his side, and grinned inanely at Lambert.

Lambert moved to the sofa, and helped manoeuvre the man into a sitting position. 'Let me take that for a bit,' he said, tearing the whisky glass from Sackville's grip.

Sackville glared at Lambert, as if he'd just insulted him. Seconds later and his concentration had wavered. 'Michael,' he said, again.

'Jesus, how much of this have you had?'

Sackville smiled, and held his hands a metre apart. 'About this much.'

Lambert ordered the officer to brew a pot of coffee. 'Make

it strong,' he said. He wanted to lecture Eustace, tell him that he wasn't honouring Moira by drinking himself into oblivion, but how could he lecture a man who had nothing. He sat in silence and watched the drama unfold on the television. The obligatory car chase held his interest for a time as he counted the different, now non-existent, car models.

It was an hour later before he could get any sense out of Sackville. He practically had to force him to drink the coffee and even now the man was slurring when he spoke. 'There's been some developments, Eustace.'

'Oh yes?'

'I met Mia Helmer again.'

'Lucky you.'

'She told me you've been suspended.'

Sackville's eyes widened, numerous lines spreading across his forehead. 'What, suspended? What the hell?'

'Sorry, Eustace, she didn't give me the details. Can you think why?'

'Because she's a jealous... Ah, what does it matter. I wouldn't want to go back there now. What's the point?'

Despite the outburst, Lambert thought Sackville wasn't that surprised. His protestations were a bit of a show, exacerbated by Sackville's alcohol intake. Helmer had mentioned Sackville hadn't been providing copy for months now and Lambert presumed she'd finally had enough, though he marvelled at her timing.

Lambert opened the cover of his iPad and uploaded a picture. 'Do you know this man, Eustace?'

Sackville produced a pair of glasses from a side table. He put them on and squinted at the image on the screen. 'No, should I?'

The picture was of Neil Lennox, taken by his care worker weeks before his death. Lennox didn't look well in the picture. His face was gaunt. Beneath his hollow eyes, and crusted lips, flaps of skins hung from his neck.

Lambert loaded the photo from Lennox's police file. It was staggering the damage time had caused. In the old picture of Lennox, he looked fit and healthy. 'This is him thirty years ago.'

Sackville adjusted his glasses and stared at the picture. His eyes diluted, and he shifted in his seat. 'I remember him. DI Lennox. Nasty.'

'Good memory, Eustace. Nasty?'

Sackville took off his glasses and focused as best he could on Lambert. 'Because that is what he was. He was a nasty piece of work. He was on the take, hands in all sorts of pockets. I tried to...' Sackville shook his head, his eyes moistening. 'Let's just say, he didn't enjoy me questioning his actions.'

'Did you run a story on him? We didn't find him on your files.'

Sackville shook his head. 'They would never have run it. You think I would get a story out about one of your lot back then? Jesus. He'd have had to murder someone in cold daylight for me to have had a chance. I had some stuff on him, but nothing I could ever print or corroborate.'

'What sort of stuff?'

'I just told you. Backhanders, that sort of thing. It was endemic, but Lennox was in with some evil people. Everyone hated him, even his own team and they were mainly like him. Can I have a drink now? Bad memories and what have you.'

Lambert poured him a small measure of the single malt. Sackville grabbed the drink, took in a deep whiff, and downed it in one.

'He's dead, Eustace.'

'Good,' said Sackville. 'Sorry, that's a bit insensitive, but he was not a nice man, Michael.'

'It's not what I meant. He's dead. The same way as Moira, as the Dempsey family. His wrists were slashed'

Sackville struggled to his feet, making his way to the sideboard where he retrieved the bottle of whisky. He drank long and hard, paused for breath, and drank again. 'When?' he said, his breathing rapid.

'Six months ago.'

'Same?'

Lambert took the bottle from him. If he let him drink any more tonight then he might as well go home. 'We think so. It looked like a suicide, but there was no weapon. It was possibly the first murder'

Sackville collapsed on the sofa, his eyes blinked rapidly. Lambert could only guess what crazed thoughts were going through his head. 'I don't understand.'

'You have to think, Eustace. What links you, Lennox, and Laura Dempsey?'

'You think this is about me?'

'Don't you? You think the killer had a grudge against Moira and let you live for the sake of it? Do you think he wanted the whole of the Dempsey family dead with the exception of Laura Dempsey?

'So it's my fault.' Tears welled in Sackville's eyes.

'No. Don't get maudlin on me, Eustace. You have to think. What links you and Dempsey, both of you to Lennox?'

A snarl appeared on Sackville's face, a coldness Lambert hadn't seen in him before. The alcohol had changed him and

Lambert feared that the conversation was essentially over. 'I can imagine loads of people wanted Lennox dead, and heaven knows I've never been the greatest man. But why Moira, what did she ever do?'

'What about Blake? Did he know Lennox in anyway?'

The bottle of whisky slipped from Sackville's hand as his eyes slipped close. Lambert reached over and caught it in time. He tilted Sackville's bulk into a makeshift recovery position. After tipping the contents of the bottle down the kitchen sink, he called for the officer. 'Keep an eye on him. He's trying to kill himself. No more alcohol is allowed in this house, you understand?'

The officer nodded.

Lambert took one last look at Sackville. 'What the hell did you do, Eustace?' he said to the sleeping figure.

Chapter 33

Lambert called Kennedy from the car. 'I need you to run tonight's debrief. I want Sackville's notes scrutinised for details on Lennox. Have we had any hits on Lennox's old cases?'

'Nothing yet, but I've tracked down his former colleague, Doug Lindsay. I've arranged to meet him tomorrow at ten a.m. He's in London for the day. He chose to meet in Leicester Square of all places.'

'Text me details and I'll meet you beforehand. Call the hospital and tell Dr Hughes we'll be back tomorrow after our meeting with Lindsay. Get together as much info on Blake, and Lennox. We need pictures, especially of Blake when he was younger. See if we can help her remember.'

He thought about the Watcher as he drove to Sophie's house. He hadn't made contact for some time. Although a normal burglary was more likely, Lambert couldn't get away from the thought that the Watcher had broken the lock on Sophie's door. It was probably designed to divert his focus. It was certainly effective but he couldn't take the risk. Lambert had been under the presumption that the killer watched as some form of revenge, but what if there was more to it? What if he had to be close to the suffering for it really to stimulate his own emotional response? Potentially, the need for revenge could be satisfied with a finite list of people. But if the killer was getting some form of satisfaction from his own reaction to the murders, it could make his list of victims endless, and could make it easier to add someone like Sophie to the list.

A plain clothes officer stopped him as he walked the pathway to his old house. Lambert showed him his warrant card.

'Sorry, sir,' said the officer.

'Anything suspicious?' asked Lambert.

'No, sir.' We've checked around the back. There is access to the house from a small dirt lane but we didn't see any damage to the fence. To be honest, sir, we're not sure why we're here. A locksmith is in the house now.'

'You checked his credentials?' said Lambert, controlling a rising panic as he rang the doorbell.

'Obviously, sir.'

'Okay, sit tight,' said Lambert, glancing in the direction of the officer's car.

Lambert was relieved to see a bedraggled looking Sophie open the door, a sleeping child locked to her chest by way of a baby carrier. Sophie's face was paler than he'd ever remembered, her skin puffy with dots of red. 'Hi,' she said, turning her back and walking down the hallway.

Sophie's mother was in the kitchen-dining area, studying the work of the locksmith with a critical eye. She glanced at Lambert with a dismissive sneer, as if he was somehow to blame for the broken door.

The locksmith stopped working and nodded at Lambert. 'Bit of a weird one,' he said to Lambert, unbidden. 'The catch seems to have snapped, see,' he said, showing Lambert a broken piece of metal which made no sense to him.

'Why is it weird?'

'It doesn't really just happen, or not that I recall anyway.'

Lambert noted the look of concern on Sophie's face. 'Is it possible it's been tampered with?'

The man grunted, rubbed his chin whilst he gave the matter his full consideration. 'I don't think so. They'd have had to open up the casing, and there's no sign of that occurring.'

'So it could be bad luck?'

'Must be,' said the locksmith, as if anything else was beyond his imagination. 'Anyway, that will hold you for now.' He moved the handle of the door up and down, locked and unlocked the door twice.

'Thanks for coming, Michael,' said Sophie, once the locksmith had left. 'I know I'm being silly.' She undid the carrier, the baby asleep. She lifted her from her body and placed her in a carrycot on the floor of the kitchen.

'Excuse me,' said Sophie's mother, lifting the carrycot and exiting the kitchen area. Sophie was on the verge of tears. He'd seen the look on her face countless times before.

'How are you sleeping?' asked Lambert. He wanted to comfort her, to hold her and offer his help, but wasn't sure about the boundaries any more. 'Sit down, I'll make some tea,' he said, with nothing else to offer.

Sophie smiled and took a seat on one of the dining chairs. 'I must be seeing a new Michael here. I can't remember the last time you offered to make me tea.'

'Don't get lippy. White tea?'

'Of course,' she said, smiling again as if all her cares had momentarily disappeared.

He made the tea and joined her. He wondered if he would ever come to terms with the situation. Sitting in a room which used to be his, with the woman who was still his wife. 'Is she sleeping well?'

'Not too bad. I'm getting up twice a night to feed, but aside from that she sleeps well and Mum has been great.' She hesitated, a gesture Lambert had become familiar with over the last three years. Ever since Chloe's death, they'd had to tiptoe around each other, both scared of saying the wrong thing.

Lambert waited, gave her the space to talk if she wanted, but she drank her tea and went silent. 'I'm sure the door's nothing to worry about.'

Sophie nodded. 'I know, but thanks for popping over. I really appreciate it. Mum's made some dinner, you're welcome to stay if you want.'

Maybe it was the separation, or his self-pity, but Lambert couldn't read the signals. He wasn't sure if she really wanted him there, and didn't want to overstay his welcome.

He made a tour of the house, checking the locks on the doors and windows. He even checked the light fittings, ceilings and walls, making a cursory glance for anything out of the ordinary.

'Thanks for coming,' said Sophie again, as she showed him out of the front door. 'A shame you couldn't stay.'

'Another time.'

Lambert took a deep breath and walked over to the unmarked patrol car. 'When are you due back?' he asked the officer he'd spoken to earlier.

'We were told to wait here until relieved. We're past shift time now, but...'

'Okay, give me thirty minutes and I'll take over,' said Lambert.

Stakeouts were boring at the best of times, despite this he

still preferred being alone. It was off the clock, and no one knew he was here. He'd bought some provisions from the local supermarket and now it was down to the waiting, without knowing what he was waiting for.

He read the newspaper, avoiding, to begin with, the pieces on the Watcher. More and more, the press were focused on creating a sense of fear and when he eventually read the pieces he was not surprised. The reporting was completely over the top. With no corroboration, Mia Helmer stated there was no direct link between the victims. Dead Lucky, she repeated. According to her, it was simply down to chance, who was killed and who was left alive. She may as well have said that the Watcher was out there, waiting, and that the whole of London was a potential victim. He scrunched up the newspaper and threw into the back of the car as the streetlights popped into life.

Lambert studied each person who passed Sophie's house, deep down knowing the Watcher wouldn't show his face so readily. Why the hell was he here? He couldn't justify the cost of other officers being here, but nor could he be here all the time. He wanted the killer to call him, to confirm his suspicions that he had Sophie's house under surveillance, but his phone refused to ring. He decided now was the time to catch some sleep. He closed his eyes, and tried to banish thoughts of the case by thinking of Sarah May, the only positive part of his life at present. He recalled the time they'd spent together in Bristol, as they both recovered from their ordeal on the Souljacker case. Despite that trauma, his time with her had been the most peaceful he could recall for a very long time. He promised himself he would call her tomorrow. He wanted to make things between them more permanent, and for that to happen he had to offer her something. Though what that was, he wasn't sure.

A banging noise on his side window woke him. His hand reached for his expandable baton, as he adjusted to the darkness and the figure peering in at him. 'Jesus, Kennedy, you trying to give me a heart attack?'

Kennedy was hopping from foot to foot, two cups of coffee in her hand. Lambert nodded to the passenger seat and Kennedy made her way round. 'How did you know I was here?'

Kennedy handed him a cup and placed the other in the cup holder. She hugged herself, swaying from side to side to keep warm. 'Bloody freezing out there. What happened to Rostron?'

'Rostron?'

'DC Rostron. He was assigned here earlier. Told me he'd seen you here.'

'Did he now?'

Kennedy took a drink. 'Something I should know?'

Lambert smirked. What could he tell her? That the Watcher had been calling him? That he had an absurd worry that his wife and his daughter's baby sister were being watched as they spoke? In the end, he went as close to the truth as he felt able. 'It's possible the back door was broken last night. I've called out a locksmith but thought I'd keep an eye on things just in case.'

'You plan to stay here all night?'

He didn't think Kennedy fully bought the story, but she wasn't about to argue with him. 'A few more hours, yes.'

'Will you be able to stay awake?'

'I will now.' Kennedy looked tired. It had been a long day for both of them. 'Go home and get some rest,' he said.

'I can stay with you. You know, if you want me to.'

'I'm sure you've got better things to be doing with your time.' He waited for her to speak, was sure she'd found him to tell him something, probably about Walker and Tillman.

Kennedy didn't respond. She sat, staring out into the desolate street.

It was comforting having her in the car but he couldn't have them both being tired for the next day. 'Go get some sleep, Kennedy. We need to see Laura Dempsey after we've seen Lindsay. You did well last time. I'm sure we'll get the answers we need.'

Kennedy went to say something and checked herself. 'Sir,' she said.

'Oh, and Matilda,' said Lambert, as she was about to close the door.

'Sir?'

'Thanks for the coffee.

Chapter 34

Lambert didn't sleep again. He managed to read three quarters of the paperback he'd purchased from the supermarket. He was thankful when he noticed movement from the living room window at six a.m. Sophie had always been an early riser, and he watched her silhouetted figure pull the blinds open. He considered knocking on the door but she would only worry if she knew he'd been outside all evening. Instead, he sent her a text message checking everything was okay which she immediately responded to.

He left the car and walked to the greasy spoon on Croydon Road, where he used to treat himself now and again when he still lived in the house. The place was already full, labourers getting their carb and protein fill before the long day ahead. Lambert ordered an English breakfast and attempted to concentrate on the newspaper he'd purchased from the newsagent next door. His pulse increased as his mobile rang. He looked at the screen and wasn't sure if he was pleased or not that it wasn't a withheld number.

'Lambert.'

'Sir, it's Walker.'

Lambert paused, wondered if his day was about to take a turn for the worse before it really began. 'Walker. What can I do for you?'

'Thought I'd let you know I'm back at work, sir. Eye is much better.'

Lambert let out a breath. 'Speak to Devlin, lots to do,' he said, hanging up.

After breakfast, he drove into the centre of London. It was not the ideal way to travel but he couldn't leave the car at Sophie's. He parked the car in a tiny underground carpark near the Southbank, and crossed the bridge to Charing Cross before making his way to Leicester Square. He took a seat on one of the benches in the square and waited for Kennedy. It had been years since he'd been here. It was quieter than it would be in the evenings, the garish neon lights of the cinemas looking lost and dowdy in the greyness of the day.

Devlin called to confirm that Walker was back at work. He hadn't heard the last from Walker. Lambert was sure that he was just waiting for the right time. Walker's black eye could have nothing to do with Tillman and Kennedy, but if Tillman had hit him, then Lambert was sure Walker would use the incident to his benefit. Walker had a Machiavellian streak, and after the case was over Lambert would make sure that he was moved to a different department. Ideally another location entirely.

'Ah, the bringer of gifts,' said Lambert, as Kennedy approached carrying another coffee. 'People will talk if you keep spoiling me like this.'

'Here,' she said, handing him the cup which was still piping hot. She looked fresher than last night. Her red hair was tied back tight in a bunch, her pale skin unblemished. She wore a patterned scarf around her neck, and a long buttoned winter coat.

'Where are we meeting him?'

'Just over there,' said Kennedy, pointing to the shop front of a coffee house chain.

Lindsay appeared twenty minutes later. An elderly man dressed in tweed, he was accompanied by a woman of similar age. He lifted his head straight as introductions were made. The woman was his wife, Eileen. 'How long will we be?' he asked, not yet taking a seat.

'Half an hour at most,' said Kennedy.

'Okay. Half an hour, Eileen,' he said to his wife and sat at the table.

'Thanks for taking the time to see us,' said Lambert.

Lindsay nodded. He carried an air of authority about him which was less to do with age, and more to do with his personality, which Lambert imagined had been shaped by his time on the force. 'You're working on this Watcher case?'

'Yes.'

'And you want to speak to me about Lennox.'

'Yes, Mr Lindsay, but this is very confidential at the moment. You know how Lennox died?'

'Not until DS Kennedy here called me. I didn't even know he was dead. You think it was this Watcher fella?'

'Possibly.'

Lambert saw a flicker in Lindsay's eyes, a sense of excitement. 'So what do you need from me?'

Kennedy opened her iPad. 'As you've probably read, there have been six victims so far, seven if you count Lennox. You okay seeing these?'

Lindsay frowned and took the iPad from her.

'The first victim was Moira Sackville, wife of Eustace

Sackville. Then Laura Dempsey's husband and two children, and finally Dempsey's parents, Mr and Mrs Patchett.'

Lindsay scrolled through the images, with a look of morbid fascination. 'Sackville and Dempsey were made to watch?'

Lambert nodded. 'Laura Dempsey watched her husband and children die, but not her parents.'

'Small mercies, eh?'

'Does this mean anything to you?'

Lindsay placed the iPad on the counter. 'No, should it?'

'You never saw anything in your time with Lennox like this?'

Lindsay squinted his eyes. 'I've seen worse things than this, unfortunately, but I don't recall such an MO. I know Eustace Sackville, at least I knew him up to twenty or so years ago. He was an over-eager young journalist when I was working with Lennox.'

'Did you have much dealing with him?'

'Not really. He was a bit of a loud mouth, from what I remember. Lennox hated him. Then again, we hated most journos.'

'Ever seen Laura Dempsey before?' asked Kennedy, finding a more recent shot of Laura on the iPad.

Lindsay shook his head slowly. 'It's possible, but you know how it is. I met thousands of people.'

Kennedy showed him a picture of a much younger-looking Laura Dempsey. 'Maiden name was Patchett.'

Lindsay shook his head again. 'Sorry.'

'What can you tell us about Lennox? Would you know why anyone would want to harm him this way?'

'Yes, I'm afraid I do. He wasn't the nicest of men. He abused his power, and I regret to say I was implicit in that as I often turned a blind eye. I wasn't one of the boys, you see. They used to tolerate me, but I never joined in their little games.'

'Games?'

Lindsay stared hard at Lambert. 'You know what I'm talking about. How long have you been in, twenty years? I imagine it wasn't so bad then, but you'd have heard what went on before. A crooked cop could sometimes get away with a lot.'

'Such as?' asked Lambert.

'Everything.'

'So Lennox was involved in criminal activity?'

'I'm not going on record about anything, whether that man's dead or not. Life's too short. It is now, and it was then. That's why I got out. I couldn't see the line any more.'

'You ever hear from Lennox after you left?'

Lindsay lifted his chin, a sign of defiance. 'I saw him. He used to pop by now and again, to check up on me. He wanted to see if I would talk, but I'd moved on. I'd met Eileen and we had children. I wasn't about to jeopardise that.'

'When did you last see him?'

'Long time ago. Probably twenty years. I was only a potential threat for a year or so.'

'One last thing. Did you ever come across a man called Curtis Blake?'

Kennedy handed him the file picture of Blake.

Lindsay shook his head. 'I'm sorry. I hate to say it, but I'm an old man now. I never thought I'd say that. My memory isn't what it was.'

'Okay, Mr Lindsay. Thanks for taking the time to see me.'

They all stood and shook hands. 'Look, if it will help, I'll check through some of my old notebooks. I kept most of them, not sure why. Wife calls me a hoarder. I'll have a check, see if I can spot any of those names.'

Eileen was waiting outside. Lambert noticed the concerned look on her face, as Lindsay left the coffee shop. Lindsay grabbed her cheek, and she smiled. He took her hand and they moved into the growing number of tourists.

The Watcher called as Lambert drove to the hospital. Kennedy had taken her own car so he was alone when he answered the call. It was absurd but it was a relief to hear the man's voice again. He took a bitter comfort in the knowledge that the man was still out there, even if he had no idea where that was.

'You've been busy,' said the Watcher.

'Busy job,' said Lambert.

'You're starting to put things together. It took you some time, but congratulations.'

Lambert had two options. He could ignore everything the man said, or play along with him. He chose the latter. 'You mean Lennox?'

The Watcher took a deep breath. 'Lennox. Lovely man. He didn't change, right up to the end. It was a pleasure watching him die.'

It was the first time the man had directly confessed to a crime. 'What did he do to you?'

The Watcher made a sound, an imitation of a laugh. 'I'm not going to do your job for you, Lambert. You'll be pleased to know that I don't tar everyone with the same brush. I appreciate the fact that you haven't disclosed our conversations.'

'Give me something to go on then.'

'I've already rewarded you for your honesty, Lambert.'

'Really.'

He laughed again, the same hollow sound. 'How's Sarah May, Matilda Kennedy and her daddy? Safe? How's your wife, Michael? She's still your wife, isn't she? How's the little baby?'

Each question was like a punch to the stomach. Heat spread through Lambert's body. How could he possibly know all these details about Lambert's life? It would surely take the surveillance skills of more than one person to keep such a record. Lambert thought about the Souljacker case, and the team the killer had helping him for a number of years. Was it possible the Watcher had a team working for him as well?

'You've gone silent, Lambert.'

'Just thinking.'

'Penny for them.'

So many things swarmed through Lambert's head that even if he wanted, he wouldn't be able to share his thoughts. He tried one last approach. It was desperate, but at the moment there was nothing else to do. 'Tell me the story. Tell me what happened, why you are doing this. Let's end it here. You said you trust me. Let me honour that trust.'

The killer paused before replying, as if reading from a script. 'Some things can't be undone, Lambert. Best stay out of it. Oh, and Lambert. Next time you need a locksmith, let me know. I know a great guy.'

Chapter 35

Lambert called Devlin from the hospital and told him to place a patrol car outside Sophie's house. 'If she leaves, tell them to follow her.'

He heard the hesitation from Devlin. He had to give a reason to assign such manpower, but he wasn't about to tell Devlin anything. Lambert knew he should get Tillman's approval, but he wasn't about to tell his young DC that. 'You have my authorisation on this, Devlin. Get on with it.'

'Sir.'

Lambert regretted the outburst but the conversation with the Watcher had thrown him. Lambert felt vulnerable and there was nothing he could do about it for the time being. The threat was implicit. He didn't want to share details of their conversations. He could put Sophie in protective custody, but he couldn't put everyone he knew in, and taking Sophie out of the equation would just divert the killer onto someone else. He would keep them under surveillance for now.

He met Kennedy in the ward. 'DCI Lambert, DS Kennedy,' said Dr Hughes, welcoming them outside Laura Dempsey's room, the lilt of her accent making it difficult to decipher if the warmness was genuine. 'Mrs Dempsey has been receiving psychological care. She is still in a very fragile state. I agreed to this, but if it is not completely necessary then I would ask that you postpone.'

'We'll be in and out as quick as possible. The killer is still at large, and Mrs Dempsey could be the closest thing we have to identifying him,' said Lambert.

Laura Dempsey was sitting up in her bed. Lambert was surprised to see her reading a book. He hadn't been able to concentrate on anything for longer than a couple of minutes following Chloe's death. It had been months before he'd picked up a book. He'd spent hours in front of the television, the words and pictures little more than white noise. It was heartening to see that Laura could escape, even for a small time, into another world.

Dempsey shut the book. She looked better than the last time they'd seen her, a hint of colour in her skin, her eyes fresh, almost welcoming.

Kennedy moved to the side of the bed. 'Sorry to disturb you again, Laura. We just wanted to ask you some questions.' Kennedy sounded compassionate and genuine. Lambert was not sure if he would have come across as so empathetic.

'Ask away,' said Dempsey.

Kennedy showed her a picture of DI Lennox on her iPad. 'Do you recognise this man?'

Dempsey took the iPad. 'Should I? This picture is years old,' she said, but her eyes didn't leave the screen. 'Is he dead?' she asked, finally taking her eyes away from the image.

Kennedy nodded.

'The same way?' said Dempsey, choking back tears.

'Do you recognise him?'

Dempsey began to cry. She wiped the tears away, in short

angry movements. 'Sorry,' she said, as if she had anything to apologise for. 'I think I do remember him. You know how some things stick in your mind. His eyes are different colours, see?'

Lambert hadn't noticed the difference of colour in the man's eyes. One eye was brown, the other hazel.

'He was a police officer?' said Dempsey.

Kennedy looked at Lambert, her eyes full of optimism.

'That's correct,' said Lambert. He didn't want to ask any questions of her just yet. He wanted the account to be her own recollection, unburdened by leading questions.

'I don't know his name. He came to the care home where I had my first job. I saw him twice, maybe three times.' Dempsey looked up at Kennedy as if for support. Kennedy smiled and nodded.

Lambert could have screamed at her. Dempsey was taking her time with the revelation, like a master storyteller.

The colour in Dempsey's skin changed as she recalled what had happened. Dr Hughes had noticed it, and inched closer to the bed. Dempsey scratched her neck. 'He was investigating some trouble at the home. There were some accusations. He looked into them, but nothing ever came of it.'

Hughes edged nearer to her patient. 'What were the accusations, Laura?' asked Lambert.

Dempsey shook her head. 'I...'she hesitated, and out of nowhere vomited onto her bed.

'That's all for now,' said Hughes, ushering them out and calling for a nurse.

As Lambert retreated out of the room, he saw Laura looking at the puddle of vomit on her bedsheets in total confusion, as if she'd just exorcised some alien life form from within her.

Chapter 36

Lambert summoned everyone to the incident room as they drove back from the hospital. He needed to make everything clear in his mind. Laura's revelation was the first direct link between the surviving victims. She'd met Lennox before. That was enough for Lambert.

Despite that, he had to keep an open mind. Too much was on the periphery, not fully accounted for. No one could be eliminated at this point, and he had to ensure that the case didn't only follow his intended route.

The incident room was alive with anticipation when they returned. Devlin bounded over to him. 'I've details on the children's home where Laura Dempsey worked. It was called St Matthew's in Dalston. It's a retirement home now. We have teams looking into all former members of staff, and we're trying to locate the names of the children who used to live there. The council are struggling to locate any files from the time it was a children's home.'

Lambert took the file. He was impressed with the initiative and quick result. He rewarded Devlin with a slight nod of the head.

The room quietened as Lambert moved to the centre of the office. 'As you're aware, we have a direct connection between three of the parties involved in the case.' On the murder board, he drew a link between Laura Dempsey and the former police officer Neil Lennox. He drew a second line between Lennox and Sackville. 'All our focus is now on exploring these links, and extending it out. Devlin, where are we on Eustace Sackville's notes?'

Devlin stood, a growing confidence in his stature. 'We're going through his reports from the time period where Laura Dempsey was working at the home. Naturally, we've searched through his files for hits on Dempsey, Blake, Robinson, Whitfield etc... and now Lennox and the children's home. The name Lennox appears a few times, but just as lead detective on cases Sackville was reporting.'

'Work through each of those cases in detail. We met with one of Lennox's former colleagues, DS Lindsay, this morning. Add him to the mix as well.'

'Sir.'

Lambert continued assigning duties. Walker was in attendance, the bruise on his eye still ripe. 'Walker, do some more research on Robinson and Whitfield. Whitfield in particular. I know he's incapacitated at the moment, but I don't want to rule out his involvement just yet.'

The disappointment on Walker's face was palpable. He obviously knew he was being side-lined, and for the time being that was exactly where Lambert wanted him. Lambert sneaked a look at Kennedy whose face remained impassive.

She approached him after he'd wrapped up the meeting. 'Are we going to the home?'

'St Matthew's? It's a retirement home now,' said Lambert.

'Devlin is struggling to find any details from the council.'

'Okay, I'll make an appointment for after lunch. I have a few things to do.'

Back in his office, Lambert began reading the files he'd downloaded on Kennedy's father. He focused on the period where Laura Dempsey was working in the children's home. Not sure as to what he was looking for, Lambert searched for mentions of Lennox, Sackville, Dempsey, Robinson, and the care home.

He spent thirty minutes on the search before deciding there was way too much data for him to make any kind of inroad. He set up a number of cross searches linking the assistant chief with everyone on the case, and paused. Was this what the Watcher wanted him to do? If there was something of relevance he could find on the assistant chief, he was sure it wouldn't bring him any closer to finding the killer. It would be too coincidental for Kennedy's father to be involved in any relevant capacity. He was convinced it was a diversionary tactic. Why else would the Watcher give him such insight? He saved the searches he'd made and logged out, refusing to be distracted any further.

He found Kennedy in the canteen, eating alone. 'Join you?' he said, placing his lunch on the table opposite her.

Kennedy nodded and continued eating.

'I've made an appointment at the building which used to be the children's home for one-thirty,' he said. 'It's a retirement home now, so not sure what we'll get out of it.'

Kennedy finished her lunch and pushed her plate an inch forward. 'Curtis Blake has a birthday this weekend,' she said.

'So I hear.'

'Sixtieth. A surprise party by all accounts.'

Lambert wondered if there was any significance to the date. 'That gives me a thought. I'll see you at St Matthew's,' he said, getting to his feet and leaving the room.

Chapter 37

Matilda watched Lambert leave then ordered her third cup of coffee that morning. They'd only been working together for a few weeks but in that brief time she'd come to trust and respect the man. Something she couldn't say about the majority of people she'd previously worked with.

The thing with Tillman was getting out of hand. She'd spent the night at his place again. There was a side to Tillman he never showed at work, would never dare. It was a caring, almost vulnerable side. Yet he was willing to share that part of himself with her, and she was finding this side of him more and more attractive. She wouldn't be the first junior officer to sleep with a superior but there were protocols in place and if they were caught they would both suffer consequences, though she imagined he would take the brunt of any investigation into their relationship. She didn't want to give it up but every time she saw Lambert she felt like she should tell him. She only hoped he wouldn't see it as a betrayal if the truth was eventually revealed.

She sensed someone following her as she walked back to her table. She sat back down, unsurprised to see the beanpole like figure of DS Walker hovering before her. She wanted to sigh but she kept her body language positive. She would not be intimidated by the man, especially not here at her place of work.

'We need to talk,' said Walker, sitting down uninvited.

Matilda lifted her head and made no secret that she was staring at Walker's right eye, more specifically at the black and purple smudge which surrounded it. Walker's hand involuntarily touched the bruised skin, realising what he'd done too late. He brought his hand back to the table, his face contorting into a grimace.

'Do you approve of your boyfriend's handiwork?' he said.

Matilda tensed. Walker had called Tillman her boyfriend. She didn't want to provoke Walker too much but he had to realise she couldn't so easily be rattled. 'You were harassing me. You wouldn't take no for an answer,' she said.

'Me? I was just trying to help you. You were the one pissed out of your head.' He looked so incredulous that maybe he believed the lies he was telling. He was right that she'd been drunk. She'd been thinking more and more about that over the last forty-eight hours. She had had a lot to drink, but her unsteadiness that night and her subsequent amnesia was not a normal occurrence.

Tillman had explained it away. His father-like explanation that it occasionally happened like that had enraged her.

'You do talk some nonsense, Walker.'

'Ask anyone, Kennedy. You were pissed that night. You were downing G&Ts like they were going out of fashion.'

'Even if that's true, it doesn't give you an excuse to harass me.'

Walker snorted. 'You believe what you want.'

'I will,' said Matilda, 'and if there is nothing else?'

Walker didn't move. Back straight, he planted his hands on the table and continued staring at her. Some of her colleagues at the other tables had stopped what they were doing and were looking over, probably looking for some confrontation to brighten their day.

Walker had accounted for his black eye by saying he'd been caught by a stray elbow in a five-a-side game of football, but not many people believed him. At least three officers asked Matilda where Walker had caught the shiner and this most public of confrontations was doing neither of them any favours.

'What is this all about, Walker?' she said through gritted teeth.

'It's easy to blindside someone, Kennedy, especially if you're someone's superior officer.'

Matilda shrugged and held her palms face up. 'Why then?' she said softly. 'Why are you always on my case?'

Walker grinned. 'Because I hate abuse of power,' he said, once again with a sense of righteousness. 'I'll be watching you, Kennedy,' he said.

Matilda remained seated as Walker sloped off. She ignored the stares from her work colleagues, pretending to check messages on her phone.

Chapter 38

The Watcher was directing him, moving him from one house to another, from protecting Sophie to worrying about DS Kennedy's father, when his focus should be elsewhere.

Lambert searched for the positives. He must be getting close. They had a link now, however tenuous, between Lennox, Sackville, Laura Dempsey, and the children's home. Next, he had to question Sackville, then back to Dempsey.

Tillman was waiting for him in his office, leaning back on his chair as if defying gravity. 'Caught him yet?' he said.

Lambert ignored the flippant comment. 'I need to see Harrogate.'

Tillman pulled himself upright, groaning with the effort. He looked smarter than usual. He was wearing a suit Lambert hadn't seen before, the cut suggesting it was custom made. He wore a crisp shirt, striped tie pressed tight against his throat. Lambert wondered who he was trying to impress. 'We've gone through that, unless you have more for me.'

'There is a surprise birthday party for Blake this weekend.'

'Not much of a surprise if you know about it.'

Lambert waited a beat. He wanted to gauge Tillman's reaction to what he had to say next. 'Actually it was Kennedy who found out about the party,' he lied.

Tillman didn't even so much as flinch. 'That reminds me, why were you checking up on Kennedy's father?'

'Don't change the subject, Glenn.'

Tillman scratched his chin. Lambert was the only person below Tillman's rank who could get away with calling Tillman by his first name. He'd learnt to use the honour sparingly. 'Okay, there's a party. I'm sure Harrogate already knows. I'll speak to his team and let you know if he wants to discuss it with you.'

'Sir,' said Lambert, standing up.

'Not so fast, take a seat. Kennedy's father, the assistant chief constable.'

Lambert sat, tried not to smile at being caught out. 'Yes.'

'Don't be facetious. Why the search on The System? These things go beyond me sometimes, especially when you're flagging up someone like that.'

'I was just curious.'

It was Tillman's turn to smile. 'Curious? Why didn't you ask me, rather than creating a record?'

'Is there something you need to tell me, sir?'

Tillman ground his teeth. 'That's not the question. The question is: what are you not telling me?'

'As I said, just curious as to whom I was working with. Though I'm becoming more curious now.'

'Just lock that curiosity in place for the time being and concentrate on the case.'

'Sir.' Lambert stood again, and was at the door when Tillman spoke again.

'By the way, I'm transferring Walker.'

Lambert nodded, thinking that was a problem for another time.

Lambert returned to his office and decided on his next

move. If he had his way, he would visit Blake again but for the time being it was more trouble than it was worth. Restless, he left his office and headed to the canteen and ordered a coffee. He checked in with the officers watching his house, and thought again about the last call he'd received from the Watcher. How the killer seemed to have eyes in multiple places at once. Lambert glanced around the room, at the officers and civilian staff, and thought about the type of person who could conduct such a surveillance, who could know where he was at any given time. A professional, certainly, but there was more to it than that. Could there be more than one person involved in the killings? Could the killer be part of a group, even? If so, what sort of group could have the resources to hack into police mobile phones, to have eyes on a senior officer whilst at the same time monitoring his family?

He didn't find it as easy as he would hope to dispel his initial theory. A professional team, with great surveillance capabilities, could easily describe The Group or some unknown subset.

Lambert had once been part of a team monitoring the activities of a corrupt vice team in the South-West of England. Obviously, if it was such a team they were working to a different agenda but he'd come across too many corrupt officers before to completely dismiss the possibility.

The only other team he could think of at present was the mini-militia installed at Curtis Blake's compound.

A uniformed officer, Thornton, approached and broke his thought process. 'Sorry to disturb you, sir. There's been a bit of an incident. I thought you should be made aware.'

Thornton was a desk sergeant, somewhere in his late fifties to early sixties. He looked nervous, which was odd for him. He had a detached and cynical personality. Lambert was surprised anything could bother him. 'Don't keep me in suspense, sergeant.'

'Yes. Well, it's Eustace Sackville, sir.'

Lambert placed his coffee on the desk and gave the man his full attention.

'I just received a call out of Holborn. It seems there was a bit of an altercation, and Mr Sackville has been arrested.'

Smokers loitered outside the building and glanced at Lambert as he strode into the station. He bypassed the queue and displayed his warrant card to the desk sergeant, a jaded looking woman with a distant stare. 'You have Eustace Sackville in custody?'

'Yes,' said the sergeant, not having to glance at the arrest sheet. 'He's sleeping one off.'

'I need to speak to the arresting officer.'

'Take a seat.'

Lambert sucked in a breath. He was about to ask for the most senior officer on duty when a familiar face rescued him from an outburst.

'Lambo,' shouted a voice, silencing the general murmurs of the waiting crowd.

DI Wallace Greig stood with his hand on his hips. He had a full head of white hair, and wore a pair of steel-rimmed glasses.

'Don't tell me you've been getting your hands dirty, Wally,' said Lambert, walking over to the man.

'God, no,' said Greig, in a thick Glaswegian accent. 'I saw them haul poor Eustace to the cells. I heard what happened to him so looked up his case. Much security clearing later I discovered your mob are in charge. Come on through.'

Lambert followed the man through to the open-plan office area within the station. Greig had put on at least a couple of stone since he'd last seen him over ten years ago. He'd been a DI then, and it appeared his career had stood still in the interim. He wore a cheap, tired looking suit, his supposedly white shirt faded into a dull grey.

'Get you a coffee?'

'I'm fine, Wally.'

'Okay, son.' Greig patted him on the back. 'I'll get the sprightly young thing who took Eustace down. Why don't you meet us in the interview room over yonder?'

Greig returned two minutes later, followed by a uniformed officer who looked like he was still going through the final flush of puberty. His skin was a battleground of pits and red sores. His pale green eyes darted around the room as if he'd been hauled in for interrogation. 'PC Brenton. First month on the job, eh, son?'

'Sir,' said Brenton.

'What can you tell me, Brenton,' said Lambert, pointing to a seat.

Brenton looked at Greig, who nodded, and took a seat. He went to open his notebook when Greig swiped it out of his hand. 'Get a grip, son. Tell DCI Lambert here what happened. Use your goddam memory.'

Lambert suppressed a grin, as Brenton began to speak. 'We were called to the Byrne Lyle Chambers earlier this morning, eleven-twenty I believe. The head of chambers had reported a disturbance and I was in the vicinity. When I arrived, I saw a man, now identified as Eustace Sackville, trying to attack one of the members of staff at the chambers.'

'You tackled him all by yourself, didn't you son?' said Greig, dripping with sarcasm.

'You were alone?' asked Lambert.

'Let's not get into that, shall we,' said Greig. 'Brenton's supervisor was spending a penny at the time, isn't that right, Brenton?'

'Sir.'

'And the man he was attacking, Charles Robinson right?' said Lambert.

Brenton's eyes widened. 'Sir.'

'You were expecting this?' asked Greig.

'Not quite. Sackville is supposed to be in protective custody.'

Chapter 39

'You need to speak to him?' asked Greig.

'Please. Can you give me five minutes? I need to read the riot act.'

'Come on, son, enough heroics for today,' said Greig, leading Brenton out of the room and closing the door.

Lambert sighed and called DS Wilkinson who was supposedly looking after Sackville. The officer answered. 'Sir, how can I help?'

Lambert hid his incredulity. 'Just checking on Sackville. How is he?'

Wilkinson went silent. 'What do you mean, sir? You told us to release him.'

'I told you?'

'Your office, sir.'

Lambert gripped his phone, his knuckles whitening with the effort. He managed to keep his tone level. 'So, my office called and told you it was safe to allow Sackville out of protection.'

'Sir.'

'Are you kidding me?'

Wilkinson went silent. 'DC Devlin, sir.'

'Devlin called you?'

'Sir, I don't know what this is all about. Devlin called. We went through all the necessary checks. I called the two numbers

I was given and received confirmation. I considered calling you but I didn't want to waste your time.'

Lambert released his grip on the phone. Was it possible that the calls between Wilkinson and the office had somehow been hacked? 'What did you do with Sackville?'

'We returned him home as per his instructions. He didn't enter the building but headed straight for the pub. I was hardly in a position to argue with him.'

The Watcher was playing games with him. 'After you hang up, take your phone to your station where it will be collected. I then want you to return to the safe house, and secure the building. I will be sending a team over.'

Lambert hung up. There was no response from Devlin so he called Tillman directly and explained the situation.

'I'll pick the phone up personally and get a tech team over now to check the house. You actually think the killer has orchestrated this? You know the amount of insight and knowledge needed to achieve that?'

It was too late to tell Tillman now about the calls. 'Someone is interfering.'

'Sackville's safe?'

'Sleeping it off in the cell.'

'I'll arrange another safe house. We'll take no chances this time.'

Greig was waiting for him outside the interview room. 'We've woken Sackville for you. He's a bit groggy, poor bastard. Who can blame him? Says that Robinson was doing his wife?'

'It seems so.'

'Fucker deserves it then. I guess that's why he doesn't want to press charges. Would rather get a beating than have his name tarnished.'

'His name is tarnished,' said Lambert, following Greig to the holding cell.

'Oh, shit,' said Sackville, as he entered the room. He was sitting with his back to the stone wall, hugging a blanket. His hair was dishevelled, his eyes sunken and drawn.

Lambert glared at the man. 'Leave me with him,' he said to Greig.

'I'm sorry if I've wasted your time, but Robinson had it coming.'

Lambert sat down, the steel block cold and unforgiving. 'I don't care about that, Eustace. Were you not surprised that we let you go?'

Sackville squinted his eyes. 'A little bit. I know what budgets are like with you lot, though, and I presumed I wasn't in any real danger. At least, not in your opinion. I thought you may have made an appearance. Why do you ask that?'

'Nothing. There's been a few developments since the last time we spoke. You might be able to help.'

Sackville took a drink from a beaker of water. 'Hangover's kicking in. How's Robinson?'

'Not pressing charges.'

'That's good of him,' said Sackville, becoming animated, pushing himself off the metal bed before collapsing back down.

'Forget him, Eustace. That's all done now. Going back to DI Lennox. Do you remember one of his colleagues, would have been a DC called Lindsay?'

Sackville considered for a moment. 'Vaguely. He left the force I believe. We stopped tracking Lennox's cases once Trev took that beating. We only reported his so-called successes.' He went to take another sip of water but the cup was empty. 'What's this about, Michael?'

'Lindsay remembers you, Eustace. And Laura Dempsey remembers DI Lennox.'

Sackville's face visibly drained of colour. 'Can you get me some more water?' he asked, his hands shaking.

Lambert knocked on the cell and made the request to the uniformed guard.

'How did she know him?'

'Can't you tell me, Eustace?'

Sackville shook his head. 'Listen, I'm too old, and too hungover for these games. I told you, I've never met Dempsey before. At least, I don't recall meeting her. Tell me the connection.'

The cell door opened and the guard gave Lambert two beakers of water. Sackville downed his cup in one, so Lambert gave him his drink. 'Laura remembers Lennox visiting her at work.' He didn't tell Sackville that he had nothing further, that sharing the information had sent Dempsey into relapse.

Sackville drank the second cup. He was rocking back and forwards. Lambert waited for him to speak, but the man's mind had wandered. His rocking intensified, his attention focused on the wall opposite. 'Eustace,' said Lambert.

Sackville jumped. 'Sorry, zoned out there.'

'Laura Dempsey and DI Lennox, Eustace. What's the connection?'

'I told you, I've never heard of Laura Dempsey.'

'She used to go by the name of Laura Patchett at the time.'

Sackville shook his head. 'I presume you've gone through my old notes.'

'Yes.'

'And no match.'

Lambert raised his voice. 'No, but that's irrelevant. Your whole life isn't in those files, not even your detailed notes. It's just finished copy in the main.'

Sackville shrugged. 'I would help you, Michael, if I could. The name is not familiar to me.'

Lambert couldn't tell if Sackville was lying or not. He doubted if the journalist knew himself. 'Laura Dempsey remembered Lennox visiting the St Matthew's where she used to work in her early twenties.'

'That's it?'

'It caused quite a reaction in her.' He pictured her pale face, the vomit on her bedclothes, the sight of Dr Hughes ending the interview.

'Put me out of misery, Lambert. Where did she work?'

'She used to work at St Matthew's children home.'

It would have been easy to have missed the subtle change in Sackville's face. Lambert spotted the narrowing of the eyes, the slight twitch of his mouth. 'You know the place?'

Sackville scratched his thigh, and straightened his back in attention. It was as if his hangover had evaporated in an instant. 'I remember the place, though I don't remember any Laura Dempsey, or Patchett. What was she, the nurse?'

'Yes.'

'Never managed to speak to the nurse. Inexperience, I guess.'

'What are you talking about, Eustace?'

'It was going to be my first exclusive. I'd received an anonymous tip. I think it was police but I'll never know.'

Lambert stood, his body language suggesting that Sackville get to the point.

'Okay, okay. There were reports that some of the teenage girls at the home were being used.'

'Used?'

Sackville sighed, his whole body shaking. 'Prostitution. Someone was running the girls out of the home. Everyone was turning a blind eye. I believe Lennox came to the home and questioned the staff but didn't bother continuing the investigation.'

'And you?'

Tears came before words. They dribbled down Sackville's stubble pitted cheeks. 'I had a report of sorts. I even spoke to some of the poor kids.'

'Why wasn't it published?'

Every inch of the journalist was shaking. 'I was warned off and at the time I was too much of a coward to pursue things.'

'Who warned you off, Eustace?'

Sackville went rigid. He looked up at Lambert for the first time in the last few minutes. 'Blake. Curtis Blake.'

Chapter 40

Lambert clutched his head in his hands. 'Blake?'

Sackville nodded.

'He was running a prostitution ring out of that home?'

'It was part of his operation, I'm sure of it.'

Lambert sat back down. No wonder Laura Dempsey had such a visceral reaction to his questioning. 'How did Blake stop you publishing the story?'

Sackville stood and began unbuttoning his shirt. He removed it and turned his back to Lambert. The flesh of his back was blotchy and discoloured, a number of incision marks crisscrossed his skin, the rest of the flesh on his back was burn tissue.

'Jesus, I'm sorry,' said Lambert.

Sackville dressed. 'I've watched that man over the years. It's the ruthless ones who succeed. That's why I was making a last attempt at a story on him. I thought I'd nothing left to lose.'

'You have the story anywhere?'

'I have another file,' said Sackville, his eyes drooping. 'You think Blake's after that? You think…'

'I don't know what to think at the moment. Where's the file, Eustace?'

Sackville told him where he'd hidden the file at his house.

'You're going back into protective custody.'

Wilkinson was waiting for him outside the room with Greig. 'Sorry, sir,' he began, before Lambert stopped him.

'He's not to leave your sight, now, and he needs to be moved to a different house.' Lambert took out his card and wrote a six digit number on it. 'Sackville is not to be released unless the code is offered to you. Do not ask for it.'

He left the station and headed straight to Blake's house. En route, he called Lindsay and left a message telling him about Lennox and the children's home. It was possible the retired officer knew something about what had happened back then. Next he called Devlin, to confirm he hadn't given permission for Sackville to be released out of protective care.

'No, sir,' said Devlin, sounding worried.

'Tighten up the security measures,' said Lambert, not revealing the code he had given to Wilkinson. There would have to be an internal investigation at some point. Somehow, the Watcher had infiltrated the phone system. He hung up and was in Hampstead twenty minutes later.

He didn't need Harrogate's permission to speak to Blake, and wasn't about to ask for it. Lennox, Dempsey, Sackville and Blake were all linked to the home and Blake was the only one not to have suffered yet. He was either somehow responsible, or his family were in danger. He would reserve judgment until he'd spoken to the man.

He parked two streets away, and walked the short distance to Blake's house. The street was deserted. If Harrogate was hiding, he was doing a good job of it. He rang the doorbell outside the two steel gates, and smiled to the camera knowing he was being watched. 'DCI Lambert for Mr Blake.'

'Do you have an appointment, Mr Lambert?' The voice from

inside was familiar. Lambert recognised it as that of Blake's head of security, Will Atkinson.

'I don't have an appointment, but it is in Mr Blake's best interest if he sees me now. I don't want to have to return with a warrant.' Lambert rested his hands on the cold steel gates, which were industrial strength with jagged ends.

Five minutes later, Lambert spotted the suited figure of Will Atkinson walking towards him, flanked by two of his ex-militia henchmen. 'This is most unorthodox, but Mr Blake will see you,' said Atkinson, opening the gates. He had a smirk on his face, his two flanking guards stony-faced, their eyes never leaving Lambert's.

Lambert heard the gate click shut behind him as he walked across the gravel pathway. A petite lady in a tight fitting dress was getting into the back of a black BMW, the door being held opened for her by a driver. As the driver shut the door he glanced over at Lambert, a confused look on his face as he held Lambert's gaze for a second too long. Lambert continued staring once the driver had diverted his attention to the car's ignition and steering wheel, taking in as much information as he could. The driver's lithe body shape, the bald patches on his scalp, the steep contour of his nose and the darkness in his eyes.

'You coming?' said Atkinson. The head of security led him to the same foyer as before. 'Wait there.'

Lambert remained standing, holding Atkinson's gaze until the man eventually retreated. Preparations for the party were already in full swing. Through the garden doors, Lambert saw a team of men erecting a vast tent in the grounds. If it was a surprise, it was a poorly concealed one.

A hand touched Lambert on the shoulder, applied a sense of pressure before letting go.

'Sixty, if you must ask,' said Blake. 'It's supposed to be a surprise but you can't invite three hundred people to your house and keep it secret now, can you?'

'I guess not.'

Blake was wearing jeans and a dark t-shirt, his feet covered only by sandals. 'You know you're welcome any time, DCI Lambert. No need for the threats.'

'Tell your staff that.'

Blake was unsmiling. 'However, I am busy so if we could get down to the exact purpose of this visit.'

Lambert recognised the tactics. The subtle changes in perspective, welcoming then impatient, vague then specific, all designed to keep the subject off guard and uncomfortable. He'd used it many times in interrogation. 'Can we go somewhere private?'

Blake rubbed his face, the loose skin on his face stretching and distorting his features. 'Follow me.'

Blake's office was as ostentatious as the rest of the house. An oversized antique oak table took centre stage. Blake sat on a racing-green leather armchair behind the desk. Behind him was a gold framed picture of a woman sitting on a bench. The rest of the room was decorated in gold-edged wood.

'I met with Eustace Sackville again today,' said Lambert, taking a seat uninvited.

Blake sighed. 'Must we? Again?'

'He showed me something I found quite interesting.'

'Humour me.'

Lambert counted to ten in his head. 'His back.'

'His back, you say?'

'Yes, what's left of it.'

'I think we're having two separate conversations here, DCI Lambert. I have no idea what you're talking about.'

'I think you do, Mr Blake. But in case you don't, let me elaborate.'

Blake leant back in his chair, and lifted his legs so his sandals were on the desk.

Lambert told him about Sackville's investigation into the use of children from St Matthew's as prostitutes. He withheld the other information, wanting to assess Blake's reaction.

Blake kept his relaxed pose. He shook his head, a fake look of disappointment on his face. 'This is twenty, thirty, years ago?'

Lambert didn't respond.

'But you do have a police report from this time? There was obviously a complaint, some arrests.' Blake sat up in his chair, the sarcastic look replaced by a stone-like hardness. 'No? You mean all you have is some fabricated nonsense from a failed journalist? I have to ask you, why are you fucking wasting my time?'

Lambert ignored the shouting. 'An officer was called to the home, now that you mention it.'

Blake looked away, muttering to himself.

'You may remember him. DI Lennox?'

Maybe he imagined it, but Lambert swore he saw a flicker of recognition from Blake. 'You may also have heard that DI Lennox is now dead.'

'Is that so?' said Blake, placing his elbows on the vast desk.

'His body was discovered six months ago. His wrists slashed horizontally until he bled out. Sound familiar?'

No mistake this time. Blake squinted his eyes, the slightest of twitches in his lips. Lambert waited for Blake to speak but the man held his tongue. His eyes darted across the room, his fingers rattling on the desk.

'Do you have any idea why someone would want him dead after all these years? The officer called in to investigate child exploitation at the children's home?'

'No idea,' said Blake, his voice barely a whisper.

'Or why someone would want to kill the wife of a journalist investigating the very same case. A journalist who just happened to be writing a story which mentioned your name?'

Blake reddened, a gnarly green vein appearing on the left side of his forehead. 'What the hell are you getting at, Lambert? You think I did it? You think I waited thirty years to kill some old copper? And why the hell would I kill Sackville's wife? It makes no sense.'

Lambert agreed but wasn't about to say so. 'You're the only thing linking the two at the moment, Mr Blake.'

'Fuck off,' said Blake, incredulously.

'You and Laura Dempsey. You know Laura Dempsey, right? Her husband and children were killed in front of her. Her parents killed the same evening.'

Blake shrugged. 'What-fucking-ever.'

'I'll tell you whatever,' said Lambert, struggling to hold his temper. 'Laura Dempsey was working at the same home when Lennox paid a visit. She was responsible for the medical care of those children. For those children you were prostituting.'

He knew before he'd said it that he'd gone too far. 'Get the fuck out,' said Blake, picking up his phone. 'Atkinson, get him out of my house.'

Atkinson was there seconds later. He went to reach for Lambert but stopped short. 'I'm going,' said Lambert. 'You might want to consider, Blake, who is responsible for these deaths if it isn't you.'

'Get him out.'

Lambert smirked. Walking as slowly as possible out of the office, he said, 'If I was you, I would be greatly concerned that I was a key person from that time yet to have suffered a... bereavement.'

Lambert heard the screaming and swearing all the way to the steel gates.

Chapter 41

Lambert parked the car in the station's underground carpark. He was about to enter the lift when he heard someone calling for him. 'Lambert,' screamed the voice, full of accusation.

Lambert stood still and allowed the voice to approach. The man it belonged to looked unsteady. He wore a grey suit with mismatching shirt and tie, his brown shoes scuffed and unpolished. His wild eyes bore down on Lambert as he approached, and at the last second Lambert realised he wasn't about to stop.

DS Harrogate went to shoulder charge him. Lambert managed to twist his body from the full force of the impact, DS Harrogate glancing his shoulder and stumbling two metres forward.

'What the hell are you playing at, Harrogate?'

Harrogate kept his back to him for a few seconds before turning and attacking him again, his face contorted by his rage.

Lambert had had enough. As Harrogate approached, still too fast and unsteady, Lambert lent forward and jabbed him hard in his throat. Harrogate dropped as if he'd been shot. Lambert hunched down and lifted Harrogate into a sitting position. 'Don't panic,' he said, as Harrogate made desperate attempts to suck in air, a pitiful rasping sound escaping from his throat.

A couple of uniformed officers glanced over, saw Lambert, and pretended they hadn't seen anything. Lambert held Harrogate as his breath returned. 'Get up,' he ordered, pulling the man to his feet.

Harrogate leant over on his knees and dry heaved.

'You want to tell me what the hell you think you are doing?' said Lambert.

'You were ordered not to approach Blake,' said Harrogate, his voice a dry rasp.

'Unless it was completely necessary. That doesn't excuse an assault on a senior officer.'

Harrogate pushed himself up from his knees, his face ashen. He coughed and spat out a lump of blood-coated phlegm onto the pavement. 'Report it if you want. You've fucked it up anyway.'

'I haven't fucked up anything. If you stop being so obstinate, there is a chance we can work together.'

Harrogate followed him to the offices.

'Sit,' said Lambert, shutting the door to his office.

Harrogate sat, his arms folded in a final show of defiance.

'I saw your man,' said Lambert.

Harrogate feigned surprise but Lambert knew he'd won the fight.

'The driver. Lithe body shape. Weird bald patches on his scalp. Pointed nose.'

Harrogate sat motionless.

'I could tell by the way he looked at me. How long has he been there?'

Harrogate blinked. 'Five years.'

Five years undercover. It was no wonder Harrogate was so protective. 'You've been handling him all this time?'

'Yes. We've been trying to gather evidence on Blake's operation. We've made some indirect arrests on the Croatians Blake works with but we can't go in all guns blazing. They scare off easily, could easily change who they work with. That's why you may have just fucked up five years' worth of work.'

'I don't think so.'

'You don't think so? You don't understand how these people work. They'll have Blake under surveillance twenty-four-seven. They see you go in, again, then alarm bells ring. You could have even put our man in jeopardy. I barely speak to him as it is. Way too risky. No wonder he was pissed at seeing you.'

Lambert didn't buy it. He decided to give Harrogate another chance. He explained in detail the current situation, what Blake had done to Sackville, what he'd been accused of doing at the children's home.

'That doesn't totally surprise me.' The encounter had knocked Harrogate. For the first time since meeting him, Lambert sensed a begrudging respect. 'Where do we go from here?' he asked, as he stood to leave.

'We work together. Inform each other of our movements. Something we should have done from the beginning.'

Harrogate hesitated, as if he wanted to share something. 'Agreed.'

'And don't ever pull a move like that on me again, DS Harrogate.'

Lambert found Kennedy and they took separate cars to Dalston. The former children's home, St Matthew's, was now a retirement home. Lambert had called the home earlier and requested a meeting with the owner, Joanne Kendrick, who had sounded bemused by the request. Kendrick was there to meet them as they arrived forty minutes later. A small, nervous looking woman, Kendrick carried more authority over the phone and Lambert was surprised that someone with such lack of presence could own such a business. It was possible she was just nervous because of their profession. The sight of a warrant card often did the strangest things to people. It made them act out of character, gave them a sense of guilt.

Kendrick's office was cluttered and tired looking. 'May I get you tea or coffee?' she asked.

Both officers shook their head. Lambert remained silent, exchanging the occasional smile with the woman.

'Well then. I'm afraid you've caught me slightly off guard this morning, DCI Lambert. I was surprised by your call and didn't fully understand the gist of what you were telling me.' Kendrick had regained some composure in the minutes they'd been in the office, her initial nervousness evaporating.

Lambert explained the situation again, realising how flimsy the reasons for being there were.

'Correct me if I'm wrong, DCI Lambert, but your visit is to do with something that may or may not have happened thirty odd years ago?'

Lambert nodded. 'I realise this takes a leap of imagination but it could be very relevant to a current murder investigation.'

Kendrick studied them each in turn as if it was all some elaborate joke. 'You realise we bought this building fifteen years ago. And I don't believe it's housed children for well over twenty years. When we bought the place it was practically derelict.'

'We're trying to find details of the home's occupants during the period that we mentioned,' said Kennedy. 'When you arrived were there any filing systems still here? Any records at all of the home?'

Kendrick rolled her tongue in her mouth and then proceeded to surprise them both.

'It's possible this might be your lucky day,' she said. 'After you called I spoke to my husband. I told him what you'd said, at least what I'd understood from it.'

Lambert leant forward, a wave of adrenaline filling his bloodstream.

'Well I'm paraphrasing here but it went something along the lines of "maybe now we can get rid of all that stuff in the attic."'

They waited in the home's lobby as one of the staff went to fetch a ladder from the gardens. Kennedy looked like a bundle of energy, her legs bouncing up and down to some unheard rhythm. Lambert dragged his fingers across the cloth armchair, the fabric rough and pitted. He thought of the people who'd sat in the chair before, future residents waiting to be shown the home's facilities with their children. The residents who'd touched the same fabric and no longer existed.

'What are you hoping to find?' he asked Kennedy.

'A name?'

'Don't get your hopes up. I doubt they had great record-keeping and even if they did...'

'DCI Lambert, we're ready for you.' Kendrick appeared out of the shadows, next to her a giant of a man clutched a retractable aluminium ladder as if it was made of air.

No introductions were made. Lambert followed Kendrick and the giant up three flights of stairs, flanked closely by Kennedy. They walked along a narrow corridor, across a threadbare brown carpet, until they stood beneath a small rectangular opening in the ceiling.

'This could be a bit of a squeeze,' said the giant, extending the ladder and leaning it against the wall. He climbed up, heaving with each step, and pushed through the opening. He hauled his bulk through the hole and disappeared from sight.

'Use the place much?' said Lambert.

Kendrick grunted a laugh. 'I take no responsibility if you go up there. We haven't used the place since we moved in. My husband didn't know what to do with all the files that were left. We should have thrown them out. We called the council. They promised they would come for them but they never showed. We kept them just in case.'

A light appeared from above, followed by the grinning face of the giant. 'Dusty,' he said, clambering back down the ladder.

The loft area was bigger than he'd imagined. It was big enough for at least a couple of rooms and was piled high with dust-covered boxes. The boxes nearer the loft's entrance were dated, the latest one from only two years ago which went against what Kendrick had told them about not using the area.

Lambert made his way to the rear of the space, banging his head on a low beam. Kendrick had warned them about the floor boards, and Lambert trod as lightly as possible. A flower patterned sheet covered a mound of shapes. Lambert lifted the sheet, the cloud of dust rising into the claustrophobic space. He took out a flashlight and examined the boxes below. In crude felt tip writing, someone had scrolled. 'Files from St Matthew's Children Home.'

'Kennedy,' he whispered, opening the first box. He flicked through the contents, stacks of letters and bills, and handed it to Kennedy, an excitement in his movements. He passed file after file to Kennedy, unsure what was causing his urgency, until he found something that made his heart stop. It was a file marked, 'Residents'.

He opened the cover. On the first page was a black and white photograph of an unsmiling girl. Next to the photo, in uneven typeface, were the girl's details. The unsmiling girl was called Janice Raymond. She was seven years old. She had no siblings. She had no parents.

Lambert held the file, fighting a surprising urge to grieve for the girl who would now be many years older than him, and flicked through the rest of the pages, the names of boys and girls, either orphans or from troubled households. It was probably his imagination, but he saw the loneliness, the sense of abandonment in each photo.

He handed the file to Kennedy, and took the next one of out of the box. It was the same again, dated the previous year. The discovery had energised him, and he scanned through the contents of the box, and on to the next one. He didn't know why, but he was sure he'd made an important discovery.

Trying to keep the excitement out of his voice, he said, 'Call Devlin. We need to get these back to the station.'

Chapter 42

It took them nearly two hours to retrieve all the files and pack the car, even with the giant's help. Matilda was covered in a film of sweat, her mouth coated in dust which had a sour metallic taste.

'I could murder a drink,' said Devlin, taking her by surprise.

She drove to a drive-in, and ordered two supersized meals. 'It's going to be a long afternoon and evening,' she told Devlin, as they sat eating the burgers and fries, sipping on their over-sized iced drinks. All the time, she kept thinking about Janice Raymond, the first unsmiling little girl in the photos.

'Right, bin that, we're off.'

It was late afternoon. The good weather had returned, the people of London unsure which set of clothing they should be wearing.

Her phone rang as she parked beneath the station building. 'Go get some help to carry the files,' she mouthed to Devlin, before taking the call.

'Matilda Kennedy,' said the voice on the other end.

She checked the number on the phone, which was from an unknown caller. 'Who's calling?' she said, maintaining a neutral tone whilst thinking something was off.

'It's me. The one your childish press calls, the Watcher.'

She was about to signal to Devlin but stopped. 'What can

I do for you?' It was probably a hoax. She was surprised someone could obtain her mobile number, but it wasn't unheard of.

'You can speak to your boss, DCI Lambert. Reiterate the warning I gave him.'

Blood thundered in her ears. 'What warning was that?'

The man paused. 'Just tell him I called.'

'Tell me what the warning was,' she said, desperate to keep the man on the phone.

'Only him, Matilda. No one else must know. Oh, and Matilda, do ask him why he has been checking up on your daddy.'

Chapter 43

Charles Robinson's flat was more modest than he'd expected. Situated in Hither Green, it was a part of a three storey new-build near the station. After leaving Kennedy at St Matthew's, Lambert had called Robinson's chambers and had arranged to meet the barrister at the flat. The man had sounded resigned on the phone, as if the fight with Sackville had taken all his energy.

Robinson greeted him at the door. He was casually dressed, in light cords and a pullover. His lack of business attire seemed to rob the man of his charisma. He looked smaller than Lambert remembered, his skin more wrinkled, his hair thin and dishevelled.

'Lambert,' said the man, by way of greeting, his rich Welsh tenor lacking its usual vibrancy. He extended his hand which Lambert shook, maintaining eye contact, trying not to fixate on the bruise spreading on the man's face.

'Mr Robinson, thank you for seeing me.'

'Do I need my lawyer?' said Robinson, laughing to himself as he retreated down the hallway to an open-plan living room.

The flat was deceptive. Robinson's living room extended in both directions, broadening into the width of the building. Expensive looking oak floors spread across the expanse which was lined with immaculately arranged bookcases. 'May I get you something to drink?'

'No thank you. I won't take up much of your time.'

'Please sit,' said Robinson, pointing to one of the sofas. An oil painting hung over a mock fireplace, an impressionist depiction of a ship in a storm. Everything in the room was pristine but cold. It reminded Lambert of the lobby of a five star hotel. 'This is about Eustace?'

'Partly.'

Robinson rubbed his eye. 'I told that young officer, I didn't want to press charges.'

'No, that's fine. I'll leave that between you two. It was more to do with Moira.'

Robinson collapsed into the chair opposite. 'Maybe I do need my lawyer.'

'If you want to make this more formal, Mr Robinson, then that's fine with me, but I don't think it is necessary.'

Robinson hesitated. He crossed his arms, hugging his body. 'Ask away.'

'You told me that your relationship with Moira ended some time ago, but that wasn't the case?'

'What makes you say that?'

'That bruise on your face for one. Eustace knew it was still going on, didn't he?'

'Looks that way. You must think I'm some sort of monster, but Moira assured me that her physical relationship with Eustace was dead long before I came along. Moira was looking for something that he couldn't provide. I understand why he wanted to do this to me,' said Robinson, rubbing his eye again. 'Naturally he's devastated at what happened to his wife and I'm a reasonable target, I accept that.'

'You lied to us, Charles.'

Robinson rubbed his chin, nodding. 'I shouldn't have done that. I panicked and I apologise.'

'So you were still in a relationship with Moira?'

'Of sorts.'

'Of sorts?'

'It was purely a physical thing. No romantic mini breaks or the like. We only saw each other one or two times a month, normally at her suggestion.'

'And Moira was a willing partner in this?' asked Lambert, sitting upright and leaning towards Robinson.

Robinson straightened. 'What do you mean, willing partner?'

'I don't want to pry, Charles, but from what I understand things with you and Moira were a bit more adventurous then the relationship Moira had with her husband.'

Robinson smiled, as if privy to some private joke. 'Yes, things were "adventurous" as you put it. Moira and Eustace didn't have a sex life, so anything would be adventurous in comparison.' Robinson sighed, his breath catching. 'Sorry, I shouldn't have said that. Moira loved Eustace. She didn't love me.'

'Charles, I have to ask you, and this is important. Did Moira end things with you before her death?'

Robinson looked confused. 'You have a way about you, Lambert, I'll give you that. No, we'd planned to meet later this week. Today in fact. I was supposed to meet...'

'Go on,' said Lambert.

'Nothing, we were supposed to meet.'

Lambert considered ending the meeting. He wanted the next part of the conversation recorded, but needing answers now he pressed on. 'You were seen loitering outside Moira's library, Charles. We have an independent witness. You used to wear a hoodie.'

Robinson stood up and began laughing. He walked over to a side cabinet and helped himself to a glass of brandy. 'Join me?'

Lambert shook his head.

'Role play, Mr Lambert. Moira took to it splendidly.'

'Role play?'

'It was her idea. She wanted me to stalk her.'

'Come on, Charles.'

Robinson gulped his brandy in one. 'I swear. She knew I was there. I used to follow her home when Eustace was out. I had to stop at the library when Moira thought one of her colleagues was becoming suspicious.'

'You have any way of verifying this?'

Robinson poured a second brandy. 'Of course not.'

Lambert rubbed his forehead. 'Okay, Charles. So you would follow her home. Then what?'

'She had a key cut for me. I would be waiting in the flat for her.' He started rummaging through some of the drawers. 'Here,' he said, throwing over a set of keys.

Lambert caught the set of keys. 'You know how this looks, Charles?'

Robinson finished his second drink. He looked like a man defeated. 'Why do you think I panicked?'

'Why didn't you tell us about the keys, Charles?'

'My mistake. I was in shock, and I wasn't thinking straight.'

'Anything else I should know at this point?'

Robinson lowered his eyes. 'She used to make me wear a mask.'

'Probably time for that lawyer,' said Lambert.

Robinson shrugged. 'I'll call him now. Can you take me in, avoid the fuss?'

'Save me some time, are we going to find anything incriminating here?'

Robinson straightened, thrusting out his chest. For a moment he looked the confident, unflappable barrister they'd met at his chambers. 'Of course not. I didn't kill Moira, if that is what you're suggesting. We were lovers. We were friends. I imagine what you find will be incriminating, for my career at least. I will miss her. Retirement looms.' he said, rolling out the last word as he emphasised his Welsh accent.

'We'll be as discreet as possible,' said Lambert.

Chapter 44

Kennedy had set up a second incident room at the station. Photos of children lined the walls of the new room, occasionally matched by their adult counterparts. Lambert began reading the names on the sheets. Joss Balfour, currently a school teacher in Northumbria. Mark Fran, deceased, died age twenty-one, suicide. Meredith Wyatt, deceased, died age twenty-eight, suicide. Linda Farrell, reported missing fifteen years ago. Rolf Fleming, unemployed, Newport, Gwent.

'We've teams tracking down every one of them. Obviously, we don't know what we're looking for. We've started to separate them into years of residence,' said Kennedy, not making eye contact.

Lambert updated her on Charles Robinson. 'We've got a team searching his house at the moment. We'll question him later. Next, we need Laura Dempsey down here. I want her to go through the list.'

Kennedy sighed. 'Not going to happen, sir. I spoke to Dr Hughes. Dempsey is under heavy sedation and will be under psychiatric care for the next week or so minimum.'

Lambert rubbed his face. 'What happened here? What was Dempsey involved in?'

'Devlin has searched for any cold cases but nothing appears about the home. Nothing official.'

'Nothing at all? Dempsey said Lennox visited.'

'Well, he either didn't report it or the file is lost.'

He would have to speak to Dempsey again, whatever Dr Hughes' protestations.

'What are you hoping we find, sir?'

Something in Kennedy's tone suggested she was off with him. 'I'm not sure yet. We could be looking for the first victim,' he said, but what he was really thinking was that they could be looking for the killer.

'I'll get on with it, sir.'

Lambert allowed her to walk away to begin with. She'd been calling him, 'Sir,' ever since he'd returned to the station and it had been said out of duty rather than reverence. He stopped her as she was halfway across the incident room. 'My office, Kennedy, fifteen minutes.'

Kennedy stopped to listen to the instructions, not turning to face him, and moved away without responding.

Lambert took a box of files from the desk, took them to his office and began looking through the former occupants of St Matthew's. All his thoughts were focused on Blake. Blake had been running some form of prostitution ring out of the home, and had been concerned enough to have tortured Sackville to ensure his silence. Dempsey had worked there. And now years later, the officer who had been sent in to investigate the allegation was also found dead. What Lambert needed now was some form of feasible motive. Motive would make the investigation easier, but could there ever really be a true motive in such cases? If it was Blake, then did he really need a motive to kill Sackville's wife, and Dempsey's wife and children? The scars on Sackville's back suggested Blake was a sadist of the highest level. It was conceivable he'd been committing such crimes off radar for the last thirty years and had simply started making mistakes.

Lambert retrieved a file from the box. The sullen face of a fifteen-year-old boy, Sean Keir, stared back at him. Keir had been put in care aged three following the death of his mother to liver disease. The boy would be five years older than Lambert was now. Lambert knew finding out what went on in that home, and how Dempsey and Sackville were linked to it, would give him his answers. He would find that information even if it meant locating every former resident of the wretched place.

A knock on the door distracted him. Kennedy walked in, uninvited. 'You wanted to speak to me?'

Lambert placed the file back in the box. 'Take a seat.'

Kennedy couldn't quite pull off the sulky look. She sat with arms folded, petulant like a teenager in front of the headmaster.

'Shall we sort whatever the hell is going on?' said Lambert.

'You tell me.'

Lambert took a deep breath. 'You have me at a complete loss here, Matilda. Have I done something to piss you off?'

Kennedy held his gaze in a way he'd never seen her do before. It was as if she was assessing him, searching for a sign of untruth. Lambert wondered if it had something to do with Tillman, or Walker. Eventually she relented. 'Why don't you ask my dad?'

Lambert shook his head. 'Fucking Tillman,' he said, under his breath.

'What's Tillman got to do with this?'

It was Lambert's turn to stop, to assess Kennedy. 'Right, Kennedy, stop pissing me about and tell me what you have been told and by whom.'

'I should go to Tillman.'

'What do you know, Kennedy?' said Lambert, raising his voice.

She hesitated, going through some internal struggle within her. 'I know he's called you,' she said.

'Who?' said Lambert, beginning to understand.

Kennedy pulled at the bunch of red hair by her shoulder. 'The Watcher.'

Chapter 45

They sat in an uneasy silence, exchanging the occasional look, each waiting for the other to speak.

'When did he call you?' asked Lambert.

'Earlier today. How long have you been talking to him?'

'He called me shortly after Moira Sackville's death.'

'Why didn't you share the information? I should report you,' she said, eyes full of accusation.

Lambert relaxed his pose. He was confident he'd made the right choice. 'He made direct threats against Sophie and the family, which did concern me. But primarily, I feared that if I revealed details of our conversation then I would lose all contact with him going forward. He had an impressive amount of knowledge.'

Kennedy recoiled, shaking her head. Lambert wondered what Tillman had told her. Whatever he had said, she seemed to have come to him first.

'You think that excuse would help you if Tillman found out?'

It didn't sound like a threat but Lambert knew the potential was there in Kennedy's voice.

'I did what I thought was best, Kennedy. It wasn't personal.'

'Sounds like it was exactly that,' said Kennedy. 'It looks to me as if you hampered the whole investigation because of your selfishness.'

Lambert took a deep breath. It was possible she was right. It was unlikely he would have been so forgiving if the roles had been reversed. At the moment he still had indirect access to the killer, and in the end that would prove the man's undoing. 'Given that he has contacted you directly, he has effectively given me permission to discuss all our conversations with you. He is getting arrogant, and that will help us to catch him. If you want to take it further be my guest, but consider the implications.'

Kennedy bit her bottom lip, her gaze never leaving Lambert's. 'Have you been looking into my father?'

'Let's start from the beginning,' said Lambert. He told her of every conversation with the killer from the first unknown call on his phone to the last call suggesting the killer had broken into Sophie's house.

Kennedy stretched her back. 'He's been watching us?' she said, sounding more impressed than anything.

'It looks that way.'

'Okay. First things first, I want to know what my father has to do with this.'

'I'm not sure it is anything. I've read your father's file. The killer hinted at nepotism, but I don't buy that, I know you are a very strong police officer. Is there anything you need to tell me?'

Kennedy looked up, caught in thought. 'It's a distraction tactic, has to be.'

Lambert agreed but wanted more confirmation. 'Are you sure?'

'Well, he's got us talking about it. He's had me worried I couldn't trust you, and you worried you couldn't trust me. It is divisive and distracting. It has diverted us both from where our attention should be focused.'

'There's nothing I should know then? Nothing that will crop up later?'

Kennedy frowned.

'Of course not. There's nothing to know. My father is a good policeman. He is honest and respected and has had a successful career. Obviously, he helped me with my application and I imagine it hasn't hurt my career development being related to him, but that's where it ends.'

Lambert nodded.

'Where do we go from here?' asked Kennedy.

'We move forward. We need to make some formal record of the killer's contact with us, in case it's needed for future records. I'll list my conversations with him on an encrypted file, you do the same.'

'Do you think all his conversations with you are a diversionary tactic?'

'There's more to it than that, more than just the threat to Sophie,' said Lambert, beginning to articulate something he'd only half considered before.

'It wasn't Blake's voice I heard.'

'No.'

'Voice altering software?'

'I don't think so. The voice doesn't sound computerised. I don't think it's Blake who has been calling us.'

'A proxy?'

'Possible, especially with all the surveillance Blake has at his disposal. It's pointless hypothesising at the moment. Let's process all the files from St Matthew's and see where that takes us. Let's find something we can question Laura Dempsey about. For now, let's deal with Charles Robinson.'

Chapter 46

The change in Robinson's appearance was dramatic. Shaved, dressed in a tailored suit, he was a different man to the one in his cords and jumper. Giles Lansdowne had arrived and was conferring with Robinson as Lambert entered the interview room. He didn't look best pleased as Lambert switched on the tape and ran through the preliminaries, making introductions and stating that Robinson was here out of his own free will.

Lansdowne went to protest but Robinson placed his hand on the man's arm. 'It's fine, Giles, let's get this over and done with.'

Lambert relayed the conversation he'd had at Robinson's flat. Robinson confirmed everything, despite Lansdowne's protestations.

'Mr Robinson, as you agreed, we have searched your premises and have taken in a number of items for examination.' Devlin was coordinating the search. He had retrieved two leather masks from Robinson's premises which had been sent for testing.

'As we discussed in the flat, you withheld some information at the beginning of this investigation. If you have anything else you need to tell us, Charles, you need to do it now. Full co-operation would go a long way at this juncture.'

'I've nothing to hide, Mr Lambert.'

'You've already wasted police time,' said Kennedy.

'I beg your pardon, but my client has wasted no time whatsoever,' said Lansdowne, his face colouring.

'He told us his relationship with Moira had ended, which is clearly not the case.'

'He was under no obligation to divulge details about his private affairs.'

It was Kennedy's turn to be indignant. 'His private affair with a murder victim?'

'Let's move on, shall we?' said Lambert. He handed Robinson's colleague a file. 'Some unpleasant images in there, Charles.'

'If there is anything of Moira then I can't look.'

Robinson looked genuinely upset at the prospect, but Lambert was not being put off so easily. 'Open the file, Charles.'

Robinson looked at Lansdowne, before opening the cover of the file, revealing a picture of Laura Dempsey's husband. 'Exactly same MO as Moira, Charles. Keep looking.'

'Oh, Jesus,' said Robinson, studying the images of the two Dempsey children.

'Laura was made to watch all three die, Charles. She was accompanied by a man in a mask.' As he spoke, Lambert searched for information on Robinson's face, a hint of recognition, or even a glimpse of pride in his handiwork. All he saw was grief and misery. Lambert turned over the next page to an image of Laura Dempsey. 'She used to work at a children's home, St Matthew's in Dalston. Mean anything to you?'

'No,' said Robinson, flicking through a number of photos of the home's former residents.

Again, Lambert searched for a hint of recognition but came up blank. 'Do you know Laura Dempsey, Charles?'

'No.'

'Really, this is quite enough. I think we are going to end this conversation now,' said Lansdowne. 'You are clearly grasping at straws. My client has admitted to an ongoing affair with Mrs Sackville. He has broken no laws, and unless you have something you wish to charge him on, we are leaving.'

Lansdowne stood, but Robinson remained sitting. 'Look, I apologise if I've wasted your time on this. I should have told you about Moira and me. I'll do anything to help you find who was responsible for killing Moira, but it wasn't me.'

Lambert had heard such pleas of innocence many times before, but had nothing to hold the man with. 'I want your client to report to this station once a day,' he said to Lansdowne.

'Anything to help,' said Lansdowne, a humourless smirk spreading across his face.

Lambert spent the rest of the afternoon and evening locked in his office, trawling through the histories of the home's former residents. It was traumatising work, each child's life caught by a black and white photo and a snapshot summary of their life. He analysed each file in meticulous detail, reading the meagre details over and over again, looking for a sentence or word that would trigger his attention. It would be so easy to miss, and he'd instructed that each file was read by at least three separate officers to ensure nothing slipped by.

In the incident room, Kennedy had placed five photos of former residents on the board, each photo was of a teenage girl. 'All have criminal records for soliciting,' she said to Lambert.

'At the time or after?'

'All after. I've managed to make contact with one of the

girls, Melissa Brady. She lives in Plaistow. I'm meeting with her tonight.'

'Okay. I'm going to stay here and work on the last box. Do you want Devlin to go with you?'

'No, I think I should go alone.'

Lambert sat in the canteen, pushing his food around his plate. He called Sophie who confirmed everything was okay in the house, and checked in with the team monitoring the house, and the second team looking after Sackville. He managed a rushed conversation with Sarah May who was working in London. She promised to pop over to his bedsit that evening if she had time.

The sensible thing now would be to return home and get some sleep but he was too restless. He returned to the office and continued searching the case histories. He felt like an intruder on the private pain of hundreds of children.

Jake Lincoln stared back at him, the same sad look as the others. Lambert entered his name and date of birth onto The System and was surprised when three potential hits appeared. Lambert clicked on each of the three files in turn until he found a match. Lincoln lived in Kent and was currently temping as a school caretaker via a recruitment agency. Lambert printed the details and added him to the file. He repeated the process with Seth Grant, now from Putney, and Celeste Rush, now in Dover.

It was painstakingly slow.

A knock on the door tore him from the latest file, Gayle Kimball, who had died twenty-two years ago. He had presumed everyone had left for the evening. 'Enter.'

'Sir, may I have a word?'

Lambert turned his attention back to his file. 'It's not the best time, Walker.'

'It's important, sir.'

'Unless it has a direct relevance to the case then I don't have time.'

'I want to make a complaint, sir. I thought I should speak to you first before I make it official.

'Sit.' Lambert placed the file down with a heavy sigh. Kimball would have to wait for the time being. 'We've been here before, Walker.'

'You heard I'm being transferred?'

'That's why you want to make a complaint?'

'No, I think you should know what the complaint is about.'

The bruising on Walker's eye had faded to a dirty yellow. 'My advice hasn't changed. You would do best to forget about all this, move to another department and get on with your career.'

Walker moved the perfect knot of his tie further towards his top button. 'It's abuse of power. I shouldn't be transferred because of this.'

'Maybe not, but you've got to learn how to play the game. You start causing a fuss now, and it will only be detrimental to your career. Moving might actually be beneficial.' Lambert wasn't totally comfortable giving such advice. He didn't like Walker, but if Tillman was responsible for the black eye, then Walker was right. Lambert didn't like abuse of power in any form. But worse things happened, and Walker would end up in an untenable position where his fellow officers wouldn't respect him.

'Never changes, does it? Old boys' club.' Walker leant in towards him, the bitter smell of alcohol drifting towards Lambert.

'Walker, go home and sort yourself out. If you want to make a formal complaint, come back tomorrow and speak to me sober. I will make sure due process is followed.'

Walker made his unsteady way to the door, which he slammed behind him. Lambert closed his laptop, a collage of fireflies filling his office room. Lambert pushed through the hallucinatory images, and followed the path made by Walker. He managed to reach the door just in time.

He locked himself in the room and fell to the floor asleep.

Chapter 47

Lambert wiped away the line of drool on his chin, his face pushed down on the hard grey carpet of his office. He rubbed his eyes, and pulled himself into a sitting position. He couldn't go on like this. If he hadn't managed to lock his office door in time, someone would have found him collapsed in a heap. The hallucinations and black outs were as constant as ever, but now he was back at work he needed to be more mindful of when they were likely to happen, and to make sure he was not at work. If his condition was discovered, medical would link the episodes to the stress of the job, which could confine him to an administrative role. The only person he'd ever told about the hallucinations was Sarah May. Even Sophie didn't know. Sarah had suggested finding a private doctor, getting checked out anonymously. He promised himself he would do that as soon as the case was finished.

He unlocked his office door. The incident room was desolate, a single neon light illuminating the open space. It was four-thirty a.m. He made his way to the kitchen area, thankful that someone had left the coffee pot on. He poured a cup, wincing at the burnt taste. He tipped the liquid down the sink, and brewed a new pot.

Back in the office, he continued his research on the former occupants of St Matthew's. It was obsessive, mundane work with no guarantee of success. It summed up much of his life in the force. Most people didn't understand the reality of his job, the endless hours of research, the administration, the false starts and wrong turns. This was the real work, the foundation which made everything else possible.

Ivy Rickard, died aged twenty-seven. Suicide.

Matthew Larder, currently a police constable residing in Leamington Spa.

Lambert picked up one last file. He would need to return to the flat for a shower and change of clothes, so this would be the last for this morning. Elaine Jacobson. The photo showed the pouty smile of a typical teenage girl. The file was heavier than the majority of the others.

Lambert turned the cover, his hand starting to shake as he viewed the picture on the next page.

Chapter 48

It was rush hour by the time Matilda made the tube journey to Plaistow in east London. She joined the throng of weary commuters returning home, spending the initial part of the journey pushed up against the chest of a suited businessman.

It was a relief to disembark at the station, the still air humid as she made the short walk to the block of flats where Melissa Brady lived.

A man she'd seen on the tube was heading in her direction, a pace or two behind. Her anxiety had been heightened by the revelations from Lambert about his conversations with the Watcher. She had already written out a record of her own conversation with the killer and the subsequent discussion with Lambert. As Lambert had suggested, she'd encrypted the file and loaded it onto a personal flash drive which she carried with her. As she walked, she thought about the Watcher's apparent ability to be in many places at once, always one step ahead.

She bent down and pretended to adjust the zip on her boot, and waited for the man to pass her. Dressed in casual clothes, Kennedy noticed the man's retro trainers. She monitored the man's progress as he continued down the road not once looking back. Her own surveillance training had told her this was irrelevant. If the man was good at what he was doing, he would never look back. If he was part of a team then he would consider his cover blown and would pass the duty onto someone else.

Kennedy scanned the immediate area. A couple, late teens, were walking hand in hand across the road moving in the opposite direction. An elderly woman pushing an old-fashioned pram followed in their wake. Behind her, a new influx of people had just left the tube station and were scattering in various directions.

Deciding she was just being paranoid, she continued. Brady lived in a ground floor apartment, the outside of which was decorated in square slabs of colour and could have easily been misplaced for the exterior of a school. Matilda rang the buzzer. A woman's voice answered.

'Hi, is that Melissa Brady?'

'Yes, come on in.'

The door opened into the brightly lit corridors which reminded Matilda of a budget hotel. She rounded a corner and saw a woman standing in a doorway surveying the corridor with a nervous shake of the head. 'Come in,' she whispered.

Matilda entered the dimly lit interior of Melissa Brady's flat, her hand brushing against the smooth walls. Brady led her into a kitchenette area which doubled as a living room. A flat screen TV hung on one of the white walls, dominating the space and drawing Matilda's eye. 'Thanks for taking the time to see me,' she said, displaying her warrant card.

'I was a bit shocked to hear from you, to be honest,' said Melissa, lighting a cigarette. 'Want one?'

Matilda shook her head as Melissa sucked greedily on her cigarette, her face breaking into a patchwork of wrinkles. 'Take a seat. Tea?'

'No, thank you.'

'Or wine?' said Melissa, pouring herself what looked like a second helping from a supermarket own-brand bottle of chardonnay.

'Still on duty.'

They sat, Matilda making out her dim reflection in the black glass of the dining table. 'Again, thanks for agreeing to see me.'

Melissa took a second drag of the cigarette, the motion almost an act of desperation. 'I haven't thought about that place in a long time. Didn't really want to if I'm being honest. What's it all about?'

'Nothing serious. We're in the process of tracking down some people we need to speak to who were in the home from that period. At the moment, we're working through a list of former residents.'

Brady took another drag before speaking. Smoking was clearly not doing her any favours. According to her file she was forty-three but the skin on her face, and in particular around eyes, made her look much older. She eyed Matilda with suspicion. 'Residents?' she said, with a throaty laugh.

In her bag, Matilda had a photo of Melissa as a girl. It was hard to equate the smiling face of the young girl in the black and white photograph with the woman before her. It looked as if she'd done okay for herself. The flat was nice enough, well decorated and clean. It could have been much worse considering her background. 'The children who lived in the home.'

Melissa stubbed out her cigarette. 'I wouldn't call it much of a home either. Who are you looking for?'

'No one in particular. We're working through our lists and trying to locate everyone. We've spoken to a number of people.'

Matilda felt the conversation running away from her. 'How long were you at the home for, Melissa?'

Melissa face twisted in confusion as she lit a second cigarette. 'I was there from the age of eight. I was taken from my mother.'

Matilda had read Brady's file. Her mother had been a habitual drug taker. Social services had been investigating her over a number of years, and had taken Melissa away from her on numerous occasions before. In the end, her mother had been sentenced to a two-year custodial sentence following her part in an armed robbery and Melissa had found herself at the home. 'How long were you there?'

'Until I was sixteen. I managed to get a job at a laundrette and managed to escape the place.'

'I know this must be difficult, but could you tell me a little about the home.'

Another drag. 'If you stop calling it a home.'

'Sorry.'

'Look, it could have been worse, I admit that. Some of the warders were kind enough but there were so many of us, so many with problems. You don't end up in a place like that unless you have sort of a problem or you're very unfortunate. You could have separated the majority of us into orphans and those from problem families. Some were what we called lifers, some passing through.'

'You lived in dormitories?'

'Yes. Chaotic. Loads of us to a room.'

Matilda pictured the scene. A room of lost girls, scared and alone in the dark. 'Can you tell me some more about the warders, Melissa? Were there any things you ever saw, anything not right.'

Brady's hand trembled as she first lifted her glass for a swig of wine, and then retrieved her cigarette. 'What do you really want to know?'

Matilda looked hard at Brady, at the frightened girl behind the stone-like front. 'We've had some serious reports about wrongdoings at the home from the period you were there. I know this may be difficult, but do you remember anything along those lines?'

Brady retrieved her bottle of wine from the fridge. 'Sure I can't tempt you?'

'No. Thank you though.'

Brady downed half her glass in one long gulp. 'Where to begin? Some of the warders were kind, but others were not. There were punishments, and I don't imagine they were legal even then.'

Matilda leant in. 'Did anything happen to you?'

'I was one of the lucky ones. I endured the odd fumbling from the older teenage boys but nothing from the adults, thank God.'

'And the others?'

Brady strained her neck forward, fighting the watering in her eyes. 'There was so much. Some of the older girls would disappear for the night. When they returned they would be different. Some of them had gifts, cheap little trinkets. Fucking pathetic really,' said Brady, laughing and crying at the same time.

'Were you ever approached by anyone outside the home?'

'Once, on my fifteenth birthday. A couple of guys used to hang around the home all the time. They would supply things for the girls. Cigs and alcohol, harder stuff sometimes. One of them started giving me the spiel. Told me I was pretty, that sort of thing. Pretended he wanted to take me to dinner, buy me gifts.'

'And you refused?'

'I tried and he didn't push it, though he tried it a couple of times. Then I got the job and I was out of there.'

'They let you leave, aged sixteen?'

'I was lucky. My aunt worked in the launderette too. Moved in with her until I found a room. She's dead now, along with Mum. I've no family left now.'

'I'm sorry to hear that.'

'Yeah.'

'I'm sorry to push you on this, Melissa but I've looked at your record.'

'I knew this was bullshit. What's this about?'

'We're investigating an accusation of a prostitute ring at the home.'

'But that's got nothing to do with me. I had long gone by the time I was arrested for that. I was still working in the laundrette and needed some more money. I got caught on my second night, some undercover cop. I accepted the charge and never did it again. The best thing that ever happened to me.'

'Okay, I understand. What about the other girls, did you stay in contact?'

Brady shook her head. 'I couldn't. I needed to make a clear break. That was the only way.'

Matilda showed the woman a picture of Blake from that period. 'Was this the man who approached you?'

Brady studied the image as if it was a lost artefact. 'I can't remember. I'm sorry.'

Later that evening, Matilda lay in bed and thought about what Melissa had told her. She'd hinted at what amounted to systematic abuse at the institution, and Matilda believed the place should be fully investigated. She decided she would talk to Lambert about passing their research over to a cold case team.

Next to her, Glenn Tillman lay on his back, the considerable width of his chest high in the air as he let out the occasional growl of a snore. She'd given in and visited him after meeting Melissa, the need not to be alone outweighing her concerns over her relationship with her superior. She elbowed the man in the ribs, and he turned onto his side rubbing the area where she'd hit him. Thirty seconds later, the snoring resumed.

She switched off the bedside lamp, comforted by the blanket of darkness. She tried to sleep but kept returning to the case. The Watcher's voice was still fresh in her head. He'd tried to destroy her working relationship with Lambert. She had called her father en route to Tillman's. He'd been surprised to hear from her and had probably sensed the concern in her voice. It was comforting to talk to him. She hoped that Lambert was correct. That the Watcher was trying to distract them, that her father was a diversion meant to take their focus away from the main case. She wasn't convinced Lambert fully believed his own theory, nor did she believe he was being totally open with her about everything.

As for the man lying next to her, he knew that Lambert had run a search on her father. Tillman had been adamant that their private and professional lives remained separate, and she'd naturally agreed but that was before her father was mentioned. She wanted to broach the subject with him but that would involve Lambert, which would lead to questions she was unprepared to answer.

The strangled cry of a vixen on heat startled her, sending a wave of adrenaline through her system. It was ridiculous being this on edge. She walked to the window, peered out of the curtains onto the twilight world and couldn't help but wonder if the killer was out there watching her.

'Will you go to sleep?' said Tillman, before returning to his snore infused slumber.

Matilda crawled in beside the gigantic man, the touch of his skin warm and clammy against her own, but she was pleased to have him next to her. She closed her eyes, and slept fitfully until her phone rang at four-thirty a.m.

She pressed the green button on the phone and sprang to her feet so as not to wake the sleeping Tillman. 'Lambert?' she said, as if dreaming.

'Get to the office, Kennedy. I think I've found the first victim.'

Chapter 49

Lambert was still holding Elaine Jacobson's file when Kennedy arrived, forty minutes after he'd called her. She was out of breath, dressed in the same jeans and top she'd been wearing yesterday. 'Here,' said Lambert, handing her the file.

He studied Kennedy's face. Her eyes narrowed, her lips tightening as she read and reread the record of Elaine Jacobson's last day on earth. 'It says suicide,' said Kennedy, handing the file back.

Lambert looked at the pictures again, the images forever branded onto his brain. Elaine had been found dead in the home's bathroom on the morning of the tenth of June, 1985. The file said she'd committed suicide. A single rusted razor blade had been found next to her body. Both her wrists had been sliced horizontally. The coroner's verdict was death by exsanguination.

'I know what it says. Did you read who discovered the body?'

Kennedy nodded. 'The head nurse, Laura Patchett, Laura Dempsey. This is incredible. What do you think it means?'

Lambert had been thinking about nothing else since he'd called her forty minutes ago, but was no closer to an answer. 'We need to speak to Laura again, find out if she thinks it really was a suicide. We need to track down anyone who was close to

Elaine Jacobson at the time, even anyone who was at the home when she died. What about that woman you met last night?'

Kennedy cross-checked her notes. 'Melissa was a couple of years younger at the time but she was there.'

'Then I'm sure she remembers. Go see her now. I'll speak to the hospital, make sure Dempsey is lucid.'

Lambert called the hospital and arranged to meet Dr Hughes at nine-thirty a.m. He rushed back to the flat, showered and changed in minutes, and was at the hospital in plenty of time. He thought about the date coincidence. It would be thirty years to the day tomorrow since Elaine Jacobson died. It was probably a coincidence but it would also be Curtis Blake's sixtieth birthday. Had he been celebrating his birthday that evening, trying out a method of murder which looked like suicide? One thing was certain. Elaine's injuries were consistent with those inflicted on Moira Sackville, the Dempsey family, and DI Lennox.

Laura Dempsey had been moved to a different section of the hospital. Lambert traipsed the antiseptic smelling corridors, past the slow moving figures of patients and visitors, until he reached the ward where Dempsey was being kept.

Dr Hughes was waiting for him. The white coat was absent, Lambert surprised to see the woman wearing casual clothes. 'Day off,' she said, reading his thoughts. 'Sort of.'

'I'm sorry if I've dragged you in.'

'No, I had to be here anyway. Is this absolutely necessary?'

'I'm afraid it is. Mrs Dempsey may hold information which is vital to finding the murderer of her family.'

'You will have to make it quick, she's only recently recovered from your last visit.'

Lambert followed the woman into the room. Laura Dempsey was sitting up watching television. She closed her eyes on seeing Lambert, her hand reaching for the remote.

'Hello, Laura.'

Laura nodded. She'd lost weight around her face. Her cheek bones were more prominent, her eyes clouded by thick bags.

Lambert took a seat by her bed. 'I am sorry to put you through this again. We've discovered some additional information.' He showed her the cover picture of Elaine Jacobson. The fifteen-year-old, weeks or days away from dying. 'Do you recognise her?'

Dempsey took the file and Lambert saw something change within her. It was different to before. Last time, she'd panicked and lost herself. This time she sighed, almost in defeat. 'Yes. I remember.'

Lambert exchanged looks with Dr Hughes who nodded, giving him permission to continue. 'Can you tell me the girl's name?'

'Elaine. Jacobson, I think. She died at St Matthew's. I called the coroner.'

'What else can you tell me?'

Dempsey shrugged. 'What's to tell? One of the boys found her in the morning. One of the warders called me to the scene. She was cold, her blood was black on the white tiles.' Dempsey was monotone, devoid of emotion.

'How long had she been there?'

'All night probably. She'd been ticked off for bedtime. She must have crept out in the middle of the night.'

'You called the police?'

'I believe they were there when the ambulance arrived.'

'Do you remember the officer?'

'No. It was a long time ago. I think there were two uniformed officers.'

Lambert scratched the back of his head. 'Did anyone look beyond suicide?'

'What? The razor blade was next to her, coated in blood.'

'Okay, Laura.' Lambert exchanged looks with Dr Hughes again. The physician was frowning. 'One thing does confuse me, Laura.'

Laura looked at him directly for the first time since he'd arrived. 'What? You think there is a link to this girl? This was years and years ago. The home was a depressing place, for everyone.' she said.

'How many suicides did you encounter at the home, Laura?' It was impossible to believe what she was telling him. Something like this would have left a permanent impression on her.

Colour rose in her cheeks. 'Three, if you must know. There were three successful suicides when I worked at the home. Elaine, Sandi Corey, and Trevor Gibbs. Sandi also slit her wrists. Trevor hung himself in the dorm. He was being bullied. I've lived with those three deaths all my life. I was there for only two years, and they were the worst two years of my life. It never once occurred to me that they could be related to what happened to my family.'

Lambert ignored the woman's indignation. He remembered the last time he'd visited her at the hospital, the conversation which had sent her into a relapse. 'Why do you think Elaine killed herself, Laura?'

Dempsey turned away, arms folded. Hughes glared at him but he wasn't about to stop now.

'We know some of the girls were being used, Laura,' he said, noting Laura squirm as he said the words. 'Was Elaine being used, Laura? Did you know about it, Laura? Is that why you're feeling guilty?'

'What was I supposed to do?' Laura screamed the words with an uncontrolled rage. 'I was so young. The girls were coming to me with their injuries. They told me what they were being made to do and I reported it. I tried to help them. I thought it had stopped.'

'Who did you report it to?'

'The warders, the owners of the home.'

'The police?'

Laura shook her head. 'But the police came.' She began crying and Dr Hughes moved to stop the interview, but Lambert held up his hand. 'Who was Elaine friends with, Laura?'

Laura shook her head, still crying.

'Please tell me who she was friends with, Laura. Any name might help.'

He let her cry for a time. She was assuaging her guilt over Elaine's death, and the deaths of her children and husband. 'There was a boy,' she said. 'He doted on her, never left her side even though he was much younger. A good three or four years. He knew what was happening.' She began crying again, the sobs short and resigned. 'I'm so sorry. He told me what was happening to Elaine. Said there was a man giving the girls gifts and taking them out. He told me he followed her one evening and saw her getting into a stranger's car. It's all my fault, you see. I do understand that. I should have done something about it, but I was too young and naïve.'

Lambert pitied her but what she said didn't excuse her lack

of action. She had now paid an awful price. 'What was the boy's name, Laura?'

Dempsey wiped the tears away, her eyes two red circles on a deathly pale face. 'Neil Barnes.'

'Okay, that's enough for now, Michael,' said Hughes, moving to Dempsey's side.

Lambert nodded, his interest was already diverted to Neil Barnes. He stopped as he reached the door. 'What was Neil like, Laura?'

'He was a sweet boy, doted on Elaine. Almost to the point of obsession, he was very intense.'

'Did he have a temper?'

'Not that I remember. He was more desperate to protect her.'

'What happened to him after she died?'

'He was devastated, naturally. I don't think I ever got the chance to speak to him properly. I left a few weeks later.'

'Okay, thank you Laura.'

'You think Elaine was murdered, don't you?'

The woman had suffered terribly, but Lambert felt torn about her lack of action at the home. Like him, she now wanted answers. He wanted answers to find the killer, and it felt like she wanted answers to alleviate her guilt.

'Thanks again,' he said, leaving the room.

Chapter 50

Lambert called as she was leaving Melissa's. 'One minute,' she said to the woman. 'Sir?'

'You still with Melissa Brady?'

'Just leaving now.'

'Did she remember the incident?'

'Sort of.'

'Ask her if she knew a boy called Neil Barnes. Apparently he was friends with Elaine Jacobson.'

Matilda remembered the name. She'd processed the boy's file yesterday. She hung up and asked Melissa the question. The woman had not welcomed her return. She'd rushed into the flat as before, embarrassed, or scared, to be speaking to someone from the police. She'd been less forthcoming than last night. She remembered Elaine's apparent suicide but refused to elaborate.

'I remember him. He was younger, used to follow Elaine about.'

'Anything you can tell me about him?'

'Nothing more than that. He changed a bit after her death. Became a bit quiet. I think she was his only real friend. She was nice to him'

'You've got my number if you remember anything more?'

Melissa nodded and shut the door.

She had the feeling again that she was being followed, as she made her way back to Plaistow station. Knowing the Watcher was out there, she was suspicious of everyone, glancing at her phone as if taunting it to ring. Waiting on the tube stop for the District line into town, she called Lambert back and told him what Melissa had said.

Lambert updated her on his meeting with Laura Dempsey. 'Finding Neil Barnes is our priority now, though we've run into a bit of a dead end with him.'

'How so?'

'No record of him since he left the home. We're trying some additional searches now.'

'Okay, I'll be back soon.' A man followed her onto the tube and sat in the seat next to her despite the carriage being close to empty. He was overweight, breathing heavily through his open mouth. Matilda sighed and moved into an empty seat halfway down the carriage. The man seemed oblivious, his attention focused solely on his iPhone. When he left the train at Stepney Green, she took a deep breath and relaxed. She was over-thinking things, panicking when there was no need.

The team were waiting back at the station. A picture of Neil Barnes placed in the middle of the whiteboard. The grainy image showed a young boy, no older than ten. It was one of the few images they'd uncovered where a child was smiling.

Lambert beckoned her over. 'Haven't found him yet. Still waiting on a couple of searches to come back. Everyone you speak to from now on has to be questioned in relation to Neil Barnes.'

She returned to her desk and noticed an email waiting for her from Glenn Tillman. It was not like him to contact her during work hours. She glanced around, making sure no one was watching, and opened the message. It was short and to the point. 'My office as soon as you get this.' She stood, the rest of the team busying away at laptops and work stations. She couldn't help but glance over at Lambert, somehow feeling guilty for speaking to Tillman without his permission. It was ludicrous considering she'd spent last night in Tillman's bed.

His office door was shut, voices from within. She knocked once and waited. She'd been on edge ever since the call from the Watcher. It had made her distrustful of everyone. As Lambert had suggested, that was probably the point. But she still couldn't get out of her mind the fact that he'd questioned Lambert about her father.

Tillman's office door opened, Tillman standing to attention as four of the Met's senior officers walked out, including, to her astonishment, the Chief Constable. None of the officers acknowledged her presence. They walked by, stone-faced, and Matilda couldn't help wondering what they had wanted with Tillman.

She poked her head around the door. 'You wanted to see me, sir?' she said.

Tillman had retreated to his desk, his natural air of authority undiminished by the senior officers.

'Shut the door,' he said.

Matilda looked down the corridor as she shut the door, again overcome by guilt for something which on the surface was innocuous.

'There've been some developments,' said Tillman.

Matilda had always been impressed by the way Tillman could separate their personal and private lives. At the office, it was as if they'd never spent any time alone together. Every encounter was purely about work. So much so that at the moment she had to remind herself she'd spent yesterday evening at the man's flat. 'I'm going to speak to Lambert after you so there are no secrets here. I may need you to do some undercover work tomorrow evening. I wanted to know how you feel about that before we went ahead.'

'This is in relation to the Watcher case?' said Matilda.

'Partly,' said Tillman. 'You'll get a full brief once I've spoken to Lambert. We need someone on the inside at Blake's party. You haven't accompanied Lambert on any of his visits to Blake's house?'

'No.'

'So there's no reason he should know your identity?'

'I suppose not. Why do I need to be there? How are you going to get me in?'

Tillman's upper lip curled upward. It was not the most becoming of looks. 'Have you ever done any waitressing?' he asked, deadpan.

'Not really.'

'It's not silver service or anything. Just drinks, canapés, that sort of stuff.'

Matilda shrugged. 'Canapés?' She couldn't see what could be gained from being on the inside at Blake's party. The man was a professional criminal and was unlikely to give away any details of his work during such an occasion.

'You called me in just to tell me this,' she said.

'Partly. I know you probably don't want to answer this but how have you found Lambert's handling of the case?'

'We talked about this, Glenn. I was uncomfortable at the

beginning and I'm more uncomfortable now reporting on my senior officer.'

'Okay, okay, I understand. Believe it or not I'm acting in an official capacity now. I need to know if there is anything untoward you've seen in his actions or behaviour.'

Matilda thought back to a few nights ago when Tillman had punched a fellow officer in the face and, although she'd appreciated it at the time, it was ironic that Tillman would ask this question about Lambert.

'He's getting a job done and doing it in a professional manner,' she said.

'Okay, that's all for now.' Tillman pointed to the door.

Matilda rose and left, leaving the door open.

Chapter 51

Lambert had noticed Kennedy leave the open-plan office. He had to trust her now. She knew the Watcher had called him and they'd both agreed not to disclose the information. Still, she had glanced around to see who was watching, as she made her way to Tillman's office.

On his computer screen pictures of Elaine Jacobson played before him on a slideshow. Twenty-seven pictures of the girl existed. Twenty-four of which were photographs of her corpse. Lambert sat unblinking as his screen moved from the semi-smiling teenage girl of the official photograph to two photographs taken of her within the home where she'd been off guard, not knowing she'd been photographed. In one she was sitting alone reading a book. In the other she was sitting with a group of girls, knees up to her chest, captured in a moment of carefree joy, the illusion of which was destroyed by the fourth photo. Her pale white body crouched in the corner of the white tiled bathroom, a puddle of black liquid surrounding her. Then the close ups: the jagged lines on each wrist, her thin pale arms, the hideous vacancy to her eyes. Her body at the autopsy, the blood cleaned from her wrists, the incisions photographed close up. Lambert shook his head and turned off the slideshow. It was too close to home for him. Seeing the wasted promise of a teenage girl could only make him think about Chloe and how her potential had been cruelly taken away.

He switched on the next file, which contained only the one photo of the ten-year-old boy, Neil Barnes, who was so far proving impossible to track.

Lambert stared at the image. He was still undecided as to whether Elaine Jacobson had committed suicide or if she was the first victim of the Watcher. He found it hard to believe that the ten-year-old boy in front of him could have been responsible for the girl's death, but he kept returning to the image.

They needed to find him. Both Laura Dempsey and Melissa Brady had said he was a close friend of Elaine Jacobson. The priority for now was trying to track Barnes and find out as much about Elaine Jacobson as possible. The boy might remember Blake.

Kennedy returned to her desk. She looked sheepish and he couldn't help but wonder what secrets she'd been discussing with Tillman. He was about to summon her to his office when Tillman called through on the internal line.

'My office in ten,' said Tillman. 'We have company. Make sure your notes about this damn Watcher case are up to date, as you'll have some questions to answer.'

Tillman hung up before Lambert had a chance to argue. He was confident enough in his work not to go through his notes. Ten minutes later he was outside Tillman's office, surprised to see Tillman loitering in the hallway waiting for him outside the office door.

'What's this about, Glenn?'

'You'll find out soon enough,' said Tillman, lowering his

voice. 'Listen, Michael, just keep things sensible when we're in here. You're going to be quizzed over Curtis Blake and your investigation into him. If I had my way this wouldn't be happening. It's not a reprimand but there's been an incident.'

'Who's in there?' said Lambert, pointing his head towards the door.

'The Chief Constable, Harrogate and Harrogate's boss Chief Superintendent Tyler.'

'Jesus,' said Lambert. 'What am I supposed to have done?'

'Well, when you saw Blake yesterday, you spotted one of our undercover agents.'

'Actually he spotted me' said Lambert, 'I mentioned it to Harrogate.'

'His name's DS Sawyer and he's gone missing.'

No one stood as he entered Tillman's office. Tillman made the introductions, starting with the Chief Constable William Mooney, who barely acknowledged his presence.

'Sit down, Michael,' said Tillman.

Lambert sat, arms folded.

'I've updated DCI Lambert on the disappearance of DS Sawyer. As I mentioned to you outside Michael, this is just an informal gathering.'

'Doesn't look very informal.'

Harrogate's Chief Super, Tyler, spoke for the first time since Lambert had entered the office. Like the Chief Constable he was dressed in full regalia. His shirt and suit jacket looked a little too snug on his body, as if he'd recently put on weight.

'DS Harrogate informs me you were the last person to see DS Sawyer?'

'I saw him but I was hardly the last person to see him. I had no idea he was an undercover officer. I did have my suspicions and I raised them with Harrogate.'

'Tell me exactly what happened,' said Tyler.

'I'd just arrived at Curtis Blake's house. I was being accompanied by his security team into the house when I made eye contact with the man I believe is Sawyer. We exchanged a look and he seemed a little panicky to see me.'

'And what was he doing at the time?' said Tyler.

'About to get into an executive car, a BBW. In the back of which was Curtis Blake's wife.'

'What happened after that?'

'I went inside to see Blake, by the time I got back the car was gone.'

'The thing is, Lambert, we haven't seen or heard from Sawyer since. He was supposed to check in with Harrogate yesterday evening.'

Lambert looked at Tillman and shrugged. 'That's hardly unusual is it? He's not going to make contact with Harrogate if he's otherwise preoccupied with his work at Blake's house.'

Tyler looked at the Chief Constable who nodded his head.

'DS Jason Sawyer's body was found in an industrial estate near Enfield early this morning. His head had been decapitated from his body.' Tyler stared at Lambert as if somehow this was his fault.

'Why the hell wasn't I told about this,' said Tillman. 'I'm sorry, Michael, I didn't know.'

Lambert lifted his hand to his boss. 'Oh my God. That's horrendous. I'm very sorry to hear it.'

'You're sorry to hear it?' said Harrogate, standing. 'You were warned not to go to Blake's house and look what's happened.'

'Sit down, Harrogate,' said the Chief Constable. It was the first time he'd spoken. Lambert had forgotten the man was from Scotland, his accent deep and booming as if his voice was caught in his throat.

'I can assure you I didn't blow his cover. He looked at me. We made eye contact. As I said. He looked slightly startled to see me but he hid it well enough. No one else was watching.'

'What the hell do you know?' said Harrogate. 'Blake has cameras all over that building. He'll have watched and re-watched your exchange.'

Lambert looked first at Tillman and then at Tyler. He wasn't about to defend his position to some upstart who ranked below him.

'There's something else going on here. There must be. Even if Blake was suspicious, he's not about to execute an officer and leave his body in broad daylight. Just one glance at his case history would suggest he's a little bit more subtle than that.'

'Where are you on the Watcher case?' asked the Chief Constable.

Lambert thought of the best way to answer, knowing anything short of 'we found him' would sound ineffectual. 'We have uncovered two very important leads,' he said. It was the only sort of language a man like Mooney would understand, even if it wasn't completely truthful.

'Is Blake a suspect?'

'Blake is involved' said Lambert.

'Tell me everything,' said Mooney.

Lambert spent the next twenty minutes recapping the case, omitting only the details about the Watcher calling him and Kennedy.

'Elaine Jacobson's autopsy report proclaimed her death as suicide, correct?' said Mooney, once Lambert had finished speaking.

'Correct, sir, but her injuries were almost identical to those suffered by Moira Sackville, DI Lennox, and the Dempsey family.'

'So you think the Watcher may have killed Elaine Jacobson all those years ago and started back thirty years later? Sounds very similar to the last case you worked on? Isn't it a bit of coincidence DCI Lambert?'

Lambert had noticed the connection with the Souljacker, who had started killing after a twenty-year hiatus, though this was a completely different set of circumstances.

'I can only go where the evidence takes me. My focus at present is on finding Neil Barnes.'

'I've heard enough,' said the Chief Constable.

All eyes fell on the man who had his hand to his chin, deep in thought. 'I need you to work closely with Chief Superintendent Tyler, and DS Harrogate. As you know, it's Blake's party tomorrow. It's possible that Blake's competitors, or his collaborators, whichever way you wish to see them, were responsible for DC Sawyer's death. I want the men responsible found. If you are so keen to investigate Blake, you can deal with this at the same time as the Watcher murders.'

'Glenn will fill you in on the details, Lambert,' said Mooney.

Harrogate and Tyler followed Mooney out in silence. Tillman went over and shut the door as they left.

'What the hell was all that about?' asked Lambert.

Tillman shook his head and sat down. 'They know the Croatians were responsible for the beheading, it's their MO. I truly didn't know anything about it.'

‘What’s this about working together with Harrogate?’

‘If it could be any other way, Michael, it would be. They’ve asked that Kennedy be present at Blake’s party tomorrow evening. We’ve got her a position working for the waiting staff.’

‘So she’s working for Tyler and Harrogate now?’

‘She’s working for all of us. That’s why Mooney wants you to work with Harrogate. She hasn’t been with you to see Blake?’

‘No.’

‘So, he won’t recognise her?’

‘I wouldn’t have thought so, unless he’s checked up on us. Is it really necessary, Glenn?’

‘She’s worked undercover before. She has an aptitude for it, and this way we’re still part of the investigation.’

Lambert relented, understanding, and disappointed, that Tillman could do nothing about it.

Chapter 52

Lambert left Tillman's office without returning to his desk. He took the lift downstairs and left the building. He was thankful no one had tried to stop him, a little disappointed he didn't run into Harrogate so he could give him a piece of his mind.

The encounter had reminded him of the reasons he'd been reluctant to return to his role at the NCA – the politics, and mind games. It was clear that Tyler was friends with the Chief Constable, and had called in a favour for him to be present. It was the only way he would have got Tillman to roll over like that. They had all but said that Lambert was responsible for the death of the undercover officer, Sawyer. It had been disrespectful, dragging him like that to face questioning, especially with a junior officer present.

It was raining again, the June weather going from one extreme to the other. Lambert stopped at a bar called The Railway and ordered a pint of lager which he downed almost in one. 'Another,' he told the bored-looking barmaid.

Lambert paid, and took his drink to a corner of the room where he could see the main entrance. He took a sip of the second drink then pushed it away. He needed to keep a clear head. He'd been in these circumstances before, higher ranks thinking they knew better. Now was the time for logical thinking, free of emotion.

In these types of cases, motive was often non-existent. If the Watcher had killed that young girl all that time ago, and made it look like suicide, then it was possible he'd got a taste for it. His only motive would be the desire to kill, and perhaps the need for someone to watch. For all Lambert knew, the Watcher could have been active for years. Experience also told Lambert that it was possible the killer wasn't working alone. Add in the fact that someone else, pertaining to be the Watcher, had been calling him and Kennedy, and the picture was more than muddied.

With Kennedy being taken off the case to attend the party, that picture was unlikely to clear any time soon. Lambert took a last drink of the lager, making a decision. He would work with Harrogate tomorrow, would make sure that Kennedy was safe at Blake's party, but then all bets were off. But first, he had somewhere to be.

The safe house was an unimposing terraced house. Lambert would have liked a bit more security in place, but the budget was stretched as it was. He'd called ahead, so the guarding officer was not surprised to see him. 'I'm afraid he's been drinking again,' said the man.

Lambert rolled his eyes, but knew there was little they could do. Depriving Sackville of alcohol at present was not really an option. 'Take some time off,' he told the officer. 'Stretch your legs and get back here in thirty.'

Sackville was sprawled on the sofa watching the news, a glass of whisky in his hand. He glanced over at Lambert before returning his gaze to the television, his eyelids hanging so low that his eyes were nearly shut.

'I'll make some coffee,' said Lambert.

'Don't bother,' said Sackville.

'At least put the drink down, Eustace, before you spill it.'

Sackville turned his head to face him, so slow as to be comical. 'Make me.'

Lambert chuckled and sat on the armchair next to the sofa. He would have asked Sackville how he was, how he was coping, but the question would be redundant. One look at the man gave him all the information he needed. Sackville was doing little more than existing and if he carried on this way he wouldn't be doing that for very long. 'We need to get you some help, Eustace.'

Sackville lifted his glass. 'I have all the help I need here, thanks.'

Lambert switched on his iPad. 'One more thing for you to look at, Eustace. Please. Put the drink down for a minute.'

Sackville sighed. 'Fine,' he said, placing his whisky glass on the floor.

Lambert showed him a picture of Elaine Jacobson. 'Elaine Jacobson was a former occupant at St Matthew's. Her body was found almost exactly thirty years ago. She had two cuts to her wrists.'

Sackville grabbed the laptop and looked at the photo of the teenage girl. 'It's been going on all this time?'

'I'm not sure. The pathologist reached a verdict of death by suicide… but like I said, I'm not sure.' Lambert retrieved the iPad and scrolled through the pictures of Jacobson's corpse until he reached the sole picture of a ten-year-old boy. 'Neil Barnes,' he said, handing the iPad back to the journalist.

Lambert saw the recognition in Sackville's eyes. He gripped the iPad tight as if its solidity depended on the strength of his grip. 'I know this boy,' he said, shaking his head.

'You met him?'

'He came to my office once, I couldn't believe it. He must have been nine or ten. He began crying. He pleaded for me to intervene. He knew I was investigating Blake. He told me a friend of his was one of Blake's girls. He thought I could stop them.'

'What did you say to him?'

'What could I do, Lambert? Blake had already given me his warning. He had the cops on his side. I told him to go away.'

Lambert's skin prickled. He tore the iPad from Sackville. 'You've seen these, Eustace?' he said, showing Sackville the images of Elaine Jacobson's corpse, the vacant face of the young girl, the appalling contrast of her white skin and the red blood. 'She was the first, Eustace. You must have known about this?'

Eustace looked at the girl, was probably transposing a picture of his wife onto the body. 'I had nothing to do with that place following this,' he said, lifting his shirt as if Lambert had forgotten the injuries inflicted on him by Blake. 'I wouldn't have heard about a suicide. I'm sure they swept it under the carpet.'

'But don't you see, Eustace. That's where it all started. That's why Moira's dead, why the Dempsey family were killed.'

Sackville stretched down and picked up his glass.

Lambert stood and swiped the glass from his hand, the glass flying into the wall and smashing. 'If I find out you knew about Elaine Jacobson, I'll come back for you, Eustace.'

Sackville refused to meet his eye.

Lambert left the man to his television, not waiting for his babysitter to return. Sackville had proved something to him which he'd been suspecting for some time. He was now convinced of the Watcher's identity.

Chapter 53

Matilda sat in the office with Chief Superintendent Tyler and DS Harrogate, going over her role for what felt like the hundredth time. It was the morning of Curtis Blake's sixtieth birthday, and she'd hoped Lambert would have arrived by now. He'd called her late last night, after visiting Eustace Sackville. He'd sounded distant, as if his mind was elsewhere. He was supposed to be in the meeting now, going over who would be at present at the party, working on secondary and tertiary plans should she run into trouble.

'One more run through of the staff,' said Harrogate, handing her a file brimming with mugshots and text.

It all seemed a bit of overkill to her. She was going undercover for the evening, but only as a member of the waiting staff. Her role was to observe and listen. She'd already memorised the list of Blake's staff. His official staff – the security team, the accountants and lawyers – and the more unofficial members. Matilda listed the names of everyone on the list verbatim, without opening the file.

'Good,' said Tyler.

'The Croatians,' said Harrogate.

Tyler and Harrogate knew less about the Croatian gang Blake was supposedly in cahoots with. Harrogate had showed her details of a five-year operation on the gang, who they believed were involved in trafficking young girls out of Croatia to work in and around London. They believed Blake had helped them set up in the city, but it looked as if the relationship had turned sour. Sawyer had been drip feeding intelligence to that effect, intelligence which had resulted in his brutal murder.

It was hard to avoid the feeling that the two men in the room with her were clutching at straws. It wasn't her place to say, but sending her in as an undercover operative smacked of desperation. She understood the need not to stand still, the desire to avenge Sawyer's death, but there didn't seem to be any feasible plan in place. It was more a case of turning up and seeing what happened. Matilda would be wired, and would let them know if the Croatians made an appearance. It seemed unlikely to her, but she played along, following instructions which she didn't believe in.

'Dalibor Perko, Mijo Babi⊠, Jakon Petric.' She'd been up until the early hours memorising the names, the case histories and the suspected crimes. The Croatians' operation was slick and cautious. It seemed unlikely to her that they would attend Blake's party. If the relationship was still a working one, then they might send one or two of their operatives as a sign of good faith. If the relationship was destroyed, as feared, then she couldn't see them attending. From everything she'd read, they worked under the radar. They wouldn't start a turf war with Blake, at least not one so out in the open.

Lambert arrived just as Tyler was wrapping up. 'Good of you to join us, Lambert,' he said, unable to hide his derision.

'I'll get the details from Kennedy,' said Lambert, either unable, or unwilling, to apologise for his late arrival.

'You need to be at the agency in just under an hour,' said

Tyler looking at his watch. He packed up his files and left, followed by Harrogate obediently in tow.

'They love you,' said Matilda.

'It's not my operation, and I'm not wasting my time on it.'

'Fair enough. Have you located Neil Barnes?' Matilda had only agreed to go undercover because of the possibility that Blake was somehow involved, and that the operation would draw out the killer.

'No, he's a ghost. Disappeared.' Lambert picked up the files. 'You've studied all this?'

'Yes?'

'What are they expecting is going to happen? Gang warfare in Hampstead?'

'I'm not sure even they know. I think it's more hope than anything.'

'I take it he hasn't called you again?'

Matilda shook her head. The Watcher had only called her the once. 'You?'

Lambert took a deep breath. 'No. You've had gun training?'

'Of course.' Kennedy had been in The Group before it was dissolved, where everyone received fire arms training.

'You need to be armed tonight.'

'Tyler hasn't suggested anything?'

'He doesn't have the clearance. I'll confirm with Tillman, make it official, but I think the Watcher has something planned for tonight.'

Matilda wasn't sure. Being armed brought with it its own dangers, being discovered for one. 'What if they search me?'

Lambert rubbed a day's worth of stubble on his face. It was the most stressed she'd seen him since the case began. His eyes narrowed as he considered the situation. 'You're probably right, I was frisked when I went there. You'll be in radio contact?'

'If I didn't know you better, sir, I'd say you were worried.' She'd never seen Lambert like this, he wasn't thinking clearly.

'Just use your head. Keep in contact, and get out if you smell trouble.'

'I better be going, need to change into my outfit.'

Lambert nodded and she left the office, an uneasy silence between them.

An hour later, she was inside the gated area of Curtis Blake's home. It was even more grandiose than she'd been led to believe. She tried to befriend some of the other waiting staff on the way in. The majority of them knew each other but she'd met a couple of girls who were on their first job for the agency.

At present, they were at the back of the house standing on a pebbled area next to the entrance to the kitchens. Two of Blake's security details were guarding the door, dressed in identical suits and sunglasses like clichéd CIA agents.

'What is this?' said one of the agency staff, a stocky young woman who looked woefully out of her comfort zone wearing a tight fitting black dress. Her arms were decorated in tattoos, her hair shaved except for a shock of black hair which spiked out on the right side of her scalp.

The guards ignored her, the staff beginning to get restless. Seconds later, the taller of the two guards lifted his hand. 'I need two lines,' he said.

'What the hell?' said the tattooed woman.

'One more word from you, and you're out,' said the guard.

The woman looked as if she'd been slapped in the face. She glanced at her colleagues for support, but the rest of the staff refused to meet her eye, the promise of the inflated hourly rate too much to risk.

Every member of staff was frisked by the guards before being allowed to enter. Two of the staff were turned away, both men in their early twenties, the guards refusing to give a reason. The taller of the guards stopped Matilda and made her hold her arms out and spread her legs. His hands were rough as he checked practically every part of her. He took off his sunglasses and made a show of looking at her. It was a cheap and obvious way of showing dominance but the tactic had worked on the rest of the staff, who were waiting in the kitchen area subdued.

'I'm on,' she whispered, hoping the minute recorders stitched into her clothing were still working.

Chapter 54

Rain battered against the windscreen as Lambert sat in the car reflecting on what Sackville had told him. He was now convinced Neil Barnes was the Watcher.

Lambert realised he'd been looking at Elaine Jacobson's death all wrong. She had committed suicide. She'd committed suicide because no one would listen to Neil Barnes' complaints.

Barnes had gone to DI Lennox and complained about what was happening at the home, only to be ignored.

He'd gone to Eustace Sackville who had been writing a story on the home and the prostitution ring Curtis Blake was running out of the place, but Sackville had let him down. Out of pure cowardice he'd refused to print the story.

And lastly Laura Dempsey, the home's nurse, who had known what was happening to Elaine and the other girls. Neil Barnes had gone to her and she too had turned a blind eye.

And because of the inactivity of those three people, Elaine Jacobson had committed suicide.

Lambert wondered if Barnes had found the girl the morning after. If he'd known what she'd planned to do. Either way, the effect on the boy's life had been dramatic. Lambert believed he'd spent the rest of his life avenging Elaine's demise. He killed Lennox as a test run, using the same method to murder him as Elaine had used to kill herself.

Once he'd got that out of his system he moved onto Eustace Sackville. He killed Sackville's wife and made Eustace watch. He'd then done the same to Laura Dempsey. He'd killed all her family and again she'd been forced to watch his handiwork. Eustace and Laura were now like the killer, perfectly alone.

The killer had told Lambert that he was like him, now he understood why. With no daughter and a soon to be ex-wife, Lambert was effectively alone in the world. But the killer meant more. Lambert still had Sophie and her child, he still had Sarah May. The comparison was meant as a warning. Curtis Blake's party was only hours away. Lambert knew he had to find Neil Barnes' real identity before then.

He logged onto The System and tried every search imaginable. It was obvious Barnes wasn't using his real name. He would have probably changed it aged eighteen and the deed poll records for name changes back then were non-existent. It was easier than people imagined to change identity, to rid yourself of the past. And it would be impossible to track Barnes that way.

Lambert strummed his fingers on the leather coating of the steering wheel, the rain still battering the car's windscreen in a constant rhythm. He needed to think, to clear his mind. The Watcher must have access to surveillance equipment. It was possible he was a member of a team, as Lambert had previously thought. He tried to dispel the idea that the Watcher was a member of the police, though it would go some way to explain how he was always one step ahead. Lambert called a colleague in the tech department, Lee Chamberlain, who owed him a favour.

'I'm going to send you some voice files,' he told the man. 'There can be no official blueprint on this.'

'And what would you like me to do with them?' asked Chamberlain.

'I know it's a huge long shot but try to trace them on the voice database.'

'That database you speak of is almost non-existent. I can analyse the voice for you. Give you an idea of age, dialect, any peculiarities in speech pattern. That's the best I can offer.'

'Can you do it within the next hour?'

'As a favour I'll start working on it now but it's not a simple job.'

'Just have a listen through, see if you can spot anything unusual.'

'Okay, I'll do my best.'

Lambert sent the files and was about to make a second call when his phone rang. Lambert waited for three rings, controlling his breathing and preparing for the conversation. He answered the phone but didn't speak.

'Moody silences,' said the Watcher. 'Let me guess. Sackville finally told you his full story. You think you know who I am.'

'I know who you are, Neil,' said Lambert.

The Watcher chuckled, a sound not without genuine mirth. 'I have to confess that I admire you, Lambert. I'm surprised you've pieced it together so quickly. What was it? The files at St Matthew's?'

'This can end now, Neil. You've got back at those people who hurt you. Let's just end it here before anyone else gets hurt.'

'Perhaps you don't quite understand after all,' said the Watcher, raising his voice.

'You were friends with Elaine Jacobson. Eustace and Laura

failed you. I understand that, even if I don't understand what you did to them.'

'It won't end until everyone responsible has paid the price.'

'You mean Curtis Blake?' said Lambert

'Who else?'

'And you think you're going to get to his family? Now I know what you want Neil, I'll do anything in my power to stop it. Eustace and Laura didn't kill Elaine, Neil. They failed you and I understand that but I'm not going to let any more innocent people die.'

Lambert realised there was little point trying to reason with the man. His life had been tainted by what had happened to Elaine Jacobson and a few well-chosen phrases on the phone were never going to undo that damage. But he wanted him to think twice before attacking Blake's family. He hoped that slight indecision would lead him to make mistakes.

'I think we've come to understand each other, Lambert. You listen to what I have to say and you'll fully understand.'

Lambert pulled the car over and waited. He tried to control his breathing, his heart hammering in his chest.

'I know you've sent over those voice recordings but I know you haven't gone official yet with our conversations. But there are contingency plans in place, Lambert. Contingency plans that will affect you directly. If anything happens to me then I'll be unable to stop them. Do we have an understanding?'

Lambert went to respond but the Watcher continued talking.

'Remember at the beginning – I said we were alike. That's not fully true, is it Lambert? You're still married despite that bastard child. You're seeing that lovely police woman. You're not totally alone in this world.' The Watcher paused. 'Are you?' he said, before hanging up.

Lambert took a few minutes to compose himself, the warning from the Watcher specific this time. He didn't have time to dwell on the conversation. He pulled away, dialling another number.

'You're alive then?' said Sarah May, answering on the second ring.

'You could say that,' said Lambert, rubbing his head, trying to organise the million thoughts playing in his mind. 'I know who the Watcher is.'

'You don't sound very pleased,' said Sarah.

'The last I know of him he was a ten-year-old boy.'

'I see.'

'Are you still in London?'

'Yes. What is it, Michael? You don't sound like you.'

'Listen I need you to do me a favour. It's probably nothing but I think Sophie might be in danger.'

'Okay. Do you want me to go and see her?'

Lambert was momentarily taken aback by the easy way Sarah accepted what he said, without hesitation or question.

'If you don't mind. If you could just watch her, but don't let her know you're watching.'

'Should I be looking out for anything in particular?'

'Not really, just anything out of the ordinary. You know the drill. But be careful, Sarah.'

'I will. Are you sure everything is okay.'

Lambert sighed, making a decision. 'I'm probably being over-protective, but I think we should move her and everyone from the house. At least until this thing at Blake's house is over.'

Again, May didn't question him. 'I'll take her and the baby to my hotel. I know this isn't the time but does she know about us?'

Sarah had met Sophie once. It had been during the Souljacker case. Sarah had been checking up on him and had visited Sophie at her place of work. He hadn't told Sophie about the last few months with Sarah. Somehow it felt like he'd betrayed Sarah by not telling Sophie. As if she was some kind of dirty secret. 'I'm sorry, Sarah, I haven't told her.'

'Don't be silly, Michael, that doesn't matter. Concentrate on the case and be safe.'

He hung up, wishing he could tell her more. With Sophie accounted for, he made his way to Hampstead where the team had set up ready for Blake's party. He recognised one of the surveillance vans, a blanked out transit favoured by Tillman. He pulled over three streets down and called Tillman. The side door opened as he walked by and Lambert stepped into the van.

Tillman was in the confined space next to Harrogate and his Chief Super, Tyler. Lambert's arrival had done little to alleviate the palpable tension within. None of the men greeted him as he sat down, only Tillman acknowledging his presence – with a glare brimming with accusation.

'Kennedy is inside,' said Harrogate, handing him a set of earphones. 'She is currently receiving security instructions.'

The sound in the earphones was mainly white noise. Beyond the rattle of general chattering, Lambert made out the voice of a clear, singular voice giving instructions in the background.

'Not exactly plain sailing. She was searched as she entered,' said Tillman.

Lambert looked at Tillman whose eyes had narrowed. The

microphones she'd been fitted with were small enough to be undetectable but Kennedy had no way of hearing them.

'Phone?' asked Lambert.

'Confiscated.'

'Shit.'

Lambert sat in the silence of the van listening to the white noise in his earphone, debating whether to share the information he had on Neil Barnes. Harrogate and Tyler were there for another reason altogether. He doubted anything he could tell them now would change their approach. They were hoping for some inroads into Blake's trafficking operation, and whilst he couldn't condemn them for that, he feared there was a more pressing concern.

'I think we should evacuate the party,' he said.

Chapter 55

Tyler pulled off his earphones. 'Have you lost your fucking mind?'

Lambert didn't respond, glancing at Tillman for support.

Tillman unbuttoned his top button. 'Would you care to divulge why?' he asked.

Lambert wasn't sure how much he could tell them. The Watcher's threat had been self-evident. Sophie was in danger if he didn't get what he wanted. But he had Sarah May watching her, and he couldn't justify not protecting the hundreds of lives inside.

'Blake is due to arrive in thirty minutes,' said Tyler. 'I am not going to let you fuck up this operation.'

Lambert stared at the man. 'What operation? This is just a whim surveillance. You're hoping Blake's partners – or rivals, you tell me which – are going to turn up. And then what? You think Kennedy is going to overhear something?'

'One of my officers is dead, Lambert.'

'Look, I realise that. Still…'

'Still nothing,' said Harrogate.

'Will everyone take a few seconds. Michael, why do you want to evacuate the party?' asked Tillman.

Lambert looked at each man in turn, and concluded there wasn't going to be an evacuation. 'I think Curtis Blake maybe in danger. Or at least, his family.' He told them about Neil Barnes, and his theory on why Lennox, Moira Sackville and the Dempsey family had been killed.

'So now you think Blake is a potential victim, not the killer?' said Harrogate. The man's voice was laced with sarcasm, and Lambert was seconds from dragging him from the van regardless of the senior officers present.

'Where are we on tracing Neil Barnes?' asked Tillman, ignoring the squabbling.

Lambert shrugged. 'The trace goes cold in his teens.'

'Jesus,' said Tyler. 'You expect us to evacuate Blake's house, declare that we've been monitoring him, on this half-baked theory? Where do you get them from, Tillman?'

Tillman was motionless. Lambert could tell Tyler was getting to his superior, but he also knew Tillman would examine the situation and reach his own conclusions regardless of allegiances. Telling them about his conversations with the Watcher may have been enough to sway Tillman, but he couldn't risk sharing that information. The Watcher's warning had been clear on that point.

'I'm sorry, Michael. There's not enough here to take such a step, you must know that?'

Lambert agreed. If someone else had proposed the idea, he would have derailed it. Even if he told them about his conversations with the Watcher, he doubted he would have been able to sway them. He pulled his earphones back on and listened to Matilda Kennedy talking to a companion within the house, at the same time updating them on the situation.

'It's a lot bigger than I'd expected,' said Kennedy.

'Yeah, huge,' said her female companion, clearly underwhelmed.

'This main room must sit nearly two hundred people.'

'Yeah.'

'Have you noticed the guards?'

'Noticed them, one of them practically touched me up on the way in. I'll be speaking to the agency when I get back, double time or not.'

'Have you seen the way they guard each entry to the main hall, and they are stationed at each of the doors in the house. At the bottom of the main staircase, by the toilets,' said Kennedy, ignoring her companion.

'Yeah,' said the woman, momentarily coming to life. 'Now you mention it, it's a bit weird.'

'I wonder if they're armed,' said Kennedy.

'Guns, you mean?' said the woman, panicked.

'Just wondered,' said Matilda. She paused, signalling that she thought they were carrying. 'I'm only kidding. They wouldn't be allowed, would they?'

Tillman was listening intently and glanced over at Lambert at the mention of guns. 'We've two armed response units ready,' he whispered, as if it would provide Lambert with some comfort.

As Kennedy continued her running commentary, Lambert logged onto The System and began scanning the copious notes from the case, desperate to find a link to Neil Barnes. He looked at profiles for Charles Robinson, and Noel Whitfield. He scanned through other names. Prue McKenzie, Moira Sackville's best friend. Sandra Levinson, the librarian Moira had worked with. Lucy Marshall, Laura Dempsey's colleague from the hospital. Mia Helmer, Eustace Sackville's boss at the newspaper.

When nothing clicked, he began searching the uploaded files of the orphans and children from St Matthew's. Photos of Elaine Jacobson and the other lost souls played before him, including Melissa Brady who Kennedy had interviewed.

A picture of Neil Barnes appeared on the screen. The Watcher as a ten-year-old, his life about to change irrevocably by the death of Elaine Jacobson, the sister he never had.

In his ear, Kennedy was talking to one of the security guards. 'Who are you expecting, the royal family?' she asked.

'Please leave me to my job, ma'am,' said the man, with the patient authority of a trained soldier.

An absurd notion came to Lambert as he listened. The voice of the soldier reminded him of the authority he'd heard from another of the people he'd interviewed. It wasn't the voice itself, more the general cadence and speech pattern.

He uploaded the file of the former police officer DS Lindsay. He recalled the meeting in Leicester Square, the dignified way Lindsay described his troubled time in the force. The corruption he'd witnessed first-hand with his superior, DI Lennox. Like many officers his age, Lindsay had worked in the armed forces before joining the force. He was a former Royal Marine who'd spent five years in active service before returning to civilian life.

Lambert scrolled through the man's records, only to reach a blank aged eighteen. He'd enrolled with the Navy on his eighteenth birthday, but there was no record, at least not present, of his life prior to this date. Lambert called Devlin. 'I want you to find out everything you can on Lindsay before he joined the Navy. I need school records, ideally a copy of his birth certificate. And get a car to his place immediately. I want him in for questioning, but be discreet and polite about it.'

It was a long shot, and it was possible he was being guided by thoughts of the Souljacker case, but at this point there was nothing to lose.

Tillman signalled him outside. Lambert's eyes took a couple of seconds to adjust to the sunlight as Tillman pulled the side door shut.

'What the hell is going on?' asked Tillman.

'I could ask you the same thing.'

The heat of the van had clearly got to Tillman. His tight fitting shirt was soaked with perspiration. 'I seem to spend half my working life giving you the benefit of the doubt, Lambert. This Neil Barnes thing, you really buy it?'

'What's not to buy? It explains everything, revenge killings mirroring Elaine Jacobson's apparent suicide.'

'What about Jacobson's family?'

'Orphaned from birth.'

'What about the original owners of the children's home? The guardians or carers or whatever the fuck they were?'

'All accounted for, mainly no longer with us.'

'And you think Barnes wants Blake next?'

'It would be the natural conclusion.'

'But if he is following the same MO then he will go for Blake's family.'

'I believe so, but maybe he'll single out Blake for special attention.'

'Jesus, this sort of shit just follows you about, Lambert. I thought this would be a simple murder case, now we have multiple victims and a dead policeman.'

Lambert went to protest, the policeman's death was nothing to do with his investigation, but the energy had left him.

'You think Kennedy's in danger?' asked Tillman, a subtle change to his voice.

'What's going on between you two, Glenn?'

Tillman shook his head, resigned. 'I should have known you would find out.'

'It's not just me. Walker wants to report you.'

'Don't worry about that jumped-up prick. I have enough dirt on him.'

'Be careful, Glenn.'

'Don't worry about me. What was that you were saying to Devlin?'

'Lindsay. He was Lennox's junior officer. We have no family information on him prior to him turning eighteen and joining the Navy. I don't think anything will come of it but I'm sure if we find Neil Barnes, we find the killer, and Lindsay may know more than he's letting on.'

The van door opened. Harrogate stuck out his head. 'Blake has left his hotel. He should be here in the next twenty to thirty minutes.'

Chapter 56

There was a shift of atmosphere within the house. One of the agency staff summoned all the workers together into the kitchen and informed them that Blake and his wife were due within the next thirty minutes. The party was supposed to be a surprise, but until Blake's arrival the guests were to be served drinks. Matilda was handed a tray of champagne flutes and sent out into the dining area.

She listened in to the conversations, desperate for a sign that her role there was not pointless. No one sounded concerned about the heightened security. They were too busy enjoying the free champagne.

Blake's children were out in the hallway, growing increasingly excited by the imminent arrival of their parents. She knew their names from her files. Jessica, aged fifteen. Mitchell, aged twelve. Josh, aged seven, and Melody aged five. All four glowed with anticipation. The children were oblivious to their father's crimes, at least for now, and for a second Matilda felt like an intruder gate-crashing a joyous family moment.

One of the security staff tore her from her regret. 'You, back in there,' said the man. From the files, she recognised him as Atkinson, Blake's head of security.

'Sorry, got lost,' she said.

Atkinson kept his eyes on her as she returned to the main

hall. She felt his gaze lingering as she turned away and served more champagne to the guests, who treated her as if she were invisible. 'I guess Mr Blake will soon be here,' she said to her colleague back in the kitchen area, for the benefit of her real colleagues who were hopefully still listening.

'Sooner this is over, the better,' said the woman. 'These guys give me the creeps. Anyone even said thank you, yet?'

'Nope,' said Matilda. 'I wonder what this Blake guy does. I presume all the guests are family and friends. No one looks out of place.'

The woman looked at her as if she was strange. 'Not sure what you mean. Anyway,' she said, taking another tray of champagne flutes.

Matilda knew her team would understand. There was no sign of the Croatians and it was increasingly unlikely they would be appearing now. She took one of the trays, half champagne flutes, half orange juice and returned to the main area. The security team looked tense. Atkinson was checking each exit point personally, nodding his approval to the guards. The tension was due to Blake's arrival. Matilda presumed it would be the time the Croatians would attack, if that was what they had planned, with Blake out in the open.

With Atkinson's attention on the guards, Matilda placed her tray down and snuck out into the hallway. Passing one of the guards, she kept her pace steady, her gaze forward as if she belonged in the area. The guard hesitated and continued walking.

Blake's children were by the door, still excited. Checking no one was watching, Matilda snuck upstairs. If she was stopped, she would say she was looking for the bathroom. She whispered details of her location to the team. At the top of the stairs she turned left, noticing the back of a guard situated outside a room to her right. She skipped along the landing until she was out of sight.

She checked the doors as she edged along the corridor, each was locked. From the window she could see the large driveway which led to the house's entrance. It was still light outside, the sky clouded. 'Two guards on the driveway, two by the gate,' she whispered. 'I can't tell if they're armed.

She heard footsteps from the stairway and continued along the corridor, trying each door as she moved, ready to use her search for a bathroom as an excuse. She rounded another corner and was presented with a second set of stairs which she duly took, the sound of a radio coming from the landing above. She wanted to slip out of her shoes, to dim the sound as they hit the polished wood of the stairs, but it would look too suspicious if she was caught. 'Oh, a second set of stairs,' she whispered, as if surprised by the development.

No one was behind her and she edged to the top of the stairs peering down the second, smaller corridor. The sound was coming from a room a few metres to her right. She stepped onto the landing, thankful for the lush carpeting. Pushing herself against the wall, she sidestepped across the corridor until she reached the entrance to the room.

The radio blasted out hits from the eighties. Beneath the prominent sound she heard the hum of electricity. She had to see what was in the room but knew one more step would reveal her location. She looked behind her. Convinced she was not being watched, she poked her head around the entrance to the room, ready to tell whoever was there that she was lost.

As she'd expected, the room was a security centre. A guard sat watching a wall full of small television screens. His back was to her, and from her vantage point she could see the numerous locations of the house: the gated entrance with its two guards, the driveway and entrance to the house proper, numerous views of inside the house, including the kitchen and at least five separate bathrooms. Nowhere was spared, and Matilda marvelled at how paranoid Blake must be to have every inch of the house under surveillance. Even the children's bedrooms were being monitored.

She was about to retreat when something caught her eye in the banks of televisions to the guard's left. The image on the screen kept on changing from inside to outside the building. It was the outside she recognised.

The guard swivelled on his chair to face her, his face painted with a smile. 'I've been watching you snoop, little lady. You think you're going to be able to steal from us?'

Matilda froze, happy to be thought of as merely a potential thief. She stepped out so she was facing the man. 'No, of course not. I was just looking for the bathroom.'

'Yeah, right,' said the guard, as a second guard placed a hand on her shoulder.

'Where are you taking me?' she said, as the second guard held her shoulder and arm with a fierce pinch.

'Somewhere you can't cause any trouble.'

'Right, I'm going home,' she said, as he guided her down the stairs to the first floor landing.

'Not yet, you're not,' said the man. He walked her along the first floor landing to a room which was being guarded by a third guard. 'Another one for you,' said Guard Two.

Guard Three stepped aside, as Guard Two guided Matilda in the room with a gentle push.

Another one of the agency staff was inside the room, sitting on a king-sized bed. 'What are you in here for?' said Matilda, as the bedroom door was slammed shut.

'They caught me looking?' said the girl, who couldn't be much more than eighteen. She was leant against the headboard of the bed, her legs pulled up tight.

'Have they done anything to you?'

'No, why? You don't think they're…'

'No, no. Sorry, didn't mean to give you a scare. They're not going to risk anything like that.'

'What did you do?' asked the girl, lowering her legs so they were stretched out on the bed.

'They caught me looking as well.' She began speaking for the team. 'So, I guess we're on the first floor in a guest bedroom. I turned right at the top of the stairs, and it was three doors down.'

'Um, I guess so,' said the girl.

'There's at least one guard outside, and just the two of us in the room.'

The girl looked at her as if she was mad. 'You planning to escape or something?'

Matilda tried the window. 'Window is locked and has three steel bars blocking entrance.'

She sat on the bed thinking, hoping she was still in radio contact.

'Do you think we'll still get paid?' asked the girl.

Chapter 57

Lambert sat in the van listening to Kennedy. Worried looks were exchanged between the four men.

'We should get her out,' said Tillman.

'Why? They only think she was stealing,' said Harrogate.

Lambert couldn't remember a time when he'd ever heard a junior officer talk that way to Tillman. Even though the man was from another team, he was pushing his luck. It wasn't the words necessarily, but the way they were spoken.

'Listen, son, you ever speak to me like that again and I'll drag you outside this van and teach you not to. Understand?'

Harrogate shrugged his shoulders, whilst Tyler studied his laptop screen pretending he wasn't there. Tillman was a big man, but he could move fast when needed. Before Lambert knew what was happening, Tillman had Harrogate in a strangle hold.

'You understand now, boy?'

Harrogate was turning purple. Tyler glanced at Lambert in a pathetic attempt to get him to intervene.

'One of my team is danger and I'll make a decision as to the jeopardy, do you understand?'

Harrogate moved his head up and down as much as he was able.

Tillman let him go, driving his face into the side of the van.

'Right, let's all calm down,' said Tyler.

Tillman sat, his chest heaving in and out, his eyes not leaving Harrogate.

'You're right, it's your call Glenn. However, I tend to agree that her cover hasn't been blown. If we go in now, they'll know we've been staking them and the Croatians won't show,' said Tyler.

'They're not going to show anyway,' said Lambert.

The four men sat in the van, muted. Lambert still had his earphones on and was listening to Kennedy talk to her fellow captive. In front of him, he was studying The System. Something was just out of reach. He scanned the pictures of the guests at the Blake household, the Croatian gang members, then switched his attention to the former residents of St Matthew's. He wasn't exactly sure what he was looking for; with nothing else to cling onto, he hoped the randomness of the search would result in something.

'We'll wait,' said Tillman. 'But I want our response teams ready. The first word of danger from Kennedy and we're in.'

Devlin called. 'Sir, Lindsay is in custody. Nottingham Central. By all accounts he's not happy.'

'Are they going to speak to him?'

'I've prepped their team. I'll be there on conference call to fill in any details.'

'Good work, Devlin. Keep me updated.'

A picture of Neil Barnes appeared on his screen. Lambert froze the image. 'Who the hell are you,' he mouthed. He zoomed in on the image, studying every pixel for a clue. The boy's hazel eyes, a faint zig zag of blood on the white of his right eye, the slight curve of his lower lip, the freckles on his cheeks and forehead, a slight nick on his left eyebrow. Would any of these characteristics have stayed with him into adulthood?

'I discovered an office full of television screens, that's how they found us,' said Kennedy, whispering to her companion. 'They've probably got this room monitored, so be careful what you say.'

'You think they're listening to us,' said the girl.

'Probably.'

'Sick bastards. This isn't on. I'm definitely talking to the agency.'

'Me too,' said Kennedy. 'Something weird is going on here. If it didn't sound crazy, I'd say they were locking everyone in rather than keeping people out.'

Lambert stopped, pushed his earpiece into his ear and lifted his hand into the air to signal the other officers.

'What do you mean?' said the girl.

'Think about it. Do you think you'd be able to walk out? They don't want us working here but they haven't sent us home. It's like they don't want anyone to leave.'

Lambert heard Kennedy sigh. She was talking directly to him. 'I don't think it's only this house they're monitoring. I think they're watching other places as well. I think they know where people are.'

'What?' said the girl.

'What is she talking about?' asked Tyler.

'Lambert?' said Tillman.

Lambert's hand was still held in the air. He was staring at the picture of Neil Barnes, trying to reconcile what Kennedy was saying. Could it really be that simple? It was so obvious that he hadn't considered it before.

On The System he typed in a name. The name of a man he'd met on two occasions. A picture appeared on the screen. Lambert pinched the screen, zooming in on the man's left eyebrow. If he hadn't been looking for it, he wouldn't have made out the mark. It was the slightest discrepancy, the legacy of a childhood scar.

'We need to stop Blake reaching the house,' said Lambert.

Chapter 58

The van fell silent.

'Now,' screamed Lambert. 'Where is he? Pull him over without the lights if possible.'

'What's this about?' said Harrogate.

'Just do it,' said Tillman.

Tyler nodded at Harrogate. 'He's on West End Lane, West Hampstead. We have an unmarked car following him,' said the DS.

'Get them to head the car off. Use the lights if necessary.'

'Want to tell me what this is about?' asked Tillman.

'Give me a second,' said Lambert, who was scrolling through the notes on the man he believed was Neil Barnes. 'Jesus,' he said, handing the file to Tillman.

'Will Atkinson? This is Blake's head of security,' said Tillman.

'Yes.' Lambert pressed a button and the screen split. 'I believe he's also Neil Barnes. Side by side, the resemblance was more pronounced but Lambert still pointed out the eyebrow scar.'

'How did you make the connection?'

'Something Kennedy said. It all makes sense now. Atkinson joined the forces aged eighteen. No school history. No history at all prior to eighteen from what I've seen. He could have easily changed his name at some point.'

Tillman showed the file to Tyler, who looked nonplussed.

'The focus has changed,' said Tillman.

'Success,' said Harrogate. 'We have the car. What now?'

'Get Blake and his wife here. Glenn, we're going to need armed response and emergency services in place,' said Lambert.

'What do you think he has in mind?'

'I think he planned to kill Blake's family tonight. It's thirty years to the day Elaine Jacobson's body was found. I believe he was waiting for Blake to arrive, and he was going to start killing. Kennedy says the place is like a fortress. He wants everyone to watch.'

'And now?'

'Now, we get everyone in place and wait.'

Lambert stepped out of the van, surprised by the light covering of fog over the common. He still had one earphone in and was listening to Kennedy.

'How many screens were there?' asked Kennedy's companion in his ear.

Tillman and Tyler had followed him outside the van and were both on their phones arranging their teams. Harrogate was still inside, no doubt smarting from the change of plans.

'At least thirty. It wasn't just this house though. I saw some other images,' said Kennedy.

'Really, like what?

'A police station I know, a house in Beckenham.'

'Beckenham. How would you know that?'

'I have a friend who used to live there.'

Lambert was already dialling Sarah May. 'Sarah, we've identified the Watcher. I think he may have the house under surveillance. I'm sending a team over to the house. Don't tell me where you are in case the call is being monitored but is everything okay?'

'Yes, everything fine here. Sophie and Jane are safe.'

'You've read this guy's background?' said Tillman, once he'd hung up.

'Impressive, isn't it?'

'Initially an explosions expert, latterly head of surveillance.'

'Doesn't exactly bode well,' said Lambert.

Atkinson had left the army ten years ago and formed his own security firm. From what Lambert could discover he'd been working for Blake for the last five years, after the mysterious disappearance of his existing head of security. Lambert marvelled at the level of planning Atkinson must have put into the project: securing the position as head of security and waiting all these years to enact his revenge, on the anniversary of Elaine Jacobson's death.

'Blake should be here in five minutes,' said Harrogate, stepping out of the van.

'We're positioning teams near the house,' said Tillman.

'Keep them out of sight,' said Lambert. 'He's capable of anything.'

'You think his team know what he has planned?' asked Tillman, taking him aside.

'They were all in the forces with him. Most have been working for him for ten years. They'll do what they're told. I'm sure there is a pay-off involved.'

In the distance, Lambert heard the screech of tyres as an unmarked car approached. It pulled up outside the van, two plain clothes officers leaving the car.

'Mr and Mrs Blake are in the back, sir,' said one of the men to Tyler.

Lambert interjected. 'Have you told them why you stopped them?'

'No. And they're not pleased.'

'Let them out.'

Blake edged out of the car, holding his hand out for his wife. 'I might have fucking known,' he said, on seeing Lambert.

'Mr Blake. Mrs Blake. Chief Superintendent Tillman and Chief Superintendent Tyler,' said Lambert, refusing to introduce Harrogate.

'Jesus, I'm honoured. You've got the big guns out to stop me attending my own surprise party. Wonderful. You don't half hold a grudge, Lambert.'

'This has nothing to do with a grudge. You need to follow me into the van. I need to show you something.'

Tyler and Harrogate wanted to follow them inside the van, but Lambert knew emotions would be running high. He could sense the pent up anger in both men. Being alone in the cramped confines of the van would be one step too far. All it would take would be the mention of Sawyer, and either would be liable to pounce. 'Sir, I think it best if I speak to Mr Blake alone,' he said, giving Tyler the option.

Tyler was taking in short breaths through his nose, his gaze stuck on Blake. 'We'll speak later,' he said to the man.

'Christ, what's his problem?' asked Blake once they were inside the van.

Lambert could still hear Kennedy in his left ear though she wasn't saying much save for the odd comment to her companion. He opened the iPad and showed Blake a picture of Will Atkinson.

'Yes. I know my own head of security.'

Lambert scrolled through to an image of Neil Barnes. 'Atkinson as a boy.'

Blake shrugged. 'I haven't got time for this, Lambert. I've a party to attend. Now if you don't mind.'

Lambert held Blake's shoulder and pushed down hard. It was only then he felt how insubstantial the man was. His suit was padded, the body beneath almost skeletal, devoid of muscle. 'I don't think your paths ever crossed, but Atkinson was known as Neil Barnes then. He was a boy of ten. He lived at St Matthew's. You know St Matthew's, don't you Curtis?'

'What is this?' said Blake.

'Neil Barnes was friends with Elaine Jacobson. You remember her, don't you?'

'I don't know what you're talking about.'

'I'm not looking for a confession, Blake. I know you used to run the girls from that home. I may not be able to prove it but I know you did it. Will Atkinson knows it as well. All those years ago he went to people for some help, help to stop you. DI Lennox, Laura Dempsey, Eustace Sackville, all authority figures who failed him. You know what he did to all those people, Blake?'

Blake began to shake, the colour drained from his face. His skin was almost translucent, the whites of his eyes clouded over in blood. 'The Watcher?'

'He has your house locked down. His team have every exit secured. Are they armed, Blake?'

'Jesus, the children.'

'Will they be armed, Curtis?'

'Yes they'll be fucking armed, of course they're armed.'

'Will they follow Atkinson?'

A look of fight had returned to Blake's features. 'I knew it was a mistake. We did our checks on him and the team. Exemplary record, but I knew it was a risk. He has the children?'

'We believe so. I need to know everything you know about the security operation. Any weaknesses, especially anything Atkinson wouldn't know about.'

Blake shook his head. 'He designed everything. The surveillance, the traps.'

'The traps?'

'What does it matter now? Some of the area is mined.'

Lambert stared at the man. 'You're serious?'

'The man's an explosives expert. Oh, Christ, I can only imagine.'

The van door opened, and Tillman squeezed himself into the back. Lambert relayed the information.

'Fuck me. What the hell were you thinking?' said Tillman, his voice reverberating around the interior of the van. He opened the van door. 'Harrogate.'

'Sir?'

'Get this fucker out of here and start working through all the details about his security operation.'

'What about my children?' asked Blake, as Tillman dragged him out of the van.

'What is it, Curtis? What's that about the children?' screamed Blake's wife as Harrogate led him away.

As if in answer, Lambert's phone rang.

Unknown number.

'Hello, Atkinson,' said Lambert.

Chapter 59

The line went quiet. Lambert waited, Tillman, Tyler and Harrogate staring at him. A breeze had picked up, and a chill ran through him as he waited for the Watcher to respond.

'Congratulations. You worked it out.' His voice was the same as ever, the accent-free, measured tone, a variation on the way Atkinson had spoken when Lambert had first met him at Blake's house.

'What do you want, Atkinson?'

'I believe you have something which belongs to me.'

Lambert was not in the mood for games. His priority was the safety of everyone in Blake's house, especially Blake's children and Matilda Kennedy. 'Blake is here, yes.'

'I warned you not to interfere, Lambert. Didn't I tell you that at the beginning?'

Tillman, who was listening along with the other officers, shot Lambert an accusing look.

'What do you want, Neil?'

'I am going to tell you what's going to happen, Lambert. Negotiation time is over.'

Lambert ignored him, refusing to give away control of the conversation.

'The house is secure, though I think you already know that.

We have Blake's children here. No one is aware of the situation yet, but that will soon change.'

Lambert looked over at Blake, who was arguing with his wife.

'You there, Lambert? This is important.'

'I'm here.'

'Nothing gets pass me, Lambert. Do you think for a moment that I hadn't spotted your DS today? That was a rather pathetic attempt don't you think? Especially after what I did to your last undercover officer.'

Tyler stepped towards him, nodding frantically.

'You killed DS Sawyer?'

'I've known about him for the last two years. He was getting close so I eliminated him. Did you think it was the Croatians?'

'You need to give yourself up, Atkinson. I know your story and I understand your reasons but this has to end here.'

Atkinson laughed. 'You know my story? You understand? How did you respond when people told you they understood about your daughter? You think they understood? Truly empathised?'

'No, I guess not. Tell me, Neil. Tell me the truth.'

Atkinson sighed. 'Elaine was the only family I ever had. That's all you need to know,' he said, his voice perfectly measured as if he was forcing back his emotions.

'Hurting all those people won't bring her back, Neil. I do understand that.'

'I'm not planning on hurting anyone other than those who deserve it. You send Blake and his wife over here, and no one else will get hurt.'

'I can't do that, Neil.'

'Then I am going to start executing his family one by one. And if you're planning on sending in the two response units I can see on my screens, be warned that the house is loaded with explosives. You've read my files, I take it?'

The scene was spiralling out of control. The guests would soon be getting restless, and it wouldn't be long before they realised something was wrong. 'You need to give me something, Neil.'

'I'm going to give you one option and one only. Send Blake and his wife over now, and I will release the youngest child. The others stay with me.'

'Come on, Neil, that's not going to happen. If you want Blake, then send all the children out.'

'He has to suffer as I did. Five minutes, or the oldest one dies.'

'Fuck,' said Lambert, as Atkinson hung up.

'We need a negotiator here,' said Tyler.

'There's no time for that,' said Lambert. 'Do we have marksmen with eyes on the house?'

'Harrogate, get that sorted now,' said Tyler.

'Would you like to tell me what the hell is going on,' said Blake, approaching him.

'I'll tell you what is happening,' said Tillman, moving towards the man. 'Because of you, a house full of people, including my officer, and your children, are in severe danger.'

Blake tensed his facial muscles and kept moving towards Lambert. 'What does he want?'

'He wants you and your wife in the house,' said Lambert.

'I bet he fucking does.'

'He offered an exchange.'

'What?'

'Your youngest, Melody.'

Blake bent over at the name of his youngest child. 'Christ,' he muttered.

Despite everything he'd done, Lambert felt a stab of compassion for the man.

'The other three?'

Lambert shook his head.

Blake stood straight. 'I'll do it but Mary's not coming. Tell him that and we've got a deal.'

The man walked over to his wife, and told her what was happening. She looked at him as if he'd made an inappropriate joke, then began screaming, punching and kicking Blake, who stood still as the blows rained down on him.

'Long range snipers in place. We have eyes on the front and back doors,' said Harrogate.

Atkinson would have planned for every eventuality. They wouldn't be left an open shot.

'We're going to send him in?' said Lambert to Tillman. It was formed as a question out of procedure, but both men knew it was a statement.

Blake's wife had stopped kicking and was allowing her husband to hold her. Blake whispered something, and she tried to cling onto him as he moved away.

'Take care of her, officer,' said Lambert, to the driver of the unmarked car which had stopped Blake.

'Let's go,' said Blake.

'I'll take the car,' said Lambert. 'Blake, you sit in the back.'

'We'll follow in the van,' said Tillman.

'You're going to give me a gun, right?' said Blake.

Lambert shook his head.

'You can't let me go in there unarmed.'

'What do you think you're going to do with a gun against a team of soldiers?'

'If I can get to Atkinson, I could end it.'

'It's too late for that, Blake.'

Atkinson called as they were approaching Blake's house. 'We have a deal?'

Lambert pulled the car over. 'Blake has agreed to take the place of his daughter. The wife stays here. Let the girl go. Tell her to walk to the main gate and Blake will meet her.'

Atkinson didn't respond and for a second Lambert feared he'd hung up. 'If anyone else follows Blake down the driveway then Kennedy will be executed with immediate effect, followed by the Blake children. There will be no second chances.'

'Understood.'

Atkinson hung up. As Lambert stepped out of the car, he heard a struggle on the other end of his earpiece.

'You, here,' said a voice to Kennedy.

'You're armed,' said Kennedy, for Lambert's benefit. She sounded calm and in control, which was a small comfort.

'She's wired,' said a second voice. 'Find it.'

'No,' said Kennedy. It sounded as if she was struggling with one of the guards. Seconds later, the line went dead.

'Shit,' said Lambert.

'The girl has been released,' said Harrogate who'd left the van along with Tillman and Tyler. 'We have eyes on her now, making her way slowly up the drive.'

'You better get going, Blake.'

'Give me a gun, for pity's sake.'

'We'll do what we can,' said Lambert. 'Go.'

Blake hesitated before moving off into the distance. Lambert followed twenty paces behind, making sure Blake didn't run away. He kept to the shadows and was able to watch as Blake punched in the key code to the steel gates.

'Daddy?' came a voice, confused and distant.

Blake bent down and kissed his daughter, and whispered something in her ear.

'Mummy,' she said, leaving the entrance to the house, the gate sliding shut.

Lambert moved towards the girl who stopped, frozen to the spot. 'Melody,' he said, softly. 'My name is Michael. I'm a policeman and a friend of your daddy's.' He showed her his warrant card, as if that would convince the girl. 'Your mummy is waiting for you. Can you come with me?'

Blake's face was pressed up against the steel gates. 'It's okay, baby. You go with the policeman.'

The girl took Lambert's hand, as Blake turned away and began walking towards the house.

'Eyes on Blake,' said Harrogate, as Lambert handed the girl over to one of the plain clothes officers.

'Blake's approaching the door. Door opening,' said Harrogate.

'We've just sent a man to his death,' said Tyler, pointing out the obvious.

Lambert's response was cancelled out by the roar of an explosion in Blake's house. Lambert shielded his ears from the deafening sound, as the heat and smoke from the explosion filled the night air.

Chapter 60

The blast was enough to send Lambert falling to the ground. He pushed himself up only for a second and third blast to knock him over again.

Tillman, Tyler and Harrogate had followed him and were scattered across the street. 'Everyone okay,' asked Tillman, dragging Lambert to his feet. 'All response units in now,' he screamed into his radio.

'Are you okay, Glenn?' asked Lambert. His superior's eyes were sunken and devoid of animation. He was talking into his radio but was acting on impulse. 'I think you may have shock.'

'Bullshit. Let's go.'

They stopped at the entrance to Blake's house, too stunned to move. One half of the reinforced gates had been completely blown away by the blast, the second half was hanging on its hinges. In front of them, Blake's house was lit up like a bonfire. As they watched, the left side of the house crumbled away, the manic flames clinging to the building, fading as a thick swarm of black smoke billowed out towards them.

'Matilda,' said Tillman, preparing to move towards the house.

Lambert held out his arm. Even from this distance, the heat was incredible. Sweat poured from him, his skin close to blistering. 'We can't,' he said, as the first of the fire engines arrived, a benefit from having the emergency services on standby.

Before he had a chance to stop him, Tillman was making a dash for it, following the path of the fire engine. Lambert followed behind, his movements slow and heavy, his lungs struggling with the fog of smoke which clouded his vision, hot tears streaming down his face.

It had to be a mistake. Atkinson wanted Blake to suffer. He was the Watcher. He wanted to execute Blake's family before his eyes, wanted to watch as Blake watched, wanted to find some solace in his brutal revenge. The explosion would not have satisfied his bloodlust. It was either a mistake, or somehow he'd managed to escape with Blake before the explosion was set off.

'Try to secure the perimeter,' he said into the radio, his arms flailing at the smoke which was getting hotter. 'Atkinson may have an escape route planned.' No one responded, and in the visionless gloom Lambert couldn't tell if the radio was even working. 'Tillman,' he shouted, his words swallowed by the smoke, the thundering sound of the flames climbing the building.

The piercing light of the fire engine guided him forwards until he was in the courtyard in front of the house. Jets of water streamed into the front of the house, soaked up by the flames as if they were fuel. Some of the party goers had escaped the house and were milling around the front of the house like the undead. Paramedics were on the scene and were chasing after the guests, attending to the silent ones first.

Lambert located a fire chief, barking orders from the side of one of the engines. 'What are we looking at?' he asked, showing his warrant card.

'Front of the house is fucked. Very unstable. We have to

get the survivors out. A third of the top floor has collapsed. I haven't seen anything like this before. This is a staged explosion. You need to get everyone out of here.'

Lambert scanned the figures, desperate for a sign of Kennedy or Tillman. He couldn't leave now. He thanked the officer, and moved off into the gloom. More engines, ambulances and police squads were arriving. He moved around the right side of the house, his skin burning, his nostrils fighting the acrid smell of the smoke, each movement laboured, until he was at the back of the house. A secondary fire team was already in place, a team of medics tending to another herd of survivors. 'Kennedy,' he shouted into the air, making his way through the wounded and dead.

A man lay on the ground, wrapped in a foil blanket, two medics trying their best to sedate him, his face a bubbling patch of blister, his skin blackened beyond recognition. A woman had her arm around a younger woman who was missing her left hand. Lambert bent down and felt the woman's neck for a pulse. He lifted her head. Her eyes were lifeless and had been for some time. Similar scenes played out all around him. He wanted to stop but had to find Kennedy and Tillman.

He stopped two uniformed officers. 'You seen Tillman?' he asked.

'No, sir.'

A group of fire officers left a side entrance, each wearing a mask, one carrying a body. 'DCI Lambert. Is it safe to go in there?'

'If you go in there, you won't be coming back,' said one of the officers, dragging off his mask. 'The smoke will get you, if something doesn't collapse on you.'

'One of my team was in there. She was locked in a bedroom on the first floor the last time we heard from her.'

The fireman shook his head. 'I'm sorry, the upper floors are pretty much gone. We'll know more when the main fire is out but it doesn't look great.'

'What did he say?'

The fireman walked off as Lambert turned to face Tillman. His shirt was untucked, and ripped at the sleeve. His eyes poked through a coating of ash, devoid of emotion.

'Come on, Glenn, you need to be checked out,' said Lambert, leading his boss to one of the ambulances.

Tillman shrugged him off. 'We've found one of Atkinson's team. Tyler's interrogating him now.'

Lambert had lost all track of time since the explosion, the scene at Blake's house dreamlike, and he questioned his own mental wellbeing.

'From what he's told us, the explosion was not part of the plan. He thinks most of the men were in the house and were killed.'

'Atkinson?'

'No sign, yet. As soon as that main fire is out, we'll start counting the bodies.' Tillman spoke with his usual professionalism, whilst looking as if he wasn't really there.

'I'm going to check the grounds at the back of the house. 'You should really see someone.'

'I think they've got enough work to do. Come on,' said Tillman, leading the way, moving as if against some invisible force.

The glow from the fire lit the grounds to the back of the house. Party goers sat on the grass, the same distant look he'd seen on Tillman etched onto their faces.

The ground stretched into the distance, a line of trees marking the border. Lambert switched on his torch, the beam of light eating into the darkness, the land vast and vacant. He scanned across the perimeter, moving forward until he caught the outline of a figure who looked as if he was scrambling over some kind of fencing. 'There,' he said to Tillman, pointing to the figure.

'Let's go,' said Tillman, 'there must be a reason he's trying to leave.'

They inched across the grass, the torch shining in front of them. Even with the help of the light, they still stumbled in the grass, which was pitted with holes, Lambert trying not to think about the mines Blake had claimed were planted in the ground.

'He's still there,' said Tillman, his breathing coming in rapid expulsions of air. The figure was still climbing the fence, as if he was stuck or was taking a rest. 'You go ahead, I'm gone.'

Lambert tried to run, but his lungs were not functioning properly. His limbs ached, heavier than he could remember. He ran as if he was in a nightmare trying to escape a foe, the normal laws of physics not applying.

The escapee looked as if he was having the same problem. Lambert closed in on the target still balanced on the fence. The man was caught in some netting, and was shaking his left leg frantically, trying to escape.

Lambert stopped twenty yards from the figure, and shone his torch. The figure turned to face the beam, an animal caught in the headlights. 'Atkinson?' asked Lambert, trying not to recoil.

What was left of Atkinson snarled back at him. His lips had been burnt clean off, as had half his face. It was a wonder he was still moving. Even from this distance, Lambert could see his revealed gums, the hint of jaw bone beneath melting flesh. Somehow, he pulled his left leg free, and fell over the fence.

'Don't move,' said Lambert, running to the fence, a dart of adrenaline driving him on.

Atkinson was up and moving away. His shirt had been burnt off his back, bits of it stuck to his flesh like an absurd collage. Lambert didn't have to run to catch up. The man was moving out of pure instinct, and wouldn't last long. 'Stop moving, Neil. We can get you some help.'

Atkinson collapsed onto the ground. His trousers were ripped at the leg, a gash of six or seven inches on his right thigh. 'I told you we were alike,' he said, coughing, his voice distorted almost beyond recognition.

Lambert took out his pepper spray and cuffs, though Atkinson had more chance of dying at the moment than escaping. 'We're not alike.'

'We're both here. Both alone. Both with no one.'

Lambert loomed over the collapsed figure. The hair on Atkinson's head had been singed, large bubbles had formed on his scalp. 'Where's Kennedy?'

'We'd moved her before the explosion. It wasn't meant to happen. Believe it or not, I didn't want anyone innocent hurt.' Atkinson's laugh turned into a rasping cough as he spat out a lump of blood soaked mucus onto the ground. 'That can't be good.'

'All you've done is harm innocent people, Atkinson. Where did you move her?'

'They weren't innocent, you must see that.'

It was pointless trying to reason with him. He radioed for medical assistance. 'Where is she?'

'I don't know. I told you, the team went to move her when I knew you had Blake.'

'Blake's family?'

'All gone, I hope. They were at the front of the house where the explosives were set.'

'Why did you have explosives there in the first place?'

'For Blake, at the end, once he'd suffered what I suffered. She was only fourteen, you know, when he first made her work for him. I was eight. She was my sister. She looked after me from the first day I arrived.'

'Didn't Blake remember you?'

'How would he? I was ten when she died. He didn't get involved in any of the dirty business himself. I only saw him once at the home, but I remembered his face. You know today's the day?'

'Thirty years since Elaine Jacobson committed suicide. It doesn't explain your actions. Moira Sackville, the Dempsey family, they weren't to blame.'

Atkinson was shivering. 'Eustace and Laura can have a lifetime to consider that, can't they.'

The medical team appeared, accompanied by Tillman. 'They found Kennedy. I went back,' he said.

One look at Tillman was enough to tell him the news wasn't good. Animation had returned to the man's eyes, his focus on Atkinson.

Lambert studied Tillman as the paramedics worked on Atkinson. 'Where is she?'

'They've taken her to A and E. Extensive burns. She may have lost an eye.'

'You should go. I can process Atkinson.'

Tillman clenched his hand. 'He's not leaving here, Michael.'

Lambert had been here before. Years ago, he'd rescued Tillman from a group who'd held him captive for two days. After being rescued, Tillman had taken Lambert's gun and executed the remaining captor who had tortured him during the ordeal. Lambert had covered for him then, but would be unable to protect the man now if he tried something. 'You're carrying?' said Lambert.

'Excuse the paramedics,' said Tillman.

The paramedics had strapped Atkinson to a stretcher. 'You're not thinking, Glenn. Atkinson won't survive the night anyway, and if he does his life is over. You try something now, and he'd have ruined your life as well.'

Tillman ignored him, the shock had taken him over. He reached inside his jacket and withdrew his gun.

The paramedics had their backs turned, treating Atkinson. As Tillman pointed the weapon, Atkinson grinned a lipless smile through his breathing mask.

Lambert didn't know if Tillman would go through with it but couldn't take the risk. He sprayed Tillman directly in the eyes with the pepper spray, Tillman falling to the ground with a scream. As he fell, Lambert took the gun from him and slid it inside his jacket before the paramedics could see.

'His pepper spray has gone off,' said Lambert to one of the paramedics. The woman exchanged a look with her colleague before tending to Tillman.

Lambert bent down as the woman applied cooling liquid to Tillman's eyes. 'You look after him. I'll help your colleague get the other man back to the ambulance,' said Lambert.

Atkinson looked disappointed as Lambert lifted the stretcher.

Atkinson watched him all the way as they carried his body through the fields at the back of Blake's ruin of a house. It was hard to imagine the man had once been a ten-year-old boy, but lying on the stretcher, his face deformed beyond recognition, Lambert caught a glimpse of that wasted innocence as the man looked at him for one final time before closing his eyes forever.

Acknowledgements

Thanks again to so many people who have helped in the writing of *Dead Lucky*:

The whole team at HQ Digital for their support and encouragement. Special thanks to my wonderful editor, Charlotte Mursell, for her insight and unending support.

All the amazing bloggers and reviewers for promoting *Dead Eyed*. Too many to name, but sincere thanks for each and every review. So many great blogs out there!

Alexia Capsomidis for her help promoting *Dead Eyed*, and the many sales she secured!

Michael Brolly, for lending his first name again.

All my friends and family who were so supportive with their feedback on *Dead Eyed*, and their continued support.

Ann Eardley, for her exemplary proofreading skills.

My children Freya and Hamish for being there.

And as always, Alison, for her expert eye and unwavering belief.

Dear Reader,

Thank you so much for taking the time to read this book – we hope you enjoyed it! If you did, we'd be so appreciative if you left a review.

Here at HQ Digital we are dedicated to publishing fiction that will keep you turning the pages into the early hours. We publish a variety of genres, from heartwarming romance, to thrilling crime and sweeping historical fiction.

To find out more about our books, enter competitions and discover exclusive content, please join our community of readers by following us at:

@HQDigitalUK

facebook.com/HQDigitalUK

Are you a budding writer? We're also looking for authors to join the HQ Digital family! Please submit your manuscript to:

HQDigital@harpercollins.co.uk.

Hope to hear from you soon!

If you loved *Dead Lucky* then turn the page for an exclusive extract from the first book in the DCI Michael Lambert series, *Dead Eyed*...

Prologue

The man hovered on the edge of the dance floor. His elongated limbs and thinning hair made him stand out from the young lithe bodies. Sam Burnham watched him from the bar, nursing the same brandy he'd ordered an hour ago.

The track ended and the man shuffled his feet. He scanned the mirrored dance area before heading towards the bar.

Burnham ordered a second drink. He sensed the man in his periphery, and turned to face him. He placed his hand on the younger man's arm, and looked him directly in the eyes.

'Can I buy you a drink?' he asked.

The man nodded, staring at Burnham. Twenty minutes later they left the club together.

'What now?' asked Burnham, pulling his jacket tight against his body. It was a late September evening in Bristol, and the temperature had dropped since he'd set out earlier that day.

'Where are you staying?' asked the man. His eyes darted in random directions, not once focusing on Burnham.

'Hotel. You wouldn't like it. Do you live near?' Burnham knew exactly where he lived.

'I'm not sure,' said the man. 'I don't know you.'

Burnham touched the man's arm again. It was the simplest of techniques, but highly effective.

The man relented. 'It's not far away. We can walk.'

The man lived in Southville, a small suburb of Bristol less than a mile from the centre. They walked in an awkward silence, peppered with the occasional question from the man.

The man stopped outside a block of flats. 'I don't mean to sound weird, but do I know you from somewhere?'

'I don't think so. I guess I must have one of those faces,' said Burnham, following him inside.

The flat was hospital clean, the air fragranced artificially. The living area was an array of various gleaming surfaces: glass, chrome, marble. Burnham accepted a glass of brandy. The man's hands trembled as he handed it over.

They moved to the living room sofa and the man made life easy for him. 'I'll be back in a minute,' he said, his voice faltering.

As soon as Burnham heard the bathroom door click shut, he removed the phial from his inside jacket pocket. He broke the seal and spilled the clear liquid into the man's drink, stirring it with his left index finger.

It took five minutes for the man to take a drink. A further five minutes for the drug to take effect. Burnham dragged him to the bedroom, the man's skeletal body insubstantial in his thick arms. He placed the man on the bed and made a phone call.

Burnham's boss arrived at the flat two minutes later carrying a small leather case. Burnham watched in silence as he removed a surgical outfit, a set of scalpels, and a second phial filled with a different substance. 'Wait in the car,' he ordered.

It was three hours before his boss left the building. Burnham hurried from his seat and opened the back passenger door for him.

'Do you need me to clean up?' he asked.

'No, not this time.'

Chapter 1

Michael Lambert waited at the back of the coffee shop. To his right, a group of new mothers congregated around three wooden tables. Some held their tiny offspring; the others allowed their babies to sleep in the oversized prams which crowded the area. Two tables down, a pair of men dressed in identical suits stared at their iPads. Next to them, a young woman with braided hair read a paperback novel. All of them looked up as Simon Klatzky walked through the shop entrance and shouted over at him.

Lambert ignored the glances. He'd arrived thirty minutes earlier, out of habit checking and rechecking the clientele. He hadn't noticed anything out of the ordinary. He stood and beckoned Klatzky over. He'd last seen him two years ago at the funeral. 'Good to see you again, Simon,' he said.

'Mikey,' said Klatzky. Like Lambert, Klatzky was thirty-eight. He'd lost weight since the last time they'd met. His face was gaunt, his eyeballs laced with thin shards of red. When he spoke, Lambert noticed a number of missing teeth. The rest were discoloured and black with cheap fillings. His face cracked into a smile. He stood grinning at Lambert. In his left hand he clutched an A4 manila envelope.

'Sit down then. What do you want to drink?' said Lambert.

Klatzky shrugged. 'Coffee?'

Lambert ordered two black Americanos and returned to the table.

'Sorry I'm late,' said Klatzky.

Klatzky had called earlier that morning desperate to meet. He'd refused to tell Lambert the details over the phone but had insisted that it was urgent. From the smell of him, it hadn't been important enough to stop him visiting a bar first.

Klatzky's hands shook as he sipped the coffee. 'I thought it best you see for yourself,' he said, looking at the envelope still clutched tight in his hand.

Lambert sat straight in his chair, scratching a day's growth of stubble on his face. It was genuinely good to see his old friend. He'd only agreed to meet him as he'd sounded so scared on the phone. Now he was here, Lambert regretted not seeing more of him in the last two years.

'How have you been, Si?'

'So-so. I'm sorry I haven't called before.' He hesitated. 'And now, contacting you in these circumstances.' He still had a strong grip on the envelope, his knuckles turning white with the effort.

'I'm not working at the moment, Simon.'

'I didn't know who else to talk to.' Klatzky produced a bottle of clear liquid from his grainy-black rain jacket and poured half the contents into his coffee cup.

Some things didn't change. 'Are you going to show me then?' Lambert didn't want to rush him, but he didn't like surprises. He needed to know what Klatzky wanted.

Klatzky drank heavily from the alcohol-fused drink, momentarily confused.

'The envelope, Si.'

Klatzky stared at the envelope as if it had just appeared in his hand. He handed it to Lambert, his body trembling.

Klatzky's name and address were printed on the front. There was no stamp. 'You received this today?'

'It was there when I got back.'

'Back from where?'

'I was out last night. Got in early this morning.' He looked at Lambert as if expecting a reprimand.

Lambert opened the envelope and pulled out a file of A4 papers. Each page had a colour photo of the same subject taken from a different angle. Lambert tapped the table with the knuckles of his left hand as he read through the file.

'It's him, Mike,' said Klatzky.

The subject was the deceased figure of an emaciated man. The skin of the corpse was a dull yellow. Wisps of frazzled hair clung to the man's cheek bones, matted together with a green-brown substance. The corpse's mouth was wide open, caught forever in a look of rictus surprise. Where the man's eyes should have been were two hollow sockets. Tendrils of skin and matter dripped down onto the man's face. Lambert recognised the Latin insignia carved intricately into the man's chest. He placed the file back in the envelope, wiping a bead of sweat from his brow.

'Well?' asked Klatzky.

'Where did you get this from?'

Klatzky poured more of the clear liquid into his cup. 'I told you. It was there this morning when I got back. Why the hell has this been sent to me, Mike?' he asked, loud enough to receive some disapproving looks from the young mothers.

Lambert rubbed his face. If he'd known what was in the

envelope, then he would never have suggested meeting in such a public place. 'I'll talk to some people. See what I can find out. I'll need to keep this,' he said.

'But why was it sent to me, Mikey?'

'I don't know.' Lambert checked the address on the envelope. 'You're still in the same flat, over in East Ham?'

'Afraid so.'

'Have you seen anyone else recently?'

'You mean from Uni? No. You're the first one I've seen since the...' he hesitated. 'Since, the funeral.'

Lambert replayed the images in his head, trying to ignore the expectation etched onto Klatzky's face. The inscription on the victim's chest read:

In oculis animus habitat.

The lettering, smudged by leaking blood, had dried into thick maroon welts on the pale skin of the man's body. Lambert didn't need to see the man's eyeless sockets to work out the translation:

The soul dwells in the eyes.

They left the coffee house together. 'Do you have somewhere else you can go?' asked Lambert.

'Why? Do you think I'm next?' asked Klatzky.

Lambert wasn't sure what Klatzky had put in his coffee but the man was swaying from side to side. He placed his hand on the man's shoulder. 'Let's not panic. These might not have come from the murderer. But until we do find out where they came from, and why they were sent to you, it would be sensible to stay away from the flat.'

'Should we tell Billy's parents or something? Christ, what are they are going to think?'

Billy Nolan had been the ninth and, until now, last victim of the so called Souljacker killer. A close friend of Lambert and Klatzky, Nolan was murdered in his final year at Bristol University where they had all studied. The killer had never been caught and everything Lambert had seen in the file suggested that he had started working again.

'Look, you need to get somewhere and rest up. Let me worry about the details.'

'I want to help, Mikey.'

'You can stay out of trouble. That will help the most. I'll contact you when I know something.' He grabbed Klatzky's hand and shook it. 'It'll be okay, Si.'

Klatzky's handshake was weak, his palm wet with sweat. He swayed for a second before stumbling across the road to a bar called The Blue Boar.

Lambert stood outside the coffee shop, his hand clutched tight to the envelope. Years ago Lambert would have jumped straight into the investigation. The responsible thing would be to locate the Senior Investigating Officer on the case, inform them that Klatzky had received the material. But he needed time to process the information, to decipher why Klatzky had received the photos.

He walked to Clockhouse station and caught a train to Charing Cross, his mind racing. Making sure no one could see him, he opened the envelope. He scanned each page in turn, studied every detail. The photographs were direct copies from a crime report. The photographer had captured the corpse from all angles. The camera zoomed in on the victim's wounds. The ragged skin around the eye sockets, the incision marks magnified in gruesome detail, the intricate detail of the Latin inscription, each letter meticulously carved into the victim's skin. It was definitely a professional job.

Reaching London, Lambert took the short walk to Covent Garden. His wife, Sophie, was waiting for him in a small bistro off the old market building. She sat near the entrance, head buried in a leather folio. 'Oh, hi,' she said, on seeing him.

'Hi, yourself.'

She shut the document she'd been reading. 'Shall we order?' she asked, business-like as usual.

They'd been married for twelve years. Sophie was half-French on her mother's side. A petite woman, she had short black hair, and a soft round face which made her look ten years younger than her actual age of thirty-nine.

They both ordered the fish of the day. 'So how was Simon?' she asked.

'Not great,' said Lambert.

'Well, don't keep me in suspense. What did he want?'

Absentmindedly, Lambert touched the document in his inside jacket pocket. 'Oh, nothing dramatic. He was thinking of putting together some sort of reunion.'

He could tell she knew he was lying. They ordered water to go with the fish and sat through the meal in companionable silence. Each avoiding discussing the reason they were there.

'Everything's booked,' she said, finally. 'The same church as last year. We can use the church hall afterwards. All the catering is organised.'

Lambert drank the water, cracking a fragment of ice which had dropped into his mouth. A shiver ran through his body as the cold water dripped down his throat. 'Okay,' he said, realising how useless the words sounded. How he was, even after all this time, still unable to deal with the enormity of the situation.

'We need to finalise the music,' said Sophie.

Lambert gripped his glass of water, tried to focus on something more positive. 'Do you remember that track she loved in the summer before she started school? She used to go crazy. Blondie, wasn't it? She used to pick up her tennis racket and play along. I can't remember for the life of me what it was called.'

Sophie beamed, reliving the memory. Then, in an instant, her eyes darkened. It had been two years since their daughter, Chloe, had died. They'd decided to hold a memorial service each year on Chloe's birthday. Sophie's mother had suggested they postpone it this year. She'd argued that rekindling the same memories every twelve months denied a necessary part of the grieving process. In principle Lambert agreed, but it was not a subject he could broach with Sophie. He blamed himself for Chloe's death, and though she insisted otherwise, he was sure Sophie did too.

Eventually they agreed on a small song list.

'I need to go,' said Sophie. She stood and kissed him on the cheek, a perfunctory habit devoid of emotion. At home, they slept in separate rooms rarely spending more than five minutes together. This was the first meal they'd shared in almost a year.

Lambert hadn't worked since Chloe's death. He'd been hospitalised, and received substantial compensation. The last time Sophie had raised the subject of him returning to work they'd argued. Now the matter was never discussed.

'I'll be home early this evening,' she said. 'Then I'm out for dinner.'

She loitered by the table and regarded him in the way only she could. Lambert saw love in the gesture, tinged with compassion and empathy. But what he saw most of all was pity.

After she left, he paid the bill and walked outside. He found a secluded spot and took out the manila envelope once more. The easiest thing would be to send the file to the authorities and forget Klatzky had ever given it to him. And if he hadn't just had lunch with Sophie, and seen that look of pity, that would have been his course.

Instead, he put the envelope back in his jacket and walked along the Strand. On a side street, he entered a small establishment he'd used in the past.

Inside, he purchased a pre-charged Pay As You Go mobile phone in cash.

From memory, he dialled a number he hadn't called in two years.

If you enjoyed *Dead Lucky* then why not try another thrilling read from HQ Digital?

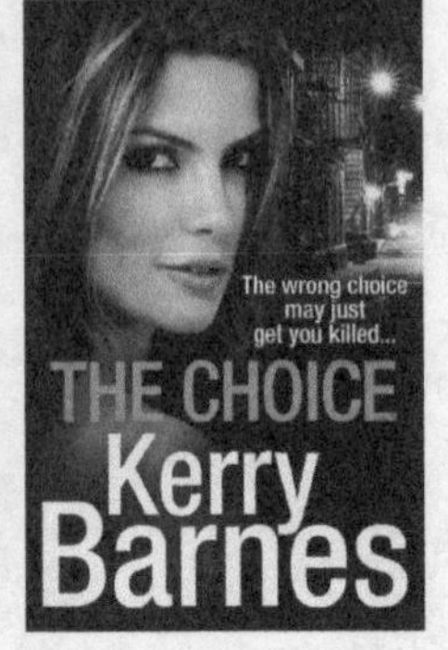

About the Publisher

Australia
HarperCollins Publishers (Australia) Pty. Ltd.
Level 13, 201 Elizabeth Street
Sydney, NSW 2000, Australia
http://www.harpercollins.com.au

Canada
HarperCollins Canada
2 Bloor Street East - 20th Floor
Toronto, ON, M4W, 1A8, Canada
http://www.harpercollins.ca
India

HarperCollins India
A 75, Sector 57
Noida, Uttar Pradesh 201 301, India
http://www.harpercollins.co.in

New Zealand
HarperCollins Publishers (New Zealand) Limited
P.O. Box 1
Auckland, New Zealand
http://www.harpercollins.co.nz

United Kingdom
HarperCollins Publishers Ltd.
1 London Bridge Street
London SE1 9GF
http://www.harpercollins.co.uk

United States
HarperCollins Publishers Inc.
195 Broadway
New York, NY 10007
http://www.harpercollins.com

About the Publisher

Australia

[illegible] (Australia) Pty. Ltd.

[illegible]

[illegible] NSW 2000, Australia

[illegible]

Canada

HarperCollins Canada

[illegible]

[illegible], Canada

[illegible]

India

HarperCollins India

[illegible]

[illegible], India

[illegible]

New Zealand

[illegible] (New Zealand) Limited

[illegible]

[illegible]

[illegible]

United Kingdom

HarperCollins Publishers Ltd.

[illegible]

London [illegible]

[illegible]

United States

HarperCollins Publishers Inc.

[illegible]

New York, NY [illegible]

[illegible]